Rosalia's Bittersweet Pastry Shop

ROSANNA CHIOFALO

KENSINGTON BOOKS
www.kensingtonbooks.com

KENSINGTON BOOKS are published by

Kensington Publishing Corp.
119 West 40th Street
New York, NY 10018

eISBN-13: 978-1-61773-938-5
eISBN-10: 1-61773-938-3
First Kensington Electronic Edition: June 2016

ISBN-13: 978-1-61773-937-8
ISBN-10: 1-61773-937-5
First Kensington Trade Paperback Printing: June 2016

10 9 8 7 6 5 4 3 2 1

Printed in the United States of America

For my dear friend "Bensonhurst."
Thank you for always believing in me.

And for my husband, Ed.
Your love is sweeter than all the pastries in the world.

CONTENTS

PROLOGUE

Frutta di Martorana

MARZIPAN FRUIT

September 4, 1955
Santa Lucia del Mela, Messina, Sicily

Madre Carmela's favorite nuts were almonds. Not only did she like the way they tasted the best among all nuts, but she loved the flavor they imparted to Sicilian desserts from cakes to biscotti, and her favorite of all, *Frutta di Martorana*—the perfect fruit-shaped confections made from *pasta reale,* or marzipan, which required plenty of almonds. Who would have thought that the base for an elegant, regal dessert like marzipan came from such a simple ingredient as the almond? But it was this nut that was the underlying flavor in many of the desserts that Madre Carmela and the nuns from her Carmelite order baked for their pastry shop, which was operated from their convent.

To collect the almonds for their baking, Madre Carmela and her fellow sisters were on one of their outings in the almond groves found in the countryside of their beautiful hill town of Santa Lucia del Mela in Messina, Sicily. In a month, the demand for marzipan fruit would soar in their shop.

As Madre Carmela and her Carmelite order of nuns busily harvested the almonds from the trees, singing their favorite hymns, she pondered on how far she and her convent had come over the years. Not only was she the mother superior of her order of nuns, but she was also the head pastry chef of the bakery she ran out of the convent. She had managed to turn their little pastry-making side business into the most famous *pasticceria,* not only in Santa Lucia, but in all the neighboring towns. Madre Carmela's pastry shop continued the tradition that dated back to the 1800s, when many convents and monasteries in northeastern Sicily also made and sold pastries. Their pastries had become famous for surpassing those of the professional bakeries in town. Long lines of patrons often waited in the courtyard of their convent, outside the pastry shop's windows where they also sold their baked goods.

Pastry making was Madre Carmela's greatest passion in life. She took the utmost pride in the confections she made, and every biscotto, *torta,* marzipan, *crostata,* and any other baked good had to be perfect—anything less would be unacceptable. Her sisters and the other workers at the convent's pastry shop knew her high standards. Mediocre work was not allowed and was cause for dismissal, but it was rare that Madre Carmela fired anyone. For her weakness was having a deep compassion, especially for those who had suffered greatly.

Suddenly, a low moan startled Madre Carmela out of her thoughts. She glanced toward Sorella Giovanna, a new nun who had entered their order only the previous month and who was standing to her right. Their eyes locked. Sorella Giovanna had heard the moan, too. And there it was again. Another moan. Madre Carmela took Sorella Giovanna by the arm, and they slowly walked in the direction the sounds were coming from. A few of the other nuns had also stopped picking almonds and were following them now, fear evident on their faces. But none of the sisters dared question Madre Carmela, since they had learned a long time ago to always trust her judgment.

The nuns continued following the sounds, which seemed to be coming from land that was just behind the almond orchard. Soon, the outline of a crumpled form came into their line of vision. It was the body of a young woman, lying by the mouth of a cave. The area was known for its many caves. Madre Carmela let out a small cry and rushed to the side of the girl, who looked to be no more than seventeen years old. She was very pale, and her lips were extremely chapped. Bruises circled her arms and legs, and scratches etched her cheeks. She wore a plain housedress that was several sizes too large on her petite, very thin frame. The dress was torn in several places and revealed one of the girl's breasts and showed she wore no undergarments. Madre Carmela tore her eyes away from the girl's exposed body as she tried in vain to cover her. While Madre Carmela did so, her gaze settled on the girl's hair. The tresses hung down to the young woman's waist, and in stark contrast to her dirty, battered body, her hair shone radiantly in its lustrous shade of black. Without a doubt, it was the most beautiful hair Madre Carmela had ever seen.

She turned to Sorella Giovanna. "Give me your canteen."

Sorella Giovanna's hands shook as she opened her canteen and handed it to her mother superior.

Madre Carmela helped the girl sit up and held the canteen up to her lips.

"*Bevi. Bevi.*" She pleaded with her to drink. The young woman barely fluttered her eyes open, but then began to drink, slowly at first, yet soon she took in quick gulps.

Madre Carmela reached into the deep pockets of her habit and pulled out two marzipans—one shaped like a small apple and the other shaped like a pear. She often threw a few marzipans in her pockets when she went on these long outings since she suffered from low blood sugar. Once she started to feel lightheaded, she'd chew on the marzipan and instantly would feel better. Well, sometimes she had a couple of marzipans even when she wasn't feeling woozy. Of all the pastries she made at the shop, marzipans were her greatest weakness.

She held out the shimmering glazed sweets. "*Prendi.* Take. The sugar in them will help you feel better."

The girl's eyes widened. She tentatively took the small apple, but left the pear in Madre Carmela's hand. She stared at it for a moment longer, no doubt in awe of the miniature dessert's perfection and marveling at how much it looked like a real apple. She took a bite out of the marzipan and stared once more in wonderment at the pastry. Then she popped the rest of it in her mouth and chewed it ravenously before swallowing. Her eyes immediately went to the pear-shaped marzipan Madre Carmela still held in her hand.

"It's very good. No?" The girl nodded her head. Madre Carmela handed her the other marzipan. This time, without hesitation, the girl took it.

"*Cosa ti è successo?*" Sorella Giovanna asked the girl what had happened to her.

In a split second, her eyes filled with terror, and she glanced over her shoulder at the cave.

Madre Carmela's gaze met Sorella Giovanna's, and she implored her silently not to take this line of questioning further.

"Don't worry. You are safe now. My sisters and I will take you back to our convent, and we will take care of you. No one will hurt you again."

The girl looked at Madre Carmela as tears fell down her face.

"Can you tell me your name?" Madre Carmela gently asked her.

The girl remained quiet. Madre Carmela reached into her deep pockets once more, and this time pulled out a plump, strawberry-shaped marzipan. A flicker of light appeared in the girl's hollow eyes. She took the marzipan and ate it just as ravenously as the other two. Once she was done, she whispered to Madre Carmela, "*Rosalia.*"

"Your name is Rosalia? Did I hear you correctly?"

The girl nodded.

Madre Carmela looked at the cave and then back at Rosalia. A shiver ran through her. She couldn't believe the irony at finding this young woman by the name of Rosalia in front of a cave. For Santa Rosalia, one of Sicily's most revered saints, was known to have lived the last years of her life in a cave. But an even greater coincidence was the fact that today—September 4—was none other than the feast day of Santa Rosalia. Could the saint herself have intended for the nuns to find this poor soul?

Tears filled Madre Carmela's eyes as she said in a soft voice, "You have a lovely name, Rosalia."

Rosalia continued to look at the ground.

Turning to the other nuns, Madre Carmela instructed them to

help the girl to her feet and take her back to the convent. She explained that she wanted to harvest more almonds and would join them later at the convent. The nuns brought a sheet they'd been using to collect the almonds and wrapped Rosalia in it. With the help of Sorella Giovanna and another nun, Rosalia rose to her feet, her legs shaking visibly beneath her. It was apparent she was suffering from malnourishment. She managed a small smile for the nuns as they cloaked her in the sheet and offered words of encouragement. Madre Carmela's heart filled with joy as she watched her fellow sisters form a semicircle around the girl, wrapping their arms around her as they escorted her to the convent. She realized what they were doing. The sheet was not only serving its first purpose of covering Rosalia's naked body, but it was also being used as a protective shroud to make her feel warm and immediately safe.

As soon as the nuns were gone, Madre Carmela entered the cave where they'd found Rosalia. She followed a long passageway. Her heart was beating fast, and she wondered what she would find, thinking perhaps she should turn back around and leave. But her curiosity at what had happened to the girl propelled her forward. She noticed there were other passageways to the left and right, but she was afraid she would get lost, so she continued walking straight along the path she was already on. After about five minutes, the narrow passageway opened up. No one was present, but there were traces of someone having lived there: kindle wood, plates, cups, and a makeshift bed constructed of hay in the corner. Madre Carmela then noticed a pile of dirty clothes in the corner. She went over and picked them up. They were a blouse, skirt, slip, brassiere, and underpants of a young woman about Rosalia's size. The blouse was missing a few buttons. The skirt and slip were torn, much like the oversized housedress Madre Carmela had found Rosalia in. But unlike the housedress, they were covered in dried-up bloodstains. Madre Carmela closed her eyes, fighting back tears. She could only imagine what terrors the poor girl had suffered in this terrible place. But she was safe now. That was all that mattered. In that moment, Madre Carmela vowed to God that she would help Rosalia find peace in her life again.

❧ 1 ❧

Minni della Vergine

VIRGIN'S BREASTS

September 25, 2004
Santa Lucia del Mela, Messina, Sicily

The winding roads of the hills were making Claudia Lombardo feel nauseous. She tried closing her eyes as Felice, her driver, chatted with her in his heavily accented English, but that only made the feeling worse. And though it was the last week in September, it was still rather warm. Then again, they were on the Mediterranean island of Sicily, where one could technically still swim at the beach as late as November, though the locals never did according to the travel guidebook Claudia had read before she left New York.

Claudia could feel her pulse racing in anticipation. Though she had spent the last fifteen years interviewing famous chefs and writing cookbooks featuring their world-renowned dishes, she felt that this next project was more special somehow. She had never traveled outside of the U.S. to interview a chef from another country. And this chef was much different from those she had previously met with, many of whom had achieved celebrity status and were often quite narcissistic.

As Felice cleared a bend in the road, Claudia caught her breath at the view in the valley below. Sprawling acres of green beckoned to her, and specks of white dotted the landscape—goats. A goat herder followed his flock, reining them in. So far the little she'd seen in the drive from the airport was what she had always envisioned Sicily to look like—verdant mountains, deep azure coastline, palm trees, and cactus pear plants. She couldn't believe she was here.

Though Claudia was half Sicilian on her father's side of the family, she never really thought about her Italian roots since she was third-generation Italian American. Her mother had Irish in her, but again Claudia's ancestors who had emigrated from Ireland had done so in the early part of the twentieth century. She just always thought of herself as American, even though her father liked to uphold a few culinary customs that had been passed down in his family through the generations like the Feast of the Seven Fish, or Fishes, which was how most people referred to the Italian Christmas Eve celebration, but she refused to call it that.

Her father's love of cooking had been instilled in Claudia from the time she was seven years old. And from the moment he'd taught her how to cook, she instantly fell in love. She watched everything her father did and in no time was taking turns with him in preparing the most mouthwatering meals for the family. As she grew older, Claudia discovered she also enjoyed writing. So she decided to combine her passions of cooking and writing to become a food writer. In addition to having *Chow Girl*—her own blog for food epicureans—she had now published eight books, several of which had become *New York Times* bestsellers.

Though the primary reason for this trip was to learn and write about the fascinating pastries Sicily was renowned for, it would also be a chance for Claudia to see the island from which her ancestors had originated. Unfortunately, any relatives her father still had in Sicily lived on the western side of the island, near Agrigento. So this wouldn't be one of those trips where Claudia would find long-lost relatives to introduce herself to, since the town she was traveling to was located in the northeast. But that was all right. She was just happy to be here and get a sense of her roots.

"Almost there, *signorina!*" Felice shouted to Claudia above the din of his car radio, which was blasting one Italian ballad after another. She had found herself tapping her foot in time to the enchanting music. She could get used to listening to Italian music. For a moment, she had to pinch herself to believe it was all real. From the perfect panorama to the bucolic valleys between the hills and mountains they were driving along to the emotion-laden pop songs playing on the radio, Claudia felt as if she were watching an Italian tourism TV commercial.

Soon, as the driver had promised, Claudia saw the road signs pointing to her destination: *Convento di Santa Lucia del Mela*—Santa Lucia del Mela Convent. The incline became steeper, and the roadway narrowed even more. Claudia's heart dropped when she noticed the Fiat hugging the side of the mountain. Immediately, she turned her head so she wouldn't see the dramatic drop over the mountain's edge.

Her pulse calmed down once she noticed the road widening again in front of her. They were entering a village that was perched along the mountains. Bicyclists and people on Vespas vied with the motorists. Right as she was thinking she would be able to get out of the stuffy car, Felice began ascending a twisty path up another hill.

"I thought you said we were almost there." Claudia tried to hide the irritation in her voice, reminding herself she was no longer in New York City, where constantly showing your annoyance to everyone who tested your patience was expected.

"We are. At the top of the hill. We have to go through the village first," Felice said before glancing over his shoulder at Claudia. "You have heard about *i dolci,* the pastries, of the Sorelle Carmelitane? *Sì?* You cannot wait to try them, no? Ha-ha!" Felice laughed.

"*Sì.* I am here to try the convent's famous pastries, but I am also a writer. I am going to write a book featuring their famous pastries and tell about the history of the convent as well as interview the head pastry chef—Sorella Agata."

"Ah! *Bravissima!* You are a writer, and you come here from New York! So far away! Make sure you write nothing but the best about our little mountain town and about the sisters. They are good women, but most of all women of God." Felice nodded his head knowingly at Claudia.

"So, Felice, you are from Santa Lucia del Mela?"

"*Si*. Born here, and I will die here."

"May I ask why you think the convent's pastries are famous? What makes their desserts more special than, let's say, the desserts in the finest bakeries in the cities of Messina and Palermo?"

Felice shrugged his shoulders and for a split second removed his hands from the steering wheel, gesturing toward the air. "Naturally, the pastries are very good. But it is more than their taste. Ahhh . . . how do you say?" Felice stammered for a moment as he tried to think of the correct phrase. "The sisters' pastries are special because of how you feel after you eat them. All the senses are engaged. How do you Americans say? Experience?" He glanced at Claudia in the rearview mirror, meeting her eyes.

"Yes, experience." Claudia nodded her head, imploring Felice to continue.

"You have a beautiful experience when you eat one of their pastries. You will see what I mean after you try them. Believe me!"

While Claudia could relate to what Felice was saying about the convent's pastries imparting an experience in addition to taste since she had trained her palate and her five senses to take in every nuance of food, she couldn't help feeling that the driver was biased and wanted to portray the pastries as being far superior to those found in the *pasticcerie* of Messina, the nearest large city. After all, he was proud of his hometown. But she was still curious as to the convent's secret to the success of their pastries.

From Claudia's research, she had learned about Sicily's longstanding history of creating the finest pastries and how wealthy monasteries and convents, especially in Sicily's capital of Palermo and in the city of Catania, had preserved the island's rich heritage of pastry making. But the convents took it a step further in the late 1800s and began selling their pastries, mainly as a way to keep their doors from being closed. For after Italian unification in 1860, much of the convents' land had been seized by the government, and many of the convents were shut down. The Convent of Santa Lucia del Mela was one of these convents that had been selling their sweets from as far back as the late nineteenth century. While their business had always done well, it wasn't until the late 1950s that word of the shop's exceptional pastries began to spread to neighboring towns outside of Santa Lucia del Mela, and even to the city of Messina. In the 1980s, the shop had managed to get the attention of several famous chefs from around the world, who had heard about the Carmelite nuns' remarkable sweets and had traveled to the sleepy hillside town of Santa Lucia del Mela to discover what all the excitement was about. And in the past decade, tourists had even begun descending upon the village just to visit the convent's pastry shop.

Claudia had first learned about Sorella Agata and her famous pastry shop, which operated from the convent where she was also the mother superior, from her friend Gianni, who was the chef at Il Grotto, one of Manhattan's esteemed five-star Italian restaurants. While Gianni had not been to the convent's pastry shop and sampled the nuns' sweets, he knew a few chefs who had and who could not stop talking about the amazing creations being whipped up there. But what really intrigued Gianni was the one dessert that all of his friends had been baffled by—the *cassata*—a Sicilian cake, originating from Palermo and Messina, that consisted of sponge cake dipped in liqueur, layered with ricotta cheese and candied peel, and covered with a marzipan shell and icing; candied fruit in the shape of cherries and slices of citrus fruit topped the cake. Not only was the cake unlike any other version of *cassata* the chefs had ever tasted, but they were convinced Sorella Agata had a secret ingredient that was responsible for its becoming the most popular of the sweets sold at her pastry shop. The chefs had looked at different *cassata* recipes, but they could not nail the unique flavor that was present in Sorella Agata's. And the ingredients listed in the recipes could not have given the cake this unique flavor.

"Felice, I take it you have tried the *cassata?*"

"Of course! That is the cake that made Sorella Agata famous. For only she has the gift to make it so delicious. My grandmother told me she's been eating *cassata* from the convent's pastry shop ever since she was a little girl—long before Sorella Agata was baking there. She said it tasted nothing like Sorella Agata's cake."

"Well, perhaps then what Sorella Agata is baking isn't really a *cassata* since your grandmother says it tasted different from the one she had years ago? Has anyone thought of that? Perhaps she is fooling you all!" Claudia laughed.

"She is a woman of God. She is incapable of deceit." Felice's voice possessed a touch of irritation.

Claudia couldn't help mentally rolling her eyes at his claim that Sorella Agata was not capable of deceit. But Claudia held her tongue, knowing how religious Italians were and how they held nuns and priests in high reverence along with the Pope.

"Maybe I have not communicated well in English what I wanted to say. It *is* the *cassata*. Anyone who has had that cake knows what it should taste like, and Sorella Agata's tastes the way the *cassata* should, but then there is another layer of flavor. You will see for yourself. You must sample the *cassata* at one of the other *pasticcerie* in the village, and then try *la sorella's* version."

"I intend to do exactly that, Felice."

Claudia was determined to get to the bottom of this mystery. She was good at what she did, especially when it came to breaking down tough chefs who were often reluctant to share secrets of what made their cuisines a success. She just needed to build a sense of trust between the chef and herself, and she had no doubt she would be able to do that even with a nun. Secretly, Claudia prayed that Sorella Agata wouldn't be one of those stern nuns her father had always told her about. He had gone to parochial elementary school, where several nuns taught, and he claimed he still had nightmares about a few of the meaner ones.

"We are here, *signorina.*" Felice came to an abrupt stop in front of a sprawling building.

Claudia quickly paid him and stepped out of the taxi. Felice took Claudia's suitcase out of the trunk.

"*Arrivederci, signorina.* Do not forget to try *la cassata.*" He chuckled as he said good-bye and got back into his taxi. He'd turned off the car stereo—no doubt out of respect for the convent. But as the car began making its downhill descent, Claudia could hear once again the notes of the Italian pop music.

She turned around and entered the tall wrought-iron gates of the convent's property. No one was outside. A mosaic-tiled walkway led to a courtyard, where Claudia could now see the magnificent structure that housed the convent. It looked even more charming than in the photographs she'd seen on the website. Porticoes lined a two-story building. The second story featured a large balcony. The off-white stone walls contrasted nicely with the shingled roof. The gardens in the courtyard were immaculately landscaped. Boxes of red bougainvillea, one of Sicily's most popular flowers, sat in each of the arched porticoes. Cactus pear plants, jade, aloe vera, and other succulents that were well-suited to the island's arid climate adorned the courtyard. There were various other plants, flowers, and trees, including lemon and orange trees. A statue of a female saint with a small bubbling fountain was situated at the back of the yard, and a makeshift shrine of vases holding flowers circled the base of the statue.

Claudia closed her eyes, taking in a deep breath. The air smelled exceptionally clean, and there was a subtle sweet fragrance of jasmine and citrus in the air. But what she enjoyed most of all was the silence. Claudia couldn't remember the last time she'd been somewhere that was this quiet—the Grand Canyon when she visited as a child perhaps? Yes, that was it. She opened her eyes and let her gaze survey the gorgeous grounds once more. A strange feeling passed over her. She couldn't quite put her finger on it, but there was something about this place—a serenity and an almost otherworldly spirituality that put her instantly at ease.

She then smelled a familiar scent—bread baking. Or perhaps cookies? Letting her nose lead the way, Claudia followed the aroma, which seemed to be coming from the side of the convent. Soon, rows of arched windows lining the side of the convent's building came into view. Long lines of people waited at two of the open windows. She then saw the head of a nun, complete in habit and wimple, peering out one of the windows as she smiled and laughed with an elderly male customer while she handed him a plump brioche wrapped in tissue paper. The man paid her and left. Claudia waited to see what the next patron would purchase, but the nun brought out a large cake box and, although she showed the customer the cake inside, Claudia was too far away to see it.

"*Mi scusi,* Signorina Lombardo?"

Claudia almost jumped out of her skin. A short nun stood before her, smiling shyly, almost like a young schoolgirl. But Claudia could tell by the few fine lines and wrinkles that were etched on her face that she was probably in her sixties. The dark circles beneath a set of large, intense black eyes also attested to the nun's age. Her smile and her eyes were kind. The nun was dressed in a chocolate-brown habit. A white coif covered her hair completely, and a white wimple covered the sides of her cheeks and neck. A black veil draped her head.

"*Si, io sono* Signorina Lombardo. *Buongiorno,* Sorella."

Claudia sent out a silent thanks to her father for making her take Italian lessons on the weekends while she was in elementary school. Then when she was in high school and was required to take a foreign language, she had figured she'd be one step ahead if she took Italian. Her high school Italian teacher, whom she managed to keep for all four years, had instilled in Claudia a deep admiration for the language, so she had decided to continue studying it in college. Just to be sure she could still easily understand the language and speak it, she had decided to take an immersion course in Italian in Manhattan. The class had been for students who already had a solid mastery of the language and wanted to refresh their skills.

"It is a pleasure to meet you. I am Sorella Agata."

So this was the famous pastry chef and mother superior of the Santa Lucia del Mela convent and *pasticceria.* The pastry shop simply went by the convent's name. Claudia didn't know why she was surprised this was Sorella Agata. She had pictured Sorella Agata to look different. Taller perhaps, and though she was a little plump, Claudia had expected her to be more portly because she was a pastry chef. Silently, Claudia scolded herself for her ridiculous assumption. Claudia was a food writer and as such was forced to taste countless dishes, and she wasn't overweight. If anything, her parents were always telling her she was too thin and needed to put on a few extra pounds. But she exercised daily, knowing how easy it would be to lose her size 4 figure with all the incredibly delicious food she was tempted with in her line of work. And she only allowed herself a bite or two, at most, when she sampled the extraordinary creations of the chefs she interviewed.

"It's a pleasure to meet you, too, Sorella Agata." Claudia shook her hand.

"I hope your trip wasn't too tiring?" Sorella Agata said in English.

"You speak English?" Claudia was surprised. Their e-mail exchanges had been completely in Italian.

"I've studied it on and off over the years. I'm more comfortable speaking it than writing. That is why when we were e-mailing I didn't do so in English." Sorella Agata's eyes met Claudia's for a moment before she quickly glanced away. Again there was that hint of shyness—another surprise for Claudia. She would've never imagined a mother superior of a convent and the head pastry chef of a shop that had gained acclaim throughout Italy to be meek. Perhaps it was her training as a nun that made her this way? After all, weren't nuns taught to be humble at all times?

"Well, we can speak Italian if you're more comfortable. Please, don't resort to English on my account, Sister. I studied Italian when I was in school, and I also took a refresher course for the past few months in anticipation of coming here. I actually rather enjoy speaking Italian."

"Thank you, Signorina Lombardo. That is kind of you. Perhaps when you are interviewing me for the recipe book, I can speak in Italian, but when we are just talking casually like we are doing now, we can speak in English? I would love to learn more and not waste this opportunity I have with an English-speaking visitor."

"That sounds like a perfect arrangement. You might have to help me as well with a few of the harder words." Claudia laughed.

Sorella Agata also laughed as her gaze met Claudia's, and this time it was Claudia's turn to glance away. There was something about Sorella Agata's intense black eyes that made her feel as if Sorella Agata knew more about Claudia than she did. But the nun's warm smile quickly put any awkwardness Claudia felt to rest.

"Let's go see your room. I'm afraid it won't be as lavish as what you are probably accustomed to when staying at hotels, but it's clean, and we actually had several of the rooms, including yours, renovated last year. We've started taking in tourists who are looking for cheap rooms to book while traveling through Sicily. Many of the convents and monasteries are doing this throughout Italy nowadays. We can always use the extra income even though our pastry shop does quite well."

"Yes, I actually read an article in the *New York Times* about the growing popularity amongst tourists of staying at monasteries and convents. Was it your idea to begin renting the rooms of your convent, Sorella Agata?"

"*Sì.* It was. I'm afraid all the business decisions are left to me. My fellow sisters do not want to be bothered by the more technical side of our operation. They are content to lead their lives of prayer, to make the best pastries possible for our village people and all those who visit our shop, and to do community work. Of course, I consulted with them and would not have opened up our doors to tourists if the other nuns weren't in agreement. We all live here together and must respect everyone's wishes. Although they agreed, they would still rather leave the dollars and cents stuff to me. I don't mind. This is part of my calling, and I am glad to serve as God sees fit."

Claudia couldn't help thinking it must be hard for Sorella Agata to take on so much responsibility alone, especially since she was getting up there in years. From what Claudia had read about the nun, she was sixty-six years old. She appeared to be in good health, although Claudia could see the slight rounding of her upper back, no doubt from all the bending over she did while making her famous pastries.

Sorella Agata led Claudia to the back of the building and through a heavy oak door. They went down a long, dark, narrow hallway. The intoxicating aroma of freshly baked goods was even stronger behind the convent's walls than it was out in the courtyard, and it only intensified the deeper they went into the convent. Claudia soon heard a din of voices and pans clanging about.

"We have to go through the kitchen to reach the rooms where you'll be staying," Sorella Agata explained.

As they entered an enormous kitchen, Claudia couldn't believe her eyes. Trays upon trays of the most heavenly assortment of sweets lined the counters either waiting to be placed in the ovens or still cooling in their pans: steaming cookies and biscotti in every shape and size; berries coated in shimmering glazes sitting atop custard tarts; fluffy swirls of cannoli cream bursting from crisp golden shells. But what really caught Claudia's eye was the fruit-shaped marzipan. She could only imagine all the time and painstaking effort it took to create the marzipan and shuddered to think of anyone's ruining their perfection by eating them, though she knew that was their purpose. Nuns and laywomen worked quickly, taking out baking sheets and pans from the ovens, icing dainty pastries, frosting cakes, stacking biscotti and other cookies on platters and wrapping them in cellophane, topped off with personalized ribbons bearing the convent's name. Claudia stopped following Sorella Agata to inspect one of the ribbons more closely. A small medallion of Saint Lucy dangled from the ribbon. Instinctively, Claudia reached for her Canon camera in her leather messenger bag and began snapping away. Forgetting all about Sorella Agata, she turned to the pastries on the baking sheets and also took photos of those.

"I see you have a passion for your work," Sorella Agata said after a few minutes had passed.

"I'm sorry, Sister. I just couldn't resist when I saw all these beautiful pastries. It's apparent you have a great passion as well."

Sorella Agata's face glowed as she observed her workers busily going about their business.

"*Si.* Baking and serving God are my true callings."

"What are these?" Claudia pointed to a platter of small round cakes, coated in pink or white icing and each topped with a maraschino cherry.

"Ah! Those are special. Virgin's Breasts."

"Did I hear you correctly?" Claudia knitted her brows in confusion, refusing to repeat what she believed she'd heard. For if she was wrong, the nun would no doubt be offended.

Sorella Agata gave a soft laugh. "*Si,* you heard correctly. Virgin's Breasts, or *Minni della Vergine,* as we say in Italian. They are pastries that were created to honor the memory of Saint Agatha—or Sant' Agata as we say in Italian—who refused to marry a man and was tortured for it. Her breasts were cut off, and she became the patron saint of rape victims."

"Agata. That's your name."

Sorella Agata nodded. "She is a great saint, and I chose her name so that I may follow in her completely selfless example. Are you Catholic, Signorina Lombardo?"

"Yes, I am."

"Do you know your saints?"

Claudia couldn't help feeling she was back in grade school and was being quizzed by a teacher.

"My father would mention a few of his favorite saints and what they were famous for, but I'm afraid I don't remember the stories."

"Saint Agatha is my favorite, which comes as no surprise since I chose her name when I took my vows as a nun. She refused to marry a wealthy Roman consul because she had dedicated herself to God and wished to remain a virgin. To punish her, the Roman consul had her imprisoned in a brothel, but she still refused to give up her virginity so she was tortured and her breasts were cut off.

"Traditionally, we would only prepare these miniature cakes for the feast day of Saint Agatha, which is February 5th, but they were so popular with our customers that we decided to carry them year round. And when our town holds its annual Saint Agatha feast, the Virgin's Breasts are the first to sell out of all the food that is sold."

"What is in Virgin's Breasts?"

"They are actually miniature *cassatas,* which as I'm sure you know is a popular Sicilian cake. If you haven't guessed it already, the cherry that tops the pastry is to give it the anatomical correctness of the virgin's breast."

"Ah! Of course."

Claudia was tempted to delve right into the subject of Sorella Agata's famous *cassata,* but she needed to be patient and wait for when the moment was right. She wondered if these miniature *cassatas* meant to symbolize Saint Agatha's breasts were made with the same recipe that was used for the standard size of the cake. If the same recipe was used for the Virgin's Breasts, then they must impart the intense, unique flavor that Sorella Agata's *cassata* was famous for. Claudia leaned in to snap another photo of the miniature pastries, but this time she took a close-up. When she looked up from her camera, a tall, quite elderly nun stood in front of her.

"*Per te,*" she said to Claudia, imploring her to take the small plate holding two Virgin's Breasts. Her voice was raspy and very low as if much effort was required to utter a full sentence.

"*Grazie,* Sorella."

"Signorina Lombardo, this is Madre Carmela."

"*Piacere.*" Claudia bowed her head toward the old nun, who bowed her head in return and smiled. Then she walked away slowly, shuffling her feet. It occurred to Claudia that Sorella Agata had referred to the old nun as *madre*. She was confused. Wasn't Sorella Agata the mother superior at the convent?

"I'm sorry, Sorella Agata, but I noticed you referred to her as Madre Carmela. I thought you were the mother superior here?"

Sorella Agata smiled. "I am, but Madre Carmela was my predecessor. I still choose to call her *madre* out of respect."

"Do the other nuns address her as *madre* as well?"

"No, I am the only one. And you'll see the other nuns do not address me as Madre Agata. When I became the mother superior, I insisted they continue to call me Sorella Agata."

Hmmm. Claudia found this interesting. It was as if Sorella Agata was not comfortable with setting herself apart from the nuns, but rather wanted to remain on an equal footing with them.

"Go ahead. Try them." Sorella Agata motioned with her head toward the pastries on Claudia's plate.

"I'll just have one. Since I work with food, I have to pace myself."

Sorella Agata frowned, and then gave Claudia a head-to-toe assessment, no doubt noticing how thin she was. Unlike Claudia's parents, she refrained from scolding her, but her face held enough reproach.

Claudia broke off a piece of one of the Virgin's Breasts with her fork and placed it in her mouth. Immediately, her mouth burst with flavor. Every taste bud was awakened. The miniature *cassatas* were beyond incredible! Surely, they had to be made from the same recipe as the regular-sized *cassata* cake that had made Sorella Agata famous. Claudia had gone to several authentic Italian-American bakeries in New York City before coming to Sicily and had tried their *cassatas*. While a few stood out more than the *cassatas* from other bakeries, they all still shared a common flavor. If Claudia had been blindfolded, she would have known each of those cakes was a *cassata*. She took another bite of the light but intensely sweet pastry, and again, each of her senses felt completely engaged. It was just as Felice, the cab driver, had described it. Before Claudia realized what she was doing, she had polished off both of the miniature *cassatas*. When she was done, she stared at her empty plate, realizing only then that she'd broken her earlier promise to have just one of the pastries. Sorella Agata was staring at her with a sly smile.

"They're very delicious, *si?*"

"*Si, sono incredibili!* I don't think I've ever tasted pastries quite as delicious as these."

Sorella Agata looked pleased with Claudia's comment. "You will probably say that with many of our sweets here. They are quite unique, especially in comparison to the American desserts."

"You know about our desserts?"

"Yes, well, not personally. But I like to research and learn as much as possible about all pastries, not just Sicilian or Italian sweets. I make my own versions of apple pie and chocolate cake. But I'm sure they must not be as good as the ones you have in America."

"You should make them for me some time, and I can tell you how close yours are to the American versions. Sorella Agata, you are quite a renowned pastry chef from what I've heard. There aren't many pastry shops that have had world-class chefs visit them to sample their desserts, which brings me to the question I cannot wait to ask you, especially after sampling these heavenly pastries. I know we've only just met, and I haven't officially started our interview, but I must ask you about your famous *cassata*."

"*Si, si.* Everyone wants to know about that cake." Sorella Agata sighed as she said this. No doubt she was tired of everyone's asking her what her secret ingredient was, but that didn't stop Claudia from posing the question.

"So then I will not be the first person to ask you, Sister, what is your secret ingredient for making the *cassata* surpass all other recipes that have come before? And I take it you are using the same recipe you use for the standard size of the *cassata* for these Virgin's Breasts, which you said are just miniature *cassatas*."

Claudia noticed a few of the other women had stopped their

work and were eavesdropping on her conversation with Sorella Agata. Sorella Agata looked in their direction and frowned. With a wave of her hand, she motioned to Claudia to follow her out of the kitchen. Remaining silent, Sorella Agata led Claudia to a hallway filled with bedrooms. Claudia was surprised none of the doors to the rooms were shut. Sorella Agata finally stopped at a room at the end of the hall and gestured for Claudia to enter.

"This will be your room while you stay with us."

Claudia was surprised to see the room was quite spacious, and she could tell from the distance of the next room in comparison to the others that this one was much larger. No doubt Sorella Agata wanted to give her a nicer room. Except for an ivory china vase filled with fresh daisies that sat atop a chest of drawers and sheer lace window panels, the décor was quite sparse. A crocheted white blanket covered the bed. Above the bed's headboard, a cross made out of wood hung. The stems of two purple silk rosebuds were entwined around the cross's center and were tied in place with a white ribbon.

"What a beautiful cross." Claudia walked closer to examine it better.

"That was a gift." Sorella Agata's face looked sad as she let her eyes rest for a moment on the cross before saying, "I will let you rest and get settled. I'm sure you must be tired from your long trip. Please do not hesitate to let me or one of the other sisters know if there is anything you need."

Claudia realized this was the sister's way of telling her they would not be discussing right now the subject of the *cassata*. Usually, Claudia did not back down so easily when she was interviewing, and she had learned in her journalism courses that persistence was key. But this was an entirely different situation. She needed to show respect to Sorella Agata, and while the nun had exhibited meekness earlier, Claudia sensed she would not tolerate aggressive or disrespectful behavior. So all Claudia said for the moment was, "*Grazie mille.*"

Sorella Agata turned to leave, but Claudia stopped her.

"Oh, Sister?"

Sorella Agata paused, looking over her shoulder. "*Si,* Signorina Lombardo?" She seemed in a hurry to leave.

Claudia paused for a moment. "I'm sorry if I offended you with my pertness and impatience. I can imagine how frustrating it must be to always have everyone ask you about that cake, but you can understand their curiosity?"

"That is all right. No need for you to apologize. I was not offended, and I am sorry if I gave you that impression. The *cassata* is my most popular pastry at the shop, and its success has helped to make the business a prosperous one. I am very grateful for that. But I take pride in all of our baking. I have a . . . how do you Americans say something that is sour and sweet? I know there is a word for it."

"Bittersweet?"

"*Si,* bittersweet. I have a bittersweet relationship with the cake. But that is another story. The truth is, Signorina Lombardo—"

"Please, call me Claudia, Sister."

"Very well, as you wish. The truth is, Claudia, there is no secret ingredient. I'm sorry to disappoint you as I have no doubt disappointed the chefs who traveled here from as far as even Paris and Vienna to discover what sets my *cassata* apart from any other that has been made."

"A few of the chefs have claimed you do not want to reveal your secret, which I wouldn't blame you for, since it is after all your trademark dessert."

Sorella Agata vehemently shook her head. "I tell you, there is *no* secret ingredient. I don't like swearing to God, but if I were one who swore, I would take that oath. Maybe it is the ingredients we have here in Sicily?" Sorella Agata shrugged her shoulders before continuing. "You can watch me make the cake, and I will show you my recipe, which is in a recipe book that all of my workers use. I keep it in the kitchen. I have no secrets from anyone."

"Forgive me once again, Sister, if I am being rude, but if that is true, why did you stop talking about the cake once you noticed the workers in the kitchen were listening to our conversation?"

"I refuse to give in to this ridiculous speculation, and it has caused my workers to question me in the past. That is not what we are about here at the Convento di Santa Lucia del Mela. I won't have it. I have told them what I am telling you now. That is the end of the discussion. They should be focused on producing the finest pastries and serving our village, not on silly gossip created by a bunch of pompous, jealous chefs!"

Sorella Agata's face was flaming beet red now. She walked over to the window and opened it. Taking a few deep breaths, she closed her eyes.

"I'm sorry, Sister. I did not mean to upset you. As a food writer and interviewer, I have an inquisitive mind. Of course, I want this book to be special and I—"

"You thought the secret ingredient would be the magic to ensuring the success of your book?"

"Our book, Sister. This book will be your book as much as it is mine, and your name will appear as the coauthor."

"That won't be necessary, Claudia."

"But you are contributing to the book. These are your pastries I will be writing about, and it is your story that will appear on the pages. After trying the Virgin's Breasts, I can tell you are an extraordinary pastry chef and have a special gift. Why won't you take the credit you deserve?"

"You forget, Claudia, I am a nun, and as such, the only credit I allow myself is that I am doing God's work and serving Him as well as the people I strive to help. That is enough for me. I must confess. I had reservations about doing the book."

"So why did you agree?"

"We could use the money."

"Really? But the pastry shop seems to be doing so well from all the baked goods I saw in the kitchen and the lines of customers waiting to buy at the courtyard's windows. You said so yourself earlier, and you are now taking in tourists as boarders. Surely, there must be enough income?"

"We are doing well. But the money would not be for the convent or the pastry shop. There is an organization we work with in town, and I would like to donate my share of the book's proceeds to this organization."

"That is very noble of you, Sorella Agata."

"It is not out of nobleness that I am doing this. The organization does wonderful work. I would hate to see them have to close their doors after all they've done for the people in this village as well as the neighboring towns."

"I understand." Claudia was about to ask what kind of work the organization did when Sorella Agata said, "If you will please excuse me now." She turned to leave, but Claudia stopped her again.

"One more thing, Sister. Would you mind if we began our interview after I'm settled? That is, if you won't be busy with anything else? If I hope to cover everything, including watching you prepare the recipes you'd like me to include in the book, we'll need to get started right away. I'm sure after all the years you've been here your story must be a long one."

Sorella Agata's eyes held a distant look as she responded. "That will be fine. Meet me in the courtyard in an hour. That should give you enough time to get settled and give me time to tie up a few things in the kitchen."

"That's perfect. Thank you, Sister. I'm really looking forward to hearing your story and seeing you create your recipes."

Sorella Agata managed a small smile. "Yes, this will be something new for me as well. I hope to learn from you, too, Claudia."

And with that Sorella Agata turned around and shut Claudia's door quietly behind her.

Claudia let out a long sigh. She had almost blown it by bringing up so soon the secret ingredient in Sorella Agata's *cassata*. But she was beginning to think the nun was telling the truth about not having a secret ingredient, if only for the fact that she was a woman of God and most likely averse to lying. But she was also human. Claudia sensed there was something else about that cake that unnerved Sorella Agata other than everyone's claiming it possessed a secret ingredient. She had to tread carefully, but Claudia was determined to find out the full story behind this mysterious cake.

~~ 2 ~~

Biscotti all'Anice

ANISE COOKIES

Sorella Agata poured three and a half cups of flour onto her work surface—a marble butcher block she had custom made from the local craftsman. She shaped the flour into a small mound, and then, using her index finger, she swirled a hole in the center. Cracking four eggs expertly with one hand into a wooden bowl, she beat them vigorously with a fork until they turned the same golden hue as the marigolds that sat in a vase on the convent's kitchen window ledge. Marigolds were her favorite flowers, and she loved looking at them when she was busy working. She dropped the egg mixture into the hole she had dug in the flour before adding sugar, olive oil, and a teaspoon of anise oil. No matter how much of a rush she was in, Sorella Agata always took the time to smell the licorice scent of the anise oil. But today the oil served a dual purpose as its fragrance soothed her frayed nerves.

Though she was meeting Claudia in under an hour, she decided to quickly make anise cookies. She would serve them to Claudia piping hot and would take pleasure in seeing the surprise on the writer's face that the cookies had just come out of the oven. But that wasn't her only reason for making the cookies. She needed to calm down before she sat down with Claudia. As she worked the dough for the biscotti, she instantly felt her muscles relax, and soon her racing thoughts slowed down. She had trained herself long ago in this form of meditation. While she prepared her prized sweets, she emptied her mind of all worries and just focused on the task before her.

She had to be careful when she kneaded dough that should not be overworked, as was the case with the dough for the anise cookies. If she was really preoccupied, she would keep kneading and kneading away, taking her frustrations out on the dough, only to discover later that it was too tough and useless to make the perfect biscotti. Instead of throwing out the dough and wasting it, Sorella Agata would still make the cookies, but would save them for her and the nuns to consume. After all, she could serve her customers nothing but the best.

Shaping the cookies into small braids, she spaced them a few inches apart on rimmed baking sheets lined with parchment paper, and then brushed egg wash over each one. After placing the sheets into the oven, she found her thoughts inevitably turning to her conversation with the writer.

"*Stupida!*" she muttered to herself.

Why did she let Claudia's interrogation about the *cassata* affect her so much? Surely, she should be accustomed to all the speculation about the blasted cake.

They should be focused on producing the finest pastries and serving our village, not on silly gossip created by a bunch of pompous, jealous chefs!

Sorella Agata's words came back to her, and she could feel her face flush again. How could she have called the chefs who had visited her pompous and jealous? She was letting her pride over her work take hold—a feeling she strived, as a nun, to keep at bay. Closing her eyes, she prayed, softly speaking the words aloud.

"Please, God, forgive me. Help me to remember that my work is done to serve You and others. I promise I will try harder not to let my anger get the better of me."

Sorella Agata wished she could give Claudia, as well as the other chefs who had visited her, the answer they wanted. She wished she did have a secret ingredient that made her *cassata* taste as wonderful as it did. But she was just as baffled as the rest of them as to why her cake surpassed all others that had come before it. While the *cassata* had made Sorella Agata and her pastry shop famous, she still refused to cave in to the requests to make it available year-round as she was now doing with the Virgin's Breasts pastries and even the marzipan fruit. She only baked *cassata* three times a year: for Valentine's Day, Easter, and Christmas. And that was too much for her. As she had told Claudia, making the cake was a bittersweet task for her.

From preparing the pale-green marzipan that was used to line the sides of the cake pan and gave the *cassata* its trademark color to ensuring the ricotta cream she used for the filling had the right amount of sweetness, Sorella Agata loved everything about making the *cassata* that had come to symbolize her beloved Sicily—for it was one of the island's most treasured desserts. And she took great pride in the elaborate designs she created on the cake once it was assembled and a lemon icing was spread over its top. She liked to fill a piping bag with melted chocolate and then create a border of decorative swirls around the cake. Then in the center, she used candied fruits and arranged them in the shape of a flower. The cake was a stunning work of art once it was completed. Yet whenever she made the *cassata,* an overwhelming sadness took hold of her.

As a deeply spiritual woman, Sorella Agata did not believe in superstition, which was hard since Sicilians steadfastly adhered to decades-long superstitions. But she was beginning to think the cake had some sort of *malocchio,* or evil eye, attached to it. *Malocchio* was usually cast by a jealous person. Perhaps she wasn't so far off in accusing the pastry chefs—who had visited her and claimed she had a secret ingredient that she was loath to share—of being jealous?

"*Basta!* Enough! It is just a cake and nothing more!"

"*Sorella Agata, stai bene?*" Madre Carmela stood before her, looking concerned.

"*Si, si,* Madre. Just talking out loud—as usual. I am fine. There is nothing to worry about." She managed a smile for the elderly nun.

Madre Carmela had been the mother superior at the convent and the head pastry chef of the shop until 1985, when she relinquished both roles to Sorella Agata. The success of the pastry shop had begun with Madre Carmela and, as such, she would always hold a special place in the convent. It saddened Sorella Agata to see the senior nun's increasingly failing health due to her dementia and rheumatoid arthritis. But Madre Carmela still insisted on doing whatever she could manage in the pastry shop's kitchen.

"Signorina Lombardo is waiting for you in the courtyard. She was worried you had forgotten since you were supposed to meet at four."

Sorella Agata glanced at the large round clock that hung above their pantry. It was fifteen minutes past the hour. She wasn't that late, but she supposed the writer was anxious to get her work started.

"I'll be there shortly."

"Shall I let her know?"

"No, that's all right, Madre Carmela."

The old nun's gaze wandered around the kitchen, as she tried to assess what she could do. Sorella Agata tried to give her work that wouldn't be too taxing. She noticed a batch of *Ravioli di Ricotta*— Sweet Ricotta Turnovers—that had just been fried and were draining on a plate of paper towels.

"Madre, those ravioli need to be dusted with powdered sugar."

"*Sì.* I will do so right away." Madre Carmela walked slowly over to the pantry, where she located the powdered sugar. She then took a small fine-meshed sieve off one of the many hooks that hung around the kitchen's walls and held various cooking instruments from pans to colanders. Sorella Agata watched her as she transferred the drained sweet ravioli to a decorative serving platter. With shaky hands, she used the mesh sieve to sprinkle the powdered sugar over the fried pastries. Sorella Agata had no doubt there would be uneven clumps of sugar on the ravioli. But Madre Carmela was the only worker in the pastry shop from whom she did not expect perfection. Sorella Agata wondered how much longer Madre Carmela would be able to continue helping out in the kitchen.

Turning her thoughts away from Madre Carmela, she checked on the anise cookies in the oven. About five more minutes until they were ready. Spotting Veronique, one of their apprentices in the pastry shop, walking by in the corridor with a pile of just laundered towels, Sorella Agata called out to her.

"Veronique! Can you please come here?"

Veronique was only nineteen years old, but she was very devoted to her work in the pastry shop. Her stunning good looks often led others to believe she was older, and while she was bright and intelligent, she still had a certain naïveté about her, especially in her habit of asking too many questions or slightly inappropriate ones. Sorella Agata credited this to her immense curiosity, which got the better of her at times, and she prayed in time Veronique would improve. But she could never be irate with her. For the young woman held a very special place in her heart, and even the other nuns had a soft spot for her. They all thought of her as their little sister, even though she had no intention of taking vows to become a nun.

"Sorella Agata, who is that beautiful woman sitting in the courtyard?"

One would think that with Veronique's inquisitive nature, she would have known by now that Claudia was writing a recipe book about the convent's pastry shop and was here to interview Sorella Agata. But the older nuns also frowned upon her excessively nosy behavior and kept as much as they could from her. "It's for her own good, after all," they would say. Sorella Agata couldn't help feeling the other sisters were being petty and should understand that Veronique's young age accounted for much of her naïveté. She was after all still a teenager, and she'd been through a lot in her short life.

"Her name is Claudia Lombardo. She is a food writer from America—New York City, in fact—and she is here to write a book featuring our pastries as well as the history of the pastry shop."

"A writer? From New York City? How wonderful! I must tell everyone." Veronique turned to leave, but Sorella Agata stopped her with a firm grip to her shoulder.

"Wait! You do not need to tell them. They know already. Besides, I need your help here. When the timer goes off, please take the anise cookies out of the oven and bring a few out on a plate to Signorina Lombardo and me. And please, Veronique, do not ask her any questions. She is here to interview me, *not* the other way around."

"*Va bene,* Sorella Agata." Veronique sighed, not even attempting to hide her extreme disappointment. "I'll just take these towels first to the linen closet."

"Let me. I am all done sprinkling sugar on these ravioli."

Madre Carmela took the towels from Veronique and held them up against her chest so that her arthritic hands wouldn't drop them.

Sorella Agata walked over to their espresso and cappuccino machine and poured two demitasse cups of espresso for Claudia and herself. They had only been able to purchase the expensive machine two years ago. Before they had the machine, the job of several workers in the kitchen was strictly to make espresso so that a few pots were always brewed and ready to serve their long lines of customers. But now that they had the machine and could make espresso and cappuccino in half the time, they were able to put the workers to use elsewhere in the kitchen.

As she stepped out into the courtyard, she observed Claudia seated at one of the café-style tables the convent kept for their patrons who wanted to eat their pastries while enjoying the outdoors and their garden. Veronique was right in noting that the writer was beautiful. Her long chestnut brown hair was clipped up in a sloppy French twist, but its imperfect shape suited her relaxed style. She wore jeans that hugged her tall, lithe frame and a sleeveless top in a stunning shade of coral. A leather messenger bag rested on the empty seat beside her. Sorella Agata expected to see a laptop, but to her surprise Claudia was writing on a legal pad. Large, oval brown sunglasses covered her eyes. Sorella Agata hoped she would remove them when they began their discussion. She hated not being able to read people's expressions, and she was already feeling a bit anxious about their interview.

"I'm sorry I am late, Claudia." Sorella Agata placed the cups of espresso on the table and sat down opposite her guest.

"That's all right. But I must admit I was a little nervous I had scared you off with our earlier conversation and that you had changed your mind completely about the book." Claudia smiled shyly as she took off her sunglasses.

At the mention of their awkward discussion, Sorella Agata felt bad once more at how she had reacted.

"I should be the one to apologize, Claudia."

"No, please don't, Sister." Claudia reached out and patted her hand.

"Excuse me." Veronique quietly spoke as she approached the two women. While she was doing her best to keep her gaze lowered and not stare at Claudia, Sorella Agata could see she kept stealing sidelong glances as she placed the plate of anise cookies on the table.

Taking pity on her, Sorella Agata said, "Claudia, this is Veronique, one of our apprentices in the shop."

Veronique was so surprised that Sorella Agata had acknowledged her presence, she merely stared at Claudia and remained silent.

"Pleasure to meet you, Veronique." Claudia extended her hand, which Veronique took, but not before glancing first at Sorella Agata for her approval. Sorella Agata gave a slight nod of her head.

"Perhaps I can ask you a few questions during my stay here, with Sorella Agata's permission of course? It would just be a few questions about your work in the pastry shop."

"Yes, I would like that very much, Signorina Lombardo."

"Please, Claudia."

Again, Veronique looked to Sorella Agata for approval.

"If Signorina Lombardo wishes to be called Claudia, by all means you must honor her request, Veronique. Now, please excuse us. We have a lot to cover before dinner."

"Have a nice day," Veronique softly said before walking away.

"And you as well," Claudia said, smiling warmly. She noticed Veronique had an accent that didn't seem completely Italian, but she couldn't quite place it.

Sorella Agata waited until she was certain Veronique was out of earshot before saying, "You must forgive her . . . How do you say in English . . . enthusiasm?"

"Yes, enthusiasm."

"You must forgive her abundant enthusiasm. She still has a lot to learn, but she is a bright young woman. I have high hopes for her."

"I'm sure. You do not mind that I would like to talk to her and a few of the other workers—just to get their experiences as well?"

"No, that's perfectly fine."

Claudia bit into one of the anise cookies. "Oh, these are to die for! And they just came out of the oven!" She closed her eyes, savoring the cookies' sweet licorice flavor from the anise oil.

Sorella Agata smiled, pleased that her intention of surprising Claudia with the warm cookies had worked.

"I thought you might like these with your espresso. They have an—"

"Anise extract. Yes, I can taste it. They're heavenly."

"*Grazie.* We actually use anise oil here instead of extract. I feel its essence is purer and imparts a stronger flavor."

"Anise oil. Interesting." Claudia scribbled on her pad.

"So I was thinking we could start with the pastries first, then proceed to biscotti and cakes, and cover the specialized desserts like *gelati* and *granite* last. Oh, I forgot my recipe book." Sorella Agata began to get up, but Claudia stopped her.

"Actually, Sister, I would like to start with your story—the history of the pastry shop, how you fell in love with pastry making, and of course a little about your life."

"But we have a lot of recipes to cover."

"Yes, but as I mentioned to you in my e-mails, your story is important for this book, too. I don't want this to just be a straight recipe book. People who know about you and what you have done with this pastry shop are fascinated. I not only want to share with the world your wonderful pastries, but also the inspiration behind them as well as your passion for what you do. I know I've only just arrived here today, but I sense there is a strong familial bond between the sisters and even the lay workers you employ in your kitchen. I want this book to convey the intimate story behind the pastries and the love you all share for them."

Sorella Agata's face looked pensive. "I see. I am touched you could see all of that since you only just arrived today."

"I am a writer. It's my job to be observant." Claudia winked at Sorella Agata before reaching into her messenger bag and producing a tape recorder.

"So if you are ready, Sorella, let's begin."

Sorella Agata finished the last of her espresso. Folding her hands in her lap, she said, "I am ready whenever you are, Claudia."

"Where did your inspiration for pastries come from? Naturally, as a nun here I know you would've had no choice but to help with the shop. But what I want to know is your true inspiration for taking this shop and turning it into the success it is today. I want to know when it was that your passion for the art of pastry making began."

Sorella Agata took a deep breath. "Well, it all started with a young woman by the name of Rosalia. I guess you can say she was my muse."

3

Lulus

SICILIAN CREAM PUFFS

October 5, 1955

Rosalia was back home. Her family surrounded her: Mamma and Papà, her older brother, Luca, and her little sister, Cecilia. Rosalia hopped up and down while her family held hands and danced the *tarantella,* circling around her first in one direction, and then in the other. Sicilian folk music played, and when the tempo picked up her family danced even faster, closing the circle in on Rosalia—her cue to switch places with another family member. Her eyes locked onto Luca's and in a split second they made the switch. Now her brother was the one they circled around. Rosalia, her parents, and Cecilia could not stop laughing. Whenever Luca was in the center of the *tarantella* circle, he made a spectacle of himself as he contorted his expression into various silly faces and danced like a madman.

Rosalia laughed harder and harder even as a fierce wave of vertigo took hold. But soon her laughter became a piercing shriek as she felt herself pulled out of her family's embrace and sucked into a dark hole.

"Rosalia! Rosalia! Wake up, my dear girl. It is just a dream. You are here at the Convento di Santa Lucia del Mela. You are safe now." Madre Carmela stroked the young woman's long bangs, which were wet with perspiration, off her forehead. Her lush dark locks were braided, reminding Madre Carmela of two shiny pieces of black licorice. Working in the pastry shop for so many years, she had made a habit of comparing everything in life to food.

Rosalia's gaze wandered around the room. Then her eyes met Madre Carmela's. She stared at her for a moment, but once familiarity set in she exhaled a long sigh.

"Are you hungry? I've brought you something very special today." Madre Carmela left Rosalia's bedside and went over to the dresser, where a bowl covered with a linen napkin sat.

Curious, Rosalia sat up in bed, straining her neck to see what delicacies the good nun had brought her today. These past few weeks, since Madre Carmela and the other sisters had found Rosalia by the cave, her only comfort had been in the daily sweets they brought to her. She had always loved her mother's baked goods, but what the sisters had here was a whole new world of pastries Rosalia had never heard of. It was almost like La Festa dell'Epifania, the Feast of the Epiphany, where La Befana—or the good witch—brought gifts to all the small children. Rosalia remembered that her parents were always careful to save their money lest hard times fall on them. But they always managed to ensure that La Befana brought gifts to their children. The presents ranged from the ripest, largest oranges or pears to pistachios, almonds, and sweet dates to a shiny new red ball for Rosalia and a perfectly chiseled wooden car for Luca to race. One year, little Cecilia even received a porcelain doll that came all the way from Palermo, Sicily's capital. Though Rosalia was no longer a little girl, she still felt that same sense of excitement whenever the nuns unveiled their pastries.

Madre Carmela brought the covered bowl over to Rosalia. A subtle, sweet aroma reached Rosalia's nose. Her mouth watered in anticipation of whatever culinary surprise Madre Carmela had for her today. Instead of waiting for the sister to unfold the napkin, Rosalia pulled it back herself and almost gasped when she saw what delights were in store for her. Puffy clusters of dough in vanilla and chocolate were piled one on top of the other to form a misshapen pyramid. Chocolate and vanilla cream oozed from a few of the pastries.

"Ha-ha! I see you couldn't wait." Madre Carmela gently teased Rosalia, who quickly looked up, her cheeks turning the same hot pink hue as the sugar roses the nuns had painstakingly created this morning for a wedding cake.

"That's all right, my child. I'm happy to see you are feeling more comfortable here. Go ahead. Have as many as you like."

Rosalia wondered which one she should try first—the chocolate or the vanilla. She'd always loved anything vanilla, so she opted for one of those first. Instead of taking a small, tentative bite out of the pastry, as she would have done her first few weeks at the convent, she popped the whole sweet at once into her mouth, eliciting another hearty laugh from Madre Carmela. But this time, Rosalia wasn't embarrassed. She closed her eyes, savoring the pastry's airy, flaky crust and the rich sweetness of the vanilla cream. Her sadness over her dream was quickly dissipating.

"What are they called?" Rosalia asked in a soft voice as she took a bite out of one of the chocolate pastries.

Madre Carmela was surprised. The girl had only spoken a few sentences since they found her. She mostly nodded or shook her head whenever Madre Carmela or the other nuns asked her a question. Sometimes, Madre Carmela had been able to coax a small smile out of her, but that was it. This week marked a month since they had rescued Rosalia. Madre Carmela was beginning to worry she might not ever get through to the terrified young woman. Her hope had been in the pastries. Whenever Rosalia ate one of the shop's creations, Madre Carmela detected a flicker of light in her eyes. Now at last it appeared that the sweets had managed to crack through Rosalia's shell.

"They are called *Lulus*."

"*Lulus?*"

"*Sì.* You'll never forget that silly name." Madre Carmela smiled before continuing. "They are *bignè* or cream puffs, but these are Sicilian cream puffs, and they are baked. When we fry *bignè,* they are known as *sfinci.*"

"I remember my mother used to make *sfinci*." Rosalia's eyes filled once more with sadness.

Fearful that she would lose her again, Madre Carmela returned to the subject of the *Lulus*. "As you tasted, they're filled with cream—vanilla in the lighter ones, and chocolate hazelnut in the chocolate puffs."

"They are very delicious." Rosalia took another chocolate one. As she ate, her brows creased together, and her eyes held the vacant stare Madre Carmela had become accustomed to seeing when she entered Rosalia's room. She couldn't help wondering what thoughts were flashing through the young woman's mind.

"*Si*, Rosalia. They are very delicious. I knew you would love them. I am so overjoyed you are feeling better. If you want, you can come down to the kitchen later and watch me make a few of our pastries."

Rosalia didn't seem to hear Madre Carmela. She had lost her again. Just as Madre Carmela's spirits began to sink, Rosalia said, "Why hasn't my family come to see me?"

"Your family?"

Rosalia nodded her head. "Where are they?"

"Rosalia, we haven't been able to notify your family. You haven't remembered your surname, and it seems like there are fragments of your memory that are missing. I, and the other sisters, have asked you a few times about your family and where you live. At first, I thought it was just that you weren't feeling well enough to tell us, but later I could see you were struggling to try to remember. You've forgotten all of this?"

The past few weeks were mostly a fog for Rosalia. She did remember the nuns rescuing her by the cave and how weak and sore she had felt. Her body had ached terribly. She remembered Madre Carmela and the wonderful sweets she brought her every day. Suddenly, visions of the nuns sitting at her bedside, sponging her body, and feeding her spoonfuls of minestrone came back to her. They had talked to Rosalia, but their words were a jumble. She even remembered they had prayed aloud for her. Their prayers would often wake her, and at night their prayers would lull her to sleep as she watched the nuns fingering each bead of their rosaries.

"Rosalia, if you remember now your surname and where your family lives, I can let them know right away you are safe." Madre Carmela looked at Rosalia, concern filling her large, almond-shaped eyes.

Rosalia liked the nun's face. She felt immediately comforted when she saw her, much as she had whenever her mother greeted her every morning. At the memory of her mother, a stab of pain pierced her heart. She had to return home right away. Her family must be worried sick about her.

"I live in . . ." Rosalia's mind went blank. Of course she knew where she lived. She had known no other home since she was a baby. It was the home she had dreamed of returning to every day since . . . No! She couldn't, wouldn't, let her mind go back to that horrible place. She tried once more. "I live in the town of . . ." Nothing.

"That is all right, my child. It will come to you. Don't worry."

"How long have I been here now?"

"A month."

"A month? I need to go home. My family must think the worst has happened to me." Rosalia pressed her fingers to her forehead as if willing herself to remember her name and her family's town. Tears spilled onto her cheeks. Madre Carmela reached into her pocket and took out a handkerchief. She patted the tears dry, then sat down on the bed. Taking Rosalia's chin in her hand, she gently lifted it, forcing the girl to look her in the eyes.

"Please, don't pressure yourself. You have had a horrible ordeal. Your mind is just tired. Allow it to get more rest. Your memory will return."

"How can you be so sure, Madre Carmela?"

The mother superior pursed her lips. She began to speak, but then paused. Since that first day when she had found Rosalia, a fierce protectiveness had taken hold of her. But she knew the day would come when she couldn't shield Rosalia from everything.

"Rosalia, when we brought you back to the convent, our first priority was feeding you since you looked so malnourished. I also wanted you to feel safe here, and I did not want to do anything that would cause you alarm. But by the end of the first week, I knew I had to have a doctor examine you, especially when Sorella Giovanna found a large bump on your scalp while she was washing your hair. Upon closer inspection, I saw your scalp was swollen, and it was badly bruised. So I asked the local doctor to come and examine you. Do you remember that?"

Rosalia shook her head.

Madre Carmela wasn't surprised that Rosalia had forgotten the doctor. At first, she had refused to let the doctor anywhere near her, though Madre Carmela and the other nuns had repeatedly assured the young woman he would not hurt her. But she had become like a wild beast, shrieking and trying to evade capture by its predators. She had run from one corner of the room to the next, looking for an escape. The doctor had been forced to tranquilize her with a sedative. Once she was unconscious, he had examined her. Madre Carmela had remained in the room, but had asked the other nuns to leave. Though she had already seen the bruises and cuts that covered Rosalia's entire body, she had still winced when the doctor removed her nightgown so that he could fully examine her.

The doctor had confirmed Madre Carmela's suspicions. Rosalia had been severely beaten, and her head injury was most likely the result of being hit with a blunt object. Rosalia had a concussion, and he believed that was the cause of her memory loss. He had assured Madre Carmela that Rosalia's memory would return.

"Rosalia, the doctor confirmed for us that you were badly beaten. Someone hit you in the head, and you suffered a concussion. That is why you are having problems now with your memory. But the doctor believes your memory loss is temporary."

"So I will have my memory back?"

"He believes so."

"Is that why I have been so dizzy?"

"You have been dizzy?"

"It comes and goes."

"*Sì*, the concussion must be causing the vertigo as well."

"What will happen to me if I don't remember where my family lives?"

"You will. Please, Rosalia. Place your trust in God."

"But what will happen to me?"

"You will live here with the sisters and me."

Madre Carmela's words seemed to calm Rosalia for the moment.

"All I want you to focus on now is getting stronger. And I think you are ready to leave your room and explore the grounds of our convent. We have a vast library. I'm sure you can find a few books you will enjoy reading. And our courtyard is beautiful. I have been bringing you flowers from our gardens every day." Madre Carmela gestured to a simple white vase filled with miniature pink rosebuds. "I thought you might like roses since your name begins with Rosa."

A memory suddenly returned to Rosalia. Her father brought her roses from her mother's garden every year for her birthday. He would tie them with a purple ribbon. Purple was her favorite color. That she remembered. And there was something her father used to say when he presented the flowers to her. What was it? "Beautiful roses for my beautiful rose."

"I remember. My father always gave me roses for my birthday."

"See. Your memory *is* coming back. Now just rest." Madre Carmela placed a kiss on Rosalia's forehead and turned to leave.

"*Grazie,* Madre Carmela."

"You don't need to thank me, Rosalia."

"Madre, you mentioned earlier that I might be able to come to the kitchen and watch you bake. If you are not too busy now, I would very much like to see how you make your pastries."

Madre Carmela's face beamed. "Now would be the perfect time."

With the help of Madre Carmela, Rosalia carefully stepped out of bed. It felt strange to have her bare feet touch the cold floor. She had been lying in that bed for so many weeks now. Letting Madre Carmela wrap her arm protectively around her back, Rosalia slowly stood up. Though her legs felt shaky, she knew she had to push herself to regain her strength, and that wasn't going to happen if all she continued to do was lie in bed. Her family was waiting for her, and she was not going to let them down.

❦ 4 ❦

Ossa dei Morti

BONES OF THE DEAD

November 1, 1955

Rosalia was in the kitchen, helping the nuns and the laywomen who worked at the pastry shop. Since that first day when she decided to live again rather than waste away in her bed, she had come down to the kitchen and helped with whatever the workers needed. Immediately, she became fascinated with the art of pastry making. She had no doubt in her mind that it was an art and marveled at how the workers on a consistent basis could bake and create such beautiful little treasures of sweets. Her favorite part was when it came time to decorate the fancier sweets like the marzipan fruit or the elaborate cakes such as *Trionfo di Gola*—Triumph of Gluttony.

She soon learned that the pastry shop operated on a calendar, in particular, the religious calendar. Pastries were made either to honor a saint's feast day or for a religious holiday like Christmas or Easter. Today was the first of November and was also All Saints' Day—a church holiday that honored all the saints. The weeks leading up to this religious holiday were among the busiest for the convent's pastry shop. Though the nuns and other workers had been preparing for a month, they were still baking and decorating marzipan and *Ossa dei Morti*—Bones of the Dead cookies made to resemble bones. These cookies were consumed every year on November 2nd for All Souls' Day, which was tomorrow. Both the marzipan and the bone-shaped cookies had been selling out. For the past two weeks, long lines of customers had waited to purchase the brightly colored, realistic-looking marzipan fruit and the white, hard bone-shaped cookies.

While marzipan was one of the pastry shop's most popular sweets and was sold throughout the year, the demand for it soared in late autumn. On November 2nd, All Souls' Day, children in Sicily woke up to find baskets containing marzipan, *pupi di zucchero*—or sugar dolls—and other toys and treats. The baskets were supposed to be gifts from their ancestors who had passed away. On the afternoon of All Souls' Day, families descended upon cemeteries with picnics and flowers to celebrate the memory of their loved ones who had passed on.

Rosalia's parents had also taken part in this long-held Sicilian custom, but they had never been able to afford a basket for each of the three children or the marzipan fruit that was sold at their local pastry shop. Instead, they prepared one large basket containing apples or pears, and her mother made her simple *Taralli* cookies that were more savory than sweet and meant to be dipped in wine or coffee. Rosalia did not even know that the tradition was to add marzipan fruit to the baskets until Madre Carmela told her. The families of her school friends were poorer than hers, and many of the other children did not receive a basket on All Souls' Day.

Tears fell down her face. Rosalia lifted the apron tied to her waist to wipe her tears, but she didn't notice that a teardrop had fallen onto one of the raw bone cookies that she had neatly lined up on a baking sheet. When she lowered the apron, her head suddenly began to throb. Closing her eyes, she rubbed her temples. A fuzzy image of a shop flashed before her. Customers were walking out of the shop holding hangers of men's trousers or suits that looked as if they had been freshly pressed. The shop's sign came into view, and she could make out the letters. They spelled "Sarto DiSanta."

Rosalia opened her eyes. "Sarto," she said aloud to herself. Of course, her father was a tailor. That was his shop she had just seen in her mind. "Sarto DiSanta," she whispered once more. Her heart raced. She remembered. DiSanta was her last name. Rosalia DiSanta. Yes, that was it!

She ran out of the kitchen, much to the dismay of the nuns, who shouted after her, "Rosalia! Where are you going? We still have much work to do!"

Running out into the corridor off the kitchen, Rosalia bumped hard into Sorella Domenica—one of the few nuns she still hadn't met. But she had noticed her during the past few weeks in the kitchen. She always seemed to stay apart from the other nuns, and sometimes Rosalia caught her glowering in her direction. Then again, Sorella Domenica often had a scowl on her face. Rosalia had not given her much thought since she was always busy in the kitchen and focused on her work. She knew her name only because she'd heard the other nuns talking to her.

"Excuse me," Rosalia said in a low voice as she tried to hurry past Sorella Domenica. But the towering nun continued to block her path. At 5´11˝, Sorella Domenica loomed over Rosalia's petite frame.

"Excuse me, *Sister.* You *must* always address me and the other nuns as 'Sister,' " she said in a very harsh tone.

Rosalia was taken aback by her demeanor. Until now, all the other sisters she had come into contact with at the convent had been nothing but kind to her.

"I'm sorry, Sister. My name is Ro—"

"Rosalia. I know who you are." Sorella Domenica looked angry. "You must never run in the convent—or even in the courtyard. This is a place of God, and as such, we must always respect it as well as carry ourselves in the most dignified and humble manner. The Carmelite Sisters do not call attention to themselves, and we expect everyone who resides and works here to abide by our rules."

"I understand, Sister." Rosalia looked down at her feet. She could feel her face burning up.

"So why were you running? What is so important that you could not walk?"

Rosalia glanced up into the sister's face. Her expression still looked contemptuous. Rosalia did not want to tell her. She wanted

Madre Carmela to be the first to hear the news that she remembered her surname and the name of her father's tailor shop. But she knew she had to tell Sorella Domenica something if she hoped she would clear her path.

"I was just looking for Madre Carmela." Rosalia silently prayed that would be enough explanation for Sorella Domenica to let her be on her way. But Sorella Domenica remained fixed in place as she stared at Rosalia, making her feel as if she could see right through to her soul. Rosalia was tempted to look away, but she knew that might give the nun cause to think she was lying. So with all her willpower, she stared back at Sorella Domenica, doing her best to maintain a wide-eyed, innocent stare.

After a few seconds of silence, but what felt like an eternity to Rosalia, Sorella Domenica said, "Very well. But remember what I told you."

Sorella Domenica stepped aside. Rosalia bowed her head in the nun's direction and walked away, doing her best to take slow steps. She could feel Sorella Domenica's stare on her back for as long as it took her to reach the end of the long corridor. When she reached the corner, she stole a sideways glance to see if the nun was still watching. She was. How strange!

Once out of Sorella Domenica's sight, Rosalia resumed running. She wasn't going to let the likes of Sorella Domenica intimidate her—well, at least when she was far away from her peering gaze. Rosalia ran to the tiny office that Madre Carmela used. She had told Rosalia that the office used to be a linen closet that she had cleared out so she could take care of the convent's affairs. Madre Carmela was often in here in the late afternoon.

Though the door was slightly ajar, and Rosalia could make out Madre Carmela making entries with a pencil into her ledger, she still knocked gently on the door.

Madre Carmela looked up. Unlike Sorella Domenica's perpetual scowl, Madre Carmela's face instantly beamed when she saw Rosalia.

"Ah! Rosalia! Come in. Is it time for *cena* already?" She glanced at the clock that hung on the wall to the side of her desk—the only adornment in the room.

"No. It's not suppertime yet. I'm sorry if I'm disturbing you, but it is important, Madre Carmela."

She waved for Rosalia to enter. "You can always come to me, my child. Don't ever be afraid." She smiled warmly.

Rosalia's heart lightened. She thanked God every day that Madre Carmela had found her. While she was anxious to be reunited with her family, she had quickly grown fond of the nun who had cared for her these past couple of months.

"I remembered my surname, Madre Carmela! DiSanta. That is my family's name!"

"Ah! That is wonderful, Rosalia! See, I told you your memory would come back!" Madre Carmela stood up and went around the desk. She wrapped Rosalia in a tight embrace.

"There's more! My father is a tailor of men's clothes. He owns a shop called Sarto DiSanta. I still don't remember the name of my hometown." Rosalia's happiness from a moment ago was quickly overshadowed by the realization that she still had not remembered where she lived.

"That is all right. I will contact the local police now that I know your surname and even the name of your father's shop. They can make inquiries here and in the neighboring towns. We are closer to finding your family. And who knows? Maybe you'll even remember everything by the time the police are done with their inquiries." Madre Carmela squeezed Rosalia's shoulder encouragingly as she lowered her head to peer into her face. "Don't be discouraged."

"*Sì,* Madre. I must be patient. I'm sorry. I do not want you to think I cannot stand being here. I just miss my family so much, and I know they must be very worried about me."

"Naturally, your place is with your family, Rosalia. I will call the police first thing in the morning."

"*Grazie,* Madre Carmela."

"It's nothing. So is it still crazy down in the kitchen?"

"*Sì!* I should return. I abandoned them in my excitement over remembering. I wanted you to be the first to know." Rosalia smiled.

As Rosalia and Madre Carmela made their way back to the kitchen, they walked arm-in-arm. Madre Carmela had a habit of telling Rosalia a saint's story whenever they worked side by side in the kitchen, and since today was All Saints' Day, it was even more fitting. Madre Carmela was about to tell Rosalia the story of Saint Rita when an idea suddenly came to her. Taking a deep breath, she knew she was taking a chance and that Rosalia might not be ready. She quickly uttered a silent prayer to God before beginning.

"Have you ever heard of Saint Maria Goretti, Rosalia?"

Rosalia shook her head.

"She was made a saint by the church only five years ago, in 1950. Well, Maria and her family were very poor—so poor that they had to share a house with another family after Maria's father died when she was nine years old. The family they lived with had a teenage son, Alessandro. He was nineteen years old when he began pressuring Maria to have relations with him. Maria was merely eleven years old. Alessandro made advances toward her on three separate occasions, but each time she adamantly refused, telling him it would be a mortal sin. But on the third occasion, Alessandro became livid. He choked Maria and threatened to kill her if she did not sleep with him. She still refused. That was when he stabbed her many times."

Madre Carmela paused and looked at Rosalia, whose face had gone completely ashen. Madre Carmela tightened her grip on Rosalia's arm. She wondered if she should continue the story. But Rosalia looked at her when she hesitated, waiting to know what happened next.

"Maria was rushed to the hospital. The doctors were amazed she was still alive, but her injuries were so grave they could not do anything for her. Before she died, she forgave Alessandro. Although Alessandro did not manage to rape Maria, she is also considered to be the patron saint of rape victims as well as of chastity, young girls, purity, poverty, and forgiveness."

Rosalia stopped walking. Her eyes held a vacant stare—the same stare she had when they found her by the cave. Madre Carmela instantly regretted telling her the story of the saint. Rosalia was still not ready. Though her plan of telling Rosalia the story of Saint Maria Goretti in hopes that it would stir up forgotten memories of whatever terrible fate had befallen her before she was rescued had worked, now it seemed that Rosalia was regressing again.

But just when Madre Carmela began thinking the worst, Rosalia spoke.

"What happened to him?"

"Alessandro?"

Rosalia nodded.

"He was arrested and sent to prison. After three years, he repented and said Maria had visited him in a dream. Maria's mother had interceded on his behalf, and instead of receiving a life sentence in prison, he was only given thirty years. After he was released, he went to Maria's mother and asked for her forgiveness, which she granted. He later became a monk."

Rosalia pursed her lips tightly. Anger flashed across her face.

"So he was able to continue living his life while that poor girl lost hers. How could her mother have forgiven him? If that were my daughter, I would never forgive anyone who had hurt my child like that."

Breaking away from Madre Carmela's embrace, Rosalia walked a few feet before stopping. She wrapped her arms around her waist and brought her chin to her chest. Rosalia's lustrous, waist-length dark locks swung forward, covering her face like a mourning veil. Madre Carmela could see her shoulders shaking. And then the sobbing began, softly at first, but soon the sobs became anguished moans. Madre Carmela rushed over and pulled Rosalia tightly against her chest.

"Shh! Shh! Everything will be okay. I promise you." Madre Carmela stroked Rosalia's hair, which had an immediate soothing effect on Rosalia. She continued to cry, but quietly now.

Madre Carmela led Rosalia back to her room and helped her into bed.

"Get some rest. Don't worry about the kitchen. I will tell them you weren't feeling well. I'll bring something up for you to eat later." Madre Carmela was about to turn off the lamp on the night table and leave when Rosalia reached out for her arm.

"Wait, Madre. Don't go yet. I want to tell you what happened to me."

"You remember?"

Rosalia nodded. "I never forgot. It's just that I tried to push it out of my mind. I didn't want to remember what happened to me in that cave." She closed her eyes tightly as if she was still trying to block the horrible memories.

"You don't need to tell me, my child."

"I think I must if I ever hope to find peace again."

Madre Carmela nodded. Sitting down on the edge of the bed, she took Rosalia's hand in hers and held it tightly as she listened to Rosalia recount the nightmare that would forever change her life.

5

Nacatuli

ENGAGEMENT COOKIES

"There was a young man who came into my father's tailor shop one day. He needed to have his Sunday dress pants hemmed. I was at the shop that day, helping my father press the clothes that he had finished tailoring. We took turns in my family, helping my father at the shop. My mother and I knew how to sew, so we would help with some of the basic stitching the clothes needed. My brother, Luca, who is nineteen—two years older than me—had been my father's apprentice, but when he turned eighteen, he decided he wanted to become a priest. We had a seminary in one of the neighboring towns, and that was where he went to live and study. So he was not able to help in the shop so much.

"Luca and I were very close from the time we were toddlers. We were always hand-in-hand, skipping and singing. And whenever one of us was done with our chores at home, or even in my father's shop, we would help the other. We were all very close in my family." Rosalia paused for a moment. Her eyes filled with tears.

"Would you like me to get you a glass of water?" Madre Carmela asked.

"No, that's all right. Thank you. I'm sorry. You must be patient with me. It hurts so much that I have been away from my family for this long, and now that my memory has been coming back, it hurts even more to remember the many good times we shared."

"You must let those memories sustain you, my child. And you will be with them again soon, so there's no need to feel such despair," Madre Carmela said softly. Rosalia thought she could hear the good nun forcing back tears.

"As I was saying, we were a very close family. My mother gave birth to another child when I was ten. Cecilia. Mamma and Papà let Luca and me choose the name. I'll never forget the first time I laid eyes on my baby sister. She was born with a full head of black hair, just like mine. She was so sweet, and she only grew sweeter as she became older. Even little Cecilia did her part in Papà's shop by dusting and sweeping. Luca had made a short broom for her." Rosalia laughed. "Every time we watched her sweep, we giggled. She took her work seriously and was proud to do her part in our family.

"So the day this young man came into my father's shop, I was alone at the counter while Papà went out to buy fabric. My father had taught me how to take measurements and pin clothes so that when he needed to leave the shop as he did that day, I could handle the customers. So this man came in. He looked to be in his early twenties. I found out later he was twenty-three. I asked him to step into the dressing room and try his pants on so that I could pin the hem. He kept staring at me, and at first I thought nothing of it since I had been accustomed to the boys in my village looking at me. But when I was pinning the hem of his pants, I glanced up to ask him if the length that I was taking in for the pants was fine, and he had this strange look in his eyes. Something about it sent shivers down my spine. I had to ask him twice if the hem length was fine before he answered me.

"I was relieved when my father returned to the shop while the man was changing back into his street clothes. I remember when he stepped out of the dressing room, he seemed mad when he saw my father.

"Papà told me I could go back to finishing my pressing. Though I was in the back of the shop, I could hear the young man give my father his name for his receipt. Marco Salerno. He was making small talk with Papà, asking him how long he'd had the shop and if his whole family helped him. My father answered him pleasantly, and I was relieved my father didn't give him my name when he said his daughter helped him as well as my other siblings and mother. Marco then took his receipt and wished Papà a nice day.

"I went to my father's shop three to four times a week, and ever since the day Marco first came to the shop, he would walk by and look into our windows. And whenever Papà stepped out, Marco would come visit me. I could tell he was lurking around outside and waiting for my father to leave. The first time he came to visit me, I politely responded to his questions about how I was and agreed with him about the weather we were having. But I continued doing my work, hoping he would see I was busy and had no time or interest in talking to him. He asked me my name on that first visit. I didn't want to tell him, but I didn't want to be rude either." Rosalia stopped talking and shook her head. "Sometimes being polite is the most dangerous thing one can do." Rosalia paused a moment before continuing.

"So I told Marco my name. On his fourth visit, he asked me if I would take a walk with him in the piazza that was a few streets over from the tailor shop. I told him I couldn't leave the shop unattended. He told me it would just be for a few minutes, and probably no one would even come by since it was almost time for midday dinner, and people would be preparing to eat rather than worrying about getting their clothes tailored. But I told him my father trusted me, and I must watch the shop. In an instant, the sweet expression Marco maintained whenever he talked to me changed into the same angry expression he had had when he'd seen my father had returned to the shop that first day he'd come by.

"But he must've noticed the alarmed look on my face, because then he laughed and said, 'All right, Rosalia. You are a good daughter. How about I come by your house on Saturday, after siesta, and ask your father if you may accompany me to the cinema?'

" 'I'm sorry, but my father would not allow it,' I said.

" 'Why not? I come from a respectable family, and I am asking him for his permission before taking you out. What harm can there be in going to the cinema?'

"I wanted to tell him that only a moment ago he had had the audacity to ask me to take a walk with him in the piazza while my father was away, but I dared not. He'd shown how quickly his mood could change, and something inside me warned me not to stir his temper.

"So instead I said to him, 'Marco, it's not you. My father does not wish young men to begin courting me until I am nineteen, and he doesn't approve of the cinema.'

"He asked me, 'How old are you now?'

"When I told him seventeen, I couldn't help smiling a little, feeling as if I'd won.

"Again, Marco's face flared with anger. He put his hands in his trousers' pockets and began circling the front of the store. I could see he was desperately trying to think of a way around my age.

"Then he said, 'Maybe if I talked to your father he would have a change of heart?'

"Marco's voice sounded desperate. I didn't want to encourage him. Though I was afraid to be honest with him, I knew I had to, for he was determined to court me.

"So I said, 'Marco, you seem like a nice boy, but I am also not ready to be courted. I'm sorry.' I kept my gaze lowered as I said this.

" 'I am a man, *not* a boy!' he shouted as he pounded his fist on the counter, causing me to take a quick step back.

"I held my hands up, saying, 'I did not mean to offend you, Marco. I'm sorry. Please, calm down.'

"He shook his head fiercely and said, " 'You are just afraid of your father, Rosalia. I can see that.'

"In my head, I was screaming, *No, I'm afraid of you!* But I refused to let him see just how fearful I was.

" 'Don't worry, Rosalia. We will find a way to be together,' he told me before coming around the counter and toward me. I continued backing up, but he firmly placed his hand on my wrist, squeezing so hard that I had no choice but to stop.

"He lowered his face near mine, and I squirmed, turning my head to the side. But he still managed to plant a kiss on my lips. In that moment, my own fury was unleashed and, with my free hand,

I struck him across the face. He let go of me and rubbed the cheek I had slapped. I ran to the front of the shop and opened the door, screaming, 'Get out! I never want to see you in here again!'

"I began to relax when he walked toward the door. He was about to step outside, but then hesitated and said, 'You are not feeling well today. I am not upset with you. I'm sure you will be feeling better the next time I visit.'

"And with that he left. I closed the door and locked it. My body was shaking all over. When my father returned, I told him what had happened. I was terrified of Marco, especially after that day, and I didn't want to be alone at the shop the next time he came by. I also told my father how I'd noticed Marco was spying on us every day, waiting for his chance to come visit me when I was alone in the shop.

"So the next day, my father told me to stay at home. My brother, Luca, was visiting from the seminary. Papà asked Luca to accompany him to the shop. I suspected they were going to warn Marco to stay away from me.

"That evening, when my father and brother came home, Luca told me, 'Don't worry. That beast will no longer bother you.'

"I breathed a sigh of relief, but I still felt a bit uneasy. Marco had managed to give me a good scare. My parents thought it best for me to stay away from the tailor shop for a few weeks just in case Marco was crazy enough not to heed my father's and brother's threats to stay away from me. This way, he would see I was no longer at the shop.

"I asked Luca one day what he and Papà had said to Marco.

"He said, 'I told him I would break his legs if he came near you again, and Papà said he would make sure no one in town would ever hire him for any work.'

"I asked Luca how he could've threatened to hurt Marco since he was studying to be a priest.

"He said, 'I know I sinned, but I went crazy thinking of how he made advances toward you when you were all alone. Besides, he needed to realize that we were serious.'

"Luca had always been my greatest defender. When we were children, a few boys and girls were teasing me because I was the shortest one in class. One day, Luca heard the kids teasing me. They had formed a ring around me and were taking turns pushing me so hard that I fell each time. Luca ran over and yelled at them and told them if he heard them make fun of me or lay a hand on me again, they would be sorry.

"So a few weeks went by and all seemed fine. I hadn't seen Marco, and my father told me he had not noticed him skulking around outside the shop. We thought he'd understood that he was never to show his face again. I told Papà I could go back and help him, but he would only allow it if my mother or Luca were with me. He still regretted leaving me alone that afternoon in the shop when Marco kissed me.

"One morning, I was hanging laundry to dry in our yard. My mother and father were at the shop, and they had taken my little sister, Cecilia, with them. When I was left alone in the house, I would turn up the radio very high and sing along to the music while I did my chores."

Rosalia stopped talking as she squeezed her eyes shut. Tears still managed to stream down her face.

"If this is too much for you, Rosalia, we can stop for today." Madre Carmela spoke in a gentle tone.

Rosalia opened her eyes. "No, I need to get it all out now."

"*Va bene.* All right. Go on when you are ready." Madre Carmela waited patiently.

"Carla Bruni's song 'Mambo Italiano' was on the radio. Oh! How I loved that song! Luca and I would always dance to it, making Cecilia laugh. Even Mamma and Papà would join in sometimes. So I was singing that song as I was hanging sheets I had just laundered. I was so wrapped up in the song that I didn't notice the shadow on the other side of the sheet. And then without warning, Marco pulled the sheet off the clothesline and was standing before me with the most malicious smile. I almost screamed from the fright he gave me.

"I asked him, 'What are you doing here, Marco? How . . . how did you find out where I live?' My heart was pounding so hard against my chest. I don't know how I even managed to get those words out.

"He smiled as he said, 'I followed your father home one night.' He actually looked quite proud of himself.

" '*Sei pazzo!*' I yelled.

"He calmly said, 'I am not crazy, Rosalia. Please don't ever say that again. I'm sorry if I scared you, but surely you must see this was the only way for me to find you. Why haven't you been at the shop? It wasn't because of me, was it?'

"I told him, 'My father and brother warned you to keep your distance from me. You should leave before they come home. They will be back any minute now.'

"Naturally, I was lying. Luca was back at the seminary, and Papà and Mamma would be at the shop until our midday meal, which we always had at one o'clock. It was only ten in the morning. Worse, I suspected Marco knew that my father wouldn't be back until later since he had continued to spy on us and had even followed my father home. But I was desperate, and I hoped that the insane part of Marco would perhaps believe my lie.

"He didn't seem to be deterred and said, 'That's all right, Rosalia. I will wait for your parents. I realize now I handled matters the wrong way that afternoon I last saw you. I should have come to your home first and spoken to your father. Look, I even brought something for you and your mother.'

"Marco lifted a small box from a *pasticceria*.

"I looked away and picked up the sheet Marco had tossed to the ground. I threw it over the clothesline and began smoothing out the wrinkles from it. I was about to place a clothespin on one corner of the sheet when Marco's hand closed over mine.

" 'You are working too hard here. Your hands are dry. I could give you a better life, Rosalia—an easier one. You haven't even looked inside the box. Have you ever had pastries like these before?'

"I couldn't resist stealing a sidelong glance at the box that he now held open. The box was filled to the rim with the most beautiful cookies I had ever seen. A few were shaped like flowers; others were shaped like fish, and a few were oval shaped, but I wasn't sure what these last ones were supposed to be. Each of the cookies had a slit cut into it, and contained a filling. I was so in awe of the cookies that I forgot about the sheet I was hanging and that Marco's hand was still on mine.

"He came even closer to me and whispered, '*Sono belli, ah?*' A wicked grin broke out across Marco's face. He knew he'd intrigued me with the cookies, but I refused to give in.

" 'I have seen far more beautiful cookies,' I said as I shrugged my shoulders and then I went back to placing clothespins on the sheet, but not before I wrested my hand free from Marco's grip.

"But he pleaded with me, '*Dai,* Rosalia. Come on. Try one. I bought them in Lipari and carried them all the way here on the ferry.'

"I couldn't help laughing and said, 'You went all the way to Lipari to buy cookies? You really are crazy, Marco.'

"I don't know what came over me, but suddenly I was no longer afraid of him. Instead, my anger was taking hold at his stubborn refusal to accept that I had no interest in him.

"His eyes darkened before he responded. '*Si,* I went all the way to Lipari. Doesn't that show you how much I care about you and what a good impression I want to make on your parents, that I would go to one of the finest *pasticcerie* and bring these as a gift? And they're not just *any* cookies. They're *Nacatuli.* On the island of Lipari, they serve these at engagement parties. Each of the different shaped cookies symbolizes a good omen for the couple. The roses symbolize love, the fish good luck, and the oval-shaped cookies are for fertility.' Marco smiled.

"Once more, he seemed proud of himself, but I was horrified as I realized why he had brought these particular cookies to my home. And my suspicions were confirmed by what he said next.

" 'Rosalia, we will be very happy together once we're married and settled into our home. Once your father agrees to give me your hand in marriage, we can have the proper courtship until our wedding day.'

"My fury was completely unleashed at this point. I yelled, 'I am never marrying you, Marco! And my father will never allow you to marry me! Never!'

"Marco's face went as white as the sheets I was hanging. For a few minutes, he said nothing. My fear returned, but I refused to let him see it. I turned my back to him and resumed hanging laundry. Perhaps my outburst would convince him finally to leave. If only I had been so lucky.

"He came up behind me and whispered into my ear, 'You think you are too good for me, don't you? But you're nothing more than a tailor's daughter. You should be honored that I am interested in you. Do you even know how much money my family has? You could live like a queen instead of being your parents' slave at home and in the tailor shop. What is the matter with your father? Having you take men's measurements and letting you get so close to them?'

"I turned around and beat my fists against Marco's chest. 'You pig! Get out! Get out before I call the police!'

" 'The police?' Marco said, laughing loudly before adding, 'Go ahead. A few of the police officers are my good friends.'

"I couldn't stand there any longer, listening to him. I ran toward my house, but he ran after me and caught me by the arm, pulling it roughly behind me. I winced aloud in pain.

"His voice then rose. 'Why are you making this so hard, Rosalia? Can't you see I just want to make you happy? Give it some time. You are young and inexperienced. Surely, you will come to see I am the only man for you.'

"I grew desperate and decided to appeal to any sense of decency he might have. 'Please, Marco, you're hurting my arm. Let me go. If you truly care about me, you will come back when my family is here and do the respectable thing.' My voice trembled as I said this.

"He said, 'That is what I am trying to do, Rosalia, but you refuse to listen to me. I was hoping to do this differently, but I can see now there is no other way. You are right about your father. He will continue to stand in our way. I was a fool to think I could persuade him otherwise.'

"And then I felt a sharp prick in the back of my neck. Before I could realize what was happening, I passed out. When I woke up I was in that horrible cave." Rosalia stopped narrating her story. She squeezed her eyes tightly shut as if trying to block out the memories that had returned.

"Rosalia, you don't need to tell me further what happened to you." Madre Carmela reached into the pocket of her habit and pulled out a handkerchief. She wiped the tears running down Rosalia's face.

"I am all right. I just need a moment."

Madre Carmela waited patiently for Rosalia to continue.

"I woke up and had no idea where I was. It was pitch-black, and it felt like I was lying down outside on the cool ground. I screamed, but no one seemed to be near. I crawled, trying to make my way in the dark. Then suddenly, I heard the strike of a match, and Marco was standing before me, lighting a candle.

"I screamed, 'Where have you taken me? Take me back home! You will be arrested and go to prison for kidnapping me!' I was hysterical, but Marco remained calm, ignoring me as he proceeded to light several more candles that were in a semicircle on the ground.

"Now that I could see, I was able to make out that he had taken me to a cave. My eyes searched frantically for an escape, but all I could see was a long, narrow passageway, which I assumed probably led to the cave's exit. I realized then he had taken me deep into the cave, and I feared I would get lost if I tried to make a run for it. For I was certain there must be other passageways, and how would I know which would lead me back outside? I also felt weak. I now realized Marco had drugged me earlier when I felt something sharp prick my neck. Whatever Marco had injected me with had left me feeling groggy and lethargic. No, I needed to wait patiently before I escaped. That was my first mistake. I should have tried to run then. If I had succeeded in getting away from him, that might have prevented what happened next."

"Don't punish yourself, Rosalia. There is no way of knowing what would have happened."

Rosalia looked into Madre Carmela's face. "Perhaps." From her tone, she didn't sound quite convinced. Sighing deeply, she continued her story.

"After Marco was done lighting the candles, he proceeded to show me around the cave." Rosalia laughed. "Can you imagine that? It was as if he had brought his new bride home for the first time and was proud of where they were living. And that was exactly what he was thinking. He had me, and no one would stand in his way now.

"Marco said to me, 'Rosalia, I know it will take some time for you to get accustomed to being here, but this is only temporary. I need to make arrangements, and then we will leave and go where we can start fresh. You will be happy being married to me.'

" 'How many times do I need to tell you I will never marry you? Do you understand you have committed a crime by kidnapping me?' I cried as I said this.

" 'Once you become my wife, the authorities won't care,' Marco said, shrugging his shoulders. He wasn't even looking at me. Instead, his eyes stared off into space, and he had this sick smile.

"I became so enraged in that moment and did not think about my safety. I threw myself at him, scratching his face, pulling his hair, kicking him. He let me have my way for a little while, but then without warning, he struck my face so hard with the back of his hand that I fell. That should've frightened me, but it only made me angrier. I crawled over and bit his leg. He pulled me by my hair, forcing me to stand." Rosalia placed her hand on the back of her head as if she were feeling the pain all over again.

"Then he turned me around, and pulled my arms behind me. He nudged the back of my legs with his knees and said, 'Walk!'

"I remained rooted in place, but then he jerked my arms back so hard I thought my shoulder was going to dislocate.

"He screamed again, 'Walk!' I stepped forward. He kept nudging me forward until we came to a spot in the cave that had what looked like a bed made of hay with blankets laid on top."

Madre Carmela closed her eyes, remembering the makeshift bed of hay and the bloody clothes she'd found when she examined the cave after she and the other nuns had discovered Rosalia.

"Marco pushed me so hard that I fell onto the hay bed. He then slapped me a few times. I fought back, kicking and scratching him. But it was no use. He was stronger than me. He tore my clothes off and . . ." Rosalia's voice trailed off. She looked at Madre Carmela, who was weeping silently. "I think you know what happened next, Madre."

Madre Carmela took Rosalia in her arms. She held her close as Rosalia sobbed uncontrollably. "He stole my innocence. He took away the girl I used to be."

"Shhh! Shhh! No one can take away who you are, Rosalia. Remember that! No one! You still have the same pure heart of the girl you were before this monster came into your life."

"Thank you, Madre," Rosalia said before pulling away and continuing her story.

"Over the next few weeks . . . Well, I imagine it was weeks. It felt like I was there a long time. You found me by the cave in September, Madre? Is that right?"

"*Si*. It was September."

"So I was in the cave for a month, since I remember it was early August when Marco kidnapped me. He continued to beat me over the course of those weeks. He beat me often for no reason. After he raped me, I was too afraid and in too much despair to fight back like I had on that first day. He seemed to take pleasure in hurting me. He didn't rape me again after that first time. I thought that was strange since he continued to beat me. Then I realized he was deluding himself into thinking we had a pure relationship. He actually apologized for forcing himself onto me." Rosalia shook her head.

"He said, 'I hope you will forgive me, Rosalia, for taking you against your will. We will not sleep together again until we are man and wife.'

"I asked him, 'Why did you do that, Marco?'

"Naturally, I did not expect a rational answer from a lunatic. I had no doubt that he was absolutely mad in addition to being evil. But I still had to ask him why, especially now that he was telling me he would wait to have relations with me until we were married.

"He said, 'Rosalia, you must see I had no choice. It was the only way. Your father will now have to agree to let me marry you. For who else will have you now that you are no longer a virgin?'

"My heart sank when I heard those words, and a cold shiver ran throughout my body. I had heard of girls who had disappeared in neighboring villages, and then they were found, but were suddenly married off. People whispered that the girls were no longer virgins, and they had to marry the men who had kidnapped them because they were now ruined. My mother told me it was a barbaric custom, and she could not believe the poor girls were forced to wed the men who had violated them. But she dared not voice her opinion to anyone else but me. In our village and the neighboring towns, people held fast to their customs. My mother didn't want to become an outcast. The only comfort I had in that moment was remembering my mother's being horrified by this act. She would never allow me to marry Marco, and I could not see my father giving his permission either. This emboldened me.

" 'My father would never let you marry me even after what you did to me. You do not know my parents. They love me and will always protect me.' I said this calmly.

"He laughed and said, 'Ah, Rosalia. You might now be a woman, but I see you still have the mind of an innocent child. Everyone lets us down in this life—even those closest to us.'

" 'You're wrong! You're wrong!' I screamed.

" 'Stop screaming!' Marco yelled at me, covering his ears. 'When will you start trusting that I am the one who has your best interests at heart, *not* your parents? When?'

"He grabbed me by the shoulders and shook me so hard. Then with one last thrust, he banged my head against the wall of the cave. I blacked out.

"After that, things only got worse. He continued to beat me, but he began to hardly feed me. I think he did this to make me weaker so that I could not escape. He would leave me alone during the day to go to work, which surprised me since he didn't have a job when he was spending all of his time spying on me at my father's tailor shop. He had also suggested before he kidnapped me that his family had plenty of money, so I didn't think he needed to work. But he explained to me one day he was saving money so that after we got married we could move far away and he could give me a grand house. I then realized he must've lied about his family's being well-off in an attempt to impress me.

"One day while he was at work or wherever he was, for I still had my doubts about whether he really did have a job, I decided to try to escape. I walked down the narrow passageway I had noticed the first day he brought me to the cave. But as I suspected, there were other passageways. I refused to give up. I couldn't take his beatings anymore, and I was constantly hungry. And when I thought about my family and how worried they must be about me, I found what little strength I had left in me to keep walking through that cave. But I was getting disoriented and could not keep track of the different passageways I had gone down. Then I heard Marco calling to me, 'Rosalia! Rosalia! Come out now! I will find you.'

"I began running, trying to get farther and farther away from his voice. But it was no use. He found me.

"He said, 'Did you really think you could get away from me, Rosalia? I have taken care of you. How do you think you would last alone out there? Ah? You don't even know where we are. I will tell you. We're in the middle of a deep forest. The nearest town is miles away.'

"I know now he was lying since you and the sisters found me, and your convent isn't too far from where he took me."

Madre Carmela nodded her head. She looked pale. Rosalia wondered if this was all too much for her to hear. But there was no stopping now. She had to relay the whole story.

"Marco led me back to where he'd been keeping me in the cave. He tied me to a wooden chair he sat on when he was with me. At night, thankfully, he didn't sleep with me. He slept on the ground on the opposite side of where my hay bed lay. After he tied me, he brought his face close to mine, and then he pressed a hunting knife against my throat.

"In that moment, I prayed silently. *God, please let him kill me. Please let this ordeal finally end.*

"Can you believe that, Madre Carmela? I prayed for death. I couldn't go on living like that any longer, and, when I thought about how he'd stolen my maidenhood, I wanted to die as well.

"But God didn't answer my prayers that day. All Marco did was keep the knife pressed against my throat while he threatened my family and me.

"He said, 'If I catch you trying to escape again, I will give you the worst beating yet, and I will make sure your family pays, too.'

"Every day afterward, he threatened me with a possible scenario

of what he would do to my family. He even told me he would kidnap my little sister, Cecilia.

"He continued to starve me. I begged him, 'Marco, please, I'm
so hungry. I need to eat more.'

"But all he fed me were those *Nacatuli* cookies—one a day. The
thought of those cookies now makes me want to vomit. And to
think I had thought they were so beautiful when I first laid eyes
upon them before he kidnapped me. I was also very dehydrated for
he only gave me one cup of water for the entire day. I became so
desperate that I began telling him what he wanted to hear.

" 'Marco, when are we getting married? When are we going to
start our lives together and leave this cave? You were right. I want
to be your wife. Only you can make me happy,' I said, doing my
best to sound as convincing as possible.

"He looked pleased when I said this. He came over and kissed
me on the lips. I wanted to die. He began caressing my arms and
back, and I thought, *Oh no! What have I done? He will rape me
again.* But he didn't. Then in an instant he snapped and punched
me in my stomach. I collapsed on the ground, writhing in pain. He
kicked me a few times and then dragged me to the chair and tied
me up again.

"When I was no longer sore from the last beating, I vowed I
would find the exit to the cave. After my first attempt to escape, he
tied me every day. And on some days, he would keep me bound
even after he'd returned from work.

"He kept the chair I was tied to against the wall of the cave,
never thinking I might try to use the jagged edges of the cave wall
to gnaw away at my ropes. And that's exactly what I did. I became
so tired from the effort of rubbing my wrists against the wall. My
arms were scraped, but I ignored the stinging. Once I got free, I
stood up. My legs were shaking so badly, and I felt very dizzy, so I
got down on my knees and crawled.

"I don't know how long I crawled, but I managed to find a dim
light coming through a crack in one of the passageways in the cave.
Finally! I knew this had to be the passageway that would lead me
outside. I struggled to get to my feet once more, hoping I could get
out of the cave faster. My heart raced as I stumbled along, holding

onto the wall for support. As I kept walking, the light became brighter, and I knew I was definitely on the right path.

"Once I stepped outside, I was so overcome with relief. I fell onto my knees again and cried. I didn't even care that I was in the middle of a forest—that much of what Marco had told me was true. I was just so happy to be out of that cave. But when I tried to stand back up again, I blacked out. The next thing I remember was your face, Madre."

Madre Carmela was crying again. Wiping her tears with the back of her hand, she shook her head before saying, "I suspected you had been violated, Rosalia, and the bruises and the bump on the back of your head told me you had been beaten. And yes, I could tell from your emaciated body, you were severely malnourished, but even though I suspected all this, it still did not prepare me to hear how much you suffered at the hands of that man. I'm so sorry, Rosalia."

"If you hadn't found me that day outside the cave, Madre Carmela, who knows where I would be now? I wouldn't put it past Marco to have killed me. His rage seemed to be growing."

"Do not think about that. What is important is that you are safe now. I am going to leave and let you get some rest—unless you would like me to wait until you fall asleep?"

"No, that is all right. You can go, Madre. You are right. I must get some rest, for I will have a big day tomorrow, especially now that I remember my surname and the name of my father's shop. That should help the police find the town where my family lives much quicker. Don't you think?"

"Absolutely, Rosalia. We will soon learn the name of your hometown, and you'll be reunited with your family once more. You can then put this nightmare behind you."

"I don't know about that, Madre. How can I put what happened behind me until Marco is caught? I'm afraid he will find me. But I haven't been afraid here at the convent. There's no way he would find me here, Madre. Still, my place is with my family. I cannot let my fear of Marco keep me apart from them any longer."

"For all you know, Marco might be long gone. When he discovered you had escaped, I'm sure he was terrified that you went to the police and that they would be looking for him."

"I hope you're right."

Madre Carmela kissed Rosalia on the forehead. "*Buona sera.* I will bring you some food later. But see if you can sleep for a bit. You will feel better when you wake up. I promise you."

Rosalia smiled. "*Grazie,* Madre Carmela. I will miss you and the other sisters who took care of me these past few weeks."

"We will miss you, too, my child. Now get some rest."

Madre Carmela turned to leave. Before she closed the door behind her, she glanced at Rosalia. Her eyes were closed, and she still looked like an innocent child. But Madre Carmela knew Marco had stolen Rosalia's innocence in more ways than one, and Rosalia would never again be the same young woman she once was.

As Madre Carmela made her way back down to the kitchen, she silently prayed, *Please, God, help Rosalia gain strength and courage. Please protect her for the rest of her days. She has suffered enough.*

Though Madre Carmela believed in God and realized she could not understand why bad things happened to good people like Rosalia, her faith was tested whenever she heard such horrible stories. Taking a deep breath, she entered the kitchen and did what she always did when her spirits were especially low: She sampled a sweet. She decided to try one of the *Ossa dei Morti*—Bones of the Dead cookies—that had just come out of the oven.

As Madre Carmela crunched down on the hard, sugary cookie, she was taken aback. Turning to Sorella Domenica, who was pounding away at an immense ball of dough—no doubt taking her frustrations out on it as she always appeared to be doing—Madre Carmela asked, "Who baked this sheet of *Ossa dei Morti?* Do you know, Sorella Domenica?"

Without looking up from her kneading, Sorella Domenica said, "It was your new disciple, Rosalia."

Madre Carmela frowned. Sorella Domenica's sarcasm was not lost on her. Though no one was immune to Sorella Domenica's sour temper, Madre Carmela still expected respect. After all, she was the mother superior. And frankly, Madre Carmela had just about had it with the nun's nasty temperament. She prayed for Sorella Domenica and had hoped she would soften as she aged, but instead her behavior only seemed to be getting more abrasive.

"Do *not* talk to your mother superior in that tone, Sorella Domenica. I will not have it! And if I hear you say anything disparaging toward that girl again, you will be punished. In fact, your behavior needs to change. There will be repercussions if I don't see you making more of an effort to act kindly toward the other sisters and even our lay workers. Am I making myself clear?"

Sorella Domenica's face colored, but Madre Carmela knew it was not from shame. For nothing shamed her. Instead, her change in complexion was due to the fact that she was absolutely livid.

"*Mi dispiace,* Madre," she said in a low tone as she slightly tilted her head, meeting Madre Carmela's gaze, but only for a moment before she looked back down to her dough and resumed kneading.

"Are you sure Rosalia baked these cookies?"

"*Sì,* Madre. That was all she worked on when she was here hours ago. I haven't seen her since I found her running through the corridors. She almost ran into me." Sorella Domenica paused for a moment, before quickly adding, "I'm sure she had her reasons for running though."

Madre Carmela pursed her lips. "I see. *Grazie,* Sorella Domenica." She knew the nun was dying to make some comment about Rosalia's disrespectful behavior of running through the convent, but had thought better of it.

"May I ask, Madre, why you want to know if Rosalia baked that last batch of *Ossa dei Morti?* Are they not to your satisfaction?" Sorella Domenica finally stopped kneading as she waited for Madre Carmela's response.

"Actually, they exceed my expectations. They are quite possibly the most delicious *Ossa dei Morti* that I've ever tasted. The girl must have a natural talent for baking." Madre Carmela smiled, enjoying the cross expression that came over Sorella Domenica's face as she said this.

"*Buongiorno,* Sorella." With that, Madre Carmela took her leave.

As she exited the kitchen, she stole a glance in Sorella Domenica's direction and caught her sampling one of the Bones of the Dead cookies Rosalia had baked. Madre Carmela softly laughed to herself. She knew what she had said to the grumpy nun was the best punishment she could dole out to her. For Sorella Domenica's weakness, in addition to her quick temper, was to obsess. No doubt she would be agonizing all evening over why Rosalia's cookies tasted incredibly delicious.

❦ 6 ❦

Gelo di Cioccolato

BENEDICTINE CHOCOLATE PUDDING

November 26, 1955

Madre Carmela was standing over one of the gas ranges, whisking feverishly the chocolate she was melting in a saucepan of water to make *Gelo di Cioccolato*—a chocolate pudding dessert based on a recipe passed down from Benedictine monks in the eighteenth century. The pudding was one of Madre Carmela's favorite desserts, but she often made it when she was feeling down. And today was such a day—for Rosalia would finally be going home to be reunited with her family.

The police had been searching for the tailor shop Rosalia's father owned for the past four weeks. Yesterday, the police inspector, L'ispettore Franco, finally had brought Madre Carmela the good news that they had located a shop by the name of Sarto DiSanta in the village of Terme Vigliatore, which wasn't too far from Santa Lucia del Mela. Madre Carmela was surprised that Marco hadn't taken Rosalia very far from her hometown. She would've thought he'd go as far as possible to evade capture. But then again, Marco sounded absolutely insane, so she could not expect he would have been more rational.

When Madre Carmela had given the good news to Rosalia and

told her the authorities would set out the next day to let her family know she was safe, she had insisted on also going. Naturally, the poor girl was anxious to be reunited with her family. Madre Carmela would accompany Rosalia and the police to Terme Viglia-tore after they had their midday meal.

Though she was happy for Rosalia, she couldn't help feeling sad that she would not see the beautiful young woman anymore. It had pleased her so much to see Rosalia bloom back to life since they had found her by the cave. And the girl had even taken a liking to helping the sisters and the lay workers in the kitchen, where she learned to make a new pastry every day. Madre Carmela still could not believe how quickly Rosalia had taken to pastry making, but what astounded her even more was the young woman's natural tal-ent for baking. She seemed to possess a photographic memory and was able to remember the ingredients to a recipe after only learning it once. Madre Carmela had watched her bake a few of their popu-lar pastries, which they made several times a week, and every time, Rosalia remembered the ingredients.

Madre Carmela sighed. Shaking her head, she mentally scolded herself. *Shame on you! You should be happy for the girl and not feel-ing sad that you will miss her.*

The chocolate had finally melted to the perfect thick, but not too thick, consistency she wanted. She reached for a wooden spoon and scooped up a little of the chocolate. Blowing on it first so she wouldn't scald her tongue, she tasted the melted chocolate.

"Ah! *È buono!*" She closed her eyes, reveling in the rich, silky chocolate. Instantly, her mood lifted. She would put some of the pudding aside for Rosalia to take home to her family.

"*Ciao,* Madre Carmela."

"Rosalia! You look so pretty today."

She was wearing a violet-colored dress that contrasted perfectly with her raven hair, which was tied in a loose ponytail with a matching violet ribbon. The ponytail was swept to the side and lay over her left shoulder. There was an unmistakable glow in her face. She was happy.

"*Grazie,* Madre Carmela. Anunziata let me borrow this dress."

Anunziata was one of the lay workers at the pastry shop, and she also resided at the convent. Rosalia and Anunziata had formed a friendship during the past month. Madre Carmela had seen Anunziata earlier that morning, and she, too, looked sad—no doubt that she would be losing her new friend.

"That was nice of Anunziata."

Rosalia nodded her head. "I will miss her, as well as you and everyone else, Madre Carmela. But you'll see me again when I come back to return Anunziata's dress."

Madre Carmela's heart leaped for a moment, hearing that she would see Rosalia again. But she couldn't help wondering if Rosalia's family would allow her to come back. She had wondered if she should tell Rosalia to feel free to visit anytime she wanted. But Madre Carmela didn't want the girl to feel obligated and as if she were in any debt toward the convent for having nursed her back to health. After all, the sisters always helped others in service to God, and not in hopes of getting or expecting anything in return. So she refrained from encouraging Rosalia to visit.

"And we will miss you, too, Rosalia. Try some of this chocolate that I have melted for a pudding. We will have it for dessert." Madre Carmela spooned up a good dollop of chocolate and held it out for Rosalia to taste.

Rosalia leaned forward and carefully tasted the hot, melted chocolate. "*Delizioso!*"

"Wait until it is done. It will taste even better. There is no doubt you will be dreaming about it tonight."

Rosalia laughed. "I am certain of it. Thank you, Madre, for everything. I will never forget all that you and the other nuns have done for me."

"I am just happy your health has been restored and that you will be with your family soon. You must be so excited."

"I am. I hardly slept last night in anticipation."

"Well, soon enough, you will be back home."

A few hours later, Rosalia was seated at one of two long rectangular tables where the sisters and the lay workers who lived at the convent took their meals. The convent had no formal dining room, and there was no space in the kitchen for the tables, so the only place the nuns could fit them was in a corridor. Fortunately, the corridor was only a few feet from the kitchen, so that the nuns weren't forced to walk a long distance carrying heavy pots and platters filled with food.

Madre Carmela had insisted Rosalia, as the guest of honor, sit at the head of the table where Madre Carmela normally sat. Rosalia couldn't help but notice Sorella Domenica frown when Madre Carmela had first suggested she sit in her seat. Her new friend, Anunziata, sat to her right.

"Rosalia, I was thinking maybe I can come visit you on my days off. You can show me around your town." Anunziata was twirling her long braid around her finger, something Rosalia had noticed she did habitually whenever she seemed anxious. Anunziata's hair reminded her of the amber color of honey.

"I would love it if you came to visit me in Terme Vigliatore, Anunziata. And I will come visit you and everyone else here, too."

"You must promise, Rosalia. We have had people here who were passing by and swore they would come back, but never did. Please swear you won't be one of those people." Anunziata held her stare.

"I promise. Besides, I could never turn my back on the women who saved me." Rosalia reached over and squeezed her new friend's hand.

Anunziata smiled before excusing herself. "I'm going to help the sisters bring the food out."

"Let me help, too." Rosalia began to stand, but Anunziata placed a firm hand on her shoulder.

"You are the guest of honor."

Rosalia thought of protesting, but knew it wouldn't amount to much. Madre Carmela and everyone else had treated her like a guest of honor for most of her stay at the convent. She was almost surprised they had let her help out with the pastry making. Rosalia sighed. While she was thrilled she would be with her family again soon, she was also a bit sad that she would no longer be a part of creating the most amazing pastries. She had thoroughly enjoyed watching the workers and learning from them. And when she made a sweet, and it came out just as it should, Rosalia felt a tremendous sense of fulfillment she'd never felt before.

Her eyes traveled around the two immense dining tables. Each seated twelve people. There were fifteen nuns and five lay workers in residence at the convent. But the convent also employed six workers from the village who did not live on the premises. All the lay workers were women. At nineteen years old, Anunziata was the youngest of the lay workers. The convent had taken her in along with two other orphan girls during the war. Anunziata's father had been killed while he fought as part of Mussolini's army in Ethiopia. And her mother had died while giving birth to Anunziata's still-born brother. The other two orphans had left the convent when they turned eighteen and had found jobs that would allow them to live on their own. Though Madre Carmela had encouraged Anunziata to pursue other opportunities outside of the convent, she had no interest in leaving. She was also a skilled baker who had a talent for adding new twists to classic pastries.

The oldest lay worker was a woman in her sixties whose real name was Mariuccia, but everyone called her Mari. Anunziata had told Rosalia that there had been some scandal in Mari's youth that had brought her to the convent, but Anunziata had not been able to pry from the other nuns or lay workers what Mari's sordid past was. Though Rosalia was curious, she didn't think it was right for Anunziata to be snooping around and hoping that the other workers would gossip with her and reveal what Mari's secret was. Mari was quite tall with a lithe body and graceful movements, almost like a dancer's. She always wore her hair, which was completely white, in a braid wrapped around her head. Her large black eyes were striking even in her advanced age. Rosalia could tell just from looking at her eyes that Mari had been through much suffering. Besides exchanging small pleasantries with Rosalia and the other women in the kitchen, Mari wasn't much of a talker. She often hummed to herself while she worked, and it was in these moments that Rosalia noticed she looked the most content.

Then there was Lidia, a widow in her thirties whose husband had fought and died in the war. She had struggled with her finances after her husband died and lost her home. With just a small suitcase, she had walked the streets for two days, going from neighborhood to neighborhood, asking for work at all the shops and restaurants she came across. Then on the third morning, she was lured by the aromas coming from the windows where the pastry shop sold its goods. She went up to one of the nuns behind the windows and asked if they needed a dishwasher. The nuns put her to work not only washing dishes, but also helping out with whatever menial tasks the bakers needed done. She worked from dawn, when the nuns rose to begin their baking, to when they closed the shop in the evenings at six p.m., right before the nuns left for their vespers. Then she slept outside in the village, wherever she could find a quiet, hidden spot where no one would bother her. She never told the nuns she was homeless. But one day, Madre Carmela had caught Lidia late at night in the kitchen making the most exquisite sugar roses for the wedding cake of a customer. Lidia thought she would be fired and had cried when she explained to Madre Carmela that she used to make wedding cakes for the women in her town and could not resist making a few sugar roses for their customer's cake. Instead of firing her, Madre Carmela appointed her the decorator for all their special-occasion cakes and even bumped up slightly her wages. That was when Lidia finally confessed to Madre Carmela that she had nowhere to live, and asked the mother superior if she could forgo the increase in her wages and instead stay at the convent. Madre Carmela had given her a room.

Elisabetta and Teresa were the last two lay workers living at the convent and the ones who intrigued Rosalia the most. They were sisters, but were worlds apart even though only two years separated them in age. They were both in their twenties. Elisabetta was the younger sister. She had rich chestnut-colored hair that she wore down whenever she wasn't working in the convent. And when she was working, she kept it pulled back in a severe, high bun, which emphasized her aquiline nose and high cheekbones. Elisabetta's demeanor was very reserved—even more so than that of many of the nuns at the convent. She was not mean like Sorella Domenica, but she wasn't exactly warm either. Madre Carmela had told Rosalia that Elisabetta was seriously considering becoming a nun. Before Rosalia had learned Elisabetta was younger than Teresa, she had assumed she was the older sibling because of her serious manner and the way she carried herself. She'd also seen Elisabetta ordering Teresa around in the kitchen. And Teresa always seemed to take Elisabetta's lead as if Elisabetta were the older sister and Teresa had much to learn from her.

Teresa didn't resemble her sister at all. With emerald green eyes and blond hair the color of rich zabaglione—the decadent custard that Madre Carmela sold at her shop—Teresa was a natural beauty. Even when she was covered in flour and had chocolate stains on her face and in her hair, she looked absolutely stunning. Rosalia couldn't help staring at her, not just because of her breathtaking looks, but also because she kept trying to find a trait that Teresa shared with her younger sister. Nothing. Even their bodies were shaped differently. Elisabetta was tall with broad shoulders and a quite exaggerated pear shape, whereas Teresa was petite with a perfect hourglass figure. Rosalia had seen a few of the male customers trying to flirt with Teresa when she was selling pastries. Teresa always looked pleased that they had noticed her, but she didn't flirt back except for one day when Rosalia saw a handsome young man with light brown curly locks talking to her for quite some time at the seller's window, much to the dismay of the other customers waiting in line. Teresa had seemed to be talking to the man as much as he was talking to her. Then, she had glanced over her shoulder, making sure no one saw her, and she had slyly snuck a few extra marzipans into the man's box of pastries. After that day, Rosalia saw the same young man visit the pastry shop at least three times a week, and when Teresa wasn't at the window, he always looked sorely disappointed. But what shocked Rosalia the most about Teresa was when she learned that Teresa had once been a nun! She had been a nun at a convent in the town of Barcellona Pozzo di Gotto. And when she had decided to renounce her vows, the mother superior had asked Madre Carmela if she could take her in as a boarder and employ her at the pastry shop. What Rosalia still didn't know, however, was how it came to be that Elisabetta had also ended up living at the convent with her sister.

As for the nuns, Rosalia hadn't learned much about them yet. They all seemed to blend in, with their uniform habits and daily routines. The only two who had stood out to Rosalia were Madre

Carmela and Sorella Domenica, and like the sisters Elisabetta and Teresa, they couldn't have been more opposite. While Madre Carmela radiated serenity and happiness, Sorella Domenica exuded nothing but doom and gloom. Rosalia wondered why she was so angry all the time and where it stemmed from.

The dinner bell startled Rosalia out of her thoughts. Every day, as soon as all the food had been laid out on the table, one of the nuns would ring a small bell made out of porcelain, alerting everyone it was time to eat.

"Sorella Domenica, would you be so kind as to lead us in the blessing today?" Madre Carmela asked the grumpy nun.

"In the name of the Father, the Son, and the Holy Ghost. Thank you, Lord, for giving us this meal. Amen."

Without looking up, Sorella Domenica immediately picked up her spoon and began scooping up her minestrone. The other sisters looked to Madre Carmela for permission before beginning to eat.

"Sorella Domenica? That was a lovely blessing. We must always be grateful for having food, especially when so many go hungry. But I was thinking perhaps you could say a prayer for Rosalia since this will be her last day with us at the convent."

Sorella Domenica froze midway while scooping up more soup. Her brows knitted furiously. Slowly she lowered her spoon. With a slight nod of her head in Madre Carmela's direction, she said, "As you wish, Madre.

"Dear God, please bless Rosalia and her family. May she find peace in her life again. Amen."

"*Grazie,* Sorella." Madre Carmela picked up her spoon, signaling to the other nuns they could begin eating. Of course, Sorella Domenica once again did not wait for the mother superior's cue as she greedily slurped up her minestrone.

"May I say something, Madre Carmela?" Rosalia timidly asked.

"Of course, my child. Go ahead."

"I just wanted to thank Sorella Domenica for the lovely blessing, and I wanted to thank all of you for helping me, especially when I was so . . ." Rosalia struggled to find the right words. ". . . especially when I was not feeling well. I will never forget your kindness."

"We are just happy you are healthy again and returning to your family and home," Sorella Giovanna said.

Rosalia remembered Sorella Giovanna's was the other face she had looked into that day when she woke up by the cave. She had tended to Rosalia those first few weeks when she was still so weak.

They ate in silence until it was time for dessert. Rosalia found it funny that the nuns made this exception to their rule of not speaking while eating. When dessert was brought to the table, the mood instantly lightened, and the nuns began chatting animatedly. Usually, the discussion centered on the particular dessert they would be indulging in that day. They even laughed and shared stories, often about some fluke that had occurred in the kitchen earlier. When Rosalia had seen that the nuns didn't abstain from having sweets every day after their midday meal, she couldn't help but express her surprise to Madre Carmela.

"We work very hard in the pastry shop, as I'm sure you've noticed in the short time you've been here, Rosalia. I cannot expect my sisters to create these wonderful pastries and deny themselves as well. The only time we abstain from eating sweets is during Lent and on Fridays throughout the year. I think having this little reward to look forward to helps inspire the sisters in their work. You must remember, Rosalia, we are human, too."

Rosalia had thought of Madre Carmela's words often since that day: "We are human, too." She didn't know why, but for some reason, these words had resonated deeply with her. She had come to think of Madre Carmela as a saint and an angel—*her* angel—for rescuing her and bringing her back from near death and the depths of despair. But, of course, Madre Carmela was right. She and the other nuns were not perfect merely because they had taken vows and had devoted their lives to God. Naturally, Madre Carmela and the other nuns must have their own stories about what had brought them to the convent, just like the lay workers did.

After everyone ate Madre Carmela's chocolate pudding, the nuns and the lay workers began leaving the table one by one until Rosalia and Madre Carmela were the last still seated. But no one had cleared the dessert dishes from the table.

"Where did they go?" Rosalia asked Madre Carmela.

"You will soon find out." Madre Carmela smiled.

After a few minutes had elapsed, the nuns and the lay workers returned. Each of them held a pastry box from the shop. They smiled as they took turns walking up to Rosalia and presenting her with a box.

"For you and your family," they each repeated.

She then realized they were giving her gifts. Each box contained a different pastry as was noted in ink on the top of the boxes. Rosalia was so moved that she began to cry as she thanked everyone.

"*Grazie. Grazie mille.*"

"*Auguri.* Best wishes, Rosalia." Lidia kissed Rosalia on both cheeks, and soon the other lay workers joined in.

Even Elisabetta, who was always so reserved with her emotions, managed a small hug for Rosalia. "You should keep on baking at home."

"*Grazie,* Elisabetta."

Mari, in her usual quiet way, merely said, "*Buona fortuna.*" She shook Rosalia's hand and began to turn around, but then stopped and said, "Go forward. Do not look back." Her gaze met Rosalia's, and instantly, Rosalia knew what she meant. She nodded her head.

"I will try to remember that, Mari. *Grazie.*"

"Do not try. You must remember that if you hope to survive." She drew Rosalia's face in close to hers as she whispered these last words. Rosalia could not help but feel a slight shiver run down her spine.

There was a loud knock at the convent's door, which almost made her jump out of her seat.

Madre Carmela looked at Rosalia. "That must be the police. Oh, my, where did the time go?" She hurried to let them in.

Rosalia's heart skipped a beat. It wouldn't be long now before she was in the warm embrace of her family.

The nuns and the lay workers followed her and Madre Carmela out into the courtyard as they said their final farewells. Rosalia thought back to that day when the nuns had found her by the cave and how they had wrapped her in the sheet, protecting her much like a mother protects her newborn baby. And now they were sending her back into the world.

7

Marmellata di Tarocchi di Nonna

GRANDMA CATERINA'S
BLOOD ORANGE MARMALADE

Rosalia's head was pressed up against the glass of the car's side window. Madre Carmela watched her, worried that the police's interrogation at the start of their trip had been too much for her. L'ispettore Franco had asked Rosalia if she would mind answering a few questions during the drive. Madre Carmela had seen her hesitation, but then Rosalia had nodded.

Sensing her trepidation, L'ispettore Franco had said, "I'm sorry. I know this is difficult, but if we hope to find Marco, we need your full cooperation."

Rosalia had replied, "I want nothing more."

So she had relayed the events leading up to Marco's kidnapping her and her ordeal in the cave. Though Rosalia had complied, Madre Carmela had noticed how anxious she looked as she recounted what had happened. She told L'ispettore Franco everything—except for the rape. Madre Carmela had already informed the inspector of the crime and asked him not to specifically ask Rosalia about it. She'd been through too much and needed to get emotionally stronger before she should be forced to recount to the authorities Marco's violation against her. And if they did capture Marco, she would have to give testimony in court. Madre Carmela shuddered. She couldn't imagine how Rosalia would be able to recount in detail what she'd been through, especially in front of a courthouse audience.

Now as Madre Carmela watched Rosalia, deep in thought, she wondered what was flashing through her mind. Hoping to lighten the mood, she asked Rosalia, "Tell me more about your family. From what you've shared with me, they sound wonderful. I cannot wait to meet them."

Rosalia turned away from the car window and smiled. "*Sì.* I am fortunate to have such loving parents. And my brother, Luca, is my best friend."

"He sounds like a special young man."

"We're all so proud of him, even Papà. Though I know he must've been a little disappointed that Luca decided to become a priest and not a tailor and someday take over his shop."

"I'm sure your father understands. And it is quite an honor to have a son who will become a priest and devote his life to spreading God's word."

Rosalia nodded.

"And what is your mother like?"

"Very kind. She always has put our needs before her own. Though we work very hard, and my parents have been able to provide our meals and keep a roof over our heads, they still struggle to ensure they can continue doing this. She is a wonderful cook. She doesn't make too many sweets though, and the ones she makes are simpler, like the *Taralli* cookies we dip in wine or when we have *caffè con latte,* or her *pan di Spagna.* She also bakes a lemon cake whenever it is our birthday or our namesake saint's day. Sometimes, she also surprises us and makes it for Easter." Rosalia smiled at the memory.

"We make simpler desserts, too, Rosalia. And sometimes they can be just as satisfying as the richer sweets."

Rosalia tapped her forehead with her hand. "How could I have forgotten my favorite—*Marmellata di Tarocchi di Nonna*—Grandma Caterina's Blood Orange Marmalade. The recipe was passed down to my mother from her mother. Mamma told me when I was a little girl she would catch me sticking my fingers into the jars of marmalade she made. She used to joke that we should call it *Marmellata di Tarocchi di Rosalia* because I loved it so much. When I was recovering at your convent, Madre, I even dreamt about it one night. It's so good." She closed her eyes for a moment. "I can't wait to have it again. We used to spread it over some toasted bread in the morning or on some *pan di Spagna* Mamma had made, and then we ate it in the evening. She also made cookies filled with the marmalade. Papà would take us to the orange orchards in the country, where we would harvest the blood oranges. It took three days to make the marmalade. I always helped Mamma. Even though it was a lot of work, I looked forward to it. We joked and laughed a lot as we worked side by side, and Mamma told me stories about her childhood and when she first met Papà. I loved hearing how my father courted her." Rosalia's eyes suddenly filled with tears.

"Don't be sad, Rosalia. You will be with them again in just a matter of minutes."

She shook her head. "It's not that, Madre Carmela. I can't help thinking how it will all be ruined for me someday when I meet someone special. Marco ruined me."

She wiped the tears that were now falling steadily with the back of her hand, but she kept her voice low, not wanting the police captain and his officer to hear. Fortunately, they had the radio on and were talking between themselves.

Taking hold of Rosalia's hand, Madre Carmela said, "*Don't* say that again. You are not ruined, and someday you will find a special man to love you. What happened in that cave is in the past. It is unfortunate this happened and that you had to suffer so much, but you must overcome this. Believe in yourself, and when you find yourself faltering, think of my words and me. God will also help you, and He has already. Pray to Him. He will give you strength."

Madre Carmela squeezed Rosalia's hand. Rosalia squeezed back and managed a small smile. "*Grazie,* Madre. I will remember what you have said."

Madre Carmela noticed they were going through the streets of a bustling village. She saw a sign welcoming them to Terme Vigliatore.

"This is it. This is my town." Rosalia looked out her window and pointed to one of the shop windows.

"There! That's my father's shop!"

L'ispettore Franco heard her and pulled over.

"There is a 'closed' sign on the door," he said.

Rosalia looked disappointed that her reunion with her family would be further delayed.

"A few other shops are closed, too. Your father is probably still taking his siesta."

"Ah. I had forgotten the time. *Si.* Everyone should still be at home—except for Luca, who is at the seminary. He only comes to visit us every other Sunday. What day is it today, Madre? I haven't been keeping track of the days while at the convent."

"It is Saturday."

"On to your home, then?" L'ispettore Franco looked at Rosalia in the rearview mirror.

"*Si.*"

Rosalia instructed L'ispettore Franco how to get to her home from the tailor's shop. Soon, they pulled up to a row of stand-alone stone houses. The street was quiet except for a couple of stray dogs looking for whatever food scraps they could find. Madre Carmela noticed a woman opening her blinds, and soon she could see a few of the other villagers doing the same. People were awakening from their siestas.

They came to the end of the street. Rosalia barely waited for the police captain to brake before she swung open her door and ran to her house.

"Rosalia! *Aspetti!*" Madre Carmela hurried out of the car and called out, but it was no use. The girl was running fast and was at her front door in an instant.

Rosalia knocked after trying the door and seeing it was locked. Madre Carmela and L'ispettore Franco joined her. They waited, but no one answered. She knocked again, harder this time, and shouted, "Mamma! Papà!" But still no one came to the door.

The inspector walked around the house and tried peering into the windows, but all the shades were drawn.

"Perhaps they're not home?" He furrowed his brows as he asked this.

"The only other place where they could be at this time would be the tailor shop, and no one was there. Maybe they are still sleeping?" Rosalia now banged on the door with her fist.

"Do they normally sleep this late during siesta?" L'ispettore Franco asked.

Rosalia stopped banging as she pondered his question. "No, we usually do not sleep for more than an hour. Papà is always anxious to get back to the shop and get ready for any evening customers. Where could they be?" Rosalia's voice filled with concern.

"Don't worry. I'm sure there is an explanation as to why they're not home," Madre Carmela said, trying to keep the worry out of her own tone.

She noticed L'ispettore Franco was knocking on one of the neighbor's doors. A woman opened the door and looked afraid when she saw the police. The captain gestured toward Rosalia, who was now pacing around, her arms crossed in front of her chest.

"Rosalia?" the woman said in a startled voice, then held her hand over her mouth.

"Signora Tucci!"

Rosalia ran toward her. Signora Tucci walked past the police and took a close look at Rosalia, not believing it really was her.

"Where are my parents? We even went to the tailor shop, but it was closed. Is everything all right?"

Signora Tucci continued to stare at Rosalia, and then looked over to Madre Carmela and frowned when she noticed her habit.

"Please, Signora Tucci. Where is my family?" Rosalia pleaded with her neighbor.

"I'm sorry, Rosalia. You've given me a bit of a shock. I never thought I would see you again. None of us did."

"And why is that, Signora?" L'ispettore Franco asked.

"She's been gone for so many weeks. And then . . ." Her voice trailed off.

"And then what?" Rosalia sounded desperate and irritated. Madre Carmela was worried she was about to start shaking Signora Tucci if the woman didn't give more information soon.

"Your parents searched for you and so did the police—our local police." She looked at L'ispettore Franco, who gestured with his hands impatiently for her to continue.

"Even the neighbors helped. We all searched for you. Your parents suspected that . . ." Again, her voice trailed off. She swallowed and then said, "They suspected that man—what was his name?"

"Marco," Rosalia said softly.

"*Sì.* They suspected he had taken you. As soon as your family realized you were gone, your father and Luca went to the authorities and told them how Marco had been stalking you at the tailor shop and how he'd made an advance toward you. The police then went to Marco's home, but the family said he hadn't returned home the day before. They even inquired around town but no one had any useful information to offer. The police continued to check in with his family and anyone else who knew him over the course of the weeks following your disappearance, but again no one had seen or heard from him."

Madre Carmela immediately realized the last time anyone had seen Marco was before she and the nuns had found Rosalia at the cave. No doubt he had run off after discovering Rosalia had escaped. And from the expression on Rosalia's face, she had made the same deduction. She blanched visibly and took a step back. Madre Carmela went to her side and put an arm around her, steadying her.

"Your poor parents were beside themselves, and little Cecilia kept asking everyone when you were coming home. She even wandered to my house one day and walked right in." Signora Tucci's eyes filled with tears. "Even she was looking for you."

"But where are they now, Signora? I'm back. I want to see my family." Rosalia turned her head, looking up the street for any signs that her family was returning home.

"May I ask, Rosalia, where is Marco?" Signora Tucci's lips pursed tightly together in a grimace. The sadness that had filled her face a moment ago when she spoke of Rosalia's family's searching for her was now gone.

Rosalia was stunned by her neighbor's question. Shame filled her face, and Madre Carmela knew she was remembering Marco's violation against her. And the way Signora Tucci was peering at

Rosalia, it was as if she, too, knew what he'd done. But Signora Tucci was looking at Rosalia as if she were the criminal.

Madre Carmela's protective instincts toward Rosalia kicked in, and she spoke up.

"How should she know where that horrible man is? Can't you see her recoiling at just hearing his name?" Madre Carmela did not attempt to disguise the anger in her face as she challenged Signora Tucci.

"I'm sorry, Sister. I meant no offense. I'm about to explain, and you will see why I drew the conclusion I did. Rosalia's parents received a letter from her saying that she had found out she was pregnant, so she ran away with Marco, and then they decided to elope."

"I never sent such a letter!" Rosalia shouted. "Never!"

L'ispettore Franco and his officer looked her over, their eyes resting on her stomach as they tried to assess if she was indeed pregnant. Rosalia noticed and shook her head.

"Lies! Marco lied. I am not pregnant, nor did I elope with him! And I never sent a letter to my parents!"

"The letter was in your handwriting, Rosalia. Your father was certain of it since you handled his customers' receipts."

Rosalia put her hands to her temples as a fuzzy image came to her. She remembered feeling so weak as Marco pulled her off her makeshift hay bed and forced her to sit up in the chair he'd used to tie her to at the end of her days in the cave. He had placed something heavy and hard on her lap, and a sheet of paper rested on the object. Then he placed a pen in her hand and told her to write the words he was repeating to her. She remembered feeling groggy, and it had been the greatest effort just to keep her eyes open. She could barely write and had dropped the pen a few times. But Marco had picked it up and screamed at her to do what he said. That was all she remembered. She didn't remember the words he'd told her to commit to paper. He must have drugged her so she would write the letter, but in that state she couldn't see how she would have been able to write legibly and in her own handwriting, which her father recognized. Surely, her father must've noticed the handwriting was distorted?

"This is too much for her." Madre Carmela held Rosalia close to her.

"It is all right, Madre. I need to know everything. It is coming back to me now that Marco forced me to write something, but he must've drugged me. I remember his holding my hand, forcing me to write whatever he was saying to me." She then looked at Signora Tucci before adding, "Papà had to have seen the writing was shaky even if it was my own handwriting?"

"I don't know, Rosalia."

"So they believed his lies?"

Signora Tucci averted her gaze. "I don't like to gossip or eavesdrop." She paused as if weighing carefully what her next words would be.

Madre Carmela seriously doubted the woman didn't like to gossip or eavesdrop—for how else had she known that the letter had been in Rosalia's handwriting? Madre Carmela could not see Rosalia's parents sharing the content of the letter with their neighbors. They would more likely have avoided this out of shame, fearing that everyone would believe the worst about their daughter.

Signora Tucci continued. "I overheard your parents arguing the night after they'd received the letter. It was so loud that I could not help but hear, as I'm sure a few of the other neighbors did, too. Your mother was saying she didn't believe what was in the letter. She was hysterical and kept screaming over and over, 'Not my Rosalia. She would never dishonor us that way.'"

"And my father?" Rosalia's voice sounded very faint.

"He was pleading with your mother, asking her to keep her voice down. I'll never forget how calm your father sounded. I didn't know how he could maintain such composure after learning what he had. He explained to your mother that they could not dispute the fact that the letter was in your handwriting. That was all he said."

Rosalia was weeping silently now.

"*Coraggio,* Rosalia. Have courage. Don't despair. When your parents hear the truth that Marco kidnapped you and how he beat and starved you, they will no longer believe the lies in that horrible letter," Madre Carmela said as she glared at Signora Tucci.

"*Dio mio!* So Marco really did kidnap you as your parents first thought?" Signora Tucci asked while making the sign of the cross. "And he beat and starved you, too?"

Madre Carmela nodded grimly.

"Dear girl, I'm so sorry." Signora Tucci was now looking at Rosalia with pity.

"Our doctor examined Rosalia shortly after the other nuns in my convent and I found her, passed out in front of a cave—the same cave where Marco kept her prisoner for a month. She not only had bruises and cuts, but a severe concussion. That is why she does not clearly remember writing that letter. Marco beat her severely and starved her. She was on the brink of death when we found her. We would have told her parents immediately that we had found her and she was safe at our convent, but Rosalia couldn't remember her surname or where she was from. Her memory has only come back recently."

Madre Carmela knew Signora Tucci didn't deserve an explanation of what had really happened to Rosalia, but she also knew that the woman would run to the neighbors and tell them word for word what she had said. And Madre Carmela didn't want anyone doubting Rosalia's innocence any longer—though she also realized there would be a few people who would still choose to believe the ugly lies over the truth. She wondered sadly why it was that humans often preferred to think the worst about others.

Signora Tucci shook her head as if not believing the enormity of all she had heard. But Madre Carmela sensed there was something else that was troubling the woman.

"Would you happen to know where the family is, Signora Tucci, and when they will be back? As you can see, the girl is anxious to be reunited with them again, and we would like to question them as well. Since Marco held Rosalia in our jurisdiction, we will be working with your local authorities to find and apprehend him," L'ispettore Franco said.

Signora Tucci looked at Rosalia, but when their eyes met, once more she looked away.

"I'm afraid they're gone."

"Gone?" Rosalia's voice sounded panicked. "What do you mean?"

"Your family no longer lives here. They left Terme Vigliatore two weeks ago."

Madre Carmela's heart sank.

"No, that can't be right, *signora*. They would never leave without me and without knowing what happened to me." Rosalia kept shaking her head as if to convince herself of this truth.

"But, Rosalia, they thought they did know what happened to you. They thought you left of your own free will and went off to be with Marco." Signora Tucci said this gently.

"No, no. You said my mother didn't believe that. You heard her! She refused to believe I would do such a thing!"

"It wasn't just the letter, Rosalia. As you know, Terme Vigliatore is a small village, and word spreads quickly, especially when a scandal occurs. People can be so mean." Signora Tucci's voice cracked a little. Madre Carmela could see the woman now was truly being sincere and possibly even regretted that she had believed the worst about Rosalia earlier.

"The villagers blamed your parents for your wayward behavior. They said they hadn't been strict enough with you, and that your father should have never allowed you to work at the tailor shop where you would come into contact with many men. A few people were so bold as to even insult them directly to their faces. Your poor mamma. She broke down one day and told me how a group of women had taunted her while she was in the piazza on the way home from the shop. They circled her and kept chanting, '*Madre di una puttana!* Mother of a whore!' Your mother yelled at them and stood up for you, but it was no use. She was outnumbered, and the women were relentless, until she could take it no more and broke out of their circle and ran away."

Madre Carmela looked at Rosalia. She was completely ashen now. This was all too much for her, and she held the same vacant stare she'd had for all those weeks after they found her.

"Then your father began losing customers at the shop. They were struggling. Luca halted his studies at the seminary so he could find work and help your parents. But no one in town wanted to hire him. So your father had no choice but to leave Terme Viglia-tore and start over again in a new village where no one knew of the scandal. I'm so sorry, Rosalia."

"Do you know where they moved to?" Rosalia asked.

"They left in the middle of the night without saying a word to anyone. I was a little surprised they didn't say good-bye to me since unlike the other neighbors I had remained on friendlier terms with them, especially your mother. But I think they wanted to slip out quietly without alerting the villagers to avoid more insults being hurled their way. Your mother had told me a week before they left that they were looking to move, but she never told me that they had already found another home or the city where they were going to. I think that was her way of saying good-bye to me, so that it wouldn't come as a complete shock that they were just gone one day." Signora Tucci sighed before continuing. "And I was even surprised that the house had been sold that quickly and without my knowledge of it."

"My house was sold?" Rosalia looked over at her childhood home—the only home she'd ever known.

"*Sì.* The new owners were here yesterday, taking measurements. They will move in at the end of the week."

Madre Carmela had no idea either how Rosalia's parents had kept concealed from the mean-spirited, nosy villagers that they were selling their house. This was all too sad. Rosalia had lost her family and her home. And she had no idea where they were now.

"But what about my things? My clothes?"

Signora Tucci shrugged her shoulders. "Your parents must've taken them." She looked at Rosalia thoughtfully, then glanced at the inspector.

"Perhaps the police could get a warrant so that you could enter your home and see if anything was left behind that you might want to take?" Signora Tucci asked.

"Would that be possible?" Madre Carmela's eyes pleaded with the police captain. If there were anything in the house that Rosalia could have as a token of her family . . . Or maybe there might even be a clue as to where they had moved.

"A warrant would take forever, and by then the new occupants will have moved in, and I'm sure they won't appreciate anyone's wanting to enter and search their home." L'ispettore Franco rubbed his chin with the tips of his fingers, contemplating.

"I suppose it would be all right if you were to enter the house, Rosalia, since the new occupants haven't moved in yet and the locks have not been changed. So we can say in essence this is still your home, and you have the right to be here. The only obstacle is getting into the house."

"I think I might be able to help there. I know that your mother often hid an extra key under the terra-cotta planter that sits beside the front door. Perhaps there is a key still there?" Signora Tucci asked this with an exaggerated, wide-eyed expression.

Madre Carmela suspected that Signora Tucci knew without a doubt that the key was still under the terra-cotta planter because she had let herself into Rosalia's house so she could satisfy her nosy nature. She wouldn't put it past the woman.

"I remember. Mamma would leave the key there when Luca and I were in school, in case she and my father didn't return from the shop in time. Sometimes they would get held up with a customer who had walked into the shop shortly before they would leave for our midday meal. But wouldn't my parents have given all the copies of the keys to the new owners?"

"It doesn't hurt to check. They might've forgotten about that key," Signora Tucci said.

Rosalia ran off to the terra-cotta planter. She tried pushing back the heavy planter, but it wouldn't budge. Her strength hadn't fully returned yet since her ordeal in the cave. L'ispettore Franco came over and easily tilted back the planter. The sunlight cast a gleam on a shiny brass key.

"It's here!" Rosalia's voice held a glimmer of hope.

But Madre Carmela feared little would come of their search of the house. She prayed silently she was wrong.

With shaky hands, Rosalia inserted the key into the keyhole. The latch turned, and as Rosalia pushed the door open, it creaked eerily. Tentatively, she stepped in, sensing this was no longer her home and she was somehow invading. Signora Tucci was about to enter the house, but the inspector stopped her.

"Signora Tucci, it would be better if you waited outside."

She was taken aback by his request. Then she tilted her head in Madre Carmela's direction and raised her eyebrow as if to indicate to L'ispettore Franco that the nun also had no business inside the DiSantas' home. But the inspector ignored her, and motioned to Madre Carmela to step inside. He must've suspected as well that Signora Tucci knew for certain that the key was under the terra-cotta planter and had let herself into the house on previous occasions.

Madre Carmela followed Rosalia and noted the disappointed look on her face every time she discovered a room was empty. Her clothes were gone from her bedroom, and there were no signs that this room had once belonged to her and her little sister, Cecilia. All the furniture was also gone. Madre Carmela was surprised that none had been left behind, since it sounded like not much time had passed between when the DiSantas had decided they'd be moving and the actual move. Then again, from what Signora Tucci had said about Signore DiSanta's losing business at his tailor shop, they must've sold their furniture to have some extra money.

L'ispettore Franco and his officer also looked around, but they too seemed to find nothing of interest. The last room Rosalia searched was the kitchen, although Madre Carmela didn't know what she hoped to find there besides a forgotten bottle of rotten milk in the icebox or some other spoiled food.

Rosalia paused at the kitchen sink. Madre Carmela could see her shoulders shaking, and soon she was sobbing out loud.

Madre Carmela went over and took her in her arms. Rosalia held on to Madre Carmela and continued to cry uncontrollably. L'ispettore Franco and his officer stepped into the kitchen, but, when they saw Rosalia crying, they left. Madre Carmela heard them go out the front door and was thankful they were giving Rosalia some time to collect herself. But her sobbing only seemed to intensify. Madre Carmela waited patiently, letting her have her moment of grief.

Finally, Rosalia pulled away. Madre Carmela reached into both pockets of her habit. In one hand she held a handkerchief, and in the other she held two cherry-shaped marzipans. Rosalia smiled when she saw the marzipans and took them and the handkerchief from Madre Carmela. Of course, she remembered the day Madre Carmela had given her marzipans when she found her by the cave. After wiping her tears, she took a small bite out of one of the cherry marzipans and slowly chewed it. For a few minutes, neither Rosalia nor Madre Carmela said anything.

"You really do love marzipan so much." Rosalia broke the silence.

"It's my greatest weakness, I admit. But I also carry a few with me everywhere I go to help with my low blood sugar. But even when I'm sad, they seem to make the pain hurt a little less."

Rosalia nodded her head. "It still hurts, Madre Carmela, but it's true. While I ate the marzipan, I found myself calming down."

Madre Carmela reached into her pocket once more, and this time took out a few raspberry-shaped marzipans. She popped two into her mouth and held the rest out for Rosalia.

After Rosalia was done eating the marzipans, she sighed. "I'm still in shock, Madre Carmela. How could my family have moved without me? How could they have left me behind? I was only gone for a few months. They gave up on me after a few months."

"Rosalia, it sounds like your parents had no other choice if they hoped to make a living and provide for your family. Remember, they still have little Cecilia to care for. Look how bad things had gotten here for them. Even your brother could not secure work."

"Luca! He wanted nothing more than to serve God and become a priest, and because of me, his dream has been destroyed. Everything that's happened to my family is my fault!" Rosalia began crying again.

"It is not your fault! You didn't ask Marco to kidnap you and keep you from your family! None of this is your fault."

"I don't know what hurts more, Madre—the fact that they're gone and I have no idea how to find them, or that they believed the lies in Marco's letter."

"You don't know that for certain. Signora Tucci even said she heard your mother saying she didn't believe you would ever do such a thing."

"But it sounded like my father believed I had run off with Marco."

"He knows in his heart that you didn't do such a thing." But Madre Carmela's voice lacked the conviction she hoped it would convey.

"If he believed there was a chance Marco had taken me against my will, he would've kept searching. He wouldn't have moved even if they were having difficulty at the tailor shop. It was easy for him to leave because he believed I had abandoned them, Madre. Don't you see that?"

"Rosalia, there is a chance you might be right. I will not tell you what you want to hear. But there is also a chance you might be wrong. We just don't know for certain how your parents felt. The only people who know are your parents. And until you see them again, you cannot torment yourself by believing they thought the worst of you."

Rosalia took a deep breath. "I suppose you're right, Madre." She walked around the kitchen, her eyes resting on different spots in the room. Madre Carmela could see what she was doing. She was remembering the times she had shared with her family. Rosalia went over to a wooden icebox that stood opposite a pantry door. She opened the icebox and gasped. Madre Carmela could not see her face since the door was blocking her view.

"What is it, Rosalia?" Madre Carmela hurried to her side and peered over her shoulder.

The icebox was empty except for the middle shelf, which contained a neatly lined up row of six jars. Madre Carmela leaned in to get a better view of the jars. It was her turn now to gasp when she saw the labels on each of the jars. A square white piece of linen was tied to each of the jars with two thin strips of purple ribbon. Embroidered on the center of the linen label were the words *Marmellata di Tarocchi di Rosalia.*

Madre Carmela picked up each of the jars. They were all full with Rosalia's mother's signature blood orange marmalade, and the seals had not been broken on any of the jars' lids.

"Do you know what this means, Rosalia?"

"I think so," she whispered before her eyes met Madre Carmela's.

"Your mother hoped you would return and find these jars. That's why your name is on the jars and not your Nonna Caterina's.

She left them here for you. This was not a mistake, Rosalia. Your family took everything in the house. No other food is in the icebox. The blood orange marmalade is all that your mother left behind, and she knew how much you loved it. She was trying to give you a message. Do you understand? These jars of marmalade were a sign from your mother to let you know she still loves you."

Rosalia's heart felt like it would burst. She had suspected on her own all that Madre Carmela had said, but had been too afraid to voice the words. She had also noticed that the labels on the jars were tied with purple ribbons—her favorite color. Surely if Madre Carmela had come to the same conclusion as Rosalia had, she couldn't be wrong. And if she were right about this, then perhaps Mamma still believed Rosalia had not dishonored her family by running off with Marco. Rosalia had not abandoned them, and she would *not* abandon them. Somehow she would find her way back to her family.

❦ 8 ❧

Cannoli

October 8, 2004

Claudia was taking a stroll through the convent's courtyard. Every day since she'd arrived in Sicily, she had made it a point to do so. Her mind felt clear, and she was relaxed as she walked around the convent's property and enjoyed its peaceful surroundings. She needed to take some time for herself when she returned to New York and have these solitary moments instead of rushing from one task to another.

Though she woke up early with the nuns to watch them at work in the pastry shop, she still felt rested and rejuvenated here. It must be the fresh mountain air and the serenity of the convent. While she was kept busy between watching the workers bake their heavenly creations during the day, and then conducting her interviews with Sorella Agata in the evening, she wasn't as exhausted as she was when she was just as busy back home.

A bluethroat flew by, startling Claudia from her thoughts. The bird landed on the ground and began pecking at a puddle of rainwater that had collected earlier this morning when there were a few showers. There were many birds on the convent's property, but this was the first time Claudia had spotted a bluethroat. Her father was a birdwatcher and, when she was a child, he used to point out pictures of birds to her in the books on birdwatching he collected. There were a few birds that were her favorites—the cardinal, the blue jay, and the bluethroat—all birds that stood out to her because of their beautiful colors. And the bluethroat's most striking feature was the band of iridescent blue combined with black, white, and burnished orange color on its breast. Her father had explained to her that bluethroats were mainly found in Europe and Asia, and a few had been spotted in western Alaska. She slowly inched closer to the bird to get a better look. The bird paused from drinking and glanced at her for a moment before flying off. Claudia shivered slightly. That was odd. It was as if the bird had stared right into her eyes.

Pushing the bluethroat from her mind, she thought about Rosalia. Ever since Sorella Agata had begun recounting the story of the young girl the nuns had rescued by the cave, Claudia could not stop thinking about her. She couldn't imagine how that poor girl had survived that ordeal with Marco's keeping her hostage in a cave of all places and raping her, only to then lose her family. Though Claudia was absolutely riveted by Rosalia's story, she was confused as to how Rosalia had influenced Sorella Agata's pastry making. All she could imagine was that Sorella Agata must've learned pastry making from Rosalia when she joined the convent. Did that mean that Rosalia had been at the convent for a long time before she was reunited with her family? Claudia knew there was no one at the convent named Rosalia. She had made it a point to introduce herself to all the nuns and the lay workers.

Claudia couldn't help wondering how long Rosalia's story was. She needed to start learning more about Sorella Agata if she hoped to get all the information she needed for this book. At least she was making swift progress watching Sorella Agata make her pastries. Claudia had already begun typing up the recipes and adding the history of the pastry and anything else that Sorella Agata felt was important to convey about the sweets.

Claudia still hadn't observed the nun make her famous *cassata*.

But she trusted Sorella Agata and knew she would let Claudia watch her make the cake. There was something about the nun that made Claudia feel very comfortable in her presence. It wasn't just that she was a spiritual woman; it was just . . . Well, Claudia couldn't quite put her finger on what it was about Sorella Agata that made her easy to talk to, although Sorella Agata had been the one doing most of the talking.

Claudia glanced at her watch. She'd taken a longer break than she should have and had told Sorella Agata she would be back in the kitchen soon so she could watch her make cannoli.

"You cannot have a book about Sicilian pastries without including cannoli!" Sorella Agata had laughed when she told Claudia yesterday that they would cover cannoli today.

Claudia had had her fill of cannoli growing up with an Italian-American father and living in New York City. So it would be interesting to see how they tasted here in Sicily.

She made her way back to the convent's kitchen. As she walked among the worktables and counters, she still marveled at how dedicated all the workers appeared to be. Everyone seemed as if she was enjoying her work, and no one appeared to be giving a half-hearted effort.

Claudia spotted Sorella Agata at a small table in the back of the kitchen. Her back was turned toward Claudia, but Claudia could see she was scooping out curds of milk and putting them into a colander lined with cheesecloth. Sorella Agata must've gotten impatient waiting for Claudia to return from her break and had begun making the ricotta for the cannoli.

Claudia was about to apologize to Sorella Agata, but then she froze when she saw the nun was weeping silently. She picked up her apron and wiped her tears, but then a new set of tears sprang. Not wanting to make her feel uncomfortable, Claudia turned around to leave, but kicked a cookie cutter that someone had dropped onto the floor. The cookie cutter slammed against the leg of a cabinet that stocked baking supplies.

"Ah! Claudia! There you are. I was beginning to think you were just going to enjoy the day and not come back to the kitchen."

Claudia glanced over her shoulder and saw that Sorella Agata was quickly wiping the tears from her face. Claudia stood and waited where she was, pretending to rub out a nonexistent stain from her shirt, until Sorella Agata was ready to look up.

"*Vieni!* Come! Why are you standing so far away? Don't you want to see me make the ricotta?"

Sorella Agata was lining a second colander with three layers of cheesecloth before she finally turned to Claudia. Though her eyes were red, the tears were all gone now.

"I'm sorry I'm late. I didn't notice the time. I don't know what it is about Italy, but it's easy not to glance at your watch." Claudia smiled as she picked up a spare clean apron that hung from a nail on a wall near the baking supplies cabinet.

"That's good! It shows you are relaxing more instead of rushing all the time. I know how you Americans are always hurrying and don't stop to enjoy life. We work hard here, too, as I'm sure you've noticed, Claudia. But we also know work is only one part of life."

Sorella Agata began pouring milk into a saucepan and telling Claudia the measurements for each ingredient to make the ricotta. Claudia was still amazed that Sorella Agata rarely had to refer to her recipe book and could remember most of the measurements off the top of her head.

"How is it, Sorella Agata, that you can remember most of your measurements without looking at your recipe book?"

"In Sicily, we bake differently. Every time we bake, the measurements could be off by a little. But we know here and here how much to add of an ingredient." Sorella Agata pointed to her eyes and her heart.

"Really? But in America, I've always heard baking is an exact science, unlike cooking, for which you can estimate how much of an ingredient is needed by looking. I've always heard that in order for your baking to come out right you must measure your ingredients exactly."

"*Si.* That is why I said in Sicily we do it differently. I know how bakers measure everything in America. But our way is more . . .

Ah! I cannot think of the word. We become one with our creations, and how can you create something truly extraordinary if you're not using your senses to do so? Even though I'm looking to see how much flour or sugar or whatever other ingredient to add, I also listen to my heart. That is how you can create something truly wonderful."

"Maybe that's the secret to your *cassata!*" Claudia laughed, but Sorella Agata frowned at the mention of the cake that was such a sore point for the nun to discuss.

"We all bake by memory. Only the newer nuns and workers refer to the recipe books, and, in no time, they soon can remember the recipes by heart. It is not like I am only doing this for the *cassata.*"

"I was just making a joke, Sister. I'm sorry."

Claudia remained silent as she listened to Sorella Agata explain how to make the ricotta. Once Claudia was ready to scoop out the curds from the milk and transfer them to the second colander lined with cheesecloth, Sorella Agata took out of the refrigerator a large bowl of ricotta that had been made yesterday.

"Now is the fun part. We sweeten this ricotta and then we fill the cannoli shells. Ah!" Sorella Agata hit her forehead with her palm. "I didn't show you how to make cannoli shells. I don't know what's the matter with me today. This is the second thing I've forgotten."

"That's all right. You can just tell me how the shells are made. I don't need to watch you make those. Why don't we fill the shells for now, and you can give me the recipe for the shells later?"

"*Va bene.*" Sorella Agata nodded her head as she added sugar to the ricotta. Once she was done sweetening the filling for the cannoli shells, she scooped large spoonfuls of ricotta into a piping bag. Expertly, she filled a cannoli shell.

"Now, you try." She handed her piping bag over to Claudia. Claudia wasn't accustomed to chefs letting her actually try to make their recipes, but Sorella Agata encouraged her with every recipe she'd shown her. Claudia was enjoying it immensely, and she was reminded of when she used to cook and bake with her father when she was a child. She needed to get back to cooking more when she returned home instead of working all the time.

They worked side by side, filling dozens of cannoli shells that lined several trays.

Claudia decided to take a chance. Though she didn't want to pry, she also wanted to get to know Sorella Agata better.

"I'm sorry, Sister, for asking. But I happened to notice you were crying earlier. Is everything all right?"

Sorella Agata paused a moment while filling a shell and looked up at Claudia. Shrugging her shoulders, she lowered her gaze and resumed her work. But after a few seconds, she surprised Claudia by saying, "I was just thinking about Rosalia."

"What happened to her? I know there is no one here with her name."

Sorella Agata kept her focus on her piping. Claudia was amazed at what a steady hand she had. But then again, she'd been doing this for so many years.

"So last night I left off with Rosalia's discovering her family had moved away. *Si?*"

"Yes, you said Rosalia was determined to find her family. I take it she came back to the convent with Madre Carmela?"

"Naturally. So Rosa—"

"I'm sorry for interrupting, Sister. But I was wondering, shouldn't Madre Carmela be telling me more about Rosalia since she was so close to her? Or is it too painful for her?"

This time, Sorella Agata stopped filling her cannoli shells and nodded.

"*Si,* it is painful for Madre Carmela to talk about Rosalia, but also her memory isn't what it used to be. In addition to her rheumatoid arthritis, she is becoming more and more senile. You must be patient with me for a little while longer, Claudia. I know it hasn't made sense to you why I am telling you so much about this young woman when you are dying to know more about me. But as I mentioned at the start of our interviews, Rosalia influenced me greatly. Since we have so many shells to fill, I might as well continue with her story now instead of waiting for this evening. If you want to stop filling the shells and go get your notebook, you may do so."

"No, that's all right. Like you, I can remember a lot by heart." Claudia smiled.

Sorella Agata returned her smile before continuing to relay Rosalia's story.

"So Madre Carmela and L'ispettore Franco brought Rosalia back to the convent that would now become her home . . ."

9

Biancomangiare

MILK PUDDING

November 28, 1955

As Rosalia followed Madre Carmela and L'ispettore Franco back to the car, she kept glancing up at her house, trying to sear its image in her head. She must not forget how it looked. With each step she took toward the car, her spirits sank further. Her resolve from a few moments earlier to find her family was faltering as insecurity and grief took hold of her heart.

As L'ispettore Franco's car made its way through the village of Terme Vigliatore, no one said a word. Madre Carmela and L'ispettore Franco knew what a crushing blow it had been for Rosalia to discover her family was gone and, worse yet, that the family possibly believed she had gone willingly with Marco. The trip that had started out with so much anticipation and elation had now become a somber one.

Rosalia kept her eyes focused outside her passenger window, which was lowered halfway. Though it was a cool, breezy day in November, she didn't care. For she was already shivering, but not from the cold. Never had she felt so alone—not even when she was Marco's prisoner in the cave.

As she'd done with the image of her house, Rosalia tried to

freeze the landmarks of her town in her mind. Suddenly, memories came rushing back with each of the sites they passed: her school, where she and Luca had spent many days laughing and running in the playground; the bread shop where she had often stopped after working in the tailor shop to bring a loaf of bread home for the family's midday meal; the produce stall where she and her mother had shopped side by side, comparing the fruits and vegetables; the church where they had gathered every Sunday morning to pray as a family. She noticed as she stared at the church a bride getting out of a car. Her father helped her up the steps to the church. Once they reached the top, the father's and daughter's eyes met. He was beaming, pride evident across his features. He leaned over and kissed his daughter on the cheek before they linked their arms together and made their way into the church.

Rosalia would never have that moment with her father. Even if she did learn to trust another man again and agree to marry him, she couldn't help but feel as though her father—her entire family—was lost to her forever.

And with that thought, she let the tears flow freely from her eyes, not bothering to wipe them even though Madre Carmela pressed her handkerchief into Rosalia's hand. She felt numb, much like she had those weeks after the nuns had found her at the cave. Though her body had then been severely battered and malnourished, this felt much worse. Without her family, she felt cold. Marco might as well have killed her in that cave. For she wished she were dead now.

L'ispettore Franco's car drove into the courtyard of the Convento di Santa Lucia del Mela. Before leaving Rosalia's family's home, Madre Carmela had asked Signora Tucci if she could use her phone to call the convent and alert them that she and Rosalia would be returning. She didn't want Rosalia to be bombarded with questions as to why she had not stayed in her hometown. Madre Carmela grew sadder as she watched the life slip out of Rosalia. Guilt also weighed heavily on her mind when she remembered how secretly a part of her wished she would not be losing Rosalia when she returned to her family. She turned her head away lest Rosalia see the tears sliding down her face.

She'd never forget how pained Rosalia's voice had sounded when she had asked her, "Where will I go now? I have no home or other family to stay with."

Rosalia's parents had both been only children, so there were no aunts, uncles, or cousins. And the grandparents had all died.

Madre Carmela had not hesitated and immediately replied, "You will come back to the convent with me, Rosalia."

Rosalia had shaken her head. "It will only be temporary until I find my family. I don't want to take advantage of your hospitality, Madre."

"You can stay as long as you want. We've all enjoyed having you with us. Do not think of yourself as a burden. You are a part of our family."

Rosalia looked pensive. No doubt she was thinking she wanted to be with her biological family and not with a group of women she barely knew.

"*Grazie,* Madre."

And those were the last words Rosalia had spoken since they had left her house. Signora Tucci had given them a small box so Rosalia could take the jars of blood orange marmalade her mother had left for her. As they walked back to the car, Rosalia had hugged the box tightly to her chest and had refused to let the inspector place it in the trunk. She kept it by her feet during the ride to the convent.

The car came to a stop in the courtyard, which was empty, unlike when they had set out on their trip earlier and all the nuns and lay workers had bid farewell to Rosalia. L'ispettore Franco helped Madre Carmela carry the boxes of pastries that the nuns and lay workers had given as gifts to Rosalia into the convent. Rosalia followed them, holding her box of marmalade. She walked very slowly, staring straight in front of her.

Madre Carmela hurriedly walked ahead, entering the kitchen before Rosalia did. All the workers stopped what they were doing. Their heads turned as they looked for Rosalia.

"Please. Give her time," she said in a low voice, glancing over her shoulder to ensure that Rosalia wasn't within earshot. "She's received a terrible shock. I will answer your questions later. And no one is to ask Rosalia anything about her family. Is that understood?" Madre Carmela said in her most stern voice.

"*Si,* Madre," the workers answered, lowering their gazes and returning to their work.

She saw a few of them shaking their heads in disbelief. Naturally, they sensed Rosalia's family reunion had not been a success.

Sorella Giovanna could not help muttering, "It is such a shame, Madre. The poor girl."

Madre Carmela went out into the corridor, but Rosalia was nowhere to be found. She rushed to Rosalia's room, where Rosalia was sitting on the edge of her bed, staring at one of the marmalade jars.

Madre Carmela went over and tried to gently pry the jar from her hands, but Rosalia held on to it with an iron grip.

"It is all I have left of my family, Madre. I don't even have a photograph of them."

"I am just going to place the jar on your dresser, Rosalia. Please, get some rest now. You've had a long day. We will talk more tomorrow when you're refreshed. All is not lost. Try to remember that, my dear child."

"All is not lost," Rosalia whispered.

She let Madre Carmela help her out of her clothes and into a nightgown. Since Rosalia had only left a few hours ago, the sisters had not had time to clean out her room. The nightgown she'd been wearing and a few other items Madre Carmela had lent her were still in her dresser.

Rosalia got into bed. Madre Carmela drew the blinds shut. It was only six o'clock, and the sun was still burning brightly.

"I will come back up a little later and bring you something to eat. But if you are sleeping, I won't disturb you."

Madre Carmela waited for Rosalia to say something, but she merely stared up at the ceiling. The young woman she'd brought back from death a couple of months ago was now slipping back into her shell.

Madre Carmela had to be patient. She knew from her own experience that Rosalia needed time to grieve the loss of her family and to fully feel the pain. She could not pressure the girl. But she feared it would be a long time before Rosalia could be reached.

Sighing, she made her way back down to the kitchen and busied herself with work, which always seemed to lift her spirits. But today no matter how much she tried to lose herself in her passion for baking, her sadness refused to budge.

A thought then came to Madre Carmela. She rushed over to one of the glass cabinets and took out a set of custard cups. She then took a plump lemon from one of the bowls that held citrus fruit and pulled out her box grater from a shelf beneath one of the worktables. She quickly ran the lemon against the box grater, inhaling the intense citrus aroma from the zest.

An hour later, Madre Carmela checked in on Rosalia and was glad to see she was sleeping. She let her sleep for another hour before she returned with a tray holding a pair of custard cups.

"Rosalia. Rosalia. Wake up." Madre Carmela gently shook her shoulder.

Rosalia woke up with a start.

"It's all right, my child. It is only me. I'm sorry if I startled you, but I brought something that I thought would make you feel better." She gestured to the custard.

Rosalia looked at the custard, but then turned her head away. Madre Carmela frowned. Even when Rosalia had still been recovering from her ordeal in the cave, she'd taken an interest in the daily sweets Madre Carmela had brought to her.

Taking one of the custard cups, Madre Carmela sat on the edge of Rosalia's bed. She scooped up some of the white custard, which was garnished with chopped pistachios, candied citrus peel, and chocolate shavings. She held the spoon out to Rosalia, but Rosalia shook her head and whispered, "I'm not hungry."

"Just taste it, Rosalia. For me?" Madre Carmela lowered her face so that her gaze met Rosalia's.

Rosalia sat up and took the spoon from Madre Carmela. Her eyes flickered for a moment upon tasting the custard. She then reached for the cup in Madre Carmela's hand.

Madre Carmela smiled. She could tell the sweet was already soothing Rosalia's broken spirits.

"What is it?" Rosalia asked.

"*Biancomangiare.* It's a milk pudding my mamma used to make for me when I was a very small girl and was not feeling well. It always managed to make me feel better, no matter my ailment."

"What was your mamma like?"

"She was beautiful, but her hard life rarely made her smile. Her hair was the color of rich chestnuts, and she always wore it in a high bun. One night, I couldn't sleep and went to my mother's room. Her door was ajar, and I could see her brushing her hair. It was the only time I had ever seen her hair down. She used to wear it in a braid when she went to bed. Her hair was gorgeous and hung down to her waist. I watched in awe as she brushed her hair. My mother finally noticed me watching and beckoned to me with her hand to enter her room. My father was already fast asleep, snoring deeply as he always did. Mamma took me in her lap and let me brush her hair for her. It's one of the few memories I have of my mamma." Madre Carmela's voice seemed to catch a little, and Rosalia could see by the distant look in her eyes that she was still in her mother's room, brushing her hair.

"Did she die when you were young? Is that why you have few memories of her?"

"No. My father was a cobbler and was always struggling to make ends meet. There were six of us, four boys and two girls. I was the youngest. My sister was the oldest. It came to a point at which my parents couldn't feed all of us. I remember there were holes in the walls throughout our little shack of a house. As a child, I didn't think much of it until one day I saw Mamma making dough to make bread. She didn't know I had entered the kitchen. I saw her tearing some plaster from one of the holes in the wall and adding it to her flour mixture. She was trying to stretch her flour to make it last longer. Can you imagine that?" Madre Carmela wiped away her tears with the back of her hand before continuing. "My parents had to give me and two of my brothers away. I came here. My brother Gaetano went to a monastery and Bruno, my other brother, went to a farmer who had no children and needed someone to help him."

"That's terrible, Madre. I'm so sorry."

"Many families were forced to do this back then."

"How old were you?"

"I was only six years old." Madre Carmela gave a soft laugh. "I didn't know it, however. I thought I was as old as my elder siblings. When I realized my parents were giving me away, I pounded my mother's chest with my fists. I told her I could help her like Angela, my older sister. Angela and my brothers Michele and Giuseppe were staying with my parents since they were the oldest. My parents didn't want their youngest children to continue to go hungry. I remember my stomach often hurt, but I was too young to realize it was because I wasn't eating enough. For as long as I could remember, my stomach had ached, so it seemed normal to me. That is why Mamma often made *Biancomangiare* for me. Of course, she could not afford to top it off with nuts, chocolate, and candied citrus peel as I did with yours."

"Were you mad at them for giving you away, Madre?"

"Terribly. I cried myself to sleep every night. I thought they would come back for me when things got better for them, but I guess things never did since I remained at the convent."

"Did they visit you?"

"At first, Mamma did. But I think it became too hard for her—and for me. Each time, I hoped she would be taking me back home with her, and when she didn't, I went into a rage. The nuns couldn't console me. I don't know this for certain, but I suspect the nuns might've told my mother to stop visiting. It was just too difficult for both of us."

"So where is your family now?"

Madre shrugged her shoulders. "I don't know. When I was a teenager, I asked the nuns if I could go visit them. But my mother superior found out my mother had moved with my other siblings after my father died. He had a heart attack about five years after they gave me away. Since my mother had stopped visiting me, I didn't know this until I was fourteen and was looking to reconnect with them again."

"Did you try to find them?"

"No. I chose to accept that this was the fate God had intended for me. I knew by then that I wanted to become a nun, and I decided to put all of my energies into that."

"I'm sorry, Madre. But I cannot understand how you were able to do that."

"The circumstances were different from yours, Rosalia. I was much younger when I lost my family. Though I was devastated, I didn't have all the years of memories you have had with your family. I think part of me had still not forgiven them for giving me away. I have forgiven them now, but it took many years. I made my peace and decided to focus on the new family I had formed with my sisters."

"I must find my family, Madre. I will never stop searching for them."

"Of course, Rosalia. We all must do what we feel is right in our hearts."

"So you understand some of the pain I am going through, Madre."

"I do. It still hurts me to this day, but I am happy with how my life has turned out, and I would not ask for it to be any different."

"Thank you for sharing your story with me, Madre. I feel some comfort in knowing someone can understand how I feel."

"You are not alone, Rosalia. I know it must seem that way. But we are all here for you. Remember that."

After Madre Carmela left Rosalia's room, Rosalia thought about the nun's sad childhood. She couldn't imagine losing her family at such a young age. For if it hurt as much as it did now and Rosalia was seventeen, how must it have hurt for a child who always ached for the love of her mother? As she drifted off to sleep once more, her last thoughts were about Madre Carmela's milk pudding. Just as with Rosalia's mother's marmalade, Madre had a sweet to remember her mother by. The nun was right, but Rosalia hadn't dared admit it to her. The pudding had made her feel a bit better. But Rosalia knew it was a temporary balm, and the pain of losing her family would still be with her when she awoke in the morning.

❧ 10 ❧

Buccellati

SICILIAN CHRISTMAS FIG COOKIES

December 9, 1955

There was a buzz in the convent and pastry shop now that they were in the middle of the Christmas season. But this year, there was also a cloud hanging over the festive air. For the nuns and the lay workers at the Convento di Santa Lucia del Mela were sad for the newest member of their family—Rosalia.

Though they were happy to have her in their fold again, they also knew how much the young woman was suffering. Seeing the devastated expression on Rosalia's face since she'd returned hurt everyone. And, no matter what encouraging words they offered, she had chosen to remain in her bedroom for the past week and a half.

Rosalia felt extremely desperate over her situation. While she still had every intention of finding her family, she didn't know where to begin. And all she could think about was that horrid letter Marco had forced her to write and the possibility that her family believed she had willingly gone off with him. So she stayed in bed and slept. For it was in her dreams that she was reunited with her family.

Madre Carmela and the other nuns came to bring her meals and try to coax her to join them in the kitchen. Thankfully, they hadn't forced her to leave her room. Even Madre Carmela's bringing a new sweet every day to Rosalia had failed to draw her out of her thoughts. She hardly ate her meals. When she thought she couldn't bear the ache over her loss much longer, she would have a teaspoon of her mother's blood orange marmalade. In that brief instant, she would be back home with Mamma, Papà, Luca, and Cecilia, enjoying the good times they shared. But she only allowed herself one teaspoon of marmalade. She had to make it last—for that was all she had left of her family.

Rosalia had woken up early today. The aromas coming from the kitchen below shook her out of her deep sleep. Though it smelled heavenly, she still had no desire to go downstairs and sample what they were making.

She walked to her window and opened it wider. Rosalia loved looking out onto the convent's beautifully landscaped grounds. Though she could tell from the steady breeze that the seasons were beginning to change, December in Sicily was still quite comfortable.

Suddenly, a bird came into her line of vision, startling her. She could see, from the beautiful colors that were displayed on its chest, it was a bluethroat. Rosalia had seen this species of bird before, and her father had told her its name. He had explained to her that the ones with a bib of blue, black, orange, and white were males. The bird perched itself on a tree branch that hung close to Rosalia's window. It tilted its head as if trying to meet her gaze. It chirped for a few seconds, looked around, and then tilted its head once more in her direction.

Rosalia walked over to her dresser and picked up the plate of cookies Madre Carmela had tried to tempt her with last night. They were *Buccellati,* named so because they were shaped like small bracelets. After the dough was molded into bracelet shapes, it was cut at intervals to display the fig filling in the cookies. Madre Carmela had explained all of this to Rosalia, and while Rosalia had feigned disinterest, she actually had found it charming that the cookies were shaped to look like a piece of jewelry. Still, her curiosity had not been enough to tempt her to try one of the cookies.

She brought one of the cookies to the window, hoping the

bluethroat had not flown away. It was still there, and its head jerked up suddenly upon seeing Rosalia had returned. She broke off a tiny crumb and reached her hand out, placing the crumb on the branch the bird sat on, but the crumb fell off. She broke off a bigger piece this time and was about to lay it on the branch when the bluethroat hopped over and pecked the crumb out of her fingers, eliciting a laugh from Rosalia.

"*Bravo!* You're a very smart bird."

The bluethroat looked at Rosalia as if it understood her, but she knew that it was silly to think so. The bird was just waiting for her to feed it again. This time she made sure to get some of the fig filling when she broke off the cookie.

While Rosalia watched her new friend pecking away at the *Buccellati* crumbs, she took one of the cookies she had not broken apart yet for the bird and took a bite out of it. She chewed it ravenously and realized how hungry she actually was. Of course, the cookie was delicious.

The bluethroat flew away to a neighboring tree and began chirping a beautiful melody. What was strange was that the bird still glanced over at Rosalia every so often, even though at the distance where it sat now, she couldn't reach out to feed it. Shivers ran down Rosalia's bare arms. She watched the bluethroat as it flitted from tree to tree, going deeper into the convent's courtyard. Curious, Rosalia decided to follow the bird.

Slipping a robe on, she quietly tiptoed down the corridor, hoping she didn't run into anyone. She wasn't ready to make small talk or to see the pitying looks on everyone's faces. She just wanted to get some fresh air and watch the bluethroat.

As she approached the kitchen, she could tell, from the commotion of the pans banging and the many orders being given by whoever was in charge of overseeing the pastries' output for the day, that most of the workers were on duty today. It was still too early for the pastry shop to be open. The selling windows opened at eight a.m. It was now barely seven. She breathed a sigh of relief, knowing the courtyard would most likely be empty.

She inhaled deeply once she stepped outside; she realized she hadn't been out since that day she had returned from her hometown. A sharp stab of pain pierced her heart. Pushing the memory out of her mind, she walked deeper into the courtyard, keeping her gaze lifted as she scanned the tops of the trees, looking for the bluethroat.

"Ah! There you are!" Rosalia said, delighted she had found the bird.

The bluethroat once more glanced at her and then resumed its singing. She saw other birds—sparrows, partridges, even a pair of striking bluebirds—but no other bluethroats were in sight. The bluethroat stayed apart from the other birds and only seemed aware of Rosalia. Again, shivers ran through her.

She followed the bird as it hopped from tree to tree, and then, when it had exhausted all the trees in the courtyard, it landed on the manicured shrubbery. Rosalia slowly walked toward the bird, hoping she could get closer to it. The bird stared at her, and this time it held her gaze. Rosalia held her hand out and began speaking softly.

"I won't hurt you. I promise."

The bluethroat took a hesitant hop forward, but then the sound of someone whistling startled it, and it flew away. Rosalia tried to run after the bird, but it seemed to vanish into thin air.

"Don't you just hate it how they can make fools of us?"

Rosalia jumped at the sound of the voice. She'd been so preoccupied by the bird that she hadn't thought to see where the whistling was coming from. A young man who looked to be about her age was standing a few feet away. He was grinning.

Rosalia stepped back a couple of feet, clutching her robe to her chest, which suddenly felt very restricted. She looked around the courtyard, but no one else was in sight.

"My name is Antonio. Antonio Bruni." The young man stepped forward, extending his hand, but that only caused Rosalia to take another step back.

"You don't have to be afraid. I just wanted to introduce myself."

He pulled his hand back, placing it in his trousers pocket. He ran his free hand over his hair, which was a little long, but seemed to suit his face, accentuating his high cheekbones and large amber-colored eyes. He was a good seven to eight inches taller than Rosalia, and he was very thin.

Rosalia wanted to leave, but she remained fixed in place. She wished she could say something to him, but the fear that had taken hold of her would not budge. In her mind, she knew not every young man wanted to hurt her like Marco had, but her heart refused to let go of that notion.

"I know. You must be mad at me for chasing your little friend away." Antonio smiled, locking his gaze onto Rosalia's. She quickly averted her eyes and scanned the treetops, pretending she was looking for the bluethroat. But it was nowhere to be seen.

"I'm sure he'll come back. I've seen him before."

"You have?" Rosalia said softly.

Antonio nodded his head. "Every day since I've been here."

Rosalia's curiosity made her forget her fear, and she asked, "What do you mean since you've been here? Why are you at the convent?"

"Madre Carmela has brought me on as an apprentice."

"But only women work here. I don't believe you. What are you really doing here?" Rosalia's brows knitted furiously; she was convinced he was lying.

"There are men on the grounds, gardening and bringing deliveries to the pastry shop."

"Oh. So you leave at the end of the day."

"No. I have a room."

Rosalia's heart skipped a beat, her fear returning.

"You don't believe me." Antonio laughed. "It's in the abandoned chapel. Madre Carmela cleaned it out for me and put a cot in there."

"There's an abandoned chapel?"

"*Si.* Would you like to see it?"

Rosalia shook her head adamantly. "No, that is all right." Her suspicions of the young man entered her mind once more.

They both remained silent until Rosalia asked, "How long have you been here?"

"Just a few days. I haven't seen you. Are you one of the lay workers in the pastry shop?" Antonio then hit his forehead and laughed.

"How silly of me. Of course you're one of the lay workers. You're not in a habit." He then took in her clothes, and his face reddened when he realized she was in her nightgown and robe. "I'm sorry. You're still in your nightgown. I meant no offense."

Though Rosalia was still not quite sure what to make of Antonio, she couldn't help but smile at his assumption. "Don't worry. I am not a nun."

"Ah. *Meno male.*" Antonio crossed himself, no doubt thanking God that he hadn't offended a nun. "So you are one of the lay workers."

Rosalia paused before answering his question. Naturally, she didn't feel comfortable sharing with this stranger what had brought her to the convent.

"*Si.* But I've been sick and haven't been in the kitchen. That's why you haven't seen me."

"I see. What is your name?"

"Rosalia."

"You have the name of one of Sicily's most revered saints—and the patron saint of my city, Palermo."

"You come all the way from Palermo?"

"Yes. It's a beautiful city."

"I have heard. Why did you come all the way over to Messina and to our small village of Santa Lucia del Mela?"

Now it was Antonio's turn to look anxious.

"I'm sorry. It is none of my business. You don't have to tell me."

"I have nothing to hide. I ran away from home."

Rosalia was taken aback. "Why?"

"My father and I did not get along. Besides, I am a man now. It was time for me to make a life for myself and not depend on him any longer."

"How old are you?"

"Eighteen." Antonio smiled. He seemed proud of reaching this milestone. "It feels good not to be under my father's thumb any longer and to be making my own decisions, especially about where my life is headed."

Rosalia nodded thoughtfully. "And your mother?"

"She died when I was twelve." Antonio looked pained.

"Do you have any brothers or sisters?"

"Just an older brother. He's still at home with my father, helping him in his shoemaker's shop. My father wanted me to learn the trade just like Salvatore, my brother. But I had no interest in it. Food has always been my love."

Rosalia took in his thin frame again and found his last statement hard to believe.

He noticed her assessing him and laughed. "While I love food, I also love to run and go swimming, which is good since I do eat a lot. But maybe I'll put on some weight here with all these amazing pastries the nuns make."

"Why do you love food so much?"

"I used to help my mamma cook. Papà hated it. Said cooking and baking were women's work. He tried to beat it out of me, but that only made me angrier and more determined not to do what he expected of me. Funny thing is he didn't mind that I cooked for him and my brother after Mamma died. But he still wanted me to become a shoemaker or at least do a manly trade."

"How did your mother die?"

"She caught pneumonia."

"I'm sorry."

"It happens." Antonio shrugged his shoulders and looked away. Rosalia noticed tears forming in his eyes.

"So what is your story? What has brought a pretty girl like you to a convent, of all places?"

Rosalia's cheeks burned. Just when she was beginning to lower her guard around Antonio and even feel sympathy for him over losing his mother and having to fend for himself after running away from home, her discomfort returned.

"I should go. It's cool out here, and I am still sick." Rosalia turned and walked quickly away.

"It was nice to meet you, Rosalia! I look forward to working with you in the kitchen!" Antonio shouted.

Rosalia stopped upon hearing his last words but, realizing that Antonio was still watching her, she merely nodded and resumed walking.

Once she was back in her room, she climbed back into bed,

pulling the covers up to her chin. But she couldn't stop shaking. Though her mind was telling her Antonio was harmless, her heart was telling her otherwise. Perhaps she could talk to Madre Carmela and Madre Carmela could send him away? Then Rosalia realized how absurd that notion was. She couldn't tell Madre Carmela whom she could hire and dismiss.

Closing her eyes, Rosalia pushed all thoughts of Antonio out of her mind. She could not think about him right now. She felt spent, and she needed to focus all of her energy on finding her family. For the sooner she found them, the sooner she could leave the convent and not have to worry about being so close to Antonio.

❧ 11 ❧

Gli Occhi di Santa Lucia

SAINT LUCY'S EYES

December 13, 1955

Today was December 13th and the feast day of Santa Lucia. In addition to the pastry shop's being busy preparing for Christmas, the past few days had been even more frenetic since they were also preparing the famous pastries that were made in honor of Saint Lucy—*Gli Occhi di Santa Lucia* or Saint Lucy's Eyes. The nuns would be selling the pastries both at their shop and to the vendors who would sell them at the Saint Lucy festival. The festival was set to start this afternoon.

Rosalia had prayed to Saint Lucy this morning and asked her to give her strength. She had resolved to end her convalescence in her bedroom and join the nuns and the other lay workers in the kitchen. Over the past few days, she'd begun to feel guilty that they were working so hard while she lay idle in her room. She owed everything to Madre Carmela, and shame filled Rosalia when she thought about how she was repaying her and the other nuns and workers by letting everyone wait on her while they already had their hands full with the pastry shop. Although the thought of seeing Antonio again and having to work near him still made her feel slightly queasy, Rosalia knew she couldn't stay locked away in her room forever either.

She twisted her long hair tightly and then coiled it into a bun at the back of her head, securing it with a few pins. Once she was done, she took a deep breath and made her way to the kitchen. Her heart beat faster with each step she took.

When she reached the kitchen, she paused a moment before entering. A row of nuns stood side by side at one of the work counters, each kneading dough with rolling pins that were no wider than ten inches. The shorter rolling pins allowed several workers to stand at the counter at a time, taking up less space and thereby ensuring more pastries were produced. At another counter, Anunziata and Mari were busy coiling dough to form the Saint Lucy's Eyes. Once they were done shaping the pastries, they placed two almonds in the center of the coils to complete the saint's "eyes."

Rosalia scanned the rest of the kitchen. Antonio was nowhere to be seen. She felt herself relax a little and stepped into the kitchen. Everyone was too busy working to notice her. But just when she thought she could blend in without a commotion, Sorella Domenica barked, "Ah! I see your vacation is over!"

Everyone glanced up from her work and looked to where Rosalia was standing. Her cheeks burned, and anger filled every pore in her body. She wanted to lash out at Sorella Domenica, but was too embarrassed. She also felt she didn't have a right to be mad at the nun since Sorella Domenica was right. Rosalia had in essence been on "vacation" while they were all working.

"Rosalia!" Anunziata ran over and embraced her. "It is so good to see you here. Are you feeling better?"

Rosalia nodded. Her embarrassment from a moment ago quickly vanished as the rest of the lay workers and the other nuns came over and told her how happy they were to see her. Rosalia glanced in Sorella Domenica's direction. A big frown was on her face, and she resumed pounding the dough in front of her.

"Are you feeling up to working? We've missed having you here." Mari placed her hand on Rosalia's shoulder and gave her a small smile, her eyes showing she understood Rosalia's pain. Once again,

Rosalia couldn't help but wonder what had happened in Mari's past.

"*Sì.* I would very much like to help you. It doesn't have to be with the pastries. I can wash the pans. Whatever you need."

Rosalia was through with the special treatment everyone had afforded her both after she'd been rescued and once she realized her family was gone. She was ready to work hard and earn her keep at the convent.

"And waste the talent you've shown us when you have helped us bake? Come. You can finish coiling more *Gli Occhi di Santa Lucia.* I must've done fifty already, and I could use a break. I'll get started on something else."

Rosalia followed Mari to the worktable where she'd been working with Anunziata. Mari showed her how to coil the eyes. Once the almonds were placed in the center of the coils, an egg wash was brushed over the pastry.

Rosalia and Anunziata worked quietly side by side. Rosalia was glad Anunziata was not bombarding her with questions. She just wanted to lose herself in her work and not think about her family for a little while.

"So, Rosalia, do you know why Saint Lucy is famous for her eyes?" Anunziata finally broke the silence.

"I seem to remember learning in school that she had been tortured, and her eyes were taken out."

"When she was still quite young, she made a pledge to God that she would remain a virgin. But her mother promised her in marriage to a pagan. When she rejected him, he denounced her as a Christian to the authorities. The judge sentenced her to a life of prostitution, but apparently her body became immobile, and guards as well as a team of oxen couldn't move her. Then the judge had her tortured, putting her eyes out, but miraculously her sight was restored. He then attempted to burn her, but the fires were mysteriously extinguished. She finally died after they stabbed her in the throat with a sword. There is another story that claims she put out her own eyes and carried them on a tray to dissuade any suitors from looking at her. That is why statues of her often show her holding a tray with eyes."

"How horrible. The poor girl suffered so much." Rosalia thought about how so many young women had suffered over the centuries for wanting to protect their virtue. She shuddered as her mind inevitably went to the cave where Marco had held her captive and inflicted his own torture on her.

"Are you all right, Rosalia?" Anunziata asked. Then realization dawned on her, and she clapped her hand over her mouth. "Oh, I'm so sorry, Rosalia. I shouldn't have told you that story."

"It's all right, Anunziata. I'm fine."

"Are you sure?"

Rosalia nodded. "Let's just finish here."

When they were done preparing the pastries, they placed them in the oven.

"I think we could use a break. How about we each get a glass of water and step out for some fresh air?" Anunziata began untying her apron.

"But it seems so busy." Rosalia looked over in Sorella Domenica's direction. She didn't want to give the impression that she was taking it easy once again.

"We all take breaks, Rosalia. If we didn't, we would never last. Come on." Anunziata took her by the hand and led her toward the icebox. She took out a glass pitcher and poured two glasses of water. She handed one glass to Rosalia and then led the way outside. They walked, arm in arm, slowly around the courtyard. Lines of patrons were beginning to form in front of the seller's windows. It was a cloudy day, but everyone seemed excited. Rosalia could hear the patrons talking about the Saint Lucy festival.

"You must come with us to the feast later. All the lay workers will be heading over as soon as we're done with lunch," Anunziata said as she raked her fingers through her hair.

"Maybe."

"I insist, Rosalia. You can't miss it. The Saint Lucy feast is one of the best our town holds."

Rosalia didn't say anything.

"I saw you talking to Antonio the other day. Isn't he nice?"

Rosalia was stunned for a moment, having thought no one had seen them outside that day. "Where were you? I didn't see you."

"I was standing behind the window and noticed."

"He told me Madre Carmela hired him to be her apprentice. Is that true? I didn't see him today."

"*Sì.* He's at the markets, buying eggs and a few other groceries we needed. He is an extraordinary baker and a very hard worker. We're lucky to have him."

"He mentioned that he's sleeping in the abandoned chapel. I didn't know there was a chapel other than the main one where the sisters pray."

"It's at the back of the property. It's very old and needs repairs, but Madre Carmela has preferred to put the money she's made from the pastry shop back toward the business. She says someday she will make the necessary renovations in the chapel. I can't imagine anyone's sleeping there." Anunziata giggled. "Imagine that! When you go to sleep all those statues are staring at you, and when you wake up, they're in the same fixed position, still staring at you!"

Rosalia laughed. It felt good. She couldn't remember the last time she had laughed. But then, in an instant, she remembered it had been with her family. Pushing away the sadness that was threatening to surface, she said to Anunziata, "He told me Madre had the chapel cleaned out for him. Perhaps the statues are no longer there?"

"I'm sure they are. Where would she put all those statues? You've never seen the chapel, right?"

"No, I haven't."

"Come on. I'll show you."

"But shouldn't we be getting back to work, Anunziata?"

"No one will notice how long we've been gone. They're all too busy."

"Sorella Domenica will notice."

"That witch. I don't know why she became a nun. She doesn't have a compassionate bone in her body. Thank God the other sisters aren't like her or I would've been gone from here a long time ago."

Rosalia followed Anunziata. Though she was reluctant to take a longer break, she was also curious about this abandoned chapel. Anunziata was right. Rosalia couldn't imagine anyone's staying in a chapel.

They approached a grassy area. Wildflowers and weeds surrounded a small wooden structure. Rosalia was surprised the grounds were so unkempt here since the rest of the property was immaculately landscaped. As they approached the chapel, she could see how weak the structure looked. It was a simple little building that still held some charm even though it was in obvious need of repair.

Anunziata walked up the three broken steps that led to the chapel's entrance and was about to open the door when Rosalia stopped her.

"Should you be going inside? It is after all Antonio's home now." Rosalia looked around in case he was returning home.

"That's true. I'm accustomed to coming to the chapel and taking a break. The door is probably locked now that someone lives here." Anunziata twisted the doorknob, but to their surprise it turned.

"I guess he doesn't mind if anyone goes inside." Anunziata smiled slyly and opened the door.

"Anunziata! Come back! I'm not coming inside with you."

But Anunziata ignored her pleas and stepped inside. Rosalia paced back and forth a few feet away from the chapel, keeping watch in case anyone came by. After a couple of minutes, Anunziata came out.

"Just take a quick look. Then I promise we can leave."

Rosalia glanced around nervously before walking quickly toward the chapel. Anunziata stepped back so she could peer inside. She'd been right. Statues of various saints stood on pedestals all around the chapel, which was quite small. A cot was pushed to the far side of the chapel. There was an empty space at the front and center of the chapel. Rosalia imagined the altar had probably once stood there and that Mass was conducted here before the chapel that the nuns presently used was built. Every Sunday, the town priest came to the chapel and said a private Mass for the nuns. At least Madre had removed the altar table to give Antonio more space and to make it feel less like a chapel, although with all those statues, it still felt very much like a house of worship.

"A radio!" Anunziata shouted as she ran toward Antonio's cot. A small transistor radio was perched at the bed's footpost. She turned it on. "Ah! Elvis!" She jumped up and down like a silly schoolgirl.

"Turn that off! Someone will hear it!"

But Anunziata began dancing like a crazy woman. Rosalia would've never dreamed the soft-spoken girl she'd befriended during her first weeks here had this daring streak.

"Let me have a little fun. You know we're not allowed to have radios in the convent." Anunziata shook her hips wildly as she danced.

Rosalia glanced outside. No one was in sight. Still, they should be returning to the kitchen.

"Dance with me, Rosalia! Just one dance!" Anunziata rushed over to Rosalia's side and grabbed her hands, pulling her closer to the radio.

Rosalia couldn't help but laugh. Here they were dancing like two madwomen to Elvis Presley in an abandoned chapel with saints' statues surrounding them.

"Looks like you're having fun."

Rosalia froze at the sound of Antonio's voice. She was too afraid to look in his direction.

"I'm sorry, Antonio. I just wanted to show Rosalia what the inside of the chapel looked like. We were just going to take a quick look and leave. We didn't touch any of your belongings—well, except for the radio. But that was my fault. I insisted. It's been so long since I've listened to music." Anunziata turned the radio off.

Rosalia finally glanced in Antonio's direction. He was smiling, much to her surprise.

"That's all right. I can't expect you girls to do nothing but work and pray all day. We all need a little fun sometimes, right?" Antonio seemed to direct the question toward Rosalia as his eyes met hers. She looked away.

"See, Rosalia! I told you Antonio was nice. He doesn't even mind that we were snooping around." Anunziata smiled at Antonio.

"We weren't snooping around. I'm sorry, Antonio. We'll leave now." Rosalia didn't wait for Anunziata as she walked out of the chapel.

"Hey! Wait! Why the rush? We could listen to a few more songs," Antonio pleaded.

Rosalia stopped and looked over her shoulder. Anunziata opened her eyes wide, signaling for Rosalia to stay.

"We've been gone a while, and we're very busy in the kitchen. Thank you, but we really must go." She walked away from the chapel as quickly as she could.

"Hey, Rosalia! Wait up!" Antonio ran after her, but she didn't slow down to make it easy for him to catch up. But in seconds, he was by her side.

"I'll walk back with you. Madre Carmela is expecting me in the kitchen. She's going to teach me how to decorate cakes."

Rosalia turned her head to see if Anunziata had caught up to them, but she was way off in the distance, taking her time walking toward them. She waved and smiled as she pointed toward Antonio. Rosalia frowned at the gesture and turned back around.

"So you are feeling better?"

Rosalia nodded, but remained silent.

"That's good. You're popular at the convent. Everyone was talking about you."

Rosalia stopped for a moment. Did he know what had happened to her?

"Why were they talking about me? What did they say?"

Antonio laughed and held up his hand. "Take it easy! Nothing bad. They were just talking about how quickly you had learned to make the few pastries they'd taught you and saying that you had a knack for it. They missed you. That's all. They were eager to have you back in the kitchen."

Rosalia sighed deeply, relieved they hadn't said more.

"I saw your friend this morning."

She looked at Antonio questioningly.

"The bluethroat. He likes to hang out on that branch that sits right outside one of the windows that overlooks the courtyard."

Rosalia already knew this, but didn't say so to Antonio. Since that day she'd first spotted the bird, it had visited her every day. She had continued to feed it crumbs from whatever pastry the nuns had brought to her room. She felt a little less lonely when the bluethroat sat outside her window. Though the nuns and the lay workers had visited her daily, she'd felt immensely alone after she'd discovered her family had left without her.

Rosalia and Antonio continued walking until they reached the convent's main grounds. Rosalia waited for Anunziata. She didn't want to walk into the kitchen alone with Antonio, especially since she'd been gone so long. She could see the likes of Sorella Domenica thinking the worst about her.

"Aren't you coming inside?"

"I'm going to wait for Anunziata. I'll see you later." Rosalia hoped he would take that as a hint and leave her alone now.

"*Va bene.* Are you going to the feast later? Anunziata told me she and the other girls would be there."

"I don't know. I have to see how I'm feeling."

"All right. I'll see you in the kitchen then. *Ciao!*" Antonio finally left.

"Why were you walking so slowly?" Rosalia asked Anunziata as soon as she joined her.

"It seemed like he wanted to talk to you. I just thought I would give you some privacy." Anunziata smiled slyly.

"You didn't need to do that."

"So what did he say?"

"Nothing."

"Nothing? I saw him moving his lips quite a bit, and he said nothing? That's fine if you want to keep it private."

"No, it's not like that. He was just telling me that everyone had missed me in the kitchen, and that he'd heard them say nice things about my baking. And he hoped I was feeling well. He was being polite. That's all."

"He's going to be at the feast later."

Rosalia didn't respond. Fortunately, they were now inside the kitchen, and she quickly walked over to Madre Carmela, whose back was turned to her as she was bent over a workstation, piping whipped cream around a cake. But when Rosalia got closer, she stopped abruptly. Antonio was standing on the other side of the table with his own cake and piping bag as he watched and copied the designs Madre Carmela was making. That was right. He'd mentioned to Rosalia that Madre would be showing him how to decorate cakes.

She was about to walk away, but then Madre Carmela, sensing someone was standing behind her, looked over her shoulder and said, "Rosalia! Everyone told me you had come down earlier. It's so good to see you here. How are you feeling?"

"Fine, Madre. *Grazie.* I was just going to help Anunziata." Rosalia looked around the room for Anunziata, but couldn't find her.

"Have you met Antonio?"

"*Si,* Madre Carmela. I have met Rosalia," Antonio said before Rosalia could respond.

"Maybe he can show you how to pipe a cake. Like you, he's proving to be a fast learner in the pastry shop."

Madre Carmela handed her piping bag to Rosalia before she could protest and walked away.

"It's easy. You have to twist the bag at the top and keep one hand placed over it, making sure to keep it shut so the cream doesn't leak out, and then your other hand is used to steady the lower part of the bag and make your design. Just practice first on the table before piping the cake."

Antonio squeezed out a swirl of cream in the shape of a leaf onto the table. Inspecting the shape, he then squeezed a leaf onto the cake.

"See. Easy!" His eyes lit up; he was taking obvious pride in his work.

Rosalia placed her hands as he had shown her on the piping bag. But she squeezed the bag too hard and a big dollop of whipped cream gushed out, looking nothing like a leaf.

"Don't worry. It takes a little practice. Try again."

Rosalia eased her grip on the bag and tried once more. While less cream was pumped out this time, it still looked like just a dollop of cream rather than a delicate leaf. She tried a few more times, but was getting frustrated that she couldn't get the desired leaf shape.

"If you wouldn't mind, Rosalia, I can stand behind you and guide your hands so you will get a better sense of how to do it."

Rosalia thought for a moment. She loved the beautiful leaves he and Madre Carmela had designed on their cakes, and she wanted to learn how to do it.

"All right."

Antonio came around to Rosalia's side of the table and stood behind her. He talked gently as he placed his arms around her and helped her grip the piping bag. His hands felt warm around hers. Rosalia's heart raced, but strangely, she didn't feel as afraid of him as she'd felt that first day when she met him in the courtyard. The more he talked encouragingly to her and guided her in piping the leaves, the more she relaxed.

After a few attempts with Antonio guiding her hand, Rosalia was ready to try to pipe the leaf design on her own.

"*Brava!* You did it!" Antonio exclaimed, clapping his hands.

Rosalia looked at her leaf design; it had come out as perfectly as one of his. She tried a few more, and each one came out just as beautifully as the first.

"Are you ready for the cake?" Antonio asked.

"*Sì.*" Rosalia laughed.

She no longer felt nervous that she was standing so close to Antonio and he was watching her movements. Focusing on the piping, she squeezed a succession of leaves in a border all around the cake. Then, she squeezed a few stray leaves on top of the cake in the center, and a few cascading down the sides of the cake.

"Wow! You're an artist! I would've never thought of the leaves cascading down the cake's sides!"

Madre Carmela came over to inspect Rosalia's work.

"*Bellissima!* It's gorgeous, Rosalia!"

Rosalia smiled. She was proud of her work. She hadn't realized how much she'd missed being down in the kitchen until now. To think she had wasted all this time feeling sorry for herself in her room when she could've been down here, making herself useful to Madre Carmela and the pastry shop staff.

"I'm going to get lunch ready. I will see you both later. Good work, Rosalia. And you, too, Antonio!" Madre Carmela patted him on the shoulder as she walked by.

"They were all right about you. You are a fast learner and have a natural talent for this."

"*Grazie,* Antonio. I'm a fast learner when it comes to learning recipes, but I think you're better at decorating than I am. I wouldn't have been able to do this without your help today."

"Anytime. I'm still learning too. Maybe we can help each other? And then we can have a contest!"

"A contest?"

"How about every time we learn a new recipe, we compete to see who can make it taste better?"

"Oh. I don't know about that."

"Come on! It'll be fun, but more important, it'll help us to master the recipes. Don't you want to become very good at pastry making? I could tell, from the look on your face after you were done decorating the cake, that you take pride in your work and that it gave you a sense of satisfaction."

"You could see all of that?"

"Of course. I can tell because that's how I feel after I've made a pastry and it's come out well. How about we start tomorrow? We'll see which new recipe Madre Carmela wants us to learn, and we can compete with that one."

"Why don't we start after siesta?"

"No one will be taking siesta today. Everyone will be at the feast, including you."

Before Rosalia could say once more that she wasn't sure if she would be going to the feast, Anunziata was suddenly standing before her with Elisabetta and Teresa.

"Rosalia, Anunziata told us you would be coming with us to the feast later. We will have so much fun. We'll be on our own away from the sisters." Teresa giggled.

Rosalia couldn't help wondering if Teresa would be meeting the young man she'd seen at the seller's windows, visiting her every day. But with her sister Elisabetta at her side, Rosalia doubted Teresa would be able to have a rendezvous with him.

As if reading her thoughts, Elisabetta chimed in. "Just because we will not be walking with the sisters at the feast doesn't mean we can run wild." She frowned as she looked at her sister.

"So it's decided then. We'll all be going to the feast, including Rosalia." Antonio smiled.

As they made their way to the dining room table for lunch, Antonio, Elisabetta, Teresa, and Anunziata were talking excitedly about the treats they would sample at the feast and how they couldn't wait to hear the live band that would be playing. But Rosalia remained silent. All she could think about was the beautiful cake she had decorated, and she began envisioning a new design she would create next time. She could see it vividly before her—whipped cream rosettes, a few raspberry marzipans, maybe even a few petals from actual flowers. She then noticed the poinsettia centerpiece on the dining table. Striking red poinsettias were arranged in a tall, rectangular-shaped glass vase. Her thoughts drifted back to Christmas last year when her father had come home from work and presented her mother with a large pot of red and white poinsettias. Mamma had been surprised. Rosalia remembered watching them as they embraced and kissed. They had been so in love. Rosalia blinked back tears, wondering what her family would be doing for Christmas this year. Would they miss her as much as she missed them?

Rosalia was still lost in her thoughts when she felt someone squeeze her hand lightly.

"Where are you right now?"

She turned to her left and saw Antonio looking at her with concern. Pulling her hand away from his, she said, "I was remembering my old life."

A marching band made its way through the narrow streets of Santa Lucia del Mela and up its winding hills. In its wake, the town priest and four altar boys followed, along with a group of sturdy men who were holding a large statue of Saint Lucy. All the sisters from the convent marched behind the procession of the saint's statue along with the rest of the village.

Rosalia and the other lay workers stayed at the very back of the procession. Lidia and Mari, the two older lay workers, walked side by side. Elisabetta kept her eyes fixed on the statue of Saint Lucy as she fingered her rosary beads. The only time her gaze strayed was to periodically keep a watch over her sister. Teresa was walking arm in arm with Anunziata, who had her other arm linked through Rosalia's. Though Teresa was talking animatedly to Anunziata, she turned her head and looked over her shoulder every few seconds as if she was expecting someone.

While she'd felt like she had no choice but to attend the feast with everyone else, Rosalia's spirits didn't match everyone else's. She could remember when she had lived for feasts, and she and her family would look forward to them. If only she could lift this heaviness that refused to budge from her heart.

Suddenly, she noticed Antonio was no longer walking with them. She breathed a sigh of relief. While he had been nothing but nice toward her, Rosalia could tell he had been watching her, and she just wanted to be left alone. But, as soon as she had this thought, he reappeared holding a white paper bag. He opened the bag and held it toward her.

"*Torrone?*"

"*No, grazie,* Antonio."

"Just a small piece. It'll make you forget your worries for a moment."

Rosalia looked surprised at Antonio. He offered a small smile and nodded his head toward the bag of *torrone.*

She didn't know why she was surprised that Antonio could tell her mind was elsewhere. No doubt her sadness was written as plain as day on her face. Perhaps she was more surprised that he would acknowledge it publicly. Everyone else at the convent walked on eggshells around her and didn't utter a word about her family.

Rosalia reached into the bag and took a chunk of *torrone,* which had been cut up into pieces by the vendor. She sucked on the *torrone,* waiting for it to soften a bit before taking a bite.

"*È buono?*" Antonio asked.

"*Si, è buono. Grazie.*"

"Teresa, Anunziata. *Torrone?*" He held his bag out toward them, but they shook their heads and resumed their conversation. Rosalia could hear they were talking about some boy, no doubt the young man Rosalia had seen visiting Teresa a few times. Elisabetta seemed too entranced in her praying and in following the procession of the statue to be eavesdropping on her sister's conversation.

"Are you enjoying yourself?" Antonio asked.

"It's nice."

"But you aren't having a good time." He said it more as a statement than a question.

Rosalia didn't respond.

"If you don't know this already, Rosalia, everyone at the convent has a story—why they ended up here, even most of the nuns."

Rosalia remained silent.

"I can tell you don't want to be here. Your heart and your head are still somewhere else. And that's all right. We all need our good memories to keep us going on the path that God has laid out for us."

"It is not that I don't want to be here, necessarily. Madre Carmela and the other sisters have been very good to me. And I enjoy working with them and learning how to make pastries. But yes, you are right. My heart longs to be somewhere else, but that isn't possible right now."

"May I ask what brought you to the convent, Rosalia?"

"I don't wish to discuss it. All I will say is that I lost my family, and I need to find them."

"You lost your family? How? Were you in a public place and you got separated from them? Can't you just go home?"

Rosalia's eyes filled with tears, but she fought them back as she shook her head.

"No, I can't just go home. They are no longer there. Please, Antonio, I don't want to talk about this right now."

"*Va bene.* I'm sorry. I didn't mean to pry. You just seem so sad, and I know sometimes it helps to talk. I promise I will not ask you about this again until you are ready to tell me." His eyes met Rosalia's, and he crossed his heart with his fingers and kissed them, eliciting a soft laugh from her.

"What's so funny? You take my oath lightly?"

"No, of course not. It is just that I did not expect you to do that. Thank you for understanding."

"So, are you ready to face off against me tomorrow in our baking contest?"

Grateful he was changing the subject, Rosalia said, "Of course I am ready—to win!" She smirked, surprised at herself that she could manage a joke. But it felt good, distracting her for the moment from the constant ache she'd felt since the day she discovered her family was gone.

"Ah! You are already overly confident! But we'll see who the true master is tomorrow."

"*Sì.* We will see."

The procession came to a halt, and the crowd became silent as the priest began praying. Rosalia bowed her head to pray, but she noticed a quick movement in her peripheral vision. Teresa was crouched low and running away from the crowd. Rosalia saw Anunziata was glancing nervously from Teresa's fleeing figure to Elisabetta, whose eyes were closed as she listened to the priest's prayers. The young man Rosalia had seen visiting Teresa at the shop waited for her by a tree. He took Teresa by the hand, and they disappeared in the shadows behind the tree.

Rosalia wondered if Teresa was in love with that man, and if he felt the same way about her. She hoped Teresa knew what she was doing. Again, she wondered what her story was and how she had ever become a nun when it was so obvious she wasn't meant for that life. Well, at least she had come to her senses and left her order.

"Amen!" The crowd responded to the end of the priest's prayer, startling Rosalia out of her thoughts.

"Now the best part of the festival is starting!" Anunziata squeezed Rosalia's arm as a live band took the stage in the town square. A male singer belted out notes to a popular song. Couples began dancing in front of the stage.

"Would you like to dance?" Antonio asked Anunziata.

"*Sì! Grazie,* Antonio. As you saw when you caught me in your place, I love nothing more than listening to music and dancing!"

Antonio and Anunziata locked hands and began swaying their hips to the music. It was a fast number, but Antonio managed to lead Anunziata perfectly in time to the beat. Rosalia had felt a bit odd when she heard Antonio ask Anunziata to dance. She tried to push the feeling away, but it only grew as she watched them dancing.

"Are you having a good time, Rosalia?" Madre Carmela appeared by her side.

"*Sì,* Madre Carmela."

"I'm so glad you came to the feast. I know how hard everything has been for you lately, but it will get easier each day."

"Have you heard anything from L'ispettore Franco, Madre?" Rosalia's voice held the same tone of expectancy as it did every time that she asked Madre Carmela this question.

"No. I will call him again tomorrow and ask if there have been any new developments, but I'm sure he would have told us if there were. And you know I would tell you right away if I heard something, Rosalia."

"*Si,* Madre."

Of course Rosalia knew she could trust Madre to give her any news about her family's whereabouts instead of hounding her with the same question. It was just that she was so desperate and wished she could be doing more herself to try to find her family. She sighed heavily, feeling frustrated.

"So, Antonio told me about the contest you two are going to have."

"He did?"

"I think that's a wonderful idea! There's no better way to master something than to have a competitor. The friendly competition will only make you strive to become better at your craft."

Rosalia looked out toward Antonio and Anunziata, who were done dancing and were making their way back to her.

"I'm going to find the other sisters. They wanted to see how our Saint Lucy's Eyes are selling at the stalls." Madre Carmela walked away.

"My heart is racing! You dance so well, Antonio!" Anunziata gushed and looked at Antonio as if he were a pop star. Rosalia couldn't help but wonder if Anunziata had a crush on him.

"You dance well, too." He smiled shyly before looking at Rosalia. "How about you? Think you're up for a dance? This is a slow song, so it won't give you the heart attack that Anunziata is currently having."

Rosalia felt panic. Before she could politely refuse, Anunziata was pleading with her to dance. "Oh, you must, Rosalia! It'll be so much fun."

"I don't really know how to dance. But thank you for asking."

"It's all right. We'll go slow, and I'll be doing most of the work leading you." Antonio took Rosalia's hand and began walking toward the stage. She could feel her face burning up. Though she had cringed slightly when Antonio took her hand, she didn't feel the terror she had felt the first day she met him when they stood so close to each other. She closed her eyes for a moment and willed herself to relax by silently repeating, *He's not Marco. I am safe. He's not Marco. I am safe.*

As if sensing her trepidation, Antonio kept some space between himself and Rosalia as he placed one hand on her right hip and held her left hand with his other. He had not done this with Anunziata. When Rosalia had watched their figures from the back, they had seemed to be pressed so close together that they could be one. But she was grateful he was not being as intimate with her.

Anunziata was right. Antonio was a good dancer, and he expertly led Rosalia through the dance. After a few seconds, she felt herself relax a little. Her hand felt sweaty in Antonio's grip, and she was embarrassed she was sweating so much. She could even feel beads of perspiration beginning to break out on her forehead. Antonio smiled and offered encouraging words.

"You're doing fine. See? You can dance!" He laughed before suddenly lifting Rosalia's hand high in the air as he twirled her quickly around. She was so caught off guard that she lost her balance for a moment and fell against his chest. She swallowed hard as she looked at Antonio. His face grew somber as their eyes met.

"I'm sorry." She stepped back, and Antonio resumed their dance as if nothing had happened. It didn't escape her notice that he seemed to have a gift for knowing when she needed some space. She couldn't help but draw a comparison to Marco who, on the other hand, had always been forcing himself into her space, never caring about her protestations. And then just taking what he wanted.

"What is it, Rosalia?" Antonio stopped dancing.

"Nothing."

"Are you sure?"

"I'm fine."

The song ended, and before Antonio could take Rosalia's hand again, she quickly said, "Thank you for the dance. I'm going to find Madre Carmela."

She quickly walked away, leaving Antonio rooted in place as he watched her hurry off. The more he got to know Rosalia, the more the mystery of her deepened. Someone had hurt her. He was convinced of it. His mother had taught him from a young age to always trust his instincts, and from the moment he had met Rosalia, he had sensed she was a frightened young woman and had been deeply hurt. Had it been someone in her family? Was that why she had "lost" them, as she put it?

He turned around and walked over to where the statue of Saint Lucy stood. Closing his eyes, he prayed silently. *Please help Rosalia. Please help her to heal and learn to trust again.*

Opening his eyes, Antonio slowly made his way back to the convent and his home in the abandoned chapel, thinking all the way about the pretty girl with the licorice-colored hair whom he was losing his heart to.

❧ 12 ❧

Pan di Spagna
con Crema Pasticciera

SPONGE CAKE WITH PASTRY CREAM

December 23, 1955

Rosalia could not believe tomorrow would be Christmas Eve already. The past month had been the busiest in the kitchen and pastry shop. She, the nuns, and the lay workers had been staying up late, working to ensure they were meeting the customers' demands and weren't running out of their most popular pastries.

Because of all the work, Rosalia and Antonio were learning quickly. Since Madre Carmela knew about their bet to see who could make the better pastry, she had appointed herself the judge and tasted their creations. At the moment, they were tied. Rosalia had won for making the better *Buccellati*—the Sicilian fig cookies that were popular during Christmas—and various other biscotti as well as individual pastries such as cannoli. Antonio seemed to be the master of fried pastries such as *sfinci,* zeppole, and Sweet Ricotta Turnovers. Today would be the first time Rosalia and Antonio would be making *pan di Spagna,* or sponge cake, as well as pastry cream.

"*Pan di Spagna* is the base of many of the cakes you will be making in our pastry shop. You must master creating a very light texture that complements the richer glazes and fillings your cakes will have," Madre Carmela said as she beat egg whites with a wire whisk.

Although the convent owned an electric mixer, she and many of the other workers preferred mixing by hand. Rosalia was amazed at how quickly Madre's egg whites were taking on the thick, airy texture that was necessary to create the perfect *pan di Spagna*.

As if reading her thoughts, Madre said, "Don't worry. It will take you time to be able to whip your own egg whites as quickly as I can. What is important is that you get this consistency, no matter how long it takes you. We won't be having you and Antonio make cakes for the shop until you've become quicker at beating, since we cannot waste time during our busiest seasons like now. But in the summer, during our slower season, I'll let you both take over making the cakes."

"I will continue to practice making at least one cake a week. I don't have time to wait until next summer," Antonio said as he cracked his eggs into his bowl.

Rosalia couldn't believe how quickly he cracked his eggs, and with one egg in each hand. She was still trying to master cracking her eggs without getting any shells into her batter.

Madre frowned in Antonio's direction. "Are you going somewhere?"

"Not anytime soon, but as you know, Madre, I have big dreams."

"Eh." Madre shrugged her shoulders. "It's good to take your time—even when you have big dreams."

Rosalia continued to focus on whipping her egg whites and acted as if she weren't paying attention to Madre and Antonio's conversation. While she was feeling more comfortable in his presence and had come to enjoy and look forward to their friendly contests, she still wanted to keep a certain distance between them. But she couldn't help wondering what Antonio's big dreams were.

"You had better pick up your speed, Rosalia, if you hope to make anything out of those sudsy egg whites." Antonio laughed.

"I will get there. Like Madre said, it will take time to whip them since we're new."

"But look how fast I've whipped mine into beautiful creamy

white peaks." Antonio lifted a dollop of egg whites with his whisk, and sure enough they were the perfect consistency.

"My Papà used to say, 'Those who boast always come last.' " Rosalia glanced at Antonio and smirked before taking her bowl and going over to a table where he couldn't observe her work.

"Where are you going?" Antonio shouted.

"Somewhere you can't watch my every move. Besides, this is a contest. We shouldn't be working so close together."

Antonio followed her, and though Rosalia did her best to shield her deflated egg whites from him, he rested his elbows on the table, placing his chin in his hands and peering straight down into her bowl.

Rosalia couldn't help but laugh. "Get out of here. Aren't you worried you're wasting precious time, even though you're already ahead?"

"I'd rather lose if it means I can be near you. What's the fun in working alone? Just look at Sorella Domenica." Antonio gestured toward the nun with his thumb and then whispered, "*That's* what happens when you work alone."

Sorella Domenica's features were pinched as usual while she smoothed an orange glaze over a cake. Her brows knitted furiously together, creating numerous lines on her forehead; her eyes squinted so that they almost looked like two slits; and her lips were tucked into her mouth so that you couldn't see them. The muscles in her neck looked taut, and the veins in her hands bulged noticeably. Rosalia had to turn her face away as a soft giggle escaped her throat.

"See what I mean? She's the only one who consistently works alone. The other nuns seem to thrive on teamwork, as do the lay workers, but not her. Whereas everyone else is chatting, even when they're crazed, or singing as they go about their work, she's all alone and looks like she's going to burst a vessel in her brain."

"Stop, Antonio! That's not nice." But Rosalia couldn't stop laughing as she wiped her eyes with her apron.

"You agree. So let's go back to working side by side and enjoying each other's company even if we are competitors."

"Fine. Fine. Anything to get you off my back," Rosalia said, but she smiled to let Antonio know she was just joking with him.

"I must say, when I came here, I thought most of the nuns were going to be like Sorella Domenica. It was a pleasant surprise to discover that she's pretty much the only nasty one. You know nuns don't always have the best reputations."

Rosalia nodded her head. "*Si*. The sisters have been wonderful to me—well, all of them except for Sorella Domenica of course. I don't know why, but I get the feeling she doesn't like me."

"It's not just you, Rosalia. She doesn't like anyone. I've even heard her give Madre Carmela attitude."

"Really? But she's the mother superior. All the nuns must show her the utmost respect."

"Sorella Domenica must think she's better than her. But Madre put her in her place."

"That's good. It bothers me to hear that anyone would speak to Madre Carmela disrespectfully."

"You look up to her, don't you?"

"I do. I owe a lot to Madre Carmela."

Antonio nodded his head. "I'll let you focus on whipping your egg whites or else you'll be here until tonight."

Rosalia raised her brow. "What happened to working side by side?"

"I'll still be right here. I just won't chew your ears off."

Rosalia smiled.

Several hours later, Rosalia was dusting the top of her sponge cake with powdered sugar. She had taken extra care to smooth the pastry cream as neatly as possible in between the two layers of sponge cake so that there were no messy drips. Antonio had finished his cake an hour earlier since he'd been able to whip his egg whites quicker. Rosalia was prepared to lose this contest to him, although from appearances, his cake didn't seem much different from hers.

"Ah! Are we ready to see who the winner is?" Madre Carmela walked over, holding a cake fork. "Whose shall I try first?"

"Ladies first." Antonio gestured toward Rosalia.

She cut a generous slice of her cake and placed it on a plate, handing it to Madre Carmela.

Madre Carmela took a bite, closing her eyes as she chewed the cake slowly. She gave no clue as to how the cake tasted. She then took a second bite, but this time kept her eyes open.

"Hmmm. All right, Antonio, yours is next."

Antonio had already cut a slice of cake for Madre and was waiting to hand it to her. Again, Madre took two bites as she usually did when she was tasting one of their sweets, but this time, she took a third bite of Antonio's cake. Rosalia's spirits sank. No doubt Madre Carmela liked Antonio's better since she had felt compelled to take a third bite, and she had never before done that with the other desserts they'd made.

"Well, I must say, both of these cakes are very, very good. But the clear winner is Rosalia's *pan di Spagna.*"

"Rosalia's?" Antonio sounded as surprised as Rosalia was, but then she realized he had been expecting her to lose, and she sent a scowl in his direction in response to which he held up his hands and gave her a bashful smile.

Even when Antonio managed to irk her with one of his jokes about her baking or in this case by expecting her to lose, he always saved himself with his irresistible smile or by saying the right words in the moment. Rosalia wondered how he could do that every time, but of course, she couldn't be mad at him. While she wanted to deny it, she knew they were becoming friends.

"Rosalia's cake has a lighter texture than yours, and if you look at it, you will see there's a slightly higher rise. Clearly, she beat her egg whites perfectly."

Rosalia couldn't help but laugh. Now it was Antonio's turn to scowl at her.

"What is so funny, Rosalia?"

"Antonio was teasing me earlier about how long it was taking me to get my egg whites to the right consistency. I reminded him what you said about not worrying how long it takes and about how it's more important to get it right."

"I see." Madre Carmela looked at Antonio and then looked at Rosalia, turning her back toward Antonio. She winked at Rosalia and smiled. "Well, let that be a lesson to you, Antonio, that you should take a little more time with your batters. Obviously, the extra time it took Rosalia to whip her egg whites must've contributed to the cake's perfect texture. I know you are in a rush to master the art of pastry making so you can pursue your 'big dreams,' but what good will it do you if you're producing average pastries at best? Eh?"

Antonio's face turned crimson. Rosalia instantly regretted saying anything to Madre Carmela about Antonio teasing her earlier. He did work very hard. Rosalia could see that.

"Well, in all fairness, Madre, Antonio's egg whites did look ready when he was done beating them. What about the pastry cream? You've only commented on the *pan di Spagna*."

"They both tasted exceptional. In that case, I think you and Antonio are tied."

Antonio looked relieved he hadn't lost as far as the pastry cream was concerned.

"You're both learning very fast and have much talent. I'm proud of both of you. Now, I must go get ready for the evening vespers." Madre Carmela patted both of them on the shoulder before taking her leave.

Rosalia cut the rest of her cake into individual portions so that they could be sold in the pastry shop. Nothing went to waste, and she took great pleasure in seeing customers buy what she had made. Antonio did the same with his cake and then began cleaning up. Rosalia joined him at the sink.

"I'll dry your bowls and pan for you."

Antonio looked surprised at her offer of help, but didn't say anything.

They worked side by side quietly for a few minutes before Rosalia said, "I'm sorry, Antonio."

"For what? Winning? That's ridiculous. You've won before and haven't apologized."

Rosalia shook her head. "I'm sorry for telling Madre Carmela about how you teased me about my egg whites. I should've just kept that to myself."

Antonio shrugged his shoulders as he rinsed off his whisk under the running water. "That's nothing. Don't be sorry. It was pretty funny actually, thinking back on it now. I like seeing you laugh. You need to laugh more often. That's partly why I tease you when we're working. I'm just trying to see your pretty smile."

Their eyes locked before Rosalia glanced away.

"*Grazie.* I just felt bad since it seemed like you thought you were going to win this contest, and then Madre Carmela was a bit harsh. I know how hard you work."

"So you've been watching me?" Antonio smirked.

Rosalia blushed. "It's hard not to notice since we are working together."

As they finished up cleaning, Rosalia took off her apron.

"I'll see you tomorrow, Antonio."

"Wait. I'll walk with you."

Rosalia frowned. "You're not allowed to come to our living quarters."

Antonio hit his forehead with his hand. "I forgot. If you're not too tired, would you like to take a walk in the courtyard? Just for a few minutes."

Rosalia thought for a moment. It would be nice to take a walk outside and look at the stars. She had rarely stepped out at night since she'd come to the convent.

"All right. For a few minutes. But let me get my sweater first."

When Rosalia returned, she and Antonio made their way to the courtyard and took a stroll around the grounds. It was more peaceful than early in the mornings when Rosalia liked to open her window and look for the bluethroat, which had become a daily visitor to her ever since that first day she'd seen it.

"That's a pretty sweater."

"*Grazie.* Mari knitted it for me. She's an expert knitter and made it in just a little more than a week."

"That was nice of her." Antonio glanced at the plain gray dress Rosalia and the other lay workers wore as part of their uniform in the kitchen and the pastry shop. The nuns gave these dresses to them. The only other dress he'd seen Rosalia wear was the pretty violet dress she had worn at the feast of Saint Lucy. His heart ached a little when he thought about how poor Rosalia was. A girl her age and with her beauty should be wearing a beautiful dress every day.

Though he knew she had been through a lot and that there was still a deep sadness in her, she seemed happiest when she was working in the kitchen, making her pastries and doing her best to beat him.

He watched her now out of the corner of his eye. He didn't want to make her feel uncomfortable. She was finally beginning to let her guard down around him, and he didn't want to risk alienating her again. She seemed to be enjoying their walk and looked relaxed. Maybe he could finally ask her the question he'd been wanting to ask since that day they had danced at the feast. Or was it still too soon? The impulsive side of him couldn't wait any longer. He would ask her and deal with the consequences afterward.

"Rosalia, I was wondering how you will be spending the day after Christmas since the shop will be closed and the nuns aren't expecting us to work that day."

"I hadn't really thought about it. I'll just rest in my room."

"Have you ever been to Messina?"

"I used to go with my father sometimes when he needed to buy fabric. He was a tailor and had his own shop."

"A tailor? That's fine work. He must've been a very good one."

"He was. He made the most beautiful men's suits."

"So you've been to the Cathedral of Messina?"

"No, I haven't. Papà said he would take me one day when we weren't so busy, but he was always in a rush to return to the shop. He did treat me to *gelato* sometimes." Rosalia felt a pang in her chest when she remembered her trips to the city with her father. She used to look forward to them so much.

"Would you like to visit the cathedral with me?"

Rosalia stopped walking. "Go all the way to Messina?"

"It's not that far."

"I don't know. Are any of the other girls coming? Like Anunziata?"

"They have plans already. I overheard them talking about what they would be doing the day after Christmas."

Rosalia was a little hurt that the other girls hadn't asked her if she wanted to join them on whatever excursion they were taking the day after Christmas. Then again, she supposed she couldn't blame them. Except for the feast of Saint Lucy, she had said no every time they asked her to go out with them.

"You'll be safe with me, Rosalia. I promise you."

Rosalia looked at Antonio. How did he know she was afraid to be alone with him? Had her fear been that evident?

She felt torn. On the one hand, it would be nice to go back to Messina and finally visit the cathedral her father had always promised he'd take her to. But on the other, she wasn't sure about spending so much time alone with Antonio.

She couldn't go. She wasn't ready. It was all too much, too soon. Just as she was about to tell Antonio she couldn't go with him, she was startled by a quick motion that flashed before her eyes.

"Look at that! The bluethroat you were following the first day I met you." Antonio pointed to the fountain that surrounded the statue of Saint Lucy, where the bird was dipping its beak as it drank. "That's odd. I've never seen him out here at night when I'm walking back to the abandoned chapel. I have spotted him a few times during the day, especially in the morning. He likes to sit on that branch by that window." Antonio pointed to Rosalia's window.

"I know. That's my bedroom. He comes and visits me every morning. I feed him."

"He likes you." Antonio grinned.

Rosalia looked at the bluethroat, which had stopped drinking and was just sitting on the fountain's ledge. It turned its head and once more seemed to be looking at her. Whenever the bird did this, she always felt a shiver go through her. But its presence comforted her more than anything else.

"So have you decided? Will you come to the cathedral with me? We could even visit a couple of the pastry shops there and compare their pastries to ours. You can think of it as an educational outing if that makes you feel better."

Rosalia could feel her resolve weakening. It was true. They could learn a lot by visiting the pastry shops in Messina. Then, a thought came to her. Perhaps her family had moved to Messina? Why not? It was a large city that no doubt needed tailors, and her father was familiar with it from all his trips there to buy fabric. The fabric store! That was it! She would go to the fabric store her father visited whenever he went to Messina to restock his tailor shop. The fabric store owner knew her father and would remember if he'd been there recently. And if she didn't get anywhere there, she could inquire at other establishments in the city to see if perhaps anyone had come into contact with her family. It was a long shot, but at least she would be actively doing something to search for them instead of waiting to hear from L'ispettore Franco.

"All right. I'll come with you."

Antonio's eyes shone. "You will?"

"*Sì*. It will be nice to visit the cathedral and see what pastries the shops in Messina are selling. It could inspire us in our own creations."

"That's true. I promise you, you'll have a good time."

"If you don't mind, I think I'll head up to my room now. We still have a busy day tomorrow since it's Christmas Eve and the shop will be closing early."

"Of course. I'll walk you back to the convent's entrance."

"That's all right. I'll be fine. *Buona notte,* Antonio."

"*Buona notte.*"

Antonio waited until Rosalia reached the convent's entrance. She looked over her shoulder and waved before stepping inside. He waved and turned around, heading to the abandoned chapel. But when he reached the fountain of Saint Lucy, where they'd been talking earlier, he stopped and looked up toward where Rosalia had indicated her bedroom window was. The light was on. He saw a shadow cast over the sheer curtains that hung behind the window, and then the light went out.

"*Buona notte,* Rosalia," he whispered before turning away and continuing home. His spirits were high as he whistled a tune softly to himself. Now he only had to get through tomorrow and Christmas before he would have Rosalia to himself for an entire day. He would make sure it was a day she would never forget.

❧ 13 ❧

Fior di Mandorla

CHEWY ALMOND COOKIES

December 26, 1955

Rosalia felt hopeful—an emotion she hadn't felt since that day she had returned to her hometown expecting to be reunited with her family. She was riding in the back of a pickup truck with Antonio. He had asked the man who delivered flour to the convent if they could get a ride with him to Messina. Though she was also a little nervous that she would be spending the entire day alone with Antonio, her hope that she would find some information about her family outweighed her anxiety.

Madre Carmela had given Antonio permission to take Rosalia to Messina. She seemed happy that Rosalia would be getting out and having a day away from the convent. Rosalia had promised Madre that she would find out all she could about the pastries that were being served in the shops in Messina.

"Don't worry about that, my girl. Have a good time. Relax. Take in the sights. Be sure to take her to the Duomo and the Santissima dei Annunziata dei Catalani church, Antonio."

"You have been to Messina?" Rosalia had asked Madre, surprised. She couldn't picture the nun anywhere other than Santa Lucia del Mela and the convent.

"Of course. It is a wonderful city."

So with Madre Carmela's blessing they were on their way. Rosalia was enjoying the ride to Messina and just feeling her hair blow softly in the breeze as she drifted off to sleep. Thankfully, Antonio had left Rosalia to her thoughts instead of talking. About an hour later, she was awakened by a blaring car horn.

"We're here!" Antonio shouted above the traffic's din.

"I can see and hear that." Rosalia smiled faintly, trying to force herself to wake up. "What time is it?"

"Just about ten o'clock. We ran into some traffic and lost about twenty minutes."

Rosalia nodded her head as she scanned their surroundings. They were approaching the Piazza del Duomo. Soon, Rosalia could see the Duomo—Messina's famous cathedral. Papà had taken her a few times to see the Duomo's clock, which was known for its mechanical figures that moved when the clock struck noon every day.

"Are you ready?" Antonio held out a hand for Rosalia as she stepped out of the truck.

"How will we get back to the convent?" Rosalia asked.

"A friend of mine who lives in Messina agreed to give us a ride. He'll meet up with us later in the day."

Rosalia pushed away the fear that seeped into her mind upon hearing she would be alone with two boys on the car trip back to the convent. She knew she would be safe with Antonio. She needed to stop worrying.

"Are you hungry? I know it's early for lunch, but I thought we could begin our research of the pastry shops right away, and while we're there, we might as well have an espresso and sample the sweets."

"*Sì.* I'm hungry." Rosalia rubbed her stomach and laughed.

Antonio reached for her hand and led her across the piazza. She felt strange holding his hand, but she didn't pull her hand out of his grasp. They entered a shop called Dolci di Duomo. Many patrons waited in line, and most of the tables were taken. Antonio spotted a couple leaving a table that was tucked in a corner of the shop.

"Quick, Rosalia." He gestured toward the table with his hand, and she hurried over.

Antonio waited in line. She hadn't told him what she wanted, but it didn't matter. She would have whatever he ordered. She saw this shop had an assortment of marzipan fruit, but their selection featured large apples, pears, oranges. The marzipan fruit at the convent's shop were smaller. Baskets of different biscotti in cellophane bags, tied with ribbons of red, green, and white—the colors of the Italian flag—stood on either end of the very long counter. She looked around to see what the patrons seated at the tables next to her were eating. Several had biscotti to go with their espressos or cappuccinos. A few had brioche with *granita;* even though the weather wasn't as hot as it was in the summer, she supposed people still loved having *granita* for breakfast. She then noticed many of the customers had puffy *S*-shaped cookies that were dusted with powdered sugar. She'd seen these cookies at the convent's pastry shop, but had not paid them much mind. But here, they seemed to be the popular sweet.

"*Mi dispiace,* Rosalia. I forgot to ask you what you wanted before you walked away, and I didn't want to lose my place in line with all of these customers. So I had to take a guess. If you don't like these, I'll get you something else. And I suppose you're all right with an espresso?"

Antonio looked worried. It hadn't occurred to Rosalia that he might have anxieties of his own about today. She was touched that he was so concerned about something as trivial as what she would eat and drink.

"I'm sure everything tastes wonderful in here or else they wouldn't be so busy." She gave him an encouraging smile. His face seemed to relax as he put down a small tray with a plate of the same cookies that Rosalia had seen most of the customers eating and two cups of espresso.

"That's funny! I was wondering what these cookies are, especially since it seems like they're the popular sweet at this shop. Madre Carmela has these in her shop, but I've never paid any attention to them and have no idea what's in them."

"So I did well then?" Antonio's face beamed with pride.

"*Sì.* This will be a good test since we don't sell a lot of these cookies at the shop. There must be a reason why they're so popular here. Maybe we can figure out their secret ingredient?"

"I like that. We can be pastry detectives today!" Antonio laughed. "Actually, when I realized I hadn't asked you what you wanted, I asked the man in front of me if he knew what were a few of the shop's most famous sweets, and he told me these were the most popular. They're called *Fior di Mandorla.*"

Rosalia took a bite out of a cookie and was surprised at its chewy texture and intense burst of almond flavor. Her eyes opened wide, showing her immense pleasure.

"That good, huh?" Antonio laughed before taking a bite out of one of his cookies. "Ah! *Buonissimo!*"

"I wonder if these taste as good at our shop," Rosalia said before taking another bite.

"Well, we'll have to see when we get back tonight. We must try them as soon as we return so we don't forget what these tasted like."

After they were done eating their cookies and drinking their espressos, they walked around the Piazza del Duomo and made their way toward the Orion Fountain. Rosalia remembered her father's telling her about the fountain one of the times they had come to see the Duomo's clock. The fountain featured statues that represented four rivers: the Tiber, the Nile, the Ebro, and the Camaro.

Once they reached the fountain, Antonio stopped walking and glanced at his watch.

"I thought we'd just take a break here and wait until noon so we can see the moving figures on the Duomo's clock. We still have an hour, so if you'd rather walk around more and come back, we can do that."

"Would you mind if we did walk around until close to the time? I wanted to do a little window shopping." Rosalia blushed slightly at her little lie. She didn't know yet how she would explain to Antonio that her real reason for wanting to browse along the main shopping thoroughfare was to inquire about her family.

"Of course. That will be fun."

Rosalia felt bad suddenly that she had lied to Antonio. Here he was going out of his way to make sure she would have a good time, and she was going to be deceitful and even try to find an excuse so she could go into the shops alone to make her inquiries.

Her thoughts then drifted to Marco. He was a liar. And she didn't want to do anything that remotely resembled his behavior.

Taking a deep breath, Rosalia reached for Antonio's arm, stopping him from walking away from the fountain.

"I'm sorry, Antonio. I'm afraid I haven't been completely honest with you about my reasons for coming with you to Messina today. I don't want to lie to you. You've been nothing but kind to me since we've met."

Antonio's eyes filled with concern. "What is it, Rosalia? Please know you can trust me with anything. I don't want you to be afraid around me, and I want you to feel like you can be honest with me."

Rosalia let go of his arm and turned her back to him as she took a few steps closer to the fountain. She focused on the sprays of water that were streaming from the fountain.

"Do you remember when I told you I lost my family and needed to find them?" She looked over her shoulder, seeing Antonio nod before she turned back around. She was afraid if she didn't keep her head turned away from him as she spoke that she would break down crying.

"I was hoping that I could ask a few of the shopkeepers here if they had seen my family, especially at the store where my father purchased his fabric for his tailor shop. I want to know if my father has been back recently. Who knows? Maybe my family decided to move to Messina, and perhaps a few of the other shopkeepers might've seen them."

"I see. We can do that, Rosalia. That's fine. But . . ." Antonio's voice trailed off. He was about to continue, but stopped again. "I'm sorry, Rosalia, but I must ask again. What happened to your family? How is it that you're separated from them? Wouldn't they be looking for you?"

Rosalia's eyes quickly filled with tears. She turned. Her gaze met Antonio's for a brief moment before she glanced away again, trying to fight back the tears, but it was no use. The thought that her family had stopped looking for her and had been able to move away so soon after receiving Marco's ugly letter was too much for her to bear in this moment.

"I'm sorry, Rosalia. I didn't mean to upset you."

Antonio placed his hand on her shoulder, and before Rosalia could think better about what she was doing, she leaned into him, letting him cradle her as she surrendered herself to her emotions. Antonio waited patiently until she stopped crying. He pulled a handkerchief out of his trousers pocket and patted her tears dry before placing the handkerchief in her hand. Again, she couldn't believe how tender he was with her.

"You didn't upset me, Antonio. It's hard for me still to accept that they're gone. I have to find them. I just have to."

Antonio nodded his head thoughtfully. She could see he still wanted to ask her more questions, but didn't want to upset her any further.

"I want to tell you, Antonio, what happened to me, but I'm not ready yet. All I will say is that I was separated from my family, and they were led to believe something false about me. They went through a very difficult time and had no choice but to leave my hometown. They . . . they thought I was gone and would not be returning. It's not like they abandoned me, Antonio."

He patted her shoulder and said, "Of course not. How could anyone abandon you? You're an angel."

She glanced down at the handkerchief he'd given her, twisting it around her index finger.

"Rosalia, you don't have to tell me everything that happened. When you're ready, I'll be here. Like I said before, you can trust me."

"*Grazie,* Antonio."

"Let's go make a few of those inquiries. Do you remember how to get to the fabric store where your father used to shop?"

"*Sì.* I'm sure the owner will remember me. I came to Messina with my father earlier this year."

They walked toward Via Garibaldi; in this neighborhood, many shops lined the streets. Rosalia felt like she was going back in time, imagining she was walking the streets with her father instead of Antonio. For a moment, she wished she were having a bad dream and that everything that had happened to her during the past few months wasn't real. She then remembered what Madre Carmela had told her. She must place her trust in God and ask Him to help her through this difficult period. Silently, she prayed.

Please, God, give me the strength to go on without my family while we are separated, and give me the strength to never give up the hope of being reunited with them again.

"There's a fabric store right there. Is that the one your father shopped at, Rosalia?"

Rosalia looked to where Antonio pointed. *Merceria Mandanici.*

"*Sì*, that's it." She stopped walking as a cold shiver washed over her. Her heart began to race. She closed her eyes and prayed to God once more. *Please, God, let me find out something.*

"Are you all right, Rosalia?" Antonio looked at her with concern.

She nodded her head. "I'm just a little nervous and hoping Signore Mandanici, the owner of the shop, can tell me something about my family—though I know the odds are slim."

"It's a start. If he has no information for you, don't be discouraged." Antonio grabbed her hand and gave it a tight squeeze before leading her to the shop.

They stepped into the store and saw Signore Mandanici was finishing up a sale. While they waited to talk to him, Rosalia inhaled deeply the scents of all the fabrics lining the shelves. They were comforting scents, for she was reminded of the times she had come here with her father, when they had discussed which fabrics to buy. They had also purchased their fabrics here for the clothes Rosalia's mother would sew for the family. Rosalia remembered buying a beautiful bolt of lavender cotton once for a summer dress her mother had made for her. Rosalia took a deep breath before the memories consumed her.

"Rosalia?" Signore Mandanici called out to her.

She offered him a small smile. "You remember me."

"Of course! Why wouldn't I? You and your father are among my best customers."

Rosalia cringed slightly at his use of the present "are." *He doesn't know anything,* a voice whispered inside her head.

"So what can I do for you today?" Signore Mandanici then took notice of Antonio and frowned. "Is your father well? Why isn't he with you today?"

Rosalia's heart sank. Her suspicions were confirmed. "He . . ."

She couldn't continue as her voice cracked. Antonio came to her rescue.

"Signore Mandanici, I am Antonio, a friend of Rosalia's. This might sound strange, but please bear with us. Rosalia was separated from her family."

Signore Mandanici's eyes widened. He was about to ask a question, but Antonio held up his hand before Signore Mandanici could speak.

"I'm afraid it's too long a story and too complicated to explain. We don't want to take up too much of your time. We know how busy you are."

Antonio's last statement appeared to placate Signore Mandanici's curiosity.

"As I was saying, she was separated from her family, and she is desperate to find them. Rosalia was wondering if her father has been in the shop in the past month? And if so, did he give any indication as to where he might be living now?"

Signore Mandanici raised his right eyebrow. He then looked at Rosalia.

"Rosalia, is everything this young man is saying true?"

"*Si.* I'm afraid it is, Signore Mandanici. Have you seen my father?"

"The last time I saw him was in November. I should've suspected something was wrong since he came in, not wishing to purchase fabric from me, but instead to ask if I wanted to buy a few men's suits that he had made. He was even offering them to me at a much lower price than what they were worth." Signore Mandanici shook his head. "He explained to me that the men whom he'd made these suits for had never returned to his shop to pick them up, and he wanted to unload them. It seemed like a plausible explanation, so I believed him."

Rosalia remembered what Signora Tucci had told her about her father's losing business at the shop. She imagined Papà had made the suits for the sole purpose of selling them.

"Did you buy the suits from him?" Rosalia asked.

"I did, but I insisted on paying him more than he was asking. As I said, the suits were worth more than the low price he was asking, and I didn't feel right paying him so little for them. Besides, your father has been a steady, loyal client to me over the years. I felt I owed him."

"*Grazie,* Signore Mandanici. You are an honest man."

Signore Mandanici waved his hand. "It was nothing. I am just so sorry to hear that your family is having a difficult time. Are you all right, Rosalia? If you're looking for them, then where are you staying?" Again, he looked questioningly at Antonio.

"I am staying at a convent in Santa Lucia del Mela. The nuns are treating me kindly and have been so generous to let me stay with them until I can locate my family. May I give you the phone number at the convent? If by any chance you see my father again, can you please give it to him and tell him I am there?"

"Of course." Signore Mandanici reached for a notebook he kept next to his cash register. He opened the notebook to a page with other contacts and phone numbers and handed a pen to Rosalia. "Write your number down here."

Rosalia then realized she didn't know by heart the convent's number. It wasn't as if she ever had a need to call the convent, since this was the first time she had been gone from it by herself. She looked at Antonio, panicked.

"I don't know the number."

"Don't worry. I do."

Rosalia breathed a sigh of relief as Antonio took the pen out of her hand and wrote the number down.

"Perhaps you should make inquiries with a few of the other shops in town that your father regularly frequented? They might have more information for you than I do," Signore Mandanici offered, but the sad expression on his face told Rosalia he doubted it.

"*Grazie,* Signore Mandanici. We will do that."

Rosalia and Antonio wished him farewell and turned to leave the shop, but Signore Mandanici called out to Rosalia.

"Wait! I want to give you these two bolts of fabric. I know it's not much, but perhaps you could make yourself a few pretty dresses."

"That is all right, Signore Mandanici."

"Please. I want to do something for Signore DiSanta's daughter.

I respect your father. He's a fine businessman and an excellent tailor. I haven't been able to sell these bolts of fabric in the past year, so you would be doing me a favor by taking them off my hands." He smiled and held out the fabric.

Rosalia knew he was telling a small lie in saying he hadn't been able to sell the fabric. As Papà had told her many times, Signore Mandanici's fabric store was the best in Messina. His business did very well.

"*Grazie molto.* I will never forget your kindness, *signore.*" Rosalia's eyes teared up.

"Take care of yourself, my child. And please, do let me know if you find your family and if there is anything else I can do for you."

Once they stepped out onto the street, Antonio took the bolts of fabric from Rosalia and held them for her.

"I'm sorry, Antonio. I wasn't thinking when I accepted the fabric from Signore Mandanici. Now you will be stuck carrying these bolts of fabric all day."

"I don't mind. And besides, I can't wait to see what beautiful dresses you will make. I didn't know you know how to make clothes. But I guess that makes sense since you are the daughter of a tailor."

"I can make basic dresses, not as beautiful as the ones my mother makes. But the true talent in our family is my father. His suits are impeccable."

"Do you want to inquire at any of the other businesses about your family?"

"If you don't mind?"

"Of course not."

They asked at the café where Rosalia and her father would stop to take a small espresso break and buy sweets for her mother when they came to the city to buy fabric. But the café owner barely remembered Rosalia and her father. They stopped at a few other businesses where her father had also visited, but no one had seen him in months.

"If you still want to see the Duomo's clock, we'd better be on our way since it's almost noon." Antonio glanced at his watch. "But if you'd rather make a few more inquiries, that's fine. I've seen the mechanical figures of the Duomo's clock before."

"No, that's all right. The few shops we have already gone to were the only places my father would stop by when we would come to Messina. My family is most likely not here, and they probably aren't even anywhere near this city. Do you believe in premonition, Antonio?"

"I guess." Antonio shrugged his shoulders.

"I have this premonition. This sense that my family is far from Messina. I don't know why, but I do. And before I learned that my family had left my hometown, I sensed something was wrong."

Antonio placed his hand on Rosalia's arm, but didn't say anything.

"How will I find them, Antonio, if they are far away?"

"I will help you."

"But how? Sicily is so large."

"I will make calls to the local authorities in every county."

"That's crazy! Besides, the police inspector of Santa Lucia del Mela is doing that already. According to Madre Carmela, nothing has come of his efforts."

"I see. I didn't realize the police inspector was involved in searching for your family."

Rosalia could see the questions in Antonio's face, but he refrained from asking her anything.

They reached the Duomo just in time for the mechanical clock to start its show. A crowd had gathered in front of the cathedral.

Unlike the other spectators who had gathered to watch the mechanical figures of the clock, Rosalia felt no elation. For how could she take pleasure in anything without having those she loved most near her? Instead, as she watched, she couldn't help feeling that she was like the figures and had no control over her own fate; rather, time was dictating her every move.

‿ 14 ‿

Cuscinetti

CITRUS-FILLED ALMOND PILLOWS

December 27, 1955

Rosalia was shifting and turning in bed, unable to sleep. She glanced at an old wristwatch, which had a small crack on its face, that she kept on her nightstand. One in the morning. Madre Carmela had given her the old watch so she could keep time. Rosalia always kept it on her night table and only used it to know what time she was waking up in the morning—or to see what time it was when she couldn't sleep. She yawned, resting her arm on top of her forehead as she turned onto her back. Thoughts of her day spent with Antonio in Messina kept flashing through her mind. While they had tried to make the most of their afternoon, there had been a cloud hanging over them. Rosalia's hopes were deflated, and she no longer believed she would find more clues. She had taken some small comfort in the fact that Signore Mandanici had seen her father, even though the news that Papà had sold a few of the suits he'd made only served to deepen her pain over the hard times her family had fallen on—and all because of her. While she knew she should listen to Madre Carmela's advice not to blame herself, it was near impossible for Rosalia not to do so.

Sighing deeply, she decided to get out of bed and go down to the kitchen. Perhaps studying the recipes in Madre Carmela's recipe book would tire her enough that she could finally go to sleep. This was a habit Rosalia had begun in the past few weeks whenever insomnia took hold. At least once a week, sometimes more, she could not fall asleep, or she would wake up in the middle of the night and be up until morning. She welcomed sleep since she often dreamed about being with Mamma, Papà, Luca, and Cecilia. But just as often as there were good dreams, there were also nightmares—nightmares that awakened her and left her feeling a terrible emptiness deep inside her.

Fortunately, none of the other nuns or lay workers who resided at the convent had problems sleeping, so when Rosalia went down to the kitchen in the middle of the night, she was all alone. But as she approached the kitchen tonight, she saw light streaming out into the corridor. Although she knew how meticulous the nuns were about ensuring the lights were turned off when not in use, perhaps one of the workers had forgotten.

A few feet away from the kitchen, Rosalia stopped. She could hear noises coming from the kitchen, a light scraping sound. Walking slowly to the entrance, she stretched her neck and peered into the kitchen. She was stunned by the sight that greeted her.

Mari, the oldest of the lay workers, was dancing! And not just any frivolous dancing, but ballet. Rosalia placed a hand over her gaping mouth as she watched the woman go from one movement to the next, completely absorbed. Mari made a deep plié, her feet turned out one in front of the other in fifth position. Her arms arched high over her head as her head tilted gracefully to the side. She leapt up and soon was dancing in semicircles around the space in the center of the kitchen. Though her leap was not very high, her skill and ability to still dance this well in her early sixties impressed Rosalia.

Rosalia knew a little about ballet, for one of her teachers had had a book on the subject and had lent it to her once. She'd loved looking at the photographs of the lithe ballerinas all decked out in their frilly tutus and dainty ballet slippers. She remembered reading about the five ballet positions and seeing the illustrations of each one. And she'd also read about pliés, chassés, and rond de jambe.

Mari ended her dance with a pirouette, but instead of completing the spin gracefully, she lost her balance and fell to the floor.

Rosalia ran over to her. "Are you all right?"

Mari looked up, confused at first to see Rosalia, but then embarrassment took over as she glanced down, nodding her head.

"I'm fine. Just a little dizzy."

"Let me help you to your feet." Rosalia held out her hand, and Mari took it as she slowly stood up.

"Did you see what I was doing?" Mari asked as she walked over to the kitchen sink and washed her hands.

"I did. I'm sorry. I didn't mean to spy on you. It's just that I couldn't sleep, and I thought I'd come down here and study a few of the recipes in Madre Carmela's books."

Mari wiped her hands dry with a clean kitchen towel before saying, "So you discovered my secret." She smiled, much to Rosalia's surprise. She rarely saw Mari smile.

"Were you a ballerina?" Rosalia asked.

Mari nodded. "In another life."

"You were beautiful."

"Ah. *Grazie.* But I can no longer dance the way I once did."

"I'm sorry if I am prying, Mari, but may I ask why it is a secret?"

Mari shrugged her shoulders. "I just haven't spoken to anyone about my former life, before I came to the convent's pastry shop. I suppose if people found out it wouldn't be that big of a deal, but then there would be more questions—questions that would lead to my having to be evasive. And I'd rather not have any speculation swirling around me. I just want to be left alone to make my pastries here."

Rosalia realized in that moment that Mari did not know there was already much speculation swirling around her. Rosalia remembered that Anunziata had told her there was some scandal in Mari's youth that had brought her here. But, from what Mari had just said, it seemed as if she hadn't told anyone about her past. So why would Anunziata and a few of the other pastry shop workers be spreading rumors that there was a scandal in Mari's past?

"I can understand your not wanting to talk about your past."

Mari looked at her for a moment. Rosalia couldn't help feeling as if Mari were seeing straight through to her soul.

"Ah, Rosalia. You have come a long way since the day the sisters found you, but I can see in your eyes you are still suffering, especially after learning that your family had moved. If there is anyone who can understand even a hint of what you are going through, that would be me. Come with me."

Mari took Rosalia by the hand and led her to one of the worktables toward the back of the kitchen.

"Before I decided to relive my days as a ballerina and almost kill myself with that pirouette, I was making *Cuscinetti*. You're not the only one who comes down here when you can't sleep."

She gestured toward three large rectangular sheets of rolled-out dough. A bowl of preserved citrons was next to the dough.

"Have you learned how to make these yet?"

Rosalia shook her head. "Did I hear you right when you said they're *Cuscinetti?*"

"*Si.* That's what they're called. Little pillows. You'll see once we're done filling them and cutting them; they resemble cute little pillows. I think these are my favorite desserts to make."

Mari smiled as she scooped up some citron preserve with a tablespoon and spread a diagonal line of it down the center of the rectangle. She then folded each side of the dough, overlapping the two edges, before taking a knife and cutting eight pieces of dough off.

"See! *Cuscinetti.* Aren't they adorable?"

Rosalia couldn't help but note the childlike glee in Mari's voice. She helped Mari fill the remaining rectangles of dough and then cut the individual little pillows.

"When I was fourteen years old, my wealthy aunt, who lived in Paris, told my mother I could go live with her and learn ballet. Zia Santa wanted to sponsor me and had high hopes that I would become a prima ballerina someday. She didn't care that I had never donned a pair of ballet slippers, and in the ballet world, fourteen was already too old to master the art. My parents were very poor, and this offer was the next best thing to a suitor's asking them for my hand in marriage. They would not have to worry about feeding another mouth if I went to stay with Zia Santa. I had three younger brothers. In fact, a few months before Zia Santa made the offer, my father had begun talking about trying to find a suitor for me."

Mari stopped working for a moment as her eyes fixed on a memory only she could see.

"My aunt had never married and had no children. Though she had many friends, there was always a loneliness about her. I suppose that's why she made her offer. Even though I was a little nervous about going to another country where I didn't know the language or even my aunt, for I had never met her before, I was relieved. I was not ready to be wed to some stranger, and that's what would have happened if I hadn't moved to Paris. So I went. Zia Santa was very kind and became like a second mother to me. She hired a tutor so I could learn French, and while it was difficult in the beginning, especially in ballet school as I struggled to understand what the teacher was instructing me to do, I learned the language enough to feel confident speaking on my own in just six months. My ballet training was rigorous, but I fell in love with it. The younger students laughed at me in the beginning since I was much older and taller than them, but knew so little. But my teacher, Mademoiselle LeJeune, encouraged me. Zia Santa always said Mademoiselle LeJeune saw something in me, and that was why she worked so hard to bring me to the level of the other students in the class. Within a year and a half, I was putting the other students to shame. They were no longer laughing at me and instead were now jealous.

"When I turned eighteen, I was offered a position with a reputable ballet company in Paris. Zia Santa's dreams of seeing me become a successful ballerina were realized. My parents were so proud of me and told me they would come to Paris someday to watch me, but they never did. They couldn't afford to take such a trip, and when I sent them the money so they could come, they sent it back." Mari's eyes filled with tears.

"Why did they do that?"

"Pride. Silly pride. But I don't blame them. Here I was the child of farmers, and now I was making so much money. My father had always taken great pride in providing for his family, even when he struggled to do so."

"How often did you come back home to visit?"

"While I was still in dance school, I came back to Sicily every summer for Ferragosto. Zia Santa even accompanied me a few times. I could tell that her visiting was uncomfortable for my parents since she had so much money. They invited her to stay in our home and, to be polite, Zia stayed, but I could tell my parents wished she had stayed in a hotel during her visits. They were embarrassed about how poor they were. But Zia didn't care. Mamma always seemed happy to see me again, even if she did feel a little uncomfortable around her sister."

"What about the times your aunt didn't join you?"

"Of course my parents were more relaxed, but there was still a strain between them and me. It was as if we no longer knew one another. That pained me a lot, and I couldn't quite understand why there was this strain, especially on my part. I should've felt that nothing had changed when I returned home, but of course, so much had changed. I had become this young woman who lived in one of the most cosmopolitan cities in the world and was learning to become a world-class ballerina. But more important, I was living under my aunt's roof in a lavish house with servants. I wore expensive clothes and had my hair done." Mari shook her head before continuing. "No wonder my poor parents felt uncomfortable around their own daughter. And I suppose now that I look back, my own awkwardness around them was because I felt guilty. Guilty that I had so much when they had so little."

"I can understand that. I feel guilty about things with my own family." Rosalia sounded very sad as she said this.

"Once I began working, it was hard for me to come back home every summer since I was often touring. So I continued to work hard, improving my dance skills and thrilling to the applause of audiences as I peformed. When I was twenty, I met a man who regularly came to watch the ballet while we performed at home in Paris. He always had a front-row seat. He had a way of managing to catch my eye as I was taking my final bows before the curtain closed.

"Finally, one day he waited for me outside the theater. He came over to my ballerina friends and me and introduced himself. Henri

Montserrat was his name. He walked me home and, after that night, he always made sure to do so when I had a performance in Paris. Soon, he began taking me out with my aunt's permission. Henri seemed to be the perfect gentleman: well-bred, wealthy—he owned a perfume factory—and impeccably polite. Needless to say I fell in love immediately, and I thought he was in love with me, too." Mari's voice caught.

Rosalia cringed, anticipating what Mari would say next.

Mari picked up two of the trays holding the *Cuscinetti* and placed them into the oven. Rosalia followed her with the other two trays. She could see in her peripheral vision that Mari was fighting back tears. Her heart went out to her.

"Mari, you don't need to tell me any more if you don't want to."

"I want to. For too many years, I have been holding on to this pain, Rosalia. It's time I let it go. And I sense my story might help you with your suffering. And if it does, that would make me happy. You are still so young, Rosalia, and I don't want to see you put yourself through the same ordeal I put myself through my whole life."

Rosalia followed Mari back to the worktable. She waited patiently until Mari was ready. Mari began mixing another batch of dough to make more *Cuscinetti* even though they already had a lot. Rosalia didn't say a word. She understood, for she had recently begun to do the same thing whenever she was upset—she had begun to use the making of the pastries as a form of healing. When she kneaded dough or prepared the shapes of the marzipan fruit or braided rows of biscotti, she felt her sadness and anxiety lift for the moment.

"As I was saying, I thought Henri was in love with me, too, but I was wrong. I was convinced he would propose to me."

"Did he tell you he would?" Rosalia asked.

"No. And he never told me he loved me even though I had told him so several times."

"Then why—" Rosalia caught herself, but it was too late.

"That's all right. You were going to ask why I thought he loved me and that he was going to propose, even though he never uttered a word to express his feelings for me or his intentions. I was foolish, and I made excuses for him: *He isn't comfortable talking about his emotions. . . . He's too busy at the perfume factory to get married to me at this moment, but when the time is right he will.* My aunt was beginning to get nervous as well and questioned his motives, but I staunchly defended him—until one day when I was enjoying a beautiful day in the park with my friends and saw him. He was having a picnic with a woman, closer to his age. Did I mention to you he was a dozen years my senior?"

Rosalia shook her head. "But I gathered he was older."

"The woman was beautiful—the complete opposite of me. She was very petite with reddish-brown curls that were pinned to the back of her head. Her face held this very wise expression. I don't know how else to put it. She had this confidence about her. Though I was becoming a celebrated ballerina, I still had insecurities and, looking back now, I'm sure they were apparent, especially to Henri.

"So I assumed she was his mistress. I was sickened at the thought, especially since I had given him my virginity. That was another reason why I thought he would marry me. I thought Henri was too honorable to persuade me to sleep with him and then not do the proper thing by marrying me."

Mari let out a wicked laugh, which startled Rosalia. She almost sounded mad, and for the first time since Rosalia had met Mari, there was a malicious glint in her eyes.

"I was such a fool. What good was all that fine education my aunt had given me if I knew nothing about life and the ways of the world? I would've learned more if I had stayed home with my poor parents on our little farm in Sicily."

"You were young, Mari. I don't think it matters where a person is brought up; we often make poor choices when we're young and inexperienced."

"I suppose. I'm sorry if I sound bitter. All these years, and I can still feel his betrayal as if it happened a moment ago." Mari closed her eyes for a moment before continuing her story. "I was about to walk away. I couldn't take watching Henri any longer in the company of this woman. But just as I was about to turn around, a breeze blew in from the Seine. It was quite a gusty day, and all the people having picnics were constantly chasing after their belongings that were getting blown away. The breeze blew up the woman's dress, revealing that she was quite pregnant. I couldn't tell before since she was seated and her dress was loose, but there was no mistaking the size of her stomach when her dress blew.

"Fortunately, my friends hadn't noticed Henri, and I told them I wanted to take a walk to the village to buy pastries. They took my suggestion, and we left. The next day when Henri came by the theater to walk me home, I confronted him with what I'd seen. And Henri confirmed what I had suspected once I'd seen that the woman with him was pregnant. She was his wife. But what twisted the knife deeper into my heart was when he told me he already had another child.

"I couldn't believe he had been unfaithful to his wife—a wife who was about to have his second child. The honorable man I thought I knew was a fraud. He told me he loved his wife, but marriage didn't suit him, and then he had the nerve to tell me that when he had first laid eyes on me he had known he had to have me. He finally told me he cared about me. Naturally, he didn't utter the word *love,* but his even saying he cared about me was the most he'd ever revealed about how he felt about me.

"I told him I could not be with a married man, and that he had betrayed me in addition to his wife. He tried in vain to convince me to change my mind, but I would not be swayed. Zia Santa didn't press me to reveal the reasons why we were no longer together. I think she had begun to suspect anyway that he was not suitable for me, and perhaps she was relieved we had ended it.

"I was beyond heartbroken and threw myself even more into my dancing. About two months after I stopped seeing Henri, I received an offer to go dance with the Bolshoi Ballet in Moscow. They wanted me to be their prima ballerina. My aunt was so proud of me. I had finally arrived. I no longer cared about finding the man of my dreams and falling in love. Henri had shattered that illusion for me, and I decided I would completely devote myself to my dancing—even more than I had before.

"I had been in Moscow for a month when I discovered I was three months pregnant. I was shocked, but not as shocked as my zia Santa, who was staying with me until I was settled. But more than shocked, she was enraged that I had let this happen, as she constantly reminded me. I'd never seen her that angry. She screamed at me and told me all of her hard work and money had gone down the drain. I wanted to lash out at her as well and remind her I was the one breaking my toes while I rehearsed constantly. I was the one constantly pressuring myself to do my best and make her proud.

"I had to resign from the dance position with the Bolshoi. I returned to Paris with my aunt, but she barely paid me any notice, and I knew it was just a matter of time before she would tell me I was no longer welcome there. I felt like such a fool, for I had misjudged both Henri and my aunt. After my ballet career was over, she no longer wanted anything to do with me. I wrote to my mother and told her what had happened. I asked if I could come back home. When I received my mother's letter, I feared she was going to turn her back on me, but she didn't." Mari wiped tears from her eyes with her apron. "The mother I had abandoned was still welcoming me with open arms. And to think I had felt awkward around her all those times I had come home to visit."

"What about your father?" Rosalia's voice sounded grave, for she was remembering how her father had believed the lies in Marco's letter.

"He wasn't happy that I was pregnant, but he didn't turn me away. I had quite a bit of money from my work as a ballerina. I gave it all to my parents when I returned home. It was the least I could do given what they were doing for me, and besides, they would need it since now I would be living with them, as would my baby once she was born.

"But it wasn't to be. I had a miscarriage in my sixth month. It was a girl. I almost died as well."

"I'm so sorry, Mari." Rosalia reached out and placed her hand on Mari's arm.

"*Grazie,* Rosalia. I think about her every day."

They remained quiet for a few moments while Rosalia waited for Mari to compose herself and continue.

"So now you know about my other life as a ballerina, living in Paris and even in Russia briefly." Mari managed a small smile for Rosalia.

"May I ask how you ended up here? At the convent?"

"I needed to find work. I couldn't keep relying on my parents to provide for me, and I wanted to be able to help them. I had heard about the pastry shop here and thought I could help with whatever was needed. I didn't live here at first. My father died about twenty years ago, and then my mother passed away a decade later. The farm was too much for me to care for, and my younger brothers had married and moved far away, so they couldn't help. I sold the farm. Madre Carmela told me I could come here to live. I gave her a generous donation after I sold the farm and insisted she take it even though she was reluctant."

Rosalia nodded thoughtfully. She was still wondering how Anunziata had known there was a scandal in Mari's past. Now, after hearing Mari's story, Rosalia saw Anunziata had been right.

"Have you told anyone else about what happened to you when you were young?"

"Only Madre Carmela. She has helped me find peace, although I still struggle at times. But I suppose the good thing to come out of what happened to me was that I was reunited with my parents. I should have never left them, and I know they grew to regret letting me move to Paris."

"And you never fell in love again?"

"No. There was someone—a young man whom I had gone to grade school with. We spent some time together when I returned home, but I just couldn't allow myself to trust again."

Mari placed her hands on either side of Rosalia's shoulders.

"Don't make the same mistake I made, Rosalia. Don't let that horrible man who kidnapped you and took you to that cave make you lose faith in others. You must learn to trust again."

Rosalia was taken aback. How had Mari known she had been kidnapped? She had only told Madre Carmela. But then Rosalia remembered what she had looked like when the nuns had found her by the cave. She had been bruised; her clothes had been torn. Her cheeks burned as she remembered she hadn't been wearing any undergarments. And in that moment, Rosalia realized they all knew. Everyone at the convent knew she'd been raped. Shame filled every pore in her body. Though Madre told her repeatedly she had nothing to be ashamed of, and that it was Marco who needed to be ashamed, Rosalia couldn't help it. She felt exposed, much as she had been on that day when she had been lying like an animal outside that cave, near death.

If the sisters and the lay workers knew that Rosalia had been raped, did that mean Antonio knew as well? She hoped not. For she was beginning to think of him as a friend, and she couldn't bear the thought of his thinking anything bad about her.

❧ 15 ❧

Chiacchiere

FRIED PASTRY RIBBONS

February 12, 1956

Carnevale had arrived, and as with other holidays, the pastry shop had been abuzz the past couple of weeks with preparing the special pastries made for the occasion. The most popular were *Chiacchiere*—delicate strips of fried dough dusted with confectioners' sugar.

Rosalia could not get enough of them and kept sneaking a piece when no one was looking. Although she and the other workers were allowed to sample the sweets, they were encouraged to only try those that were burned or did not look perfect. But each batch of *Chiacchiere* that she fried were coming out perfectly. She didn't feel too guilty for indulging since the season of Lent would begin in three days, and she, along with the other nuns and lay workers at the convent, would be abstaining from most sweets. They would only be allowed to have *Piparelli*—special biscotti that were made for Lent. Rosalia didn't know how it would be possible to stay away from the other pastries since the workers were constantly surrounded by them.

She was excited about Carnevale. For Antonio was going to take her to the festivities held in Acireale, which had the reputation of having the best Carnevale in Sicily—maybe even in all of Italy. They were going to attend with Teresa and Francesco, the young man Rosalia had seen at the pastry shop window and at the Saint Lucy feast. She wondered if Teresa had been honest with her sister and told her Francesco would be accompanying them. Something told Rosalia that Elisabetta had no idea.

As Rosalia dropped a few strips of dough into the hot oil, her thoughts turned to Antonio, and she couldn't resist a small smile. Ever since the day they had spent in Messina together, her uneasiness around him had completely faded. In fact, she felt their friendship had deepened—for he had helped her to inquire about her family, and he had even offered to phone the local authorities to see if they had any information. What amazed her even more was that he had done this without pressing her for more details as to why she'd been separated from her family.

Rosalia stepped back as a few beads of oil hissed and jumped up in the air. She had dropped her last batch of dough into the pan too quickly.

The past month she had looked forward to working by Antonio's side as they learned more pastries and had their friendly competition. Though she still missed her family and wanted to be reunited with them, she was growing to accept and even take some comfort out of her life at the Convento di Santa Lucia del Mela.

Every day, Rosalia woke up as soon as the rooster crowed. She quickly dressed, made her bed, and then joined the nuns, Anunziata, Mari, Lidia, and Elisabetta, in the main chapel, where the sisters prayed and the town priest came to say Mass. The lay workers weren't expected to join the sisters in morning prayer, just for vespers. But Rosalia and the others were usually present for the morning prayers. The only lay worker who was conspicuously absent was Teresa, but that came as no surprise to anyone.

Afterward, they had breakfast, which usually consisted of biscotti and *caffè con latte,* which they drank out of small bowls. Once breakfast was over, they began making their pastries. At eight o'clock, the pastry shop's windows opened, and they quickly transferred the baked goods over to the windows and began selling to the customers who had been waiting patiently in line for the shop to open.

Last week, Rosalia had begun to sell at the window. She didn't enjoy it, but hadn't asked Madre Carmela if she could bow out of this duty. She didn't want any special favors, especially after all the convent had done for her. But she felt a sense of dread when she looked at the customers' faces. For she kept wondering if some day Marco would be one of the patrons waiting in line. While her mind knew the chances of Marco's finding her at the convent were slim, her heart believed there was a very real possibility he might show up one day. Madre Carmela had assured her repeatedly that he must've gone far away to elude capture by the police. Rosalia only wished she could feel as certain as Madre did.

"Let me take over." Antonio came over to Rosalia and took her slotted spoon out of her hand before she could protest.

"*Grazie,* Antonio." She took her apron and patted the perspiration from her brow. She realized her pulse had quickened, probably at the thought of encountering Marco again.

"You looked deep in thought." Antonio scooped out the last of the *Chiacchiere* and then cut more strips of dough with a pastry cutter and added them to the sizzling oil.

"And you have a habit of sneaking up on me when I am deep in thought." Rosalia playfully nudged her elbow into Antonio's side. She couldn't help but marvel at how comfortable she now felt around him.

He laughed. "That is true. Well, I know better than to press you as to the mysteries in your mind."

Rosalia couldn't help feeling a small stab of guilt. She wished she could share with Antonio what had happened to her, but she was still terrified of what his reaction would be.

"So are you looking forward to Carnevale in Acireale tonight?"

"I am. Ever since I was a little girl I have dreamed of going to Acireale one day and seeing the grand festivities."

"Really? So I am making one of your childhood dreams come true then. That makes me happy." Antonio's eyes met Rosalia's as he said this.

A light flutter rippled through her belly. Startled, she pressed her hand to her stomach and then turned her back toward Antonio, busying herself with making more dough for the

Chiacchiere. This would be her job all day, for the shop was selling out almost as quickly as they were done making a fresh batch.

Besides trusting Antonio more and not feeling so awkward around him any longer, Rosalia had begun to notice what a handsome young man he was. She'd seen Teresa flirt with him, which made her mad since Teresa already had a beau. Rosalia had even noticed that a few of the female customers at the pastry shop window talked a little longer to him than was necessary. What surprised her a bit was that he had even cast a spell over the older women. But Antonio was nothing more than polite with all of them. His mother must've been a fine woman to have raised such an upstanding, good young man. He rarely spoke about his family, which she found odd since she couldn't imagine leaving her own voluntarily. But then again, he had told her things had been strained between him and his father after his mother died. Suddenly, she found herself wanting to know more about Antonio.

"Antonio, what was your mother like?"

He turned toward Rosalia, surprise etched across his features.

"She was gentle, very much like you."

Rosalia blushed.

"I miss her every day, but it is her memory and her dreams for me that give me the inspiration to make her proud of me one day. I hope she can see me wherever she is." Antonio's eyes held a distant look.

"I'm sure she is already proud of you. How could she not be? You're a hard worker and a kind person."

"You've noticed all of this about me, eh?" Antonio's eyebrow arched, and a sly smile danced across his face.

Rosalia kept her eyes lowered, pretending she was concentrating on mixing her dough.

After a few minutes, she asked, "What were your mother's dreams for you?"

"What most mothers want for their sons. She wanted me to be successful and to find a woman who would love me."

Rosalia nodded her head before saying, "I remember when we met you said you didn't want to work in your father's cobbler shop and that food was your passion. I suppose you want to be a pastry chef since you are apprenticing here?"

Antonio shook his head. "While I love learning how to make pastries, ultimately I want to become a chef. I'm saving money and hoping that I will also receive a scholarship to study at a culinary school. I want to have my own restaurant some day."

"That would be nice."

"It would. And what about you? What are your dreams for the future?"

Rosalia paused in her work. She had never really considered any dreams for herself. She had been a dutiful daughter and had taken pride in helping her father at the tailor shop. She knew someday she would marry and bear her own children, but other than that she had never given much thought to anything else. Besides, wasn't that the way it was for most young women? They either married or decided to become nuns like Madre Carmela. But at least for Madre and the other sisters, there was more in their lives besides serving God and helping those in need. They ran a thriving business and created beautiful pastries for many people to enjoy. As Rosalia had discovered these past few months, there was a great sense of fulfillment in knowing you had created something with your own hands that others appreciated. But it was more than that. She felt like she served a purpose by working.

"That many dreams, huh?" Antonio asked.

Rosalia realized he was still waiting for her answer. She smiled. "I don't really have any dreams. This is my life for the moment—until I am reunited with my family and then . . ." She let her voice trail; she didn't know what to say, for she knew so little of how her life would end up. Feeling embarrassed under Antonio's watchful gaze, she added, "I guess you could say I am content living for the moment. Whatever plans God has for me will be."

"Living for the moment. That's an interesting thought. I've never imagined doing that for myself. All I've ever wanted was to reach a certain milestone. When I was a boy, I longed to reach eighteen so I could leave home. Then I longed to land an apprenticeship so I could begin to realize my dreams of becoming a chef. Now I long for the day I am accepted into culinary school and finally become a chef. But I respect you for appreciating what you have right now and being able to surrender control over your life."

Rosalia's face clouded over upon hearing his last words. If only he knew how much fate had already dictated the course of her life and just how much control had been taken away from her.

"What is it, Rosalia? I said something to upset you. I can see it in your face. I'm sorry."

She held up her hand. "It's not you. Please don't apologize." She glanced at the clock on the wall. "It's almost time for lunch. Let's finish frying these last *Chiacchiere* and head over to the dining room."

"Are you sure you're fine?"

"*Sì, sì.*" Rosalia tried not to sound frustrated. After all, he was just concerned for her.

"We're going to be so tired by the time we go to Acireale tonight." Antonio heaved a long sigh. Thankfully, he decided to drop the subject of what had upset Rosalia.

"Are you saying you'd rather go to bed, Antonio?" She smiled playfully in his direction.

"I'm only eighteen. Not eighty. Being tired has never stopped me from having a good time."

Several hours later, Rosalia and Antonio were seated in the back of Francesco's car as he drove to Acireale. The drive took them along the coast of the Ionian Sea. Rosalia kept her eyes fixed on the blue waters. It was so beautiful. But her serenity was short-lived as her thoughts inevitably turned to her family. Whenever there was a holiday, she always wondered what they were doing. Had Mamma also fried a batch of *Chiacchiere,* letting little Cecilia help her dust the powdered sugar on top? Did Mamma think of Rosalia and how they used to work side by side in the kitchen or even in the tailor shop, laughing like the best of friends? Was Luca remembering how the two of them as children would wait with anticipation in the piazza for the village's small Carnevale parade to begin? And what about Papà? Did he have fond memories of Rosalia? Or had he completely pushed her out of his mind, believing she had dishonored the family and let him down? She closed her eyes tightly at this last thought, fighting back tears. The pain was too much to bear. Though she had plenty of distractions at the convent, they were never enough to completely block out how much she still felt the loss of her family.

"You're going to love Aci." Antonio's voice broke through Rosalia's thoughts.

She kept her head turned toward the sea for a moment longer as she composed herself.

When she was ready, she turned toward Antonio and did her best to look calm. But worry was written all over his features. She should've known there was no hiding how she felt from him. He seemed to often be in tune with her emotions. And now, he was trying to steer her thoughts to a less painful place by talking about Acireale.

"Why do you call it 'Aci'?"

"That's what the locals call it. Some even call it 'Jaci.' "

"So you've been there before?"

"I have. The churches are stupendous, and the views of the sea just add to the city's charm."

"You've traveled a lot."

"I guess you can say I'm a bit of a nomad." Antonio winked.

"So Santa Lucia del Mela is just another temporary stop for you?"

Rosalia didn't know why, but she felt sad thinking Antonio would some day leave when he got bored with the pastry shop and town.

"I already told you, Rosalia, that I want to go to culinary school. There aren't any in Santa Lucia del Mela, and even if there were, I need to become the best chef, so I must go to one of the best schools."

"That's true. You did tell me of your plans to go to culinary school. Where would you go then? It seems like you already have a place in mind."

"I would love to go to Le Cordon Bleu. It's in Paris."

"Paris? You would go all the way to France? Why not stay in Italy? Surely, there must be culinary schools in Rome or Milan."

"Le Cordon Bleu is the best. But there's a good chance I might not be admitted. And even if I am admitted, I can only go if I receive a scholarship. I know it's a long shot, but I must try."

"Of course. You must not abandon your dreams."

Just as Rosalia could not abandon her own dream—of being reunited with her family someday. She thought about how Antonio had asked her what her dreams were, and she could barely answer his question. But she could not think more about what she wanted from life until she was with those she loved most.

"Don't worry. We will be friends forever." Antonio tipped Rosalia's chin up with his index finger, forcing her to meet his gaze.

She was surprised by the action and by his words.

Seeing her surprise, Antonio said, "I can tell you're sad at the thought that I will have to leave the convent someday."

Rosalia blushed. Silently, she cursed herself for always letting her emotions show so easily, especially when she was embarrassed.

"It's not that. It's just . . ."

She didn't quite know what to say. He was right. She did feel sad at the thought that he would leave some day, but she couldn't understand why she felt this way. True, they had become good friends, and she no longer was afraid of him. If anything, Antonio had shown her she could come to trust men again—although she didn't know if she could ever be alone, truly alone, with a man. She had always thought she would marry someday and have her own family. But that was before Marco had disrupted her life. Now the thought frightened her terribly.

"So you won't miss me? Here I thought we were the best of friends." Antonio looked somber.

"Of course I'll miss you, and we are good friends."

Antonio's face glowed, and in that moment, Rosalia knew he had only been pretending to look sad. He had wanted to hear her say she would miss him.

"We're here!" Francesco yelled out, saving Rosalia from another awkward moment with Antonio.

Francesco and Antonio helped Teresa and Rosalia out of the car. Teresa then linked her arm through Francesco's as he leaned over and kissed her. Rosalia quickly looked away and walked a few steps ahead of Antonio. Perhaps this was a bad idea coming here with them? If only Anunziata or the other women from the convent had joined them, Rosalia wouldn't feel weird about being with a couple and Antonio. She stole another glance in Francesco and Teresa's direction. They looked in love, and she couldn't help wondering what that must feel like.

"Hey! Wait up for me!" Antonio quickened his steps.

"I'm sorry. I'm just taking everything in." She felt her face beginning to burn at the lie, but did her best to turn her head and take in the festivities that were already under way in Acireale, or Aci as Antonio had called it.

He glanced at his watch. "If we hurry, we might make the last show at the *Teatro dei Pupi*, before the Carnevale parade begins. Would you like to see the puppets? They're quite something."

Suddenly, a memory flashed before Rosalia's eyes. She was maybe no more than eight years old, and her father had brought home a little Pinocchio puppet made of wood. She had kept that puppet, and it had hung on one of the knobs of her bedroom dresser. Papà and Luca would take turns making Pinocchio dance, which always made Rosalia laugh.

"*Sì,* I would like that."

"We're going to catch the last puppet show. Do you want to come?" Antonio called out to Francesco and Teresa.

"I hate puppets! They scare me!" Teresa laughed and tossed her golden hair back over her shoulder, glancing seductively at Francesco. In return, he gave her a strange look. He then laughed and pulled her toward him, giving her a quick kiss.

"We'll meet you by the cathedral in the Piazza del Duomo, say in an hour? Will that give you enough time to see the show?" Francesco asked.

"That should be plenty of time. *Ciao!* Don't get lost!" Antonio waved.

"*Ciao!*" Teresa waved back and winked in Rosalia's direction.

Rosalia waved, but avoided meeting Teresa's gaze. Why had Teresa winked at her? Rosalia was actually relieved they would be apart from them for a little while. Francesco and Teresa's overt gestures of love were making her feel very uncomfortable, especially in Antonio's presence.

"Let's go." Antonio took Rosalia's hand, leading her toward the puppet theater.

She felt herself stiffen slightly, but then when she saw the large crowds everywhere, she relaxed. It would be easy to get separated from Antonio if she didn't hold his hand.

A few moments later, they were watching the puppet show play out. She watched knights, kings, queens, and court jesters interact with one another. The puppets were beautiful. Rosalia laughed with the audience at all the jokes in the show. At one moment, she saw in her peripheral vision that Antonio was staring at her, much the way Francesco had looked at Teresa earlier when she had tossed her hair over her shoulder. Rosalia swallowed hard and kept her attention on the puppets. Her stomach fluttered lightly.

After the show, they made their way to the Piazza del Duomo to meet up with Francesco and Teresa.

"Flowers for the beautiful woman, *signore?*" A woman holding a basket of assorted flowers stood before them.

"*Si.*" Antonio pulled a few *lire* from his pocket and handed them to the woman as she gave him a bouquet of daisies, marigolds, and carnations.

"For you." He smiled as he gave the bouquet to Rosalia.

She had wanted to tell him not to buy the flowers for her, but for some reason she didn't. He had been nothing but kind and generous to her ever since she'd met him, and she knew if she refused the flowers, he would be disappointed. And the thought of making Antonio sad did not sit well with Rosalia.

"*Grazie,* Antonio."

They were quiet for the rest of the walk toward the cathedral. Rosalia was feeling more and more troubled by these feelings she was having about Antonio. They were good friends. He looked out for her, almost like a brother. Yes, that must be why she felt the way she did about him. He reminded her of Luca. That was why she didn't want to disappoint him and why she knew she would miss him when he went to culinary school someday. It would be like losing her brother all over again. Antonio reached for her hand again, startling her for a moment. Her pulse raced, and once again her stomach fluttered, but the feeling was even stronger this time. Whom was she fooling? Antonio was nothing like her quiet brother Luca. And she'd never felt remotely like this when she was a child and had held Luca's hand.

Perhaps she needed to place some distance between herself and Antonio. But how could she do that when they worked together in the kitchen and pastry shop every day? And how would she explain her sudden aloofness toward him?

"Ah! There they are." Antonio pointed toward Francesco and Teresa, who were sitting on a bench in front of a fountain. They held each other in a tight embrace and were kissing.

Rosalia stopped walking toward them.

"Maybe we should wait until they're . . ." For what felt like the hundredth time today, she blushed.

"If we wait for them to be done kissing, we'll miss the whole Carnevale parade!" Antonio laughed. "Come on! Don't be shy about interrupting them."

Antonio walked ahead of Rosalia, letting go of her hand. She noticed how cool her palm felt without Antonio's pressed against hers.

"*Basta!* Enough! It's time for the parade."

Antonio clapped his hands loudly in Francesco's and Teresa's faces. They stopped kissing and laughed upon seeing him.

"Where's Rosalia? Did you have a good time at the puppet show?" Teresa asked, looking behind Antonio for Rosalia.

"*Si,* it was fun. You should've come," Rosalia said.

"Ah! We needed some time to ourselves. No offense." Teresa gave Francesco a sultry look.

A loud drum began thumping, soon followed by trombones and trumpets as the parade began. The sky had now completely darkened, making it the perfect setting for the floats, which were bright with lights and beginning to come down in a procession. This was nothing like the small parade Rosalia's hometown of Terme Vigliatore had. The floats were enormous and very elaborate. She marveled at a float in the image of the Pope. People crossed themselves when the Pope float went by as if it were the Holy Father himself. Rosalia couldn't help but laugh.

"You shouldn't be laughing at *il Papa*," Antonio whispered in her ear, before laughing himself.

Again, she felt her pulse race.

"*Maschere! Maschere!*"

"*Qui!*" Antonio shouted to the man selling Carnevale masks, raising his hand in the air.

"Please, Antonio, let me pay for these." Rosalia reached into her satchel purse that she wore wrapped around her body, but Antonio placed his hand over hers.

"I insist."

Before Rosalia could protest again, he had already paid the man.

"Now choose which mask you want."

Rosalia shook her head at him, but she was smiling.

"You're too kind to me, Antonio. *Grazie mille.*"

She scanned the masks, and her eyes were immediately drawn to one in a deep shade of purple with shimmering royal-blue sequins and feathers in the same colors. Faux sapphires and amethysts dangled from its sides.

"May I have this mask, please?"

The man handed it to Rosalia. "You chose the perfect color to complement your beautiful dark hair, *signorina.*"

"*Grazie.*" She blushed slightly at his compliment.

"And I'll take this one." Antonio pointed to a simple black mask.

Rosalia stared at her mask. It was so beautiful. It had been ages since she had owned something this pretty. She thought about her clothes and her possessions that she had left behind in her childhood home, but which were now gone. But their loss paled in comparison to the loss of her family.

"*Dai!* Let's see how our masks look on us," Antonio said as he placed the elastic band of his mask over his head and fastened it in place.

Rosalia giggled.

"That bad?"

"No, it actually looks quite good on you. I just laughed because you look so different."

And it was true. The mask made Antonio look mysterious, and even more handsome. With the mask on, his cheekbones were more pronounced and his lips looked fuller. She felt her cheeks warming up as she realized he had noticed she was staring at his lips. Antonio merely peered at her through his mask as a slow grin spread across his face.

Hoping to cover her blush, she held her mask to her face with the wand that was attached to it. Unlike Antonio's mask, hers did not have an elastic band, so she could lower it whenever she felt like it.

"*Bellissima!*" Antonio exclaimed.

She lowered her mask, but he raised her arm so she would cover her face again.

"Let's keep them on for the duration of the festivities. After all, how often can we wear masks and pretend to be someone else?"

"That's true!" Rosalia laughed.

"It seems that we've lost Francesco and Teresa." Rosalia strained her neck to try to see above the crowds in front of them, but it was no use.

"Don't worry. We can always wait for them by Francesco's car when the parade is over."

Rosalia nodded. "I have a small confession to make."

"Oh no! Should I be afraid?" Antonio clutched his heart, eliciting a giggle from Rosalia.

"It's not about you. I'm a bit relieved to have some time away from Francesco and Teresa again. I kind of feel like we're not with them anyway. They're so caught up in themselves."

"That's a polite way of putting it. But I guess that's how it is when you're in love and it's still new."

Rosalia hesitated for a moment before asking, "Have you ever been in love?"

She held her breath. Rosalia couldn't believe she'd had the nerve to ask him such a personal question, but wearing the mask made it easier. She felt protected behind it.

"I had boyhood crushes, but no, I don't think I was ever truly in love. I have escorted girls to dances and on walks, but things never progressed more. My mamma always told me never to rush love. She told me that young people are often in a rush for everything to happen: fall in love, get married, drive a car, whatever it is that most young people can't wait to do. She said love should be thought of as a piece of fruit that is waiting to ripen. Take your time with it, and when it is right, you will delight in its full essence."

"That's beautiful and sounds very wise. Your mother was a smart woman."

"She was. I miss her so much." Antonio's voice cracked.

Rosalia placed her hand on his, giving it a light squeeze. This was the first time she had heard Antonio express how much he missed his late mother. And in this moment, she felt she could relate to him only too well.

"I can't imagine how hard it was for you to lose your mother so young. I know how I am feeling about being separated from my family, but I can't imagine how I would feel if I knew there was no way I could see them again. At least I know they are alive, and someday I will see them again."

Antonio pulled Rosalia toward him and, before she knew what he was doing, he placed a kiss on her lips. Her eyes widened, but he didn't notice. She could see his own eyes were closed behind his mask. Part of her wanted to run, but another part of her felt entranced by the feel of his soft, warm lips pressed against hers. Before she could decide what to do, Antonio kissed her again, and again. She closed her eyes and pressed her hands up against his chest. The bouquet of flowers she'd been holding all night fell to the ground. Finally, Antonio broke the kiss, bending down to pick up her bouquet.

Rosalia had lowered her mask for a moment when Antonio bent down to pick up the flowers. But when he stood back up, and their eyes met, she quickly raised the mask to her features and turned her back toward him. Her mouth was very dry, and her heart felt like it would burst through her chest. Silently, she chided herself. *Why did you let him keep kissing you? Why did you kiss him back?*

"Let's go sit down on one of the benches. Are you thirsty? I can get us some water."

Rosalia nodded. She dared not speak for she was afraid how nervous her voice would sound.

Antonio took Rosalia by the hand and led her through the crowds to a bench that was far from the parade.

"I'll be right back."

She was grateful for the time alone. Lowering her mask, she pressed her fingers to her lips. They felt a bit swollen. She'd been kissed. Not that this was the first time a man had kissed her. The day Marco had kissed Rosalia in her father's tailor shop was the first time a man had kissed her. He had robbed her of what she had always envisioned that special moment would be like, just as he had robbed her of her maidenhood. She had always thought she would share that moment on her wedding night with the man she would marry someday—the man she loved. Unlike Marco's rough, bruising kisses, Antonio's had been so gentle and light. Even when he'd deepened the kiss, she could tell he had been exercising control. He was kind in everything he did toward her.

He returned with two paper cups.

"All I could find was an old lady selling *limonata*. I hope that's all right. I didn't want to go searching for water and make you wait here alone a long time."

Again, she couldn't help marveling at how thoughtful he was.

"I love lemonade, so that's perfect." She smiled, and then she realized she was no longer holding her mask up to her face. Neither was Antonio. Though her pulse raced as she thought about their kiss, she was no longer blushing.

They sipped their lemonades and didn't talk for a few minutes. Rosalia finally broke the silence.

"You were right. Aci is beautiful. The cathedral and all the churches look stunning all lit up at night. And their Carnevale celebration is absolutely breathtaking. I'm having a wonderful time. *Grazie,* Antonio."

Antonio smiled. "It makes me happy to hear that you've enjoyed yourself. I felt bad when we went to Messina that it wasn't as pleasurable an outing as I had hoped it would be."

"Don't feel bad, Antonio. I am to blame since I wanted to inquire about my family at the shops. I should be apologizing to you that I ruined the day."

"Don't be silly! It made me feel good to try to help you find your family. I see how sad you are without them, and it pains me to see you this way."

They were silent once more. Rosalia wondered if perhaps now was the time for her to share with him why she was separated from her loved ones. But she didn't want to dampen the mood. She was having a good time, and she didn't want a dark cloud to be hanging over them as it had that day in Messina after she'd asked the merchants about her family. Besides, she was still too afraid to tell him why she was estranged from her family. For that would mean having to tell him about Marco. And she definitely was not ready to tell Antonio about him.

"I'm sorry, Rosalia, if I was too forward by kissing you. I don't know what came over me. Well . . . that's not exactly true. I've wanted to kiss you for a long time, and talking about how much I miss my mother and your sharing with me how you could understand how I felt just made me lose all reason. I just wanted to hold you close. Ah! I'm embarrassing you again. I can see your face coloring up."

Rosalia patted her cheeks with her hands as if the action would make them blush less.

"I take after my mother."

"What?" Antonio looked confused.

"My cheeks burning up so much . . . how I blush over any little thing that makes me embarrassed or uncomfortable. I get that from my mother. My father always teased her about that, and then he teased me when he noticed I suffered from the same affliction. I'm cursed."

Rosalia looked at Antonio, and then they broke out laughing. They laughed so hard that tears came to their eyes. Once their laughter subsided, Rosalia realized she no longer felt flushed.

"Rosalia, I can tell you are the type of girl who needs to take her time with things, and I want you to know I am a very patient person. I would like to court you and become even better friends with you than we are now. Would you consider letting me court you?"

She was stunned. Though she'd sensed recently that Antonio might like her in that way, she had kept hoping she was wrong, just as she had been trying to fool herself into thinking that the reason why she felt strange around him, especially when he held her hand, was because he was like a brother to her. But now, after their kiss and his admission of wanting to court her, she could no longer deny it. She didn't know though if she was ready after her ordeal with Marco. Besides, what would happen if Antonio got his wish of going to cooking school in Paris? Was he just using her to make the time at the convent go by quickly? No. She knew in her heart Antonio was not like that. He was a good person. Just as she had known early on that Marco was bad.

"Antonio, I like spending time with you. I have learned a lot from you working by your side at the pastry shop. And you are so kind to me. I feel like I can trust you. But I must warn you. I'm not sure about a lot in my life right now. It is hard for me to make any concrete plans for even the near future because my thoughts are so focused on trying to find my family. I don't want to mislead you. Perhaps it might be better if we just remained the good friends that we already are."

Antonio looked crestfallen. She could see his cheeks suck in as he let out a long breath. Again, she felt sad that she was letting him down, but she knew she had to be honest with him.

"What are you so afraid of, Rosalia? You say you trust me, but you don't."

"That's not true. I do."

Antonio shook his head. "From the moment we first met, I sensed how scared you were, especially around me. I didn't see you act as nervously around the women at the convent. The only times I'd seen you anxious was around me, at least those first few weeks after we met, and then whenever one of the men who work on the convent's property or who make deliveries would walk by you. I know you feel more comfortable around me now. I don't doubt that, but I still sense you are holding yourself back and don't fully trust me. I also know, Rosalia, that someone hurt you very badly. And I suspect this is why you still don't trust me completely."

Rosalia's face paled. "What do you know?"

"Nothing. I can just tell by the way you have acted around me and, as I said, whenever another man is nearby. That day when my friend gave us a ride back to the convent from Messina, you seemed very nervous around him. Rosalia, I just want to help you."

Antonio waited for Rosalia to respond, but she didn't for a couple of minutes.

"You are right. I don't trust men easily. And someone did hurt me. But that is all I can say for now. I mean it, however, when I tell you that I trust you, Antonio. At least now, I do. I know you would never hurt me, and I feel safe when I'm with you. But just because I do trust you and feel safe with you doesn't mean that I'm ready for our friendship to become something more. You were also right when you said you could tell I need to take things slow."

"That's fine. Would you at least consider spending more time with me? I mean, spending more time with me alone, away from the convent, like that day we went to Messina. I was thinking on our days off of work from the pastry shop, we could go on a few outings. But I want it to be just us—none of our friends joining us like Francesco and Teresa. This way we can get to know each other better."

"Well, I have no objection to not inviting Francesco and Teresa. That is probably the real reason why you couldn't help yourself tonight and kissed me, since you had those two constantly locking lips in our faces!" Rosalia laughed.

Antonio laughed with her.

"You have quite a sense of humor, I'm beginning to see. It makes me happy that you can laugh and joke with me like you do. That shows me you truly do feel comfortable around me now."

They could hear fireworks erupting in the distance.

"Ah! Let's go. I don't want you to miss the fireworks."

"We can see them from here." Rosalia pointed to the sky off in the distance, near where the parade had ended.

"It's not close enough. Come on!" Antonio held out his hand. They ran through the streets as they approached the fireworks.

The sound was deafening as they arrived at the spot where the fireworks were launching into the night sky. Rosalia held her fingers to her ears as she stared at the spectacle of lights playing out above her. She then felt Antonio wrap his arms around her. Instead of fighting the feelings, she decided to surrender to them. She'd been alone for months now, without the comfort and love of her family. Except for Madre Carmela, no one else had hugged her. She leaned into Antonio and wrapped her own arms around him. And when Antonio looked down into her face, surprise etched over his features in response to her gesture, she stood on her toes and placed a light kiss on his cheek.

"Is that my answer? You never did answer my question as to whether I can court you." Antonio continued to hold Rosalia close as he spoke into her ear so she could hear above the din of the fireworks.

"You have my permission to court me." Rosalia smiled.

Antonio took her hand and kissed the back of it.

The fireworks were over, and an orchestra began playing a Viennese waltz. As people danced, they put their masks back on after having taken them off to witness the fireworks display. Rosalia couldn't help feeling like she was a character in an opera.

"Shall we dance?" Antonio bowed toward Rosalia, flourishing his hand dramatically.

She placed her flowers and mask on a nearby bench. She then placed her hand in Antonio's as she let him guide her in their waltz. As they danced, she realized she was feeling something she hadn't felt in quite some time—she felt a glimmer of happiness.

16

Piparelli

CRUNCHY SPICE COOKIES

March 9, 1956

R osalia ran in and out of the porticoed archway that lined the first story of the convent's property. As soon as she spotted Teresa chasing her, she quickly hid behind the wall of one of the arches.

"It's no use, Rosalia! I will catch you sooner or later!" Teresa called out.

Rosalia laughed before saying, "I'm too fast for you!"

She and Teresa had decided to play this silly game to quell their boredom. Ever since Lent had begun, they, along with the other lay workers and the nuns, were expected to do their work in silence as much as possible in order to reflect on their sins; they were to remember that the next forty days were to be a somber time of penance and prayer. Normally, Rosalia would have followed the rules as she'd been doing ever since she had come to stay at the convent. But they were now in their third week of Lent, and she couldn't take the morose air any longer.

The only lay worker who didn't seem to mind that they could no longer joke and talk animatedly while they worked in the kitchen or did their other hobbies when they had free time was Elisabetta, of course. She had begun her training to become a nun, and she was not going to let anything get in the way of her dream. Unlike her sister, Teresa, she intended to become the best nun, and to devote the rest of her life in service to God. Ever since Rosalia had gone to the Carnevale celebrations in Acireale, she had become closer to Teresa. But she still didn't have the courage to ask her what had happened before she came to the Convento di Santa Lucia to cause her to be defrocked as a nun.

Rosalia was getting tired and decided to surrender to Teresa. Running into plain sight, she held up her arms.

"I give up. You win! Let's take a break."

"You're not supposed to give up. What fun is that? You're supposed to let me catch you." Teresa frowned.

They walked over to the Saint Lucy statue by the fountain. It was an overcast day, but the cloudy weather did not detract from the signs of spring that were evident all around them. It was the second week in March, and the official start of the season was just a couple of weeks away. The magnolia trees had already bloomed, and tulips, daffodils, and wildflowers were shooting up all around the convent's gardens. Rosalia took some small comfort in seeing everything turn green again even if she wished she were back home, watching the flowers in her mother's garden come to life. She tried not to let herself think about the fact that it was now seven months since she'd been separated from her family. And still no word from the police about where her family had moved.

"Where is Antonio?" Teresa broke in on Rosalia's thoughts.

"Madre Carmela sent him into town to pick up a few supplies."

"You still have not told her that he is your beau?"

"He's not my beau." Rosalia blushed.

"Oh, really? One does not hold hands or steal kisses with someone who is just a friend."

"I don't want to tell Madre Carmela. I don't want her thinking we are being disrespectful on the convent's property. This is a sacred place. Besides, Antonio has plans to leave the convent someday. We are just good friends."

"You're too serious sometimes, Rosalia. You are not acting disrespectfully toward Madre Carmela or the convent if you sneak a kiss with Antonio or have a litte fun." She smirked before adding, "So you say you are just good friends and nothing more. But you do care about him?"

"Of course."

"What I meant is, you are in love with him? You get that funny feeling in your stomach whenever he is near or whenever he holds your hand. And when he kisses you, it's like you're seeing stars."

"How did you know?" Rosalia looked up at Teresa in surprise.

"Oh, Rosalia! You are still so innocent."

Rosalia's brows furrowed in anger. "I am not." And then she thought about how true it was that she was no longer innocent since Marco had robbed her of her maidenhood.

Sensing what Rosalia was thinking, Teresa softened her tone.

"I'm sorry. I didn't mean for you to think I was making fun of you. I was taken aback that you didn't realize that what you feel when you are around Antonio is love. You are falling in love with him. I know because that is how I feel when I am with Francesco." Teresa's eyes took on a dreamy, faraway look as she said this.

Rosalia hadn't considered that her affectionate feelings for Antonio were signs that she had fallen in love with him. But she knew in her heart Teresa was right. Every day that she spent with Antonio, she found her feelings and admiration for him deepening. Still. She couldn't let herself get carried away. Her future was uncertain. Until she was reunited with her family, she could not think about what she wanted. And as she had told Teresa, Antonio was planning on going to culinary school someday, somewhere far away. They were just enjoying each other's company and friendship. She knew she should put a stop to what was developing between them. She should push him away when he leaned in to kiss her or whisper how pretty she looked on a certain day. Rosalia didn't know why she hadn't. Well. Maybe she did know. She enjoyed kissing him and holding his hand. She enjoyed feeling safe in his arms. And Antonio made her feel special. He made her feel loved— something she hadn't felt since she had been in the comfort of her home and had the love of her parents and siblings surrounding her.

Deciding to deflect the attention off herself, Rosalia asked Teresa, "When are you going to tell Elisabetta about Francesco?"

Teresa shrugged her shoulders. "Maybe never." She laughed.

"So you intend to keep your relationship with Francesco a secret forever? What if he wants to marry you?"

Teresa's face grew serious. "He does want to marry me."

"He has already asked you?" Rosalia asked incredulously. "When?"

"The night of Carnevale, right after the fireworks show."

"And you are only telling me now?"

"I wanted to keep it private, especially since . . ." Teresa's voice trailed off.

"*Dio mio!*" Rosalia made the sign of the cross. "You are not with child, are you?"

"No, no! Although I would not be horrified."

Rosalia was stunned, but did her best not to show her surprise. It was obvious from what Teresa had just said that she and Francesco had been intimate with each other. Rosalia had thought every young woman would want to wait until she was married—though she knew there were a few who didn't. Then again, Teresa seemed to embrace life fully and not follow any rules of convention. Rosalia didn't know why she'd been surprised to learn Teresa wasn't a virgin. Perhaps Rosalia was a little jealous—for unlike her, Teresa had been able to choose whom she would give her virginity to. It hadn't been brutally taken from her. Tears quickly sprang in Rosalia's eyes.

"Rosalia! What is the matter?"

Rosalia wiped her tears with the back of her hand. "Nothing. Please don't mind me. I am happy for you and Francesco."

"And you could be happy, too, with Antonio. Don't you see that, Rosalia? I know you have been through a terrible ordeal—what happened to you in that cave." Teresa whispered the last phrase. "But you mustn't let what that man did to you ruin the rest of your life. Do you hear me, Rosalia?"

Once again, Rosalia's tendency to flush easily won over. Although she knew that everyone at the convent must've known or guessed what had happened to her, she still felt ashamed when she realized yet someone else knew. Would there ever come a day when the shame would disappear?

"Please, Teresa. I don't want to talk about that, and you mustn't breathe a word about it to Antonio. Have . . . have the workers and the nuns talked about me behind my back? Do you think someone said something to him?"

"No, no! We all love you."

"But how did you know about what happened to me?"

"Naturally, the nuns mentioned how they had found you when they returned from their almond harvesting that day. They described the state you were in. We had our suspicions, but no one has ever said with certainty. And the nuns wouldn't talk about it beyond that day. You know how they are. They would never utter the words to express that a man had possibly violated you. However, I see now I was right in my suspicions. I'm so sorry, Rosalia." Teresa placed her arm around Rosalia's shoulders and pulled Rosalia in to her as she embraced her.

"*Grazie,* Teresa. You are a good friend. Please, do not worry about me. I will be fine. Now back to you. Did you give Francesco an answer? Will you marry him?"

"*Sì.* I can think of nothing I want more." She glanced toward the convent's entrance and then behind her shoulders. "I will trust you. As you said, we are good friends. But you can't tell anyone about this, especially Elisabetta," Teresa whispered in an urgent voice as she squeezed Rosalia's hand.

"I swear. You have my word. I won't tell anyone."

"We are going to elope!" Teresa whispered, her voice barely able to contain her excitement.

"Elope? Where will you go?"

"Francesco has gotten a job with the municipality in Messina. We are going to live in the city! I've always wanted to live in the city. Country life has never really suited me."

Rosalia had no doubts about that.

"So he has a good job and will be able to take care of me. I won't have to slave away any longer in the convent's kitchen. I can focus on being his wife and raising his children." Once again, Teresa's eyes glazed over with a dreamy look.

"You don't enjoy making the pastries?" This came as a surprise to Rosalia since she thought everyone working at the pastry shop took pleasure in their work and loved it as much as she did.

"It's too much work. The only thing that I am grateful for about having worked here is that I'll be able to make lavish cakes and sweets for my husband and for my children on special occasions. I just need to learn how to cook. But that can't be too hard since I know how to bake."

"When are you planning on eloping?"

Teresa sighed. "We have to wait until after Easter since the church doesn't hold weddings during this cursed season of Lent! I will certainly not miss spending Lent at the convent or having to go to church and pray so much. I had enough of that when I was a nun."

Feeling emboldened now that Teresa had mentioned her previous life, Rosalia decided to finally ask her what she'd been dying to ask.

"May I ask you, Teresa, why you became a nun? And what happened that you were asked to leave your previous convent?"

Teresa's face clouded over. For a few seconds, she remained silent, before saying, "It is a long story."

"I'm sorry. If you don't want to tell me, that's fine. I didn't mean to pry. It's just that I was shocked to hear you had been a nun."

Teresa laughed. "I'm sure. You could tell even when you hardly knew me, I was not meant for that life!"

"I think we all could tell." Rosalia couldn't help but also laugh.

"I had no choice. Elisabetta and I lost our mother when I was fourteen, and she was twelve. Our father had died when we were very young, so Mamma raised us alone. She then contracted a fever and did not recover. The local convent agreed to take us in, but their order only consisted of eight nuns. The town we were from was very small, so the convent was having a difficult time finding novitiates. They agreed to take Elisabetta and me only if we promised to become nuns once we were the right age. We were desperate. There were no other family members who were willing to take us in and feed us. It was my uncle, my mother's own brother, who took us to the convent and asked the nuns if they would take us." Teresa's voice filled with anger. "The bastard. He only had one child, and he had a prosperous mill. He could have afforded to take us in. But he didn't bat an eyelash at giving away his sister's children."

Rosalia reflected on how so many people she knew had lost their families. Madre Carmela had lost hers when they gave her up as a child; Antonio's mother had died, and he had decided to forsake his father; Rosalia was estranged from her own family; and Teresa and Elisabetta had been orphaned. While Rosalia knew it was inevitable and that someday everyone would be separated from his or her family, especially once they died, this realization didn't make it easier for her to accept that her parents and siblings were no longer in her life. And that perhaps she would never see them again.

Teresa continued her story. "So, I became a nun when the sisters felt I was the right age. I hated it! The long hours spent kneeling on those hard wooden pews, saying over and over again the same prayers. The itchy cheap habit I had to wear. Having nothing to look foward to, day in and day out. At least at the Convento di Santa Lucia, the nuns have their pastry making, and they don't pray all day like the nuns at the convent where I took my orders. The nuns here don't seem as strict either—except for Sorella Domenica. She belongs at one of the more severe convents, like where I used to live. The worst was when they shaved my head." Teresa took her golden locks, which she was wearing in a ponytail today, and pulled them over her shoulder as she stroked her hair. "Can you imagine shaving off all this beautiful hair?" Teresa shuddered.

"I think most of the sisters see it as a small sacrifice to show they are giving up all vanity for God, just as they all wear the same simple habits."

"Small sacrifice? Are you out of your mind, Rosalia? Can you imagine shaving off all that lustrous black hair you have?"

Rosalia shrugged her shoulders. "There is more to life than our appearances. I know what happened to you was horrible, especially since you had no desire to become a nun. All I'm saying is that many of the sisters have made this choice, and it is something that makes them happy, gives them peace and contentment. Like Madre Carmela. I can see she is devoted to her calling and does not mind the sacrifices she has had to make."

"True. But like you said, many of them made the choice to become nuns. I was forced into it. So, secretly, I began growing my hair back. The nun who was responsible for ensuring everyone's hair was cut when it started growing back had become quite senile, and she couldn't keep track of whose hair needed to be cut next. Fortunately for me, no other sister was checking to make sure. It took two years for my hair to grow back. Once it did, I was getting restless, not to mention depressed. I couldn't take living the way I was living. I tried convincing Elisabetta that we should run away. I told her I could get a job somewhere, but she wouldn't hear of it. She had fallen in love with the life of a nun and couldn't wait until she would begin her training. I think she lost a few of her marbles." Teresa pointed to her head, and her expression became very sad.

"She changed, Rosalia, once we went to live at the convent. The little sister who had played with me and followed me around, looking up to me, became this quiet, timid child. There was a nun, Sorella Maria, who took Elisabetta under her wing. She became like a surrogate mother to Elisabetta. At first, I thought Sorella Maria just wanted Elisabetta to feel more at home at the convent, and that she wanted to be more of a mother figure for her since Elisabetta had lost her own. But soon I saw Sorella Maria had her own motives for taking a liking to Elisabetta. She wanted to mold Elisabetta into her image of the perfect nun."

"What about you? Didn't she try to be a role model for you?"

"She hated me. I think she could tell from the first moment she laid eyes on me that I was not nun material. But I guess she was right about Elisabetta. Look at her now. Elisabetta is already acting like a nun even though she is not one yet." Teresa shook her head, disgust plainly evident in her features. "I can't help but feel like Sorella Maria brainwashed my sister. In fact that whole convent brainwashed her.

"Anyway, I was not successful in persuading Elisabetta to run away with me. My despair grew until one day I noticed a young man delivering fruits and vegetables with his father. My heart leapt. He was handsome, and, when he saw me and smiled, wishing me a good day, I was elated. His father owned a farm, and the convent bought its produce from them. Sometimes, the son would deliver the fruit on his own. I began to find ways to sneak out of the convent and engage him in conversation, hiding in some spot in the convent's courtyard where none of the other nuns could spy on us."

"That was a huge risk."

"It was, but I didn't care if I was caught. I couldn't take living there anymore. But then there was also a part of me that knew Elisabetta would be affected by my choices, and I feared if I was caught, they would take it out on her just because we were sisters. So I still tried to be careful and not let the other nuns see me.

"One day, the boy convinced me to take a ride with him in his car. Sometimes I couldn't believe he saw any beauty in me while I was covered up in my habit, but he did. I could tell he liked me, too."

"You have a beautiful face, Teresa."

"*Grazie,* Rosalia. So I took a ride with him in the car. It was during siesta when the nuns took their nap—well, those who weren't praying. There were a few nuns who never took siesta and instead spent that time praying even more. I knew these nuns wouldn't notice my absence since they would be holed up in the chapel. I pretended to go to sleep so that Elisabetta and the other nun who shared our room wouldn't notice. As soon as I was certain they were sound asleep, I quietly made my way outside to the back of the convent, where the boy was waiting for me on the other side of the gate with his father's car.

"Once I was in the car and we had driven away from the convent, I took off my veil and unpinned my hair, shaking it out. I felt so free!

"The boy's eyes grew wide as he took in my blond hair." Teresa laughed. "Thank God, we met once my hair had grown back or else he would've surely run when he saw the chick's head that mine resembled after the nuns had cut all my hair off."

Rosalia laughed, wiping tears from her eyes. "You're too funny, Teresa!" She shook her head.

"Well, it's true. Anyway, my knight in shining armor took me into town and bought chocolate for me. Of course, people were staring at us because I was still dressed in that horrible habit. People must've thought I was mad since here was this nun, decked out in her full habit, but she was not wearing her wimple and veil and her hair was spread out over her shoulders. And she was in the company of a young man who it was obvious had designs on her."

"That was so bold of you, Teresa!" Rosalia placed her hand over her mouth and giggled, imagining the strange sight that Teresa must've surely posed that day.

"It was. But you have to realize, Rosalia, I was nearly to the point of killing myself. That's how sad I was at the convent. I had become reckless, and I truly believed I would get away with it that day. But there was a priest who saw me, and he immediately called the convent. When the mother superior saw I was not sleeping in my room, she knew the priest was correct in identifying one of her nuns as being in town with a young man and not wearing her wimple and veil.

"When I came home, the mother superior yelled at me and made me kneel on a wooden pew in the chapel where we prayed. I had to keep my hands on top of the bench in front of me while she repeatedly hit them with a wooden paddle. Tears slid down my face, but I refused to cry out from the pain. She then told me I was no longer a nun and that I would have to leave the convent the next day. She said Elisabetta would also have to leave. Sorella Maria tried to intervene for Elisabetta, pleading with the mother superior to let her stay, but the mother superior wouldn't hear of it.

" 'They share the same blood. She will make fools of us someday just as her sister did,' the mother superior said.

"So, as I had suspected, the convent also punished Elisabetta for my behavior. The mother superior called Madre Carmela and asked her if she would take us in and employ us in the pastry shop. She told Madre Carmela that would be our way of paying for our room and board. I was kind of surprised the mother superior didn't just throw us out onto the street, not caring where we ended up, but I think Sorella Maria might have been the one to come up with the idea of asking Madre Carmela if she could hire us. I guess Sorella Maria did care about Elisabetta, and it wasn't just for her own selfish motives that she was encouraging my sister to become a nun. I suppose I should be grateful to her for finding us room and board."

Teresa sighed before continuing. "Elisabetta has never forgiven me for what I did. She cried so much when we left the convent under the cover of night. The sisters didn't want the younger nuns to witness our leaving, and my defrocking. When we arrived at the Convento di Santa Lucia, I was relieved that Madre Carmela was much kinder than the mother superior from our old convent. And I was relieved the way of life was not as severe. I hoped that spending time here would rid Elisabetta of her desire to become a nun. But it didn't. Of course she can never go back to our old convent, but I think she is happy to be here and hopes she will be able to become a novitiate in Madre Carmela's order."

"And what happened to that boy? Did you ever see him again?"

Teresa's face lit up. "The boy was Francesco."

"Francesco!" Rosalia then remembered hearing from Antonio that Francesco's father owned a farm. "But how did he know you were here?"

"It was fate. That is how I know we were meant to be together. His father's farm is nearby, and Francesco had heard about the nuns' famous pastries. He and his father would often come by the shop to buy sweets for his mother. So he was shocked when he saw me selling at the pastry shop window."

"This is why you haven't told Elisabetta yet about Francesco?"

"Yes. Although she never knew what he looked like or his name, I know she would still not approve. I think she hopes that I will come to my senses and ask if Madre Carmela would allow me to become a nun here, even though I've told Elisabetta I would rather die first."

"I see. But she will find out once you're married, Teresa."

"I know. But things will be different then. She won't be able to do anything about it once we're married, and I think she will respect my decision more then. If I tell her now of my plans, she will just think I am being foolish and rash again. I will tell her everything after Francesco and I are married. She will then see that I truly fell in love with Francesco from the moment I first saw him and that I wasn't just being a silly young woman when I snuck out of the convent that day to be with him.

"So we plan on eloping the week after Easter. I will need a

witness, and Francesco has asked Antonio. And now that you know of our plans, I hope you will agree to be my witness at my wedding, Rosalia?"

"But how will I explain being gone from the convent that day?"

"We're going to do it on a day that we have off. Madre Carmela has let you go on your outings with Antonio. You can just act like it is another outing with him, which won't be untrue. She just won't know that I'll be there with Francesco—and neither will my sister."

Rosalia thought for a moment. "All right. I'll do it."

"*Grazie,* Rosalia!" Teresa hugged her.

Rosalia felt her stomach grumble. She had left a bag of *Piparelli,* covered up tightly, on the opposite side of the fountain so that she and Teresa could nibble on a few when they wanted a snack. Walking over to retrieve the biscotti, she was surprised to see her friend—the bluethroat—perched by the bag.

"Ah! You know what I have in this bag, don't you?"

The bluethroat looked at Rosalia, and a slight chill ran through her when the bird's eyes seemed to make direct contact with her own.

"He's so beautiful!" Teresa came to Rosalia's side. But the bird barely heeded her, instead watching Rosalia's movements as she pulled one of the *Piparelli* out of the bag and broke off a crumb to give to the bird. She held the crumb out, and the bird hopped over and quickly pecked at the crumb until it was all gone.

"He's not afraid of you!" Teresa marveled.

"Of course not. We're friends. I've been feeding him for a few months now. He's often on the branch that is just outside my window." Rosalia pointed to her window.

"I don't think I've ever seen a bluethroat on the convent's grounds before."

"Antonio told me he's seen this bird before, but no other bluethroats."

"But how can you be sure it's the same one?"

"I can tell."

Teresa reached into the bag and took one of the *Piparelli* for herself. "Ugghh! I'm so sick of these biscotti, but I'm hungry, so it'll have to do."

Piparelli were biscotti that were usually made during the Lenten season because the recipe did not call for eggs. Catholics were supposed to abstain from eating meat, fat, and eggs during Lent. Since Lent had begun, no meat or fat had been consumed at the convent. And while Sicilians still bought their sweets during Lent, although in more moderation, the sisters expected everyone who resided at the convent to only eat *Piparelli*. But Rosalia had weakened and given in to her craving for a marzipan fruit and would quickly pop a raspberry or cherry marzipan in her mouth when her back was turned toward the other workers in the kitchen.

Rosalia fed a few more crumbs to the bluethroat before finishing off the last biscotto. The bird glanced at her for a moment before flying away. Rosalia followed it with her eyes, but it was too fast for her, and she lost track of where it had flown. Every time she saw the bluethroat, it made her feel happy. She couldn't explain why.

Teresa let out a loud yawn as she glanced at her wristwatch. "I'm going to take a nap before siesta is over. All that running and chasing after you has tired me out. Are you coming inside?"

Rosalia shook her head. "I think I'm going to take a walk." She loved strolling around the convent's grounds when everyone was taking their siesta. The serenity of the convent soothed her, and it was during these times that she felt most at peace.

"*Va bene.* Remember . . ." Teresa pressed her lips together and mimicked zipping them shut with her fingers.

"Don't worry, Teresa, your secret is safe with me." Rosalia waved at her friend as she walked away.

Rosalia walked under the corridor where she and Teresa had been zigzagging in and out of the porticoes. She thought about Teresa and how sure she seemed about her love for Francesco. Then Rosalia thought about how she would miss her once Teresa married and moved to Messina. She sighed. But that was life, coming into contact with people and losing them. A quick jolt of pain pierced her heart, but she forced herself to push the feeling away. Taking deep breaths, she closed her eyes and soon felt calm again. Madre Carmela had taught her this form of meditation, not just for praying, but also for when Rosalia wanted to still her racing mind, especially when she was feeling anxious. It had helped her tremendously.

"Boo!"

"Oh!" Rosalia clutched her chest with her hands. "Antonio! You scared me!"

"That was the point!" Antonio laughed as he came closer to Rosalia and took her into his arms. He kissed the top of her head and stroked her hair. Rosalia began to push him away, still mad that he had startled her, but the moment he began running his hands through her hair, she felt her defenses melt away and instead leaned into him.

"I'm sorry! I was just having a little fun. Please, don't be mad at me." Antonio tilted his head so that his gaze met Rosalia's, his eyes pleading.

She could never be mad at him when he looked like that. She laughed.

"Is that the face you gave your mother when you were a little boy and wanted to get away with bad behavior?"

"How did you know?" Antonio grinned.

Rosalia pulled out of his embrace and resumed walking.

"Would you like to walk with me?"

"Of course. I like to do anything with you."

Antonio took Rosalia's hand in his and matched her slow pace. She couldn't help glancing over her shoulder to make sure no one saw them.

"Relax."

"I just don't want Madre Carmela or the other sisters to think we're . . ." She struggled to find the right word.

"Cavorting?"

Rosalia blushed, but she remained silent.

"We're not doing anything wrong, Rosalia. I like you a lot, and when you're ready, I think we should let Madre Carmela know. Besides, I'm sure she has her suspicions."

"What makes you say that?"

"Come on, Rosalia! We've been spending all of our free days together. I think she likes me and approves of my spending so much time with you. I'm almost certain she would give us her blessing. So there's really no need for you to worry."

Rosalia pondered what he said. It was true. She had also gotten the sense from Madre Carmela that she thought highly of Antonio, and she always seemed pleased to hear that Rosalia was going with Antonio on their outings. At first, Rosalia had believed it was just that Madre was happy she was getting out of the convent, but then she had noticed how Madre Carmela always had something nice to say about Antonio. It was almost as if she was trying to emphasize his positive attributes to Rosalia. But whenever she thought about telling Madre that there was something more between Antonio and her than friendship, she wanted to hide.

Deciding to change the subject, she said, "Teresa told me of her plans to elope with Francesco. She asked me to be her witness and told me you will stand for Francesco."

Antonio looked surprised. "She told you?"

"*Sì*. She asked me not to tell Elisabetta or anyone else of course."

"I don't know why I'm surprised. I suppose the two of you have grown close recently."

"We have. Actually, I've become close to a few of the women here—Anunziata, Mari. . . ."

"So you told her you would be her witness?"

"I did. It looks like we'll be together that day for their wedding."

"I'm happy for them. They are obviously crazy about each other."

Antonio's voice did not mirror his words. Instead, he sounded and looked sad.

"Is everything all right, Antonio?"

"*Sì*. Just tired."

"I should let you get some sleep. Teresa told me you went into town to buy supplies." Rosalia began to take her leave of Antonio, but he grabbed her hand and pulled her toward him. Before she could protest, he wrapped his arms around her waist and kissed her.

Rosalia's heart raced. He had never kissed her like this before. His tender kisses of the past few weeks and the gentle prodding of his tongue now deepened into a long, unbroken kiss. Her stomach flipped, and though she felt nervous, she also felt a wonderful warm sensation spread throughout her. Before she knew what she was doing, Rosalia wrapped her arms around Antonio and kissed him back.

When they finally pulled apart, she felt slightly dizzy. She pressed her fingers to her swollen lips. Part of her was a little sad that the kiss was over.

"I'm sorry, Rosalia. I got carried away." He blushed, a soft smile playing along his lips.

"You don't need to apologize, Antonio. I guess you could say I got carried away, too." She laughed softly.

"Don't go. I'm tired, but I love spending as much time with you as possible. Come back with me to my place. We can just relax and listen to my radio."

Rosalia hadn't been to the abandoned chapel where Antonio slept since the day she and Anunziata had trespassed. She was a little scared to be alone with him there, but then again, they had been alone on their outings on their days off. But this was different. They would be in his home, sitting on his bed. From what she remembered that was the only piece of furniture he had.

"Don't be afraid. I promise I won't kiss you. We'll just talk and listen to music."

Although she was anxious, she also enjoyed being in his presence. He made her feel safe—and loved. Her father had created a safe haven for her and her family in their home. But with Antonio, it was different. She felt that she could go anywhere with him and would never have to worry—as long as he was there with her. Rosalia knew he would always protect her. She was still in awe of how he seemed to be able to read her thoughts and sense her feelings. No one had been able to do this before . . . well, maybe except for Mamma. Antonio always knew, too, when to give her space. He had to be the most patient person Rosalia had ever met. She had noticed he was a careful listener, not just with her but with everyone. Yes. There was no doubt in her mind he was a good person, and the more she got to know him, the more she felt herself falling in love with him. His gentle ways with her and thoughtfulness had won over her trust. But it was more. She admired the kind man he was and the integrity he carried with him. Besides her family, she had never loved anyone the way she loved Antonio. Perhaps that was why she still didn't fully trust her feelings for him and was scared. For the love she shared with him felt so powerful. Though her immense feelings for Antonio still made her anxious, she knew in this moment that she wanted to spend time alone with this wonderful young man with whom she had fallen in love.

"All right. I'll come," Rosalia said softly, keeping her gaze to the ground.

Antonio beamed.

They held hands once again as they walked to the abandoned chapel. Neither of them said a word. Every few seconds, Antonio's eyes met Rosalia's, and he offered her a reassuring smile.

When they reached the chapel, Antonio unlocked the door and stood back, letting Rosalia enter first.

She could feel her pulse racing once she stepped inside. She was surprised to notice a couple of pieces of furniture now existed: a small, café-style table and a nightstand. Unfortunately, the only place to sit was still Antonio's bed.

"I'm slowly buying more things as you can see, but I don't want to accumulate too much."

Rosalia nodded her head. Of course he didn't want to collect too many things since he was planning on leaving. What was she doing? She shouldn't be letting herself develop feelings for a boy who was not going to be around.

"Sit down." Antonio gestured to the foot of the bed.

He went over and turned his radio on. An Italian pop ballad came on.

Rosalia sat at the corner of the bed, trying to look as relaxed as possible.

Antonio sat next to her, but kept some space between them.

She mulled over something to say, but for some reason her mind was blank. Usually, they talked about everything, from their families to what they had baked in the kitchen that day to their childhoods. She supposed her nerves were getting the better of her. Antonio was strangely quiet, too.

Wanting to break the awkward silence, Rosalia blurted, "So when are you planning on leaving the convent?"

Antonio looked at her, surprised, and immediately she regretted her impulsiveness.

He shrugged his shoulders. "I don't know. Not anytime soon. There is still so much I need to learn here, and I haven't saved enough money."

Rosalia felt guilty. Every time they'd gone out, he'd insisted on paying for everything.

"I suppose I'm partly to blame for your lack of funds."

"No! I want to treat you. Please! I'm happy when I can do things for you. I'm happy to buy you gifts. What kind of a man would I be if I let you pay when we went out? Don't ever say that. I like seeing you content, Rosalia. It makes me sad when you look sad."

Now it was Rosalia's turn to look surprised. "Really?"

Antonio took Rosalia's hands in his. "I care about you so much, Rosalia. And as you know from losing your own family, it hurts when you can't be with those you love, and when they are in pain, it also brings you pain. That's how I feel with you."

Rosalia swallowed hard. She was moved by his words.

"*Grazie,* Antonio. I don't know what to say. That is very kind of you."

"I'm not being kind. I'm . . ." He turned his head. His gaze rested on one of the saints' statues in the chapel.

Rosalia could not help but see the absurdity of their surroundings. Here she was sitting on the bed of a young man who made her weak whenever he kissed her, and all around them were statues of saints and even one of Jesus and Mary. And to think she was worried about the disrespectfulness of getting caught holding Antonio's hand while they walked around the convent's gardens or the few times they had stolen kisses. Where they were now was beyond disrespectful. She should leave, but her body remained rooted in place. She wanted to be with Antonio. The more time she spent with him, the more she found herself thinking about him when he wasn't around and looking forward to when she would see him next.

Rosalia took her hand out of Antonio's and traced her index finger along his cheek. She then let her hand wander up toward his hair, pushing back a few wisps of his bangs that always hung over his left eye. It gave him a mischievous, irresistible look she loved.

He turned to her, his eyes widened in surprise at her intimate gestures. She then rested her head on his shoulder.

"You're a good man, Antonio. And you are so kind to me. Sometimes I feel I don't deserve it."

"Why? You're such a sweet person."

"I know I've held myself back from you, Antonio. That is why I feel I don't deserve your kindness. I don't know what of myself I can give to you, and besides, you are planning on leaving someday."

"Nothing is set in stone, Rosalia. My plans might change. Besides, who is to say you couldn't come with me?"

Rosalia was stunned. She lifted her head off his shoulder.

"You would want me to come with you—even if you go to Paris?"

"Why not? It would be wonderful. We'd be able to experience the city for the first time together."

"I don't know, Antonio. We haven't even known each other for long. And then . . ."

"And then what?"

She remained quiet.

"You can tell me anything, Rosalia."

"I don't think I could be gone from here for a long time. This is my home now."

Antonio searched her face. After a moment, he nodded. "Your family. You're worried you would be gone if word came about them. But Madre Carmela could let you know. And we can come back. I'm not saying I want to move to Paris permanently."

"This is going too fast, Antonio. Like you said, you're not planning on leaving anytime soon. There is still so much about me you don't know. And I'm sure there is much about you I don't know. Let's just enjoy the time we have now and see what happens tomorrow then?"

Antonio glanced down at his lap. His face looked pained, and Rosalia felt her heart cringe a bit. She thought about what he had told her about feeling sad when she looked sad. She didn't want to hurt him, but she had to be honest with him. Besides, he had promised her he would take things slow.

"You're right, Rosalia. We have plenty of time. I'm sorry if you feel I'm rushing things. I guess I just wanted to let you know that I care about you a lot, and this isn't just a passing fling for me. In fact, I have been giving more thought to whether I still want to apply to Le Cordon Bleu. There is a culinary school in Palermo I could go to, and while that's a long car trip from Santa Lucia del Mela, it's at least in Italy and not in another country."

"Oh, Antonio! Please, you mustn't change your plans for me. You wanted to go to the best culinary school, and if that's in Paris, then you should go."

Antonio stood up, walking toward the statue of Saint Sebastian. The many arrows that pierced the statue's body and the pained look on his face seemed to match Antonio's miserable expression. He ran his hands through his hair before turning around. And Rosalia saw something she had yet to see in Antonio: anger.

"Don't you see, Rosalia? I wouldn't mind giving up Paris for you. That's why I can think about staying here or even asking you to come with me to Paris. I can't envision being without you. Before, you said I was being kind to you when I told you how it makes me sad when you're sad, and happy when you're happy. But I'm not being kind. I'm falling in love with you. Can't you see that? I'm crazy about you, and it's tearing me up on the inside. You're all I think about when I wake up in the morning and go to sleep at night. You're in my dreams. Even when I'm struggling over how to make a pastry better, you pop into my mind! I wonder what you would add to make it better. Then again, whom are we fooling? Your desserts are always better than mine!"

Rosalia lowered her eyes and said softly, "That's not true. You've won a few of the contests we've had. Madre Carmela wouldn't lie."

"She's getting old. Her palate is changing. I've heard the other workers who have tried your pastries express how good yours are and how they're often better than everyone else's."

Rosalia folded her hands in her lap. *He is falling in love with me.* He'd said it! Though she was frightened to hear this, she couldn't deny that she was also elated.

Antonio came back to the bed and sat down next to her. This time, he closed the space between them. He pushed her hair back behind her ear, and then took her face in both of his hands. She had no choice but to look at him.

"I love you, Rosalia. I know you say we haven't known each other long, and we need to just think about today, but I'm tired of keeping how I feel about you inside of me. I love you. And nothing is going to change that. I'll wait for you. Whenever you are ready, I will be here, and I promise you my feelings won't change. Do you hear me?"

Antonio stared intensely into Rosalia's eyes. She nodded.

He then kissed her gently. They held on to each other, letting their bodies recline back onto the bed. Rosalia felt very tired. Hearing Antonio's admission of his love for her, and feeling all the emotions that came with hearing how he felt, had sapped her of her energy. She supposed she'd always known Antonio loved her. She just wouldn't let herself believe it. But now there was no denying it.

She loved him, too. But for now, she must wait before she told him how she felt. Still, she wondered if he would still love her once he knew about her past. No. She could not tell him just yet that she had also fallen in love. For she still needed to protect herself.

❦ 17 ❦

Zeppole

SAINT JOSEPH'S DAY DOUGHNUTS

March 19, 1956

Antonio and Rosalia were rolling furiously down the hill, picking up weeds and dandelions in their hair. They laughed and screamed, fully giving in to childlike abandon. Antonio reached the bottom of the hill first, and soon after Rosalia tumbled on top of him. They continued to laugh. Once they calmed down, Antonio reached over and kissed Rosalia. She was blissfully happy. Ever since Antonio had revealed his love for her, the time they spent together felt different—magical.

Today was the feast day of Saint Joseph, and it also happened to be Monday, which was their day off from working in the pastry shop. Rosalia had packed panini and zeppole—the customary sweet that was made in honor of Saint Joseph's Day. Yesterday, she and the other workers had made several large batches of the fried sweet. Madre Carmela had told her she could take a few to share with Antonio on their outing.

"We're going to look a fright when we return to the convent!" Rosalia laughed.

"I'm sure we'll receive one of Sorella Domenica's scowls." Antonio grimaced, imitating the nun's sour expression.

"Stop!" Rosalia laughed hard, wiping tears from her eyes.

"I'm hungry after all that rolling up and down the hill. I can't believe we did it more than once. I'll probably lose my balance once I stand up. Do you want a few zeppole?" Antonio stood up, wiping the weeds and dandelion petals from his clothes.

"I can never say no to zeppole."

Rosalia stood up and pulled at a dandelion that was caught in her hair's long strands. She mentally scolded herself for not wearing her hair up today. It would take her forever to get all the weeds and petals out. Then a thought flashed through her mind. What if their appearances led the nuns to believe they had been doing more than having an innocent picnic? She looked at Antonio with fear in her eyes.

"What is it, Rosalia?" Antonio quickly came to her side.

"Look at us! What will the sisters think? We have to make ourselves look more presentable." Frantically, she began shaking out her dress until Antonio stilled her hands.

"Rosalia, calm down. We will fix our clothes and hair. There is nothing to get so worked up about."

Rosalia paused for a moment before nodding. She then felt embarrassed, realizing how crazy she must've sounded and looked.

"I'm sorry. It's just . . . I don't want them thinking the worst about me."

"I don't think that would happen. They all love you very much. You have nothing to worry about, Rosalia."

Tears filled her eyes as she shook her head. "You don't understand, Antonio."

"Then make me understand. Please, Rosalia. I want to be here for you. I think you know by now you can trust me and open up to me."

She hesitated for a moment. Could she finally tell him about Marco? Her chest suddenly felt constricted, and sweat began to bead her forehead. Breaking free from Antonio, she bent down and busied herself by laying out the blanket she had brought for their picnic. She then took out the panini of prosciutto and tomatoes she had prepared. Of course, Antonio had skipped right to their dessert of the zeppole before they had their midday meal. He had a weakness for sweets, and sometimes she wondered if he was right in wanting to become a chef rather than a pastry chef.

Rosalia was startled by Antonio's kicking a few small rocks as he walked away. The way he carried his body, and seeing his lips drawn tightly together, showed Rosalia he was angry. She thought about calling after him, but decided to leave him alone.

She stopped preparing their picnic and clasped her hands in her lap. Naturally, he was upset with her. While he never had become angry with her directly, she knew that even Antonio, who was normally so even-tempered and thoughtful, had his breaking point. It was probably just a matter of time before he would grow tired of her refusal to tell him what had happened to her and why she was estranged from her family. Tears rolled down her face. She desperately wanted to open up to him, but every time she thought about doing so, the fear took hold. She'd heard stories growing up about what happened to young women whose innocence had been compromised. And she'd also heard stories about women who were engaged, but then were attacked by another man, and their fiancés had immediately left them as if it were their fault, as if they had asked to be violated. Rosalia began to get mad. She thought about her father. From what Signora Tucci had said, Rosalia's father seemed to believe Rosalia had willingly left with Marco. Rosalia's father believed she had been intimate with Marco and was pregnant with his child. Papà should have known her. He should have known she would never do such a thing, and that she would never bring shame upon her family. But he hadn't known his daughter at all.

And here she was, desperately trying to find her family—not just to be reunited with them again, but also to prove to her father that she was not guilty of what he thought. She should have been angry that he had chosen to leave and that he had believed she really wanted to be with Marco. Papà had let her down terribly. If her own father had believed the worst about her, what would Antonio think—a young man who had only known her for a few months?

Rosalia noticed a shadow and looked up to see Antonio. He

dropped down to his knees and took her hands in his. Tears were still streaming down her face.

"I'm sorry, Rosalia. Please, don't be upset that I lost my temper."

Rosalia shook her head, taking one of her hands out from beneath his grasp and placing it on top of Antonio's hand.

"I'm not crying because you got upset. I don't blame you for getting mad at me. I'm just mad at myself that I can't open up to you. I want to. You have to believe that, Antonio, but it's still very hard for me."

"When I was walking toward you, I noticed you looked mad even though you're crying. You can be honest with me, Rosalia, and tell me if you're upset with me."

"I was thinking about my father. I was feeling anger toward him—and sadness, too." She sighed deeply before continuing. "I promise you, Antonio, I will tell you everything someday. I just need to do so when I'm ready. I hope you can continue to understand."

"Of course, I can. Like I told you that day in the abandoned chapel, I will wait for you as long as it takes. I promise."

A few flies swirled around the food Rosalia had laid out on the blanket. She swatted them away with her hands.

"Let's eat and enjoy the rest of Saint Joseph's Day."

They ate ravenously, making comments here and there about how good the food was. Rosalia's thoughts turned once again to her father. Regret began to fill her heart—regret that she had become angry with him and on Saint Joseph's Day of all days. Saint Joseph was the patron saint of fathers. On this feast day, she should have been thinking of all the good memories she had of her father. How he had shown her how to sew when she was a little girl . . . the pride he had instilled in her when she worked alongside him in his tailor shop . . . the gifts he would give her whenever he also gave one to her mother so that she wouldn't feel left out. Still, like Antonio, she was only human. She had been angry with her father for believing Marco's lies and for abandoning her. She was even a little mad with her mother and Luca for agreeing with Papà's decision to leave their hometown. But she had not been letting herself feel anger these past four months since discovering they were gone.

She then remembered Madre Carmela's words, explaining that her family had no choice but to leave if they hoped to make a living since the townspeople were no longer frequenting Rosalia's father's tailor shop. They needed to go on living—even without Rosalia. And she supposed she needed to go on living, too, without her family. But how could she when she had no idea what had become of them? Were they still struggling financially? Had her father been able to successfully set up shop somewhere else? How was Mamma faring without one of her children by her side?

No, Rosalia could not go on living until she knew that her family was safe and sound.

❦ 18 ❧

Pane di Pasqua

EASTER BREAD

April 1, 1956

Rosalia watched Madre Carmela as she quickly braided several loaves of Easter bread dough. Rosalia was still amazed at how quickly Madre worked in the kitchen. Maybe someday Rosalia would be able to work just as quickly. Her job was to insert hard-boiled eggs into the holes within each loaf of bread. Rosalia had chosen brown and white eggs to add some color. Once she was done inserting the eggs, she brushed an egg wash over the bread to make it glisten after it was baked.

Today was Easter, and the lay workers and nuns would be celebrating with a large dinner. Rosalia was glad the season of Lent and abstinence was over, and she could once again have the many sweets tempting her every day at the pastry shop. Madre Carmela had bought a lamb at the butcher shop in town and had been marinating it overnight in white wine, fresh oregano, rosemary, and thyme. She was going to roast it and prepare a special red wine sauce to drizzle over the lamb while it was cooking.

After dinner, Rosalia was going to spend the rest of the afternoon with Antonio. They were planning on taking a stroll along the beach. The temperature was expected to reach in the mid-sixties today.

While it wasn't exactly beach weather, it would still be nice enough to enjoy a walk by the shore. Rosalia would just make sure to bring a light sweater. She was looking forward to going to the beach and spending time with Antonio. Though she had tried to rein in her feelings for him since she didn't know what the future held for them, she found it near impossible. Every day they spent together, she found herself admiring him more. And she even looked forward to his caresses and kisses. He was still being the utmost gentleman and had not tried to take their physical relationship further, which relieved Rosalia tremendously.

"Will you and Antonio be going out after our Easter dinner?" Madre Carmela broke in on Rosalia's thoughts.

"We will. Since the day is so nice, we were thinking of taking a walk at the beach. Antonio is borrowing his friend's car so we can drive there."

"That will be nice." Madre Carmela knitted her brows as if she were deep in thought.

"Maybe Antonio will ask Rosalia to marry him, and they'll go live somewhere nice." Anunziata, who was using molds to shape lamb marzipans, which were popular during Easter, chimed in.

"Please, don't say that." Rosalia blushed, anger filling her. Why couldn't Anunziata just keep her mouth shut and not have to embarrass her?

"Why, Rosalia? You don't see yourself marrying a nice boy like Antonio?" Madre Carmela asked, surprising Rosalia.

Until now, Madre had not inquired much about her growing friendship with Antonio except to ask if they would be spending their free days together and where they would be going. Now Rosalia realized Antonio was right in thinking Madre suspected they were more than just friends. Still, she was surprised that Madre would be so direct, especially where Rosalia's personal life was concerned. But though she could be angry with Anunziata, Rosalia could never be mad at Madre Carmela.

Rosalia lowered her eyes as she quickly brushed egg wash onto the next loaf of Easter bread. "I don't know. Antonio is a nice boy, but he has plans, and there is still so much that is uncertain in my own life."

"You feel that you cannot think about your future until you know where your family is."

Rosalia stopped working and looked up at Madre Carmela. She could see compassion in her eyes.

"That is true, Madre. And then there's . . ." Rosalia let her voice trail off.

Her heart began to pound. This was all too much for her. She didn't want to talk about it.

"What happened to you." Anunziata finished Rosalia's sentence.

Rosalia merely nodded her head.

Madre Carmela came over to Rosalia's side. She wiped her hands with a damp towel and then grabbed Rosalia by both arms, startling her.

"Listen to me, my dear child." She brought her face closer to Rosalia's, forcing Rosalia to look at her. "Do not let what happened to you in that cave destroy any future happiness you can have. Antonio is a wonderful young man. He is not that evil person who kidnapped you. Do you understand?" Madre squeezed Rosalia's shoulders as she asked her question.

Rosalia nodded once again.

"He cares about you, and you have nothing to be ashamed of."

Tears quickly slid down Rosalia's face as she whispered, "But he doesn't know. He might not feel the same about me once he finds out."

"You are not giving Antonio enough credit. Anyone can see that boy worships you." Madre Carmela finally let go of Rosalia's arms. She returned to her loaves of Easter bread, quickly braiding them. She seemed upset.

"Do you like him, Rosalia?" Anunziata asked.

"Very much. It's just . . . I'm afraid."

"Oh, Rosalia!" Anunziata came over and wrapped her arm around Rosalia's shoulders.

Madre Carmela stopped working and looked up. Tears were in her eyes.

"I'm sorry if I was too direct with you, Rosalia, but I can tell you are still punishing yourself over what happened, and that is what makes me mad. You are not to blame at all for what that horrible man did to you. But I can see why you are afraid of what Antonio's reaction will be once he learns about it. After all, your own father seemed to believe the lies in Marco's letter."

Rosalia began to sob aloud. It was the first time since her ordeal that she had allowed herself to completely lose control. Hearing Madre voice that her father had possibly believed Marco's lies was too much for her to bear. Rosalia had been doing her best to push the pain away. Push away the pain of losing her innocence . . . the pain of losing her family . . . the pain of her father's letting her down.

"It's all right, my child. Let it out. No one is judging you here."

Rosalia was grateful the other nuns and workers weren't present in the kitchen. Madre had assigned them to clean the convent and make sure it was pristine for the holiday. Rosalia continued to cry, her chest heaving with every sob. Once she calmed down and had wiped her tears with a handkerchief Anunziata handed her, Madre Carmela held out a small plate of marzipan fruit—her usual balm for making the hurt go away. And just as with the other times Madre had given her marzipan or whatever sweet, Rosalia felt better.

"*Grazie,* Madre. And you, too, Anunziata. I'm sorry I became so upset."

"It's nothing. Please. Don't be sorry. We've all been amazed at your strength these past few months. If it were me, I would have fallen apart." Anunziata patted Rosalia's shoulder.

"Enough sadness for today. Just think about what I said, Rosalia. Give Antonio a chance, and give yourself a chance to truly be happy." Madre lowered her head, forcing Rosalia to meet her gaze once again.

"I'll try, Madre."

"Good. Now, let's celebrate our Lord's resurrection and enjoy Easter."

After dinner, Antonio and Rosalia left for the beach. They rolled down the car windows and chatted all the way to the beach. Rosalia almost forgot about the conversation she'd had with Madre and Anunziata, but every so often she would remember. Perhaps she should finally confide in Antonio and tell him what had happened to her.

Antonio broke in on her thoughts. "I have a surprise for you when we get to the beach."

"You do?"

Antonio smiled as he kept his eyes on the road.

"I guess I can't get it out of you."

"No, of course not. It wouldn't be a surprise then. Just trust me."

"All right."

Antonio took his eyes off the road for a moment and smiled at Rosalia. Steering the car with one hand, he used his free one to pick up Rosalia's hand and press a kiss to it. He held her hand until they reached the beach and it was time for him to park.

As they walked toward the beach, she noticed a few people on bicycles riding on a gravel path that began before the sand that led to the water. The path wrapped all the way around the parking lot. It was a nice day for a bike ride. Papà had taught Rosalia and Luca how to ride a bicycle when they each turned eight. He felt that was the safe age for them to learn. She remembered how jealous she had been when Luca had learned and how she had pouted. They could only afford one bike—the family *bicicletta,* as they called it, since they all took turns riding it, except for little Cecilia, who had still been too young to ride a bicycle. Rosalia still remembered her utter joy after she had mastered balancing the bike on her own. Closing her eyes for a moment, she let herself fully experience the emotions she had felt on that day that seemed so long ago now.

Opening her eyes, she was glad to see Antonio seemed preoccupied and was looking straight ahead. He hadn't noticed how absorbed she'd been in her thoughts. He stopped before what looked like a garage. People were pulling up on their bicycles while others were taking off. She then realized it was a bike rental shop. Antonio got into the line of people waiting to rent a bicycle.

"What are you doing?" Rosalia asked.

"This is my surprise. I thought it would be fun to take a bicycle ride before we go on to the beach. You do know how to ride a bike? I suppose I should have asked you that earlier." Antonio looked annoyed with himself.

"*Si, si!* I love nothing more! When I noticed the people riding on the bicycles as we were walking toward here I was remembering how my father had taught my brother and me to ride, and how much I missed it. *Grazie,* Antonio!" Rosalia reached over and placed a kiss on his cheek.

"Thank God! I was worried my surprise was ruined." Antonio smiled and kissed Rosalia back.

Once they received their bicycles, they set off. Rosalia followed Antonio's lead, making sure to keep to the right as people returning from their rides were coming in the opposite direction. After pedaling for fifteen minutes, Antonio made a left turn, and soon there were no other bicyclists on the path. They seemed to be getting farther and farther away from the beach.

"Where are you going?" Rosalia shouted to Antonio.

"There's a small park this way. Not many people know about it. I thought it would be nice to go somewhere quiet. Don't worry. We'll make it back to the beach in time for the sunset, and the beach will be quieter then too. I just want you all to myself." Antonio looked over his shoulder, flashing a grin.

She pedaled harder to catch up to him. All along the way he had been a few feet ahead of her, but he would turn around every so often to make sure she was keeping up. She realized her physical strength still had not fully returned. Mustering every bit of it, she finally caught up to Antonio.

"You're killing me, Antonio! I'm out of breath. Please, let's slow down."

"I'm sorry! I'm just used to riding fast." He slowed down.

They rode the rest of the way to the park at a leisurely pace. Soon, a small sign pointing to the park came into view. It was hard to see since a pear cactus plant stood next to it, obscuring it partially from sight.

Antonio got off his bike and held Rosalia's bicycle still while she alighted.

"How do you know about this park?"

"I overheard a couple talking about it when I was in town to buy supplies the other day."

They left their bikes perched against a tree before walking down a narrow pathway that was lined with bushes on either side. Soon the path opened up to a small field. Antonio had been right that they would be alone here.

He took off the canvas satchel he wore strapped around his chest and reached into it, taking out a rolled up bedsheet.

"Help me lay this out."

Rosalia took the opposite end of the sheet, and they placed it on the ground. She then kicked off her sandals and placed them on the corners of the sheet to hold it down. Antonio did the same with his sandals. They then sat down. Rosalia looked at the different plants, trees, and wildflowers that were planted around the park.

"And here is surprise number two." He pulled out of his satchel a bottle of white wine.

"You are full of surprises today! What has gotten into you?" Rosalia laughed.

"It's Easter."

"*Si,* Easter. Not Christmas! *Grazie,* Antonio, but you don't need to surprise me."

"I want to." His eyes met Rosalia's.

He held her gaze for a moment. Rosalia swallowed hard. He was looking at her with desire in his eyes. Was that why he had brought her to this quiet place?

As if reading her thoughts, Antonio said, "We won't stay long. I know you wanted to take a walk along the beach, and if we hope to make the sunset we'll have to go soon since we have a long bicycle ride back."

"That is true." Rosalia silently uttered a prayer of thanks.

He poured wine into two small wooden cups he had brought.

"*Salute!*" He tapped Rosalia's cup as he toasted. "To our health and happiness."

"*Salute!*" Rosalia grinned before taking a sip of wine.

She listened to the birds chirping all around them. Leaning back on her elbows, she closed her eyes, enjoying the peacefulness of their surroundings.

"You're so beautiful, Rosalia," Antonio whispered into her ear.

She opened her eyes and saw he was lying back, propped up on one of his elbows. He stared at her and, soon, with his free hand, he tucked a few loose strands of her hair behind her ear before bringing his face closer to hers and then kissing her.

They kissed a little longer before Antonio broke the kiss. Tossing his head back, he gulped the last of his wine.

"So next week is Teresa and Francesco's wedding."

"*Sì.* I can't help feeling a bit nervous when I think about it. I keep wondering what Elisabetta's reaction is going to be when she finds out her sister has eloped with Francesco."

"It will be fine. What can she do about it? Besides, Teresa is getting married; she's not running off with some hooligan. Elisabetta needs to loosen up a bit. She's too serious."

"That is who she is. Just as Teresa is who she is."

"Exactly. If only Elisabetta could accept that and not want to turn Teresa into a nun—or rather back into a nun." Antonio began laughing so hard, tears welled up in his eyes.

Rosalia joined him. "I know. It is all so crazy! Teresa will have some stories to tell her children some day."

"Do you look forward to the day you have your own children?"

Rosalia did not know how to answer. Naturally, she had always assumed she would be a mother someday. But again, she hadn't thought about children or marriage much in the past few months after all that had happened to her.

"When I am ready to have children, I will look forward to it."

Rosalia couldn't help noticing how unenthusiastic her response had sounded. Antonio looked lost in thought. Perhaps he hadn't noticed.

He opened his mouth, about to say something, but then thought better of it.

Rosalia stood up. "I suppose we should head back if we hope to catch the sunset."

"Of course." Antonio put the cork back into the bottle of wine and placed it, along with the cups, back in his satchel.

As Rosalia helped Antonio fold the sheet, she could tell he was still thinking, but she was too afraid to ask him what was on his mind. She didn't want him to ask her any further questions about her future.

As they rode back to the beach, Antonio's mood lightened once again, and he told Rosalia all the jokes he knew. She laughed at every one of them. Madre Carmela was right. He was a good man. And for the first time, Rosalia let herself imagine what a future with him would be like. She imagined him helping her with the cooking and even a few of the household chores, although she knew that wasn't the usual arrangement between married couples, but Rosalia sensed Antonio wasn't like other men. She sensed he would always help her and be by her side—a true companion, much the way her own father had been to her mother.

"I guess that was a bad one," Antonio said.

"What was a bad one?"

"My last joke. You didn't laugh."

"Ah! I'm sorry, Antonio. My mind wandered. Tell it to me again."

"That's all right." Antonio waved his hand. "I already know it's not my best joke. Besides, I'd rather hear what you were thinking about."

"Oh, nothing." Rosalia's cheeks flushed.

"Ah! You were thinking about me." Antonio flashed a wicked grin.

"I was not!"

"Don't lie, Rosalia. It's unbecoming to you." Antonio broke out laughing.

Rosalia shook her head, but didn't say anything. She knew when she'd been caught redhanded.

Once they reached the beach, they returned their bikes to the rental shop and then made their way to the shore. A few other people were either walking or standing along the shore, waiting for the sun's descent.

Antonio and Rosalia walked hand in hand. She enjoyed these moments the most—when they didn't need to fill up the quiet with constant talk. Well, she couldn't lie to herself. She also enjoyed when Antonio held her . . . and kissed her.

Reaching the shore, they walked slowly on the wet sand. Every so often, Antonio would kick up a pebble that had washed ashore.

"You're getting that wet sand on our legs."

"So what? It's already on our feet. I have a great idea! Why don't we have a wet sand fight?"

"You're crazy! I know you're not serious." Rosalia returned her gaze straight ahead, but suddenly she felt something hit her arm.

"I can't believe you!" She watched a clump of wet sand roll off her arm. Some of the sand had splattered onto her sundress.

Antonio giggled like a schoolboy as he bent over, scooping up another small mound of sand.

"Oh, no, you don't!" Rosalia quickly bent down, scooping up what she could, but he threw sand at her again before she could strike first, hitting the hem of her dress.

She stood up, throwing her small pile of sand at Antonio. But she missed.

"Looks like I'm winning already!" Antonio taunted her before throwing another clump of sand, but this time he directed it at her ankle.

Rosalia picked up as much sand as she could with both of her hands and ran up to Antonio, throwing the pile at his back.

"You aimed right for my shirt!" But Antonio looked amused.

Rosalia bent down to scoop up more sand. She hadn't had this much fun since she was a child, chasing Luca on the beach. But suddenly, Antonio wrapped his arms around her waist and lifted her high up in the air.

She kicked him lightly with her feet, screaming, "Put me down! Put me down!"

But Antonio swung her over his shoulder and headed into the water.

"Have you gone mad? The water is still too cold. And we're going to be a sight when we return to the convent. How will we explain our disheveled appearance?"

"We'll just tell them we felt like going for a swim."

And Antonio meant it, as he waded into the water until he was chest high in it. He then slowly lowered Rosalia but, knowing she was much shorter than he was, he held her rather than let her stand in the water.

"Let's go back. You must be freezing."

"You must think I'm a weakling. I'm fine, but thank you for being so considerate."

He brought his lips to meet Rosalia's and kissed her. Rosalia wrapped her arms around Antonio's neck. She didn't care any longer that they had gotten wet or about what everyone back at the convent would think when they saw them. She just cared about this moment and how happy and carefree Antonio made her feel.

"Look!" Antonio had pulled away from their kiss as he pointed out the sun setting.

As they watched the sun slowly sink beneath the horizon, Rosalia marveled at how magical it was. She wished she could freeze this moment and forget about all that had happened in the past—and not contemplate what her future still held in store for her.

❧ 19 ❧

Trionfo di Gola

TRIUMPH OF GLUTTONY CAKE

April 14, 1956

Though it was only the second week in April, the temperature had climbed to the low seventies, a good ten degrees warmer than what Sicily usually experienced during this time of the year. Rosalia wiped the beads of perspiration that were forming along her hairline with a handkerchief as she stood at the altar of a small church in Messina, watching Teresa and Francesco take their wedding vows.

Antonio stood opposite Rosalia, next to Francesco. Every so often, he caught Rosalia's gaze and smiled deeply, holding her stare. But Rosalia could not hold his gaze for long and would look away. Something about the way he was looking at her made her feel nervous. Instead, she let her thoughts drift to the couple before them who would begin a new life together.

Teresa was stunning as always, but today her beauty radiated even more. She wore a long-sleeved, white lace dress that accentuated her svelte figure and came just past her knees. The dress's neckline was scalloped, revealing her delicate collarbone. Just before the ceremony started, Rosalia had helped her with her hair. Teresa wanted it to be coiled into a bun of several thin braids.

"My hair looks so pretty, Rosalia! I wish I didn't have to cover it with this veil," Teresa had exclaimed after seeing her hairstyle. She held a short mantilla veil with a lace trim, looking at it with disdain.

"It's just for the ceremony. You know we have to keep our heads covered in church." Rosalia had bought a simple black veil when she had gone into town with Antonio on their last day off. Since she and the other laywomen who resided at the convent always attended Mass at the convent's chapel, there wasn't any need for a veil. But if she ever wanted to attend Mass in church, she would have to wear one. So at least she hadn't been spending money on something she would only wear once.

Something flashed before Rosalia's eyes, shaking her out of her reverie. Teresa was waving her small bouquet of white daisies rather impatiently in Rosalia's direction.

She took the bouquet and silently mouthed, "I'm sorry."

Francesco turned toward Antonio, who held out two gleaming gold wedding bands. Francesco went first, taking Teresa's ring and placing it halfway down her finger. He repeated the priest's words and then fully slipped the ring on. Teresa smiled, glancing down at her ring with admiration. The priest took Francesco's ring, handing it to Teresa as she repeated her vows after the priest. After she slipped Francesco's ring all the way down his finger, the priest took their hands and joined them together, saying a prayer of blessing and announcing their union. Teresa and Francesco both looked at the priest, waiting for his nod of approval before they kissed. And in true Teresa fashion, she kissed Francesco for a few seconds, causing the priest to blush before he coughed loudly.

Rosalia looked at Antonio, wanting to share her amusement with him. But Antonio seemed oblivious to Teresa and Francesco's long kiss. He stared intently at Rosalia. This time, she didn't pull her gaze away. Instead, she imagined for a moment it was them standing before the priest taking their wedding vows. An image of Rosalia's mother's wedding dress came to her mind. Tiers of lace wrapped around a voluminous ball-gown skirt that held a hoop beneath it, causing the dress to billow dramatically out to the front. Mamma's hair was pulled up into a gorgeous bun. A veil made of

Alençon lace, which had been a gift to Mamma from Papà, hung down to her elbows. Since Rosalia was a little girl, she had known she would wear her mother's dress when she got married some day. Perhaps she still could—if she found her family. She did not have to abandon all hope of that dream's coming true.

The wedding ceremony was over, and Rosalia and Antonio followed Teresa and Francesco out of the church. No one else was in attendance, and Rosalia couldn't help noting how sad it was having only herself, Antonio, and the priest witness such a momentous event in the newlyweds' lives. But that was how they had wanted it, and they didn't look like they held any regrets. They laughed as they rushed down the aisle and out into the street. As usual, they were so wrapped up in themselves that they hadn't even waited for Rosalia and Antonio. Teresa and Francesco picked up where they had left off at the altar, and resumed their kissing.

"Let's give them some privacy for a few minutes. They'll come look for us." Antonio pulled Rosalia's arm, leading her to the side of the church building.

"Are you sure they'll come looking for us? They probably forgot we even exist." Rosalia laughed.

"True." Antonio winked at Rosalia. He then took her hand in his.

"It was a nice ceremony," Rosalia said, not voicing her thoughts from a moment ago.

"I suppose. It did seem a little sad that we were the only people to witness it."

"I was thinking that as well, but the ceremony itself was nice, and they look happy."

"They do."

"I can't stop thinking about what Elisabetta's reaction will be when she finds out her sister has eloped. Actually, everyone at the convent will be surprised."

"I know. I hope I am around tomorrow when everyone discovers she is gone."

Rosalia elbowed Antonio. "You're terrible!"

Antonio laughed. "It will be fun. I'm sure you will enjoy it, too! The best will be seeing Sorella Domenica's face. I'm sure she will feel vindicated in some way and will have to say something about knowing Teresa was up to no good."

"She thinks the worst of everyone."

"Rosalia! Antonio! Where are you? Have you decided to get married next? Ah, there you are!" Teresa made her way toward Rosalia and Antonio.

"Shhh!" Rosalia scolded her as her cheeks quickly burned hot. Once again, Teresa had managed to embarrass her. Rosalia stole a sideways glance at Antonio, who was smiling slyly.

"What do you say, Rosalia? Should we make it a double wedding?"

Rosalia's eyes widened.

"I'm only teasing you. Come on!" Antonio laughed, but Rosalia couldn't help noting that his laugh didn't reach his eyes.

They walked to a *trattoria* near the church, where they had their midday meal and celebrated.

"To the happy newlyweds. *Salute!*" Antonio held up his glass of wine as he toasted Teresa and Francesco.

"*Grazie!* You both have become such dear friends to us. We must continue to see each other even though Teresa and I will be living in Messina," Francesco said.

"As long as you don't mind coming here. I don't know how welcome I'll be at the convent after today." Teresa's eyes looked sad.

"That's nonsense! I'm sure Madre Carmela would welcome you," Rosalia offered.

"She would, but I don't know about a few of the other nuns and . . ."

"Elisabetta will come to understand. You're sisters, after all, and have only each other left in your family. Just give her some time."

"Maybe you're right, Rosalia."

"Enough! Today is a happy day. Waiter! Another carafe of wine, please! On second thought, make that two!" Francesco called out.

They laughed and celebrated for the rest of the meal. Francesco became a bit drunk and began singing, even getting down on his knees to serenade his new wife. The restaurant's other patrons applauded him.

Though Teresa laughed, Rosalia heard her whisper to Francesco, "Enough!"

After the dishes had been cleared from the table, Antonio looked at Rosalia and silently mouthed the word "now."

"Excuse us for a moment. We'll be right back," he said.

"Ah! They need some time alone! Go, go, my friend." Francesco patted Antonio's back as he walked by.

When they were out of earshot, Antonio whispered, "If he keeps drinking, I'm afraid their wedding night won't be memorable at all."

Though Rosalia was surprised by Antonio's frank comment, she couldn't help giggling softly.

They entered the *trattoria*'s kitchen. Antonio spotted the owner, Signora DelAbate, who was coating the sides of a *Trionfo di Gola* cake with chopped pistachios. *Trionfo di Gola,* or Triumph of Gluttony, was a very old cake recipe passed down from nuns over the centuries. The batter was divided among three different-sized round cake pans. After the individual cakes were baked, filling was spread on top of each layer, and then they were stacked one on top of the other. Once the cake was assembled, it was then frosted with marzipan paste, and the finishing touch was the coating of the chopped pistachios around the cake. The cake's tall, pyramid shape gave it a unique, impressive appearance. Rosalia had wanted to make a cake that was more elaborate than a typical wedding cake.

"*Signora,* it looks beautiful!" Antonio exclaimed.

"I am almost done with it. You know you could have asked me to make the cake. We make some of the finest cakes in Messina even though we are a simple *trattoria*."

"I'm sure you do, but as I explained earlier, this is our gift to our friends."

"You both made this cake?" Signora DelAbate looked up, surprised. "I thought it was just your wife who made it. A man who bakes. Very nice. *Bravo!*" She nodded approvingly before returning to her work.

Antonio opened his mouth to correct Signora DelAbate, but Rosalia placed her hand on his. It was all right that the *trattoria* owner had mistaken them for a married couple. It was a natural assumption. Also, Rosalia had been the one to actually make the cake, but she and Antonio had collaborated on the recipe, especially since it was their first time making *Trionfo di Gola.*

"All done. Ah! Wait!" Signora DelAbate grabbed her cane, which was propped against the worktable, and hobbled over to a vase of large blood-red tulips. She snipped two of the tulips from their stems with a pair of kitchen shears and hobbled back to the table. She placed the flowers side by side in the center of the cake.

"One for the groom and one for the bride!" She laughed, pleased with herself.

"It's gorgeous, *signora*. *Grazie!*" Rosalia admired the cake.

She couldn't wait to see Teresa's and Francesco's reactions. Rosalia and Antonio had agreed not to decorate the cake themselves out of fear that it would get ruined when Antonio transported it to the *trattoria*. They had traveled to Messina an hour before they were supposed to meet Teresa and Francesco at the church. It had been difficult to convince them they didn't need a ride to Messina, and Antonio had told a small lie and said he needed to meet with one of Madre's suppliers in Messina. Besides, he told them if they left together it might arouse suspicion, although they'd gone out on other occasions. But Teresa and Francesco were so anxious to tie the knot and not be discovered by Elisabetta that they had heartily agreed it was for the better if they didn't leave the convent together. Antonio had borrowed his friend's car, and he and Rosalia had snuck the cake out of the convent's kitchen. Rosalia had made the cake secretly the day before in the kitchen. The other workers in the convent were too busy to notice anything out of the ordinary. Once the cake was baked, Antonio had placed it all the way in the back of the refrigerator that was used for their meals and not for the pastries the convent made. And when it was time to take the cake to the car, Rosalia had found an empty potato sack to cover it with. God had been on their side, since no one had seemed to notice them as they carried this odd-looking platter covered in burlap outside.

"Would you like me to carry it out?" Signora DelAbate asked.

Rosalia shook her head. "No. *Grazie.* We would like to do it since we are presenting it as a gift to the newlyweds."

"*Va bene.*" Signora DelAbate motioned with her hands for them to take the cake platter.

Antonio carefully picked up the cake with both of his hands.

"This is heavy. Did you put rocks in this, Rosalia?"

Rosalia narrowed her eyes at him. "Funny!"

She followed Antonio out of the kitchen. She began to feel nervous.

"I hope the cake came out good. Can you imagine if it tastes horrible, and they'll always remember their wedding cake as being this terrible cake Rosalia made?"

"When have you made anything that tasted bad, Rosalia?" Antonio said without turning his head.

She couldn't help noting he seemed nervous, too, as if afraid he would drop their treasure.

When they reached their table, Antonio and Rosalia shouted, "Surprise!"

"Is that for us?" Teresa looked at Rosalia, who nodded.

"It's beautiful! Isn't it, Francesco?"

"*Sì!* What a gorgeous cake!"

"We made it. Well, Rosalia made it, but I consulted with her on the recipe. But it's truly Rosalia's creation. And it's not just any cake. It's a *Trionfo di Gola.* A special cake for your special occasion." Antonio was beaming with pride.

"Antonio was very much a part of it. It was his idea to make you a wedding cake as our gift to you. I hope you like it. Oh, and we have Signora DelAbate to thank for decorating it. We were afraid to decorate it back at the convent and have the frosting get ruined while we transported it here. I'm sure if we had, most of the pistachios would've fallen off!" Rosalia laughed.

She then gestured toward Signora DelAbate, who waved and shouted, "*Buona fortuna!*"

Teresa waved back. "*Grazie, signora! Grazie,* Rosalia and Antonio. Wait! This was the reason why you came to Messina earlier and not with us? You weren't meeting with one of Madre Carmela's suppliers, were you, Antonio?"

"Guilty as charged! All those lies I can fully take credit for!" Antonio bowed.

"Enough talk! Let's cut into the cake!" Francesco shouted.

Signora DelAbate ran over with a large cake knife. "You must cut it together for good luck."

"Ah! Good luck! Who believes in that nonsense anymore!" Francesco barked, eliciting a glare from Teresa.

"I do! This is my wedding, and we must follow tradition, including doing everything that can ensure only good luck in our marriage." Teresa took the cake knife from Signora DelAbate and nudged Francesco with her elbow.

Francesco placed his hand over Teresa's as they cut the first cake slice.

Everyone in the restaurant was standing up and cheering the newlyweds. Rosalia was glad she had decided to make a large cake. She would offer a slice to all the patrons. Originally, she had wanted to make a large cake even though it would just be the four of them celebrating the wedding because she thought it would look nicer than a small cake. And it was, after all, Teresa's wedding. Now, Rosalia was glad that everyone in the restaurant was taking part in the celebration. Though they were strangers, it made the occasion seem more festive than just having four people at a wedding party.

Teresa broke off a piece of cake with her fork and fed it to Francesco, who paused for a moment. Rosalia held her breath. Oh no! she thought. Had she forgotten to add the rum? Or maybe she hadn't measured the sugar properly?

But then Francesco exclaimed, "*Dio mio!* This is the best cake I've ever had!"

Relief washed over Rosalia as Francesco then fed Teresa her first bite of cake. Teresa had the same reaction as Francesco. She paused and seemed to be slowly chewing the cake as if she was savoring it for as long as she could.

"Rosalia, this has to be the best dessert you've created at the pastry shop."

"*Grazie,* Teresa. I'm just happy you both like it."

Rosalia and Antonio took over cutting the rest of the cake and serving it to the restaurant's patrons, many of whom came up to Rosalia afterward and told her the cake was amazing. She couldn't help feeling like she was taking some of the attention away from the bride, but Teresa didn't seem to mind. She was too busy stealing kisses from her husband.

* * *

An hour later, Rosalia and Antonio took their leave. Teresa and Francesco were going to spend the night at a room they had rented in a small hotel. Then in the morning, they would make their way to Milazzo, where they would take a ferry to the Aeolian island of Lipari for a short honeymoon.

Rosalia and Antonio were quiet, basking in their success at surprising Teresa and Francesco with the wedding cake and how good it had turned out. Rosalia suddenly noticed they were by the marina in Messina. Antonio pulled to the side of the road and parked the car.

"What are you doing?"

"Let's sit here for a little while. It's such a beautiful night, and it would be nice to relax by the marina. There's no need for us to rush back home. No one will be waiting for us."

"All right." Rosalia stepped out of the car, taking her shawl with her. The temperature had cooled a bit, and there was a light breeze coming off the water.

They walked hand in hand until they were close to the wall that overlooked the water. Rosalia stared at the sky as twilight unfolded. She felt comforted whenever day gave way to dark. Something about the night soothed her.

"You're cold." Antonio wrapped his arms around her.

They stood silently wrapped in each other's embrace.

"*Ti amo molto,* Rosalia."

Tears sprang to Rosalia's eyes. Though it was not the first time Antonio had professed his love to her, for some reason, hearing the words tonight moved her more. Without thinking, she whispered back, "*Ti amo, anch'io.* I love you, too."

Antonio pulled slightly away from Rosalia. Surprise and joy were etched across his features. He was about to say something, but instead he kissed her. Softly, at first, then ravenously. Every so often, he would pull his lips away just long enough to whisper again and again, "*Ti amo.*"

When they stopped kissing, Antonio led Rosalia to a bench. A few other couples were walking by the marina, while others sat on benches, locked in kisses. Antonio and Rosalia sat down on the bench, and Rosalia rested her head on Antonio's shoulder.

"I feel safe with you, Antonio."

"And you should. You've made me so happy, Rosalia. Just hearing you feel the same way has made me the happiest person in the world—even happier than Francesco or Teresa."

Rosalia laughed. "I'm glad you're happy, Antonio. You deserve it. You are such a kind, good man. And you have been wonderful to me."

"It's because I love you."

"I know. I have no doubt of that." Rosalia squeezed Antonio's hand. He wrapped his fingers around hers.

"Rosalia, today has been special. Watching our friends commit to each other and seeing their happiness. I don't want to waste any more time. So I'm going to take a chance."

Antonio dropped down to his right knee. Rosalia's eyes widened. It couldn't be what she was thinking.

"Will you marry me, Rosalia? I will be devoted to you every day of our lives together. I will do whatever it takes to ensure your happiness."

Once again, tears filled Rosalia's eyes. Hearing Antonio say how devoted he would be to her brought an overwhelming wave of emotions. The tears quickly slid down her face. Antonio's expression of hope quickly changed to concern. But she placed her hand on the side of his face and whispered through her tears, "I would be honored to marry you, Antonio. I'm crying because you love me. I can see how much you love me. And I do trust you completely with my heart now."

"Rosalia!" Antonio's eyes filled with tears. He stood up and sat next to Rosalia, holding her close to him. "You've made me the happiest man in all of Italy!"

"Just all of Italy?" Rosalia raised her eyebrow, narrowing her gaze, but she couldn't help smiling a little.

"All of Europe. The whole world. No, the entire universe!" Antonio shouted, and then he stood up, lifting Rosalia high into the air.

Rosalia laughed, reveling in the feeling of elation. She was happy.

It felt good—even though she knew the feeling would always be overshadowed whenever she thought about her family. But she was too caught up in the moment to think about the practicalities of marrying Antonio. They would figure it out. For now, all she knew was that she couldn't imagine losing him and his not being in her life anymore. He had become like family. And while she still ached for the family she had lost and still hoped to find someday, Antonio made her feel safe, protected, and loved.

20

Biscotti Regina

SESAME COOKIES

Later that evening . . .

As Antonio pulled up to the gates of the convent, Rosalia was surprised to see all the lights were on. It was almost ten o'clock, and usually most of the nuns were in bed by nine. There were a few exceptions like the lay workers who often stayed up in their rooms to read, or sometimes Madre Carmela wanted to test a recipe. But to see all the lights on at this time was unusual. A sense of dread began to fill Rosalia. Teresa. That had to be the reason why everyone was up. Of course.

Teresa had left a note in the top drawer of Elisabetta's dresser. This way Elisabetta would see it when she got dressed in the morning. Elisabetta would not be wondering until the next day where her sister was, since she usually went to bed every night at eight o'clock sharp. The strain between the two siblings since they'd left the previous convent had become so great that Elisabetta barely paid any attention anymore to Teresa.

"They must realize Teresa is missing." Antonio looked at Rosalia as he said this.

"I was thinking the same thing."

"Well, I suppose we should get this over with. You are prepared for Elisabetta's and possibly Madre Carmela's being upset with us since we knew about Teresa's plans?"

"Yes, I am prepared."

Antonio parked the car, and then he and Rosalia made their way toward the convent's entrance. But they had only walked a few feet when the front door opened. Madre Carmela stepped out, her face looking grave.

Rosalia could not help thinking of the irony that only a few minutes ago, she had been elated over her engagement to Antonio. And she couldn't wait to share the news with Madre. She knew how much Madre Carmela loved and admired Antonio, and Rosalia knew she would be happy for her. But her good news would have to wait for the time being.

"Rosalia. Antonio." Madre slowly walked toward them. She glanced nervously over her shoulder.

"I'm sorry, Madre. I know we are returning later than we normally do. But we can explain. Everyone by now must know about Teresa."

Madre frowned. "Teresa?"

"*Sì.* Is Elisabetta very upset?"

"My child, what are you talking about?"

Antonio reached over and squeezed Rosalia's hand, warning her not to say more. But if Madre didn't know about Teresa yet, then why were all the lights on in the convent and why did Madre look so upset?

Then, Rosalia saw a man standing in the shadows by the front door. He stepped out, and Rosalia almost gasped when she saw it was none other than L'ispettore Franco. Her eyes then met Madre's.

Madre Carmela stepped forward. "I'm sorry, Rosalia. I wanted to warn you that L'ispettore Franco is here."

"What's happened? It's my family, isn't it? What's happened to them?" Rosalia's chest heaved, and her eyes darted frantically from L'ispettore Franco's face to Madre's.

Antonio squeezed Rosalia's hand tighter, and Madre came over and put her arm around her shoulders.

"Please, Rosalia, let's go inside and sit down."

"Tell me now! What has happened?" Rosalia broke free from Antonio's and Madre's embraces and walked up to L'ispettore Franco.

"Calm down, Rosalia. Please. It's not what you think. Let us go sit inside," L'ispettore Franco pleaded with her.

Antonio was by Rosalia's side again as he took her hand and led her indoors. Her heart pounded as she followed him. All the nuns except for Sorella Domenica were seated at the dining table; even Anunziata, Mari, and Lidia were there. A bowl piled high with *Biscotti Regina* sat at the center of the table. Sorella Giovanna was nibbling rapidly on one of the sesame cookies, a nervous habit of hers Rosalia had witnessed before. Sorella Giovanna kept her gaze averted from Rosalia, but everyone else looked at her the moment they saw her. Their faces held the same grim expression Madre's had outside. Rosalia couldn't help wondering where Elisabetta was. Had she perhaps discovered Teresa's absence already and remained behind in her room? Or maybe she was still sleeping in her bed, oblivious to the unexpected visit from L'ispettore Franco that had awakened the rest of the convent?

L'ispettore Franco led Rosalia and Antonio to a small sitting room that Madre used when she had visitors. He gestured for Rosalia to sit down. Madre came in and closed the door behind her. Rosalia saw a small cake plate with a few of the *Biscotti Regina* on it. Once they were all seated, L'ispettore picked up one of the cookies and began eating it while speaking at the same time. Rosalia frowned. Hadn't anyone taught him better manners? A few sesame seeds from the biscotto fell onto his lap, but he continued eating, even picking up a second cookie after finishing the first. Rosalia turned her focus to his words.

"As you know, Rosalia, I have been making inquiries about your family these past several months. I have not given up, but the progress has been very slow. That is why you haven't heard from me except for the phone calls I made every few weeks to Madre Carmela to give her updates and let her know I had not abandoned my search. I want you to know that." He wiped his mouth with the napkin placed next to the plate of biscotti and glanced at the remaining cookies as if tempted to eat another one, but he thought better of it and instead leaned forward, resting his elbows on his knees. Finally, his eyes met Rosalia's.

"*Grazie,* L'ispettore. I appreciate your not giving up."

"There were a few false leads in other cities. My police contacts would think they had located your family, but it always turned out to be people who had your same surname. Finally, we had a break about a month ago."

"A month ago? Why didn't you call Madre right away?"

L'ispettore held his hands up. "I am getting to that. Please, Rosalia, I ask you to be patient just a little longer."

Antonio placed his arm around Rosalia. She couldn't help thinking he was trying to brace her for whatever L'ispettore Franco was about to say.

"I began wondering if perhaps your family had decided to have a fresh start somewhere else, somewhere besides Sicily. I knew it would be even harder to locate your family if they had decided to move to mainland Italy, but naturally, I put out the word to whatever contacts I had in Calabria, Rome, Bari. I hoped, if your family had gone to the mainland, they would have stayed in the south since going farther north would cost them more in transporation expenses. And the south of Italy is more comparable to Sicily."

"The mainland? They left Sicily?"

Again, L'ispettore Franco held his hand up. "Once more, no trace of them surfaced in Italy. I even put out the word to the authorities in cities farther north. Then an idea came to me." He paused, glancing at Rosalia for a moment before looking away. He picked up what was now his third biscotto and bit into it. This time in addition to the sesame seeds that fell, a few crumbs broke off. Rosalia could feel her nerves getting more irritated by the second. Why didn't he just tell her the bad news he obviously had for her? Why was he prolonging her misery?

"Go on," she pleaded, trying to keep the irritation out of her voice.

"I wondered if perhaps they had decided to immigrate to America."

Blood rushed to Rosalia's ears. Surely, she must not have heard him correctly. She barely whispered, "America," as a huge lump formed in the back of her throat.

"It seemed plausible since they were trying to make a fresh start, and your father was struggling with his business. And with all the immigrants who are still flocking to America to build a new life, perhaps your family was among them. So I checked the ships' registers for the past few months to see if your family was amongst the passengers listed."

"And?" Rosalia was now sitting on the edge of the settee.

"Your father's name was listed. But not the rest of your family members."

"I don't understand. Perhaps they went on different ships."

"I thought of that as well, especially since it is common for the head of the household to immigrate first, get settled, and then bring the rest of the relatives over, but no. The rest of your family's names haven't been on any of the passenger lists since your father set sail for America, which was in December."

"Well, maybe Papà is not settled yet in America, especially if he has decided to set up his tailor shop there. He might be waiting until he has more money to send for my mother and siblings. That must be it."

Though Rosalia could not imagine her father's being so far away, on another continent, she felt a glimmer of hope since at least L'ispettore Franco had been able to locate one of her family members.

"There's more, Rosalia. I continued to look at the ships' registers every week, while still trying to locate the rest of your family in Sicily. Your father left from the port in Marsala. So naturally, I thought that was where he and your family had gone after leaving Terme Vigliatore."

Though Rosalia had had a gut feeling her family had gone far, she had never imagined they would travel all the way to the western coast of Sicily. The farthest she could conceive of their going was the capital city of Palermo. Had her father's search for work taken him that far? And now to hear that he had gone as far as America. She was shocked. She imagined Papà, Mamma, Luca, and little Cecilia traveling through the island like gypsies with nowhere concrete to go. Then she envisioned her father on the huge ship that had taken him to America, swaying about in the throes of the Atlantic Ocean, having no idea if he was making a mistake leaving his family behind in Sicily and traveling so far from them. Did he ever wonder if he had made a mistake in leaving Terme Vigliatore without finding Rosalia first to make sure she really wanted to be with Marco? Or at least make sure that Marco was treating her well? Her heart filled with pain. She didn't know how much more suffering she could take. Poor Mamma, Luca, and Cecilia. To think of what had become of her family saddened her immensely. Tears spilled down her face. Madre reached into the deep pockets of her habit. Rosalia expected her to produce one of her marzipan fruits that always made Rosalia feel better, but instead she pulled out a white linen handkerchief and handed it to Rosalia.

"I was able to find out that your family was working in a vineyard in Marsala. The vineyard owners paid them by providing for their room and board."

Rosalia gasped. Her hand flew to her mouth as excitement washed over her. "You found them! You found them!"

Antonio dug his fingers painfully into Rosalia's shoulders, but she ignored the sensation.

"I did, but then they simply vanished." L'ispettore Franco stood up, turning his back toward them as he paced back and forth in front of the sitting room's window.

Rosalia's joy from a moment ago was quickly replaced with a deep despair. It couldn't be. It just couldn't be. And then anger washed over her. She walked over to L'ispettore Franco, standing in his line of vision until he had no choice but to look her in the eyes.

"What do you mean they vanished?" Her voice came out shrill.

"The vineyard owners told us that your father had returned from America the last week in March, and then, a week later, he and your family had left Marsala. He had gone temporarily to America to work in the coal mines. He had anticipated being there for nine months to a year. His plan was to make some money so he could open a tailor shop again in Sicily. He never had any plans to make America his permanent home. He had been living in Virginia, where he worked as a coal miner. He got into an argument with the mine's supervisor and lost his job. Although he hadn't been in America for long, he had hated living there and couldn't imagine himself living there any longer, so he decided to just return to Marsala. But the vineyard owners were struggling financially, and they could no longer afford to keep your family on as laborers, let alone provide for their board. So your family left a week after your father returned. The vineyard owners have no idea where they went since your family didn't know either. All they knew was that they were heading east to find whatever work they could. You don't know how sorry I am, Rosalia. I wish I had better news for you. But I will keep searching for them."

Rosalia couldn't believe it. For a second time, they had narrowly missed her family. First, when she had returned home to Terme Vigliatore, and now again. It was just a week ago that her family had left Marsala. A week! Why couldn't L'ispettore Franco have found out where they were sooner? Why was God playing with her life once again? What had she done to deserve the cruel twists of fate her life had taken these past eight months?

East. L'ispettore Franco said the vineyard owners only knew that her father was planning on heading east. Maybe they were traveling closer to home? After all, didn't Papà always used to say that the county of Messina was the best in all of Sicily? He'd also said his ancestors had been born here, and he would die here. *Sì!* He was coming back home. He didn't have to return to Terme Vigliatore. He could just live in one of the many other towns in Messina. There was hope left still.

"Papà is coming back to Messina. This is where his heart has always been. He always said it was the best place to live on the island, and he planned on dying here. I can feel it. He is coming back. Perhaps he has forgiven me and wants to find me."

Madre Carmela hung her head low, slowly shaking her head. Antonio's eyes filled with tears.

"You don't believe it, but I know." Rosalia's voice was shaky, belying her confidence.

"Oh, Rosalia," Madre said as she stood up and walked over to her.

Rosalia swung her head quickly from side to side, not wanting to fully abandon her last shred of hope. "No, you are not having faith, Madre! You, a woman of God, and you have no faith!" Rosalia pointed her index finger at Madre as she screamed. "I thought you were my friend, but you don't even believe my family is coming back for me! None of you believe it!" Her eyes then landed accusingly on Antonio, who was now crying. He came over, holding his arms out to her, but instead of rushing into his embrace, she turned away and left the sitting room. The nuns and the lay workers, including Elisabetta now, were all standing just outside the door. Of course, they'd been eavesdropping. Why was it that they were privy to her life and all the pain in it? Did they feel entitled since they had rescued her that day when they found her by the cave?

"Rosalia! Wait! Please, don't go!"

Anunziata called out to her, as did several of the others, but she ignored them as she continued heading toward the front door. And in case any of them decided to follow her, she began to run once she stepped outside. But she didn't have to worry. No one followed her. She continued to run until she reached the abandoned chapel where Antonio slept. She sat down in front of a bare fig tree, the same tree Madre had told her produced the sweetest figs in the summer. She stared up at the night sky, which was full of stars, and just let herself breathe deeply for a few minutes as she waited for her pulse to return to normal. Her mind turned to Teresa. For her, tonight would be one of the most wonderful, memorable moments in her life as she sealed her union with her husband in their wedding bed. And for Rosalia, too, tonight would always remain etched in her memory because it would be the night she lost her family a second time. She had accused Madre Carmela and everyone else of not believing she would be reunited with her family. Tonight was the first time Rosalia, too, was beginning to lose faith that she would ever find them again.

❧ 21 ❧

Gelo di Melone

WATERMELON PUDDING

June 6, 1956

Rosalia was standing in a field of fragrant white jasmine flowers.
It was the first week in June, and the sun was especially hot today.
She could feel it warming her head through the cotton kerchief she
wore. A large straw basket, slung around her arm, held the jasmines
she was harvesting for the jasmine water that was needed to make
Gelo di Melone—watermelon pudding. With the temperatures well
in the eighties, the shop couldn't make enough of the watermelon
pudding that was popular with the villagers during late spring and
throughout the summer.

As she picked the jasmines from their stems, she frequently took
the time to smell them although she didn't need to do so since the
fragrance surrounded her. But she loved holding the blossoms up
to her nose and inhaling deeply. The scent seemed to ease her heavy
heart and lift her sorrow for a bit. She couldn't believe almost two
months had passed since Teresa and Francesco's wedding, and
since she had learned some news about the whereabouts of her
family. And of course since she and Antonio had become engaged.
Madre Carmela and everyone else at the convent had been happy

to learn of their engagement. And although Antonio initially was going to wait to apply to culinary schools until the autumn, Madre Carmela thought he was ready and had convinced him to begin his applications.

"After all, the sooner you go to school, the sooner you will be on your way to becoming a chef and providing for Rosalia," she had said.

Of course Madre Carmela's words did the trick and persuaded Antonio to apply. As he had continually told Rosalia since he'd asked her to marry him, he could not wait to make her his wife and for them to embark on their new life together. He had applied to culinary schools in Messina and even Palermo in case he wasn't accepted to the ones closer to home. But he knew that Rosalia wished to remain in the county of Messina. She would continue working in the shop once they were married, but naturally she and Antonio would find a small house to make their new home. At least she would not be losing the women who had become a second family to her ever since she had come to stay at the convent.

She took a break from her work and pulled out a handkerchief, wiping the sweat from her brow. A figure was making its way toward her. Antonio. She smiled and waved to him. He waved back. There was something about the way he looked at her. His eyes seemed to hold fear.

"*Ciao, bella!*" Antonio took Rosalia in his arms and gave her a long kiss.

"Is everything all right?" she asked him, pushing back the long wisps of bangs Rosalia loved on him so much, especially when they hung over his eyes.

"*Sì.*" Antonio smiled, but she couldn't help noticing that the smile didn't light up his eyes as it normally did. She decided for now not to press him as to what was troubling him. After all, how many times had he noticed she was sad, yet let her be?

"Come. Let's sit down for a bit and just hide from the rest of the world." He tugged on Rosalia's hand.

She laughed as she sat down on the ground with him, leaning her back against Antonio's chest. She held onto his arms, which were now wrapped around her. They sat silently like that for what seemed like hours but was probably no more than ten minutes before Antonio spoke.

"You know I love you very much, Rosalia?"

"*Si.* I know that. And I love you very much."

"And I consider you my family already even though we are not married yet. Rosalia, I know I cannot replace your family, but I hope in time you can come to think of me as part of your family. And perhaps . . ." His voice trailed off before he continued. "And perhaps that will lessen a bit the pain of being apart from your parents and siblings."

Rosalia turned around so that she was now facing Antonio. Placing her hands on either side of his face, she looked into his eyes. "*Grazie,* Antonio. You have already done so much to help me. I already think of you as family, as I do the nuns and my other friends at the pastry shop. You have all shown me the utmost kindness and done so much for me. I don't know what I would have done without all of you." She kissed Antonio lightly on the lips and then hugged him.

Antonio held Rosalia, stroking her hair.

"I have something to tell you."

She waited patiently.

"I have been accepted to several culinary schools."

Rosalia pulled away from Antonio, clapping her hands.

"That is wonderful, Antonio! Of course, I knew you would be! Madre Carmela and I know how talented you are. I'm so happy for you!" She threw her arms around his neck, pulling him toward her in another embrace.

But Antonio did not hug her back this time. She pulled away. He was looking into Rosalia's basket of jasmines. He took one out and smelled it.

"What is the matter? Are you not happy that you've been accepted? What is it?"

A thought then entered her mind.

"You were not accepted into any of the schools in Messina? They're in Palermo? That is all right, Antonio! We can live there until you complete school and then move back to Messina."

Antonio looked up at her. Instead of looking relieved, his face twisted a bit as if he were in pain.

"It's not Palermo." He swallowed before continuing, averting his gaze from hers. "I was accepted into Le Cordon Bleu."

"Le Cordon Bleu? The school in Paris?"

Antonio nodded. His face flushed. Finally, his eyes met Rosalia's.

"But I thought you had decided you didn't want to go there anymore. Not now that we are to be married."

"Madre Carmela thought I should still apply—if only to see if I would be accepted. As you know, she has firmly believed in me from the beginning. And—"

"Madre encouraged you to apply?" Rosalia interrupted him.

"*Sì.* I told her I shouldn't waste my time since we were getting married and planning on living here in Sicily, but she said I should see if Le Cordon Bleu would accept me. She said it would boost my confidence even more to know I was good enough for the best culinary school in the world."

Antonio's words did little to reassure Rosalia. She felt betrayed. Betrayed by Madre Carmela, who had encouraged Antonio to apply to a school in another country when she knew that Rosalia wanted to stay in Messina. Madre knew that Rosalia had no intentions of going far. How could she, especially after L'ispettore Franco had told her that her father had decided to move back east? She still believed her father was headed back to Messina and perhaps had had a change of heart and wanted to find Rosalia. No. She could not leave Messina. And to go to a strange country so far away, where she wouldn't speak the language or know the people's customs. She had come too far since the nuns had rescued her at the cave. She loved working at the pastry shop and learning from Madre Carmela. She loved the company of the women whom she had come to think of as sisters. Rosalia didn't even mind the routines of the convent: waking up at dawn and going to Mass, attending evening vespers, fasting during holy days. There was a serenity and comfort in the established rhythms of the convent that she had come to embrace. And she credited the tranquil, stable environment of her new home with helping to restore her to health emotionally.

Rosalia couldn't help also feeling betrayed by the man she loved. Why had he bothered to apply to Le Cordon Bleu if, as he had told Madre, it would be a waste of time since he and Rosalia planned on staying in Sicily? Palermo she could accept, since they had agreed it would be temporary and they would return to Messina once he was done with his education.

"Rosalia, Paris would just be temporary. We could still return to Sicily once I'm done with school."

That was true. She hadn't thought of that. Still. She did not want to go to Paris, even temporarily. At least in Palermo, she could visit Messina every month or so. It would be easier to get updates or to be reached if Madre or L'ispettore Franco received more news about her family. Though she knew they could just as easily send a telegram or call her by phone in Paris. But when she entertained even for a second the thought of moving to Paris, she felt her heart go cold.

"So you do want to go to Le Cordon Bleu? You didn't just apply so you could see if you were good enough for their program? You never truly gave up your dream of going there?"

"I did. Please, believe me, Rosalia. I had abandoned my dream of going there once you accepted my marriage proposal. But I admit I feel differently now, knowing that they have accepted me. I want the best for us. I could work in the best restaurants in Messina, Palermo, wherever, if I attended Le Cordon Bleu. We would be so comfortable financially."

"So you've forgotten about my desire to live in Messina. We had agreed that if you didn't get accepted to schools in Messina, but were accepted by schools in Palermo, we would later return to live here. And I am supposed to believe you that Paris would be temporary? How can I trust you, Antonio, especially when you did not even tell me that you had gone ahead and applied to Le Cordon Bleu? You and Madre Carmela conspired behind my back and kept this secret from me!" Rosalia's voice had risen now. Angry tears filled her eyes.

"Rosalia! It was not like that! How can you say that about Madre, a woman of God!"

"She is still human and capable of deceit," Rosalia said softly.

An immense sadness filled her then. She was disappointed. Once again, people she loved and cared about had let her down. First, it had been her father for believing the lies in the letter Marco had forced her to write. Then it had been her entire family for leaving her. Now, Madre and Antonio had disappointed her, too. Could she trust anyone?

"Rosalia, Madre and I both love and care about you very much. She probably didn't say anything to you because she believed me that I had no intentions of actually going to Le Cordon Bleu, even if they accepted me. And I did not ask her to keep it a secret from you."

"But you kept it a secret from me. Why didn't you tell me if, as you say, you were not planning on going? Deep down, you knew there was a chance you would go. But you were too afraid to tell me that. You knew how much I wanted to remain in Messina."

Antonio closed his eyes for a moment. "I guess I was lying to myself. I was trying to convince myself I would be all right with not going to Le Cordon Bleu even if I was admitted. But, Rosalia, can't you see what a wonderful opportunity this is? And how many doors it would open for me and for us? As I mentioned, I would be able to find work at almost any fine restaurant I choose. Would it be so terrible for you to go to Paris with me? I want you to be happy, so we would return to Sicily after I'm done with school. I promise."

"I'm sorry, Antonio. I know how much this means to you, and it was a dream of yours long before you met me. I do not want to hold you back. Please, go to Paris. Live your dream. This was all a mistake. I cannot marry you."

Antonio's face turned ashen. "Don't say that, Rosalia. You are overreacting. I won't go to Paris. It was a mistake. I should've never applied to Le Cordon Bleu. Nothing matters more to me than you. Forget about this whole conversation. I will go to school here in Messina."

Rosalia shook her head. "No. Do not sacrifice your dreams for me. You will always regret it, and you will become bitter. You will come to resent me. I could not live with that."

"This is all because of your family. If they come back to Messina, surely L'ispettore Franco will come to know, and he will let you know. You don't need to wait here for something that might not . . ." Antonio caught himself, but it was too late.

"For something that might not happen. It's all right. You can say it. I know that you, Madre, and everyone else do not believe that my family is returning here. And if they aren't, I know you all don't believe I will ever find them or learn what has happened to them since they left Marsala." Rosalia let out an exasperated laugh. "For women of God, Madre and the other nuns have little faith. They profess to believe in God without proof of His existence. Why then can they not believe that He will create a miracle for me and let me be reunited with my family? I can understand it more from you and the other lay workers at the pastry shop, but I would've expected more faith from the nuns. I can see it in the sisters' eyes whenever I talk about seeing my family again someday; they look at me with doubt and pity. I am tired of being pitied by everyone, including you." Rosalia turned her head away from Antonio.

"Is that what you've thought all along? That I pity you? Is that why you think I love you and want you to be my wife? Don't you know me by now, Rosalia?"

Rosalia remained silent. Though she was angry with Antonio, she knew she was being unfair toward him. Her heart softened.

"I know you love me and are not with me just because you feel sorry for me. I'm angry. You have finally been honest with me about your wish to go to Paris. And I suppose it is finally time I am honest with you. I should never have accepted your proposal. You see, Antonio, I don't think I can ever be the wife that you or any other good man deserves. I have been keeping a secret from you as well."

Antonio waited for Rosalia to continue. But every time she tried to go on and tell him what she had wanted to tell him for the past few months, she could not get the words out.

"It is all right, Rosalia. I already know." He placed his hand over Rosalia's.

"You know?" Rosalia whispered.

Of course he knew. Just as the other nuns and the lay workers had known. She'd been a fool to think that someone would not tell him. People gossiped. After all, hadn't Anunziata gossiped about Mari and the scandal in her past?

"I don't know exactly, but I have my suspicions. I had overheard the townspeople talking about how the nuns found you near death by a cave and saying that it was obvious someone had abused you. At first, I thought someone had just beaten you. But when I met you and saw how frightened you were of me and any other man who was near you, I began to suspect it was more. Though we have never been intimate, I sensed in the beginning, when we kissed, even that was a bit terrifying for you. And then there was your admission to me that someone had hurt you terribly. Rosalia, you have nothing to be ashamed of. If I am right in my suspicions that someone violated you, I will kill that man if I ever find him. I swear!"

Rosalia saw the most intense hatred in Antonio's eyes. It frightened her even though she knew the hatred was directed toward her enemy. She did not want more violence to occur after what had happened to her.

"Antonio, you are a good person. Even if you ever found out who hurt me and found him, I would not want you to seek retribution on my behalf. Don't you see? I care about you because you are the very opposite of that man. You are all good, while he was all evil."

She then cried, her shoulders shaking uncontrollably. Antonio took her in his arms.

"I will protect you, Rosalia. No one will ever harm you again. You have been through such hell. And then to lose your family. How did that happen? Did they not know what had happened to you?"

Rosalia then recounted to Antonio everything that had occurred: Marco's attempt to seduce her while she worked in her father's tailor shop; Marco's anger when she rejected him; his kidnapping her and his abuse of her in the cave; regaining her memory and returning home, only to discover her family had left, believing she had eloped with Marco and was pregnant with his child.

Once she was done narrating her past ordeal, she said, "Now, do you see why I can't marry you? I don't know if I can ever be intimate with a man again after what Marco did to me. And I am . . ."

She looked away, shaking her head. "I am ruined. You deserve a wife who has not been ruined."

"I deserve you, Rosalia! And I want you! Only you, do you hear me?"

"You have brought happiness into my life again, Antonio, but I cannot be completely content until I find my family. Now that you know what happened, can you understand better why I need to find them? I must convince my father those were lies in that letter Marco forced me to write. I must let my family know I never abandoned them and went off with that monster. I miss them so much, Antonio. How can I go on living without knowing if they are fine? I will never be whole again until they are back in my life. That is why I cannot bear the thought of leaving Messina—even if it is just temporary as you say."

"Rosalia, I hate to say this, and I'm not saying I am completely giving up hope that you will find them someday, but you must be realistic as well. You must begin to realize that there is a chance you might not ever find them or learn what has happened to them. You need to reconcile yourself with that if it happens. You've been through so much, and you have survived. Please, stop punishing yourself for what that beast did to you. I can tell you feel you do not deserve happiness because of how your family suffered in your village. You feel like you are to blame for your father's losing business at his shop. And part of me even thinks you blame yourself for what Marco did to you—as if you could have somehow prevented it. Am I right?"

Rosalia nodded.

"Please, Rosalia. You can be fully happy again . . . with me. Maybe going to Paris would be the best thing for you. You can start over there. It might be easier for you to forget what happened to you if you were in a completely different place."

"I will *never* forget! And I will never give up on finding my family! How can you even say that to me? How can you still try to convince me to move to Paris with you after all that I have told you? After I have shared my heartbreak over losing my family? You are just thinking about yourself! You just want me for yourself—like Marco! You are no different from him."

Rosalia pulled herself out of his embrace, but Antonio held on to her arm tightly.

"Rosalia, you know that's not true. Please, do not compare me to the likes of that demon. You said so yourself that I was the complete opposite of him. You are just angry with me. This is not how you really feel."

"No, you're wrong, Antonio. This is how I feel. I should never have trusted another man again. You are all the same. You only think about what you want."

Tears slowly slid down Antonio's face. "I will let you be angry. You will realize it is your anger talking. I love you, and I know you know deep down in your heart that I am different and that you can trust me. You are the one who is guilty now of not being honest, not just with me but with yourself. You are afraid. That is the true reason why you don't want to marry me or even go to Paris for a short time. You are afraid of being fully happy again and of being fully loved again. You lost your family and no longer have their love in your life, but instead of accepting my love and all I have to give you, you are pushing me away."

Antonio let go of Rosalia's hand and stood up. "I will wait for your answer. If you realize you do love me and want to marry me, I will go to school in Messina. It would not be a sacrifice for me because you are what I want most. But I will not force you to do something against your wishes because no matter what you say, I am not Marco."

Antonio walked briskly away. Rosalia watched him. Part of her thought about running after him, but her legs felt leaden. Though her heart was breaking as she watched his figure move farther and farther away, she would not chase him. No. She would let him go.

∝ 22 ∝

Torta al Mandarino

TANGERINE CAKE

November 10, 2004

Claudia was standing outside the convent's kitchen, waiting for Sorella Agata to stop crying. She had become accustomed to catching the mother superior crying; it had happened several times in the month and a half since Claudia had arrived. And every time, it had been when Sorella Agata was whipping up one of her creations. Except for the first time, when Claudia had witnessed Sorella Agata crying while she was making her cannoli filling, Claudia had refrained from asking her why she was crying. She wasn't even convinced that the real reason for Sorella Agata's crying was the one she had given while she was making cannoli: because of Rosalia. Claudia had never been one to rely on intuition, but it was telling her now there was more to Sorella Agata's tears. Then again, Claudia had almost cried several times upon hearing all that poor Rosalia had gone through.

Claudia was beginning to get impatient. While she couldn't deny that Rosalia's story was intriguing, and she was beginning to see how the young woman's natural talent for baking would've inspired Sorella Agata, Claudia's stay here in Sicily would be over soon, and the mother superior still had not gotten to her part of the story. Whenever Claudia had tried to steer the conversation toward Sorella Agata's life, the nun would hold up her hand and say in Italian, "*Pazienza!* Patience!" She said it in a stern voice, which caused Claudia to heed the sister's wishes immediately.

The fragrance of sweet tangerines reached Claudia's nose. She saw Sorella Agata squeeze a tangerine into what looked like a cake batter. Immediately, Claudia's mouth watered. She'd never had a cake made out of tangerines. Orange, yes. She and her father had made both orange and lemon cakes throughout her childhood. Why hadn't either of them ever thought about making a cake out of tangerines? It was brilliant. For tangerines were even sweeter than oranges.

"Ah! Claudia!"

Sorella Agata stopped what she was doing and quickly patted her face with a kitchen towel, making sure to turn her back toward Claudia.

"I'm getting warm with the ovens turned on." She took off her apron and fanned her face with it. Claudia was surprised at the nun's small lie.

"Those tangerines smell wonderful, Sorella Agata. I take it you're making a cake?"

"*Sì. Torta al Mandarino.* This is the second most popular cake we sell at the shop after my famous *cassata* cake. It's very sweet, but most of the flavor comes from the ripest, juiciest tangerines in season and not from too much sugar."

Sorella Agata returned to squeezing the last of her tangerines. Then she stirred the batter. Her brows were knitted furiously in thought. At first, Claudia thought she was concentrating on her mixing, but then she saw her eyes fill with tears again. She batted her eyelashes, but one tear managed to slide down her face into the cake's batter.

Claudia pulled a paper towel off one of the dispensers that were scattered throughout the kitchen. She glanced toward the other workers, but no one seemed to notice that Sorella Agata was crying. She handed the paper towel to Sorella Agata.

"Ah. *Grazie,* Claudia. I'm sorry. I don't know what's come over me." She dabbed at her tears before adding, "Just a foolish old woman."

"You're not that old, Sister!"

"I'm getting there." She laughed.

"I don't mean to pry, Sorella Agata, but I must admit I have seen you cry several times, whenever you're alone baking. It seems as if something is weighing heavily on your mind. Sometimes it helps to talk, so if you want to unburden yourself, I'm here. I promise I wouldn't put anything confidential in our book."

Sorella Agata smiled and then patted Claudia's hand.

"You are so sweet, Claudia. *Grazie.* Nothing is weighing on my mind. I suppose it's all this talk of the past that has gotten to me. That's all."

Claudia nodded. "Rosalia's story is sad to hear. When I went to bed last night, I found myself tearing up, thinking about how she let Antonio go. I know you ended at that point last night, but I'm hoping you'll tell me she really didn't leave him. He sounded wonderful. Lord knows it's hard to find a good man like that nowadays."

"Eh. That is what I hear, but what would I know, being a woman of God?" Sorella Agata shrugged her shoulders, then looked at Claudia. They broke out into laughter.

"I needed that. So there isn't a handsome young man waiting for you back home in New York, Claudia? With your beauty, I would think you would have several admirers."

Claudia blushed slightly. "I'm afraid to say I don't date much. My focus has been on my career these past few years. I date here and there, but nothing serious."

"Do you want to get married and have children?"

"Yes. Someday. For the moment, I'm content burying myself in writing my books and tasting extraordinary food from chefs like yourself."

"I'm glad you have enjoyed our pastries."

"They are without question the best I've ever tasted. I have to say even a few of the pastries that I've had before, like the cannoli and several of the biscotti, surpass what I've had when I've tried them from Italian bakeries in New York or the shops in Messina. It's not just your *cassata* that stands apart. I'm surprised no one else has noticed or commented on that."

"A few of the other nuns and our customers have said there is something unique about many of our pastries." Sorella Agata looked thoughtful as she said this.

"But none of the chefs or food critics who have visited and sampled your other sweets commented on them?"

"No. They were mainly interested in the *cassata* because they'd heard so much about it. But again, Claudia, I follow my recipes, which have been passed down from nuns throughout the centuries. You've watched me as I've made the pastries that will appear in our book, and you've reviewed my recipe book. So you know I am not hiding anything."

Claudia wanted to say that while she had watched Sorella Agata make her pastries, she had yet to watch her make the *cassata*. The *Minni della Vergine,* the miniature *cassatas* she had sampled, had been made by the other workers. Claudia was always sure to ask them who had made the miniature *cassatas* that day. She couldn't help wondering how much better Sorella Agata's *Minni della Vergine* were, since the *cassatas* she had tasted that were baked by the pastry shop's other workers were phenomenal. But it was as if Sorella Agata didn't want Claudia to taste *her* miniature *cassatas.*

Deciding to bite her tongue and wait to bring it up at a later date when she would finally be able to watch Sorella Agata make her famous *cassata,* Claudia merely said, "Yes, it doesn't appear as if you're hiding anything. Perhaps it's this place. There's some sort of magic in the air." She smiled, winking at Sorella Agata. But the nun didn't seem amused or realize that she was only joking. Instead, she looked very tired.

"We could take a break today, Sister. Why don't we just focus on the last of the recipes that will be featured in the book? You can resume Rosalia's story tomorrow."

"Well, I'm afraid that was the end of the story last night. At least, Rosalia's story."

"What? How can that be? You still haven't reached the part of the story telling how she was your greatest influence when it came to your pastry making. Did she marry Antonio? Did he stay in Sicily as he promised he would if she married him?"

Sorella Agata took a deep breath, but didn't answer Claudia. She poured the tangerine cake batter into an eight-inch cake pan, tapped it a few times on the counter to ensure it was even, and then walked over to the oven. After placing the pan in the oven, she looked up at the clock that hung high on the wall, near the ceiling. Claudia was still amazed that she never used a timer and always managed to remember when it was time to check on her baking. In the weeks since Claudia had arrived, she'd never once witnessed the mother superior burning anything.

"Let's get some espresso and go into the sitting room. We can talk more in there since it looks like we're going to get rain soon, so I'd rather not sit out in the courtyard."

"That would be nice."

Claudia helped Sorella Agata pour the espresso into two cups, and they each took a slice of plain sponge cake as well. They always had the sponge cake on a few biscotti with their espresso. Claudia's clothes were getting tight, and she knew she'd have to step up her workout routine once she got home. She'd hardly exercised here besides going for long walks and treating herself once to a swim at the local beach. But for some reason, she wasn't fretting as she would've done back home. The convent's serenity and the beautiful Sicilian landscape had done wonders in calming her nervous nature. She knew sadly though that once she returned to New York City, her stressful routine would resume.

Following Sorella Agata into the convent's sitting room, Claudia took a seat in the armchair opposite a small settee, where Sorella Agata sat.

"I must thank you, Claudia, for bearing with me. I know it hasn't been easy for you, listening to my long story about Rosalia."

"That's all right, Sister."

"So let's see. We left off in the summer of 1956. Six years later, Rosalia did get married, but not to Antonio. . . ."

❧ 23 ❧

Olivette di Sant' Agata

SAINT AGATHA'S LITTLE OLIVES

May 20, 1962
Cathedral Church of Santa Lucia del Mela

Rosalia adjusted her veil as she stood at the altar. The pins used to hold her veil in place were digging into her scalp. She was nervous, but it was a different kind of nervous. Though today would be the last day of the life she had known, it would also be the start of a new life. The woman she had known all these years would now become someone else: Sorella Agata.

Today, Rosalia would take her vows to become a bride of Christ. These last four years, the time it took for her to complete her training to become a nun, had been filled with deep introspection and reflection. She had not entered into this decision lightly. Two years after Antonio had left, she had received God's calling to become a nun, and since then, she'd had no reservations that this was her destined path. After her failed relationship with Antonio, she had no desire to fall in love again, and she had grown to love living at the convent, bonding with the women there, and learning how to make the finest pastries.

As she stood with the other novitiates from the entire city of Santa

Lucia del Mela, waiting to take their vows, her thoughts turned to Antonio. If she had remained engaged to him, she would have been standing at this altar in a long lace dress, committing herself to him rather than to God. Once again, life had surprised her—although this time she had been the one to decide what course it would follow. She had chosen not to stay with Antonio, just as she had chosen to become a novitiate and devote herself fully to God and His work. She wondered what Antonio would think if he knew that she had decided to become a nun. He would be shocked, yes, just like Madre Carmela, Anunziata, Mari, and almost everyone else at the convent had been when she'd shared with them her intentions. The only one who hadn't been shocked was Elisabetta.

Surprisingly, Elisabetta had taken the place of Teresa and become Rosalia's good friend. Rosalia had confided in Elisabetta when she first began to consider the idea of becoming a nun. Rosalia knew that Elisabetta would not judge since she, too, was planning on taking vows. Naturally, Elisabetta had been upset when she learned that Teresa and Francesco had eloped, and she had refused to see her sister when she came by to visit after her nuptials. It took Elisabetta a few months to finally write back to Teresa, and it had been too late. Teresa had stopped writing to Elisabetta. Rosalia had convinced Elisabetta to go visit Teresa, but when she and Elisabetta went to the small house that the newlyweds had been renting from a widow, they were informed the couple had moved. Rosalia was hurt that Teresa had also stopped keeping in touch with her and that she could so easily discard their friendship as well as her relationship with her sister. Was Francesco's love all Teresa really needed? This was unlike Rosalia, who had rejected Antonio and chosen to wait in Messina in hopes of her family's returning.

Though it had been six years since Antonio had moved to Paris, Rosalia's heart winced when she thought about him. True, she still cared for him, but she did not long for him as she had when they were engaged. Shortly after he left, Antonio had kept his word and written, letting her know his address and phone number. He never pressured or asked Rosalia if she had changed her mind and would be returning to him, but she knew he was still waiting for her. How she had wanted to write him back and tell him she was sorry for what she'd said to him that day in the jasmine field. Though he had told her he knew deep down in her heart she didn't really think he was like Marco, she should have told him that. But she also knew she couldn't encourage him. And that was why she never wrote back to him. She had also wanted to tell him how proud she was of him. It was as if Madre Carmela could read Rosalia's mind whenever she gave her updates about Antonio. On the one hand, it was painful for Rosalia to hear about him, but on the other, she was curious to hear if his dream of becoming a chef was coming true. But eventually, Antonio stopped writing altogether. A little more than a year after his leaving Sicily, Antonio's letters to Rosalia ceased. Even Madre's letters grew further apart until she also never heard from him again.

Rosalia's heart had ached terribly, and to try to forget the pain, she had thrown herself even more into her baking. It wasn't long before her pastries sold better with the shop's customers than the same pastries that were made by the other workers. And the questions about her methods began. The other workers couldn't quite figure out why Rosalia's pastries tasted better than theirs even though she was following the same recipes they'd been using for years. Rosalia had felt self-conscious, but Madre Carmela had told her not to pay any mind to the other workers and to just continue to do the fine work she was doing in the kitchen.

Antonio. How she had missed him while she made her recipes, missed having him beside her as they shared their friendly rivalry. She had always felt that he'd made her work better. But now she had to just remember his words of encouragement while she created her pastries alone—though she wasn't truly alone but was surrounded by all the other pastry shop workers. Still. It had been different with Antonio. She prayed for him every day and hoped he was happy. She even prayed that he had found another woman who could do right by him and love him fully. He deserved that after the way she'd hurt him.

"Are you ready, Rosalia?"

Madre Carmela came up to Rosalia and took her hands in her own.

"*Sì,* Madre."

This would probably be the last time someone would address her by her christened name. Rosalia. She felt a quick flash of sadness since that name naturally reminded her of her past: her past with her family, the tragedies she had endured, and finally the time she'd spent with the only boy she had ever loved and would ever love. She was ready to shed her old life and move forward with her new one. But Rosalia also realized that she needed to honor the woman she once had been, along with all the good and bad that had been a part of her life. She had decided to choose Agata for her new name. Saint Agatha was the patron saint of rape victims, so it was fitting for Rosalia to choose her name.

"I have a surprise for you," Madre Carmela said in a low voice, glancing over her shoulder to make sure no one heard her.

She reached into the pocket of her habit, keeping her hand curled as she drew it out. She then placed it in the pocket of Rosalia's habit.

"What are you doing?" Rosalia whispered.

"It's a little celebratory treat for you. For after the ceremony. It's natural to be nervous. I was nervous when I took my vows. Once the ceremony is over, and when you're alone, you can see what I gave you." Madre Carmela winked before taking her leave of Rosalia.

She had no time to wonder what Madre Carmela had placed in her pocket. The ceremony was beginning. Rosalia shifted her thoughts and focused on the proceedings. She prayed with her fellow novitiates as they went through the customs of the solemn ceremony: lying prostrate before the altar; pronouncing their final vows as they promised to follow a life of poverty, chastity, and obedience; accepting the ring that she would wear forever on her right hand; and finally, the last rite that would make her a bride of Christ—wearing a crown of thorns to symbolize that, like Christ, she would welcome the sufferings of the Lord and follow in His selfless example.

The crown was placed on her head. She was now Sorella Agata.

One by one, Madre and the other sisters from the convent, as well as Anunziata, Mari, Lidia, and Elisabetta—who had taken her vows last year and was now Sorella Lucia—came over and congratulated her.

"*Auguri,* Sorella Agata."

It was strange to hear her new name and title. But she liked how it sounded. She was sure it must have been odd for her friends to see her now dressed as a nun and to become accustomed to calling her by a different name.

Once they returned to the convent and had a celebratory dinner, Sorella Agata excused herself. She needed some time alone. The enormity of the occasion was beginning to settle on her.

She closed the door to her bedroom and sat on the bed. A few moments passed while she simply stared at herself in a small hand-held mirror. Gone was her long, lustrous black hair. It had been shorn the night before. The few dresses she had possessed she had given to Anunziata.

She stood up and looked down at her long habit. Smoothing wrinkles down the front and sides, she felt a few marble-sized objects in her pocket—Madre Carmela's gift for her.

Reaching into her pocket, Sorella Agata pulled out a handful of small objects that looked like candy, but upon closer inspection she saw they were marzipan, shaped like little green olives.

"*Olivette di Sant' Agata,*" Sorella Agata said aloud to herself and smiled.

Along with the Virgin's Breasts miniature *cassatas* that were made in honor of Saint Agatha and for her feast day, Saint Agatha's Little Olives were also made to celebrate the saint. There was a legend that, when Saint Agatha realized she could no longer escape death, she grasped the branch of a sterile olive tree, and because of the contact made with her hand, the tree became fertile, blossoming and bearing fruit.

Tears filled her eyes. Madre Carmela had thought of the perfect gift. And to think Sorella Agata had ever thought that Madre had betrayed her by encouraging Antonio to apply to culinary school in Paris. Sorella Agata felt ashamed and remembered how she had unleashed her anger on the poor mother superior years ago, after Antonio had told her that Madre had been instrumental in his decision to still apply to Le Cordon Bleu. Days later when she'd come to her senses, she had apologized to Madre Carmela. But Madre had told her there was no need to do so.

Sorella Agata popped one of the Saint Agatha olive marzipans into her mouth. She closed her eyes, savoring their sweet flavor. At least she would not be forced to give up pastries in her new life as a nun.

～ 24 ～

Biscottini da Tè

LITTLE TEA COOKIES

November 10, 2004

Claudia was shocked. Rosalia and Sorella Agata were one and the same. Why hadn't it occurred to her before? How stupid had she been? Of course, it all made sense now. She should have realized it all along. After all, why would Sorella Agata have gone on and on about this young woman who discovered she loved to bake as much as the nuns who mentored her and also realized she had a knack for creating the most wonderful pastries?

"So you are Rosalia."

"Yes, Claudia. I am, although I haven't been Rosalia for half my life now. Not since I took my vows and became Sorella Agata."

"Why didn't you tell me at the start of your story? No wonder I couldn't find anyone working at the convent by that name, and whenever I asked one of the other sisters or the lay workers about Rosalia, they all just shook their heads as if they had no idea who she was. But they all knew."

"Well, not all of them. Mainly the older sisters know, and I suppose a few of the younger ones must know as well. But many of our current lay workers were not with me when I was learning from Madre Carmela, so they do not know about my past. Elisabetta, who was a lay worker when I was apprenticing in the shop, naturally knows. If you remember what I told you, she was in the process of becoming a nun and has remained at the Convento di Santa Lucia."

"Which one is she?"

"Sorella Lucia."

"The cook?"

"*Si*. She discovered she preferred cooking savory foods rather than sweet, and, after becoming a nun, she followed our old cook around. Once the old cook died, Sorella Lucia took her place."

"So the other nuns kept your secret."

"Naturally. I am their mother superior, and as such, they must obey me."

"You asked them not to tell me that you were Rosalia?"

"No, I didn't. But they know better than to talk about me behind my back." Sorella Agata smiled mischievously as she took a bite out of her sponge cake.

Claudia couldn't help noticing that Sorella Agata seemed more relaxed than she had been since Claudia had first started interviewing her. Why had she been so nervous to tell Claudia about her past and to admit that she was Rosalia?

As if reading Claudia's mind, Sorella Agata said, "I'm sorry that I didn't tell you sooner. I had my reasons. You see, I wasn't even sure if I was going to tell you about my past. So I thought it would be better not to tell you right away that I was Rosalia, in case I changed my mind and decided not to tell you the entire story. It has been very painful, reliving my youth and all that I endured. I have pushed my pain away as much as I can, and I thought if it became unbearable, I would just stop."

"So what convinced you to tell me?"

"I thought it was time to try to put all of this behind me. While I have moved forward with my life as best I can, my past still weighs heavily on my mind. I was surprised to see that once I started telling you my story, it poured out of me, and then I couldn't stop, although every day I contemplated holding back."

Claudia thought for a few moments before speaking.

"What about your family? Did you ever find them or at least find out what had become of them? And did you ever see Antonio again? You mentioned you didn't become a nun until six years later. May I ask what led you to such a . . ." Claudia caught herself before she offended Sorella Agata.

". . . a drastic decision. You can say it, Claudia. It's all right. You're not the only one to have said that my choice to become a bride of Christ was a drastic one."

"It must've been a shock to everyone at the convent that you would decide to become a nun, especially since you had been engaged to Antonio and they all knew this."

"Yes. But it really shouldn't have come as a shock to them. In the two years since Antonio had left, I had been praying more and attending all the Masses with the sisters, not just the few that the lay workers were expected to attend. And then there was my service work."

"Your service work?"

"I suppose I should pick up from where I left off last night, after Antonio stormed away from Rosalia. For a few weeks, Antonio tried to persuade Rosalia—or rather me—to change my mind about not wishing to marry him anymore. But it was no use. I was so angry that he expected me to go off to Paris with him and forget about my family."

"It didn't sound like he expected you to forget about them, Sister."

"I know that now." Sorella Agata spoke quietly. "And I think part of me knew it then, too, but it was easier for me to remain mad at him. For if I stopped being mad, I was afraid I would relent and marry him."

"And would that have been so terrible? You loved him."

"I did. But I felt I wasn't worthy of him."

"Because of Marco's raping you?"

"Yes. As I told Antonio, I didn't think I would make a suitable wife to him or any man because my virginity had been compromised. You have to understand, Claudia, this was the 1950s. People thought differently then, especially about rape. You remember what I told you? When I was younger, I had heard similar stories to mine, about young women who were kidnapped, raped, and then expected to marry their rapists. It was barbaric. But that was the custom, although I still firmly believe that if my parents had known that Marco had raped me, they would not have allowed me to marry him. They were different. But then again, it appeared as if my father believed the lies in the letter Marco forced me to write. So maybe my father would have wanted me to wed Marco? I can't say for certain. But I'd rather hold on to my belief that he wouldn't have wanted that."

Claudia looked at Sorella Agata. Although she was up there in years and had had a world of experience, Claudia could still detect some innocence in her eyes—and a deep sadness. She tried to picture what Sorella Agata must've looked like when she was the young Rosalia with lustrous black hair hanging down to her waist.

"It is good to hold on to your beliefs, even when you don't know if they're true or not. After all, that is what has helped keep you going all these years. Am I not right, Sister?"

"I like to think so." She gave Claudia a small smile before taking a sip of her espresso.

"Anyway, for weeks, Antonio tried in vain to convince me to still marry him. But I wouldn't even talk to him. He would plead with me, and I wouldn't say a word." Sorella Agata closed her eyes, forcing back tears. "I was quite mean to him, Claudia. I did my best to scowl and completely ignore him. Finally, I got my wish. He gave up. The last time he communicated with me before he left for Paris was in a letter."

Sorella Agata reached into the deep pockets of her habit. Claudia couldn't help remembering how Madre Carmela had always done this and produced marzipan fruit for Rosalia to eat in hopes of comforting her. Claudia wondered if perhaps Sorella Agata had adopted Madre Carmela's practice and was going to take a few marzipan fruit from her pocket and pop one into her mouth. But instead of the delicate, perfect-looking sweets, Sorella Agata pulled out an envelope.

"You carry Antonio's letter with you?"

"Of course not. I knew I was going to share with you today that I am Rosalia, and I wanted to read his letter to you."

Sorella Agata took another sip of espresso before clearing her throat and beginning Antonio's letter.

Dear Rosalia,

Since you refuse to talk to me, I have no choice but to accept your decision that you no longer wish to be with me. I will not force you to do something against your will for I am not like Marco as you accused me of being. Again, I know deep in your heart you really do not think that. I only hope in time you come to realize that I truly love you. If you have a change of heart, I have left the address where I will be staying in Paris with Madre Carmela. Once I arrive there, I will send a phone number where you can reach me as well. But if you decide to stand by your word and not return to me, I understand and wish you nothing but the best in your life. I will continue to pray for you and hope that you and your family are reunited someday. But what I pray most for, Rosalia, is that you find inner peace— no matter what the outcome may be regarding your family. You have been to hell and back, and I can see you are still punishing yourself for everything that's happened to you. I'm afraid you will never allow yourself the happiness you deserve.

May God look after you and bless you.

Love always,

Your Antonio

Sorella Agata's voice caught at the end. She quickly blinked her eyes, and her face looked flushed. Claudia remembered that was Rosalia's trait—blushing so easily.

Claudia stood up and went over to the window. She was crying, but didn't want to upset Sorella Agata. It was too sad. Poor Antonio. And poor Sorella Agata.

"Please, Claudia. Don't cry. I'm really all right."

Claudia shook her head as she wiped her tears with the back of her hand before returning to her chair. "I just can't imagine how difficult that must've been for you, turning the man you loved away like that. I know you were afraid, and your desire to wait and see if your family came back to Messina was greater than your desire to be with Antonio, but still. I don't know. It just seems like you sacrificed so much, and like Antonio said, you punished yourself severely."

"In spite of everything, Claudia, I have had a very rewarding life. I have found happiness, although not in the traditional sense for a young woman from my generation. True, I didn't marry and have children, but God had other plans for me. I have found such fulfillment in both my work at the pastry shop and my community service. And there's something you don't know about me, Claudia."

"Another secret?" Claudia asked incredulously.

"A small one, and it's not really a secret. I just didn't get to that part of my story yet. I founded a women's shelter in town. Remember I told you when we met that I planned on donating the proceeds of the book to an organization that did tremendous work in the community? It will be to this shelter. I no longer run it, but I still visit regularly and assist in whatever way I can, mainly counseling the women now."

Claudia shook her head. "You've managed to amaze me once again, Sister. But I suppose it makes sense that you would want to help women after what happened to you when you were young."

"Yes. So God had plans for me, and I am only too happy to serve Him and those I have helped and will continue to help. This work, along with my work in the pastry shop, has given such meaning to my life." Sorella Agata paused, as if she was trying to remember something.

"I'm sorry, Claudia, but in addition to the tangerine cake, I also have a tray of *Biscottini da Tè* that are in the oven. I'll bring a few back with me so we can have them nice and hot." Sorella Agata smiled as she stood up and left the sitting room.

Claudia had thought about telling her she wasn't hungry, and besides it was late and almost time for bed. How much could one eat before going to bed? But the smile the nun had given her made Claudia bite her tongue. She reached for her belt buckle on her jeans and unclasped it, loosening it to the next notch as she mentally shook her head. The convent didn't even possess a scale, so

Claudia had no idea how much weight she'd gained in the past few weeks. She would just have to deal with it when she returned home to New York.

The aroma from the *Biscottini da Tè* reached Claudia's nose. Her thoughts returned to Sorella Agata's incredible story. She wondered if Sorella Agata would allow her to write about it in their book. Claudia was certain their readers would find the story fascinating, and the book would be about so much more than just the recipes. People would not only get to know the amazing person behind these extraordinary desserts, but they would also learn how the pastries had saved Sorella Agata's life when she was young and inspired her in her work. But Claudia would not pressure Sorella Agata to include her backstory if she didn't want to. Sorella Agata had been through enough in her life.

Sorella Agata returned with the promised plate of just-baked tea cookies. They were braided and looked like nothing more than simple cookies that would be good for dunking in tea or even in a cold glass of milk.

"They were ready as I suspected." Sorella Agata placed the plate of cookies on the coffee table and, before Claudia could protest, she placed three of the *Biscottini da Tè* on her plate.

Claudia frowned, but again remained silent. She took one of the cookies and bit into its crumbly texture. Though the cookie looked deceptively simple, it imparted a sweet flavor that was immediately addictive. Once again, as with many of the other desserts Claudia had sampled that were baked by Sorella Agata, there was an essence of something she couldn't quite put her finger on.

"You've done it again, Sorella Agata! These biscotti are beyond delicious."

"*Grazie.*" Sorella Agata shrugged her shoulders dismissively before saying, "It's from many years of perfecting my craft."

"Yes, I guess so." Though Claudia agreed with the nun, she still believed there was more to Sorella Agata's extraordinary sweets, but she had beaten the subject to death. Perhaps after she finally watched her make her *cassata*—that is, if Sorella Agata ever decided to make it in Claudia's presence—Claudia could simply accept that perhaps she and the rest of the world would never find out the cake's secret.

"Sorella Agata, I know it's been painful for you to tell me about your past. But I still have so many questions. If you don't mind, I'd like to hear the rest of your story. Tell me more about how you came to found the women's shelter."

"Very well. But first let me make more espresso. We're going to be up late. It's quite a long story."

25

Krapfen

CREAM-FILLED DOUGHNUTS

First two weeks in August, 1962

Just as Rosalia had been eager to learn the art of pastry making, now, as Sorella Agata, she was eager to find ways to serve God and those in need. She accompanied Madre Carmela in her visits to the local hospitals, orphanages, and sanitariums. While Sorella Agata found the work rewarding and she felt compassion for all those she came into contact with, she couldn't help feeling there was something else waiting for her. And she discovered what that was one day when she was in the village, shopping for supplies, and took a wrong turn down an alleyway.

"Excuse me, Sorella. Can you spare some change?"

An old bedraggled woman came out of the shadows, startling Sorella Agata. The woman wore a tattered sundress and held a crumpled-up straw hat to her chest. Her eyes looked vacant and sad.

"Of course." Sorella Agata reached into the pockets of her habit and gave the woman two *lire*.

Though Sorella Agata had been warned about beggars and pickpockets, and she did feel her heart skip a beat walking down this quiet alleyway, she couldn't refuse someone in need, especially an old woman. The woman nodded her head and turned around, shuffling away. She limped, and Sorella Agata noticed she wore only one sandal.

"Please wait, *signora!*" Sorella Agata called out to her.

The woman turned around, surprise etched across her hollow expression.

"What did you call me, Sorella?"

"*Signora.* I wanted to give you something else that you might like." Sorella Agata reached into her pocket once again, and this time produced two small watermelon-shaped marzipan fruit.

Like Madre Carmela, Sorella Agata had now taken to carrying sweets in the pockets of her habit. She couldn't resist the custom since she'd always enjoyed it when Madre had surprised her with a treat. Besides marzipan fruit, Sorella Agata also carried cookies. She loved to surprise children with the sweets whenever she ran into a group of them playing on the street. The little girls always made her think about her younger sister, Cecilia.

The old lady's eyes lit up when she saw the marzipan. She reached out to take them, but before doing so looked at Sorella Agata as if asking her if she were really certain she wanted to give these treasures away. Sorella Agata nodded her head, imploring the woman to take the marzipan.

"*Grazie,* Sorella. You are too kind."

The lady took a bite of the marzipan and closed her eyes, chewing the pastry slowly. Looking at the emaciated body of the woman, Sorella Agata thought she would have wolfed down both of the marzipan fruit in an instant.

"*Delizioso!* I remember when my husband used to treat me to these for my birthday every year."

Tears filled the woman's eyes. Instead of eating the second watermelon marzipan fruit, she placed it in her straw hat. Then, she looked over her shoulder, ensuring no one had seen.

"May I ask you, *signora,* where your husband is?"

"You keep calling me *signora.* No one has called me that in quite some time. My husband died ten years ago. After that, my life died along with him. I've been living on the streets since."

"You have no children?"

"No. God never blessed me with those, I'm afraid. But I don't want you feeling sorry for me, Sorella. Feel sorry for the young women who were forced to run away from home because of abuse they suffered by their own parents or for the women who were forced to leave their husbands who beat them. Their lives are still ahead of them, but they are wasting away on these streets. I, on the other hand, had my life, and I'm grateful to God I had some happiness when I was younger. My husband was a good man. But after he died, I couldn't find any work."

"I'm so sorry, *signora*. May I ask what your name is?"

"Giuseppina, but everyone calls me Peppina."

"I am Sorella Agata. I am with the Carmelite order of nuns. I will keep you in my prayers, and perhaps I can come again and visit you?"

"That would be nice, Sorella, although I don't know if your prayers will do any good for me anymore. It might be better you don't waste them on me, and instead pray for the younger women here."

Sorella Agata looked down the narrow alleyway, but it was deserted. Where were these other women Peppina talked about?

"I was wondering, Peppina, could you take me to where the other women are?"

She shrugged her shoulders. "If you like. You've been very kind to me. It's the least I can do."

Sorella Agata followed Peppina, who walked very slowly. She wanted to ask the old woman if it might be easier for her to take off her one sandal so her gait would be even when she walked, but she was afraid of offending her. The convent collected clothes from the villagers every month. When she returned home, she would have to see if there were shoes in the collection that might fit Peppina.

Peppina turned right, down an even narrower alleyway than the one they had come from. The glow from a lantern could be seen in the distance. Sorella Agata noticed the sky was getting darker. She should have taken her leave of Peppina and hurried back to the convent before it got dark. Madre Carmela would be worried about her. But her curiosity about the other homeless women was too great to ignore. She needed to see with her own eyes how these women were living.

Soon, one by one, women came out from the shadows. Each of them stopped when they saw Sorella Agata. No doubt her habit had caught their attention. The ages of the women ran from as old as their sixties and seventies to as young as their early teens, maybe even preteens. Sorella Agata was shocked to see that most of the homeless were these younger girls. Suddenly, the image of herself when she crawled outside the cave where Marco had taken her flashed before her eyes. She remembered how her own clothes had been torn and how afraid she had been. These girls' eyes held the same empty stare Peppina's eyes held, but there was something else present in their eyes—utter despair. She could see in their faces they had no hope. To be that young and have no hopes for the future—it was horrible. In that moment, Sorella Agata realized once again how fortunate she had been to have Madre Carmela and the life she'd given her at the convent. True, she had lost her family, but she had gained another one with the sisters and the lay workers at the convent. These young women had no one but one another.

Though the women looked at her, no one approached Sorella Agata. She kept a respectful distance. They seemed to lose interest in her and gathered in a circle by the lantern. An older woman approached the group. She held a loaf of bread. She broke pieces of the bread off and handed them to the women. Peppina left Sorella Agata's side and waited for her piece of bread. She held her straw hat so that the brims were folded in toward each other. Sorella Agata had no doubt she did so to ensure the watermelon marzipan remained hidden from view. She couldn't help noting that Peppina was like a child who didn't want to part with her prize.

Sorella Agata jumped when she felt a hand tap her shoulder.

"I'm sorry. I didn't mean to frighten you. Are you lost?"

Sorella Agata turned around and was face-to-face with a striking young woman who looked to be about fifteen or sixteen years old.

"I was, but I met Peppina, and she told me about all of you. I wanted to come by to see if I could offer some assistance. My name is Sorella Agata."

"My name is Lucrezia. Did you bring food with you?"

Lucrezia looked at the burlap bags Sorella Agata carried on each of her shoulders. She then realized with embarrassment that she was carrying groceries and baking supplies, and all she had offered Peppina were two small marzipan fruit. Sorella Agata looked at the women, each eating her one small piece of bread and taking turns drinking from a bucket of water that held a ladle. Without hesitation, she took the bags off her shoulders and reached inside, pulling out an apricot from the two dozen she'd bought to make a pie. She handed it to Lucrezia.

"Come. I have more food for you and the others."

Sorella Agata walked toward the other women. She took out the rest of the apricots as well as several round loaves of bread and various other produce. She even had a large jar of anchovies. Sorella Agata kept unloading the contents of her burlap bags until they were empty. The women gathered around her, talking excitedly. Even the older women had gleeful expressions, as if they were children waiting for La Befana to hand out her gifts for the Feast of the Epiphany.

"I brought her here! Me! I knew she would be good luck." Peppina spoke loudly above the din, pointing to her chest.

No one seemed to care that Peppina was responsible for bringing Sorella Agata to their group. They were too hungry and dazed from their sudden windfall of having more than a piece of bread for dinner that night.

A few of the women thanked Sorella Agata and shyly told her their names. Her heart swelled upon seeing how grateful they seemed and how for that brief moment their sorrowful faces looked content.

"I promise I will come back," Sorella Agata said as she began to walk away.

The women followed her down the dark alleyway.

"Be careful, Sister. May God bless you. Thank you for feeding us tonight." A few of the women called out to her as she finally parted ways with them.

One of the younger girls, who looked to be twelve or thirteen years old, ran up to Sorella Agata. "When will you come back?"

"Tomorrow. I'll come back tomorrow."

* * *

The next day, Sorella Agata returned, but Madre Carmela had insisted on accompanying her. While she had been upset at first that Sorella Agata had given away all of their groceries, she understood why she had done so. When they arrived at the alleyway, no one was in sight. Sorella Agata began to think she had gone down the wrong alley, but then the women slowly came out from their hiding places, one by one as they had done the previous night. Whom were they hiding from? Did anyone else know about their living here, hidden in the shadows?

Madre Carmela began handing out the food they were able to spare from their kitchen. Sorella Agata had a special treat for them. That morning she had fried batches of *Krapfen,* cream-filled doughnuts. While they weren't as elaborate as marzipan, the fried balls of airy dough filled with pastry cream were just as decadent tasting when one bit into them.

"*Che buono!* So good!" many of the women chanted after tasting the *Krapfen.*

After handing out their food, Madre Carmela and Sorella Agata were about to take their leave when the women invited them to stay longer.

A few of them opened up about their past lives. The older women had mainly fallen on hard times after their spouses died. But one woman, Gabriella, spat out, "My louse of a husband left me for a younger woman; he moved her into our house and then threw me out. And my son sided with his father out of fear of being disinherited. So much for marrying a wealthy man."

Everyone laughed at her last statement, but Sorella Agata could see Gabriella was still seething.

"My mother died when I was born. And then my father was killed in an accident at the mill. My uncle took me in, but then he started doing things to me. I ran away from home. I was working on the streets for a few years until Peppina found me and brought me here."

"And what is your name?" Madre Carmela asked the young woman, who looked to be in her early twenties.

"Donatella."

"Are you still working on . . . on the streets?" Sorella Agata managed to ask her.

"Sometimes." Donatella's gaze didn't meet Sorella Agata's. "But at least now I decide when I want the work. Where I was staying before I met Peppina, I had no choice but to work all the time."

Sorella Agata gathered the young woman had been living in a brothel before. Her heart ached for her lost innocence. Finding her courage once again, she asked, "How many of you are working on the streets like Donatella?"

Of the dozen women who stood before them, half raised their hands—all of them were the younger women, in their teens to twenties.

"And the rest of you?" Madre asked, directing her gaze toward the older women.

"We're ashamed to admit this to women of God such as you, but we steal what we can here and there. But we have rules. No stealing from women and no stealing from families. We mainly steal from stores and restaurants or from men who look like they are rich. They won't notice a few *lire* anyway." Peppina elbowed Gabriella, and they laughed along with the other women. Even Madre and Sorella Agata laughed.

"I suppose one must do what is necessary to survive. I'm sure if you pray to God and ask for His forgiveness, He shall grant it," Madre said.

The women lowered their heads, and a few made the sign of the cross as if Madre had bestowed a blessing upon or granted forgiveness to them.

Finally, Madre Carmela and Sorella Agata took their leave. As Sorella Agata had done the previous night, Madre promised they would return, but she told them it might be a few days until they could come back. Immediately, Sorella Agata saw the disappointed expressions on the women's faces. It hurt her greatly to see their pain.

On the way back to the convent, Madre Carmela talked about the pastries that would need to be made that week, but Sorella Agata was only half listening. She couldn't stop thinking about the women, especially the younger women who had been forced to prostitute themselves to survive. If only she could find a way to convince them to leave that life behind. But where would they go?

Over the course of the next two weeks, Sorella Agata made it her mission to visit the women every day. It was difficult for her to get away on a few of the days, particularly without Madre Carmela's noticing. Although Madre didn't mind that she visited the women every few days or so, she made Sorella Agata promise never to go alone, for she was worried about her safety, especially on her return home from that seedier part of town where the homeless women lived. But Sorella Agata had been unable to find someone who was free to escort her, and the thought of disappointing those women, even for a day, greatly distressed her. So she took her chances and snuck out of the convent, placing her faith in God to keep her safe as she made her way down the deserted dark alleys. Seeing the pleased looks on the women's faces every time she showed up was enough, for Sorella Agata, to justify taking the risk. She had never felt a sense of fulfillment as she did when she fed the women and offered words of encouragement to them. A few had even asked if they could pray with her.

One evening, as Sorella Agata made her way back out of the alleyway, she almost ran into a man. When she looked up into his face, Sorella Agata almost screamed. For she had seen that face in her nightmares. But it couldn't be. The man who stood before her looked like the same man who had changed her life forever—Marco.

"*Mi scusi,* Sorella." The man tipped his hat and hurried off, down the dark alleyway that led to where the homeless women lived.

Sorella Agata's heart pounded against her chest. She felt like she was going to faint. Walking over to the wall, she held on to it, steadying herself. Was it really Marco? It had been seven years since the last time she'd seen him. That would make him thirty years old now. The man she'd seen had looked like he could be in his late thirties, but hadn't she always heard that a life filled with evil aged one prematurely? Though Rosalia was now twenty-four, everyone told her she looked as young as she had when they'd first met her. Even the homeless women from the alley did not believe she was in her mid-twenties.

If it was Marco, he hadn't recognized her in her nun's habit. And it was getting dark. She then realized he was headed toward where her new friends resided. Fear beat through her again, but this time it wasn't for her but for the women she'd come to care for in such a short amount of time. She walked quickly back down the alley, looking for Marco, but he was nowhere in sight. When she reached the spot where the women usually stayed, she saw a few of them talking among themselves, but no one who looked like the man she'd seen was present.

"Did you forget something, Sorella?" Gabriella came up behind her.

"I thought I saw a man I once knew making his way here. Did you see a man about six feet tall, in his thirties, with a brown hat?"

"I did see someone who matched that description, but he turned down that other alleyway." Gabriella pointed to another alley that eventually led out to the main street.

"Have you seen him before?"

Gabriella shook her head.

"Do any of the men who are . . ." She searched her mind for the right word. "Do any of the men who are clients of the young girls who work on the streets ever come here?"

"No. The girls have been instructed never to let them know where they live. They are extra careful to make sure they aren't followed when they're returning home. They understand this is a safe haven for them, and as such, they must protect it at all costs. Who is this man? You seem to be frightened of him, Sorella Agata."

"I think I was mistaken. That's all. He looked a lot like someone I once knew. I just wanted to know if he lived near here. Please, don't worry, and don't say anything to anyone else. I don't want to alarm them unnecessarily. I should be going, Gabriella. It's very late. *Buona notte.*"

"*Buona notte.* Be careful, Sorella."

Sorella Agata felt a chill even though she was wearing her long habit and it was a muggy August night. Madre Carmela had been right to insist she be escorted whenever coming to the alleyway. Quickly making her way back to the convent, Sorella Agata prayed the man she had seen was not Marco.

❧ 26 ❧

Croccantini

CRISPY HAZELNUT MERINGUES

Sixteen months later . . .
December 18, 1963

Of all the sweets the pastry shop created, Sorella Agata's least favorite were *Croccantini*. She wanted to like the crispy hazelnut meringues and had tried to convince herself every time she made them that this would be the magical time that she would finally love them. But it never worked. On the other hand, the shop's patrons went crazy for them, and although she didn't like them personally, she had trained her palate so she could detect the way the egg whites, honey, sugar, vanilla, and cinnamon batter should taste.

Sorella Agata carefully wrapped the *Croccantini* in waxed paper and then placed them in a large cake box. She was going to take them to the patients in the hospital in town where she volunteered once a month. She stepped outside and walked over to her bicycle. Placing her box of meringues in the basket that sat in front of her bike's handlebars, she adjusted her habit so that she could comfortably pedal. As she pedaled into town, Sorella Agata thought about how much she had to be thankful for this year for Christmas, which was just a week away. She couldn't believe it was just sixteen months ago when she'd met the homeless women living in the alleyway. And she couldn't believe that six months after she'd met them, she had converted the abandoned chapel, where Antonio used to sleep, into living quarters for all twelve of the homeless women.

The idea of having the women come live with them had sprouted in Sorella Agata's mind as winter began to set in last year; all she could think about was how uncomfortable the women would be living outside. Although the winter months in Sicily weren't as unbearable as in other countries, it would still not be comfortable. But it wasn't just the winter months she was thinking about. She couldn't bear the thought any longer of the younger women's working on the streets where they faced danger every day. And she worried about a few of the older women who suffered from health issues.

Madre Carmela had been worried about how they could take in another dozen women, but Sorella Agata had shown her they could afford it since their profits had doubled in the past couple of years, mainly due to Sorella Agata's pastries, which were being talked about throughout the town of Santa Lucia del Mela and even in neighboring villages. Furthermore, the increase in customers meant they needed more workers. They were struggling to keep up with the demand as the pastries were selling out almost as soon as they hit the display cases. Sorella Agata proposed that the women work in the kitchen and the shop.

"*Va bene,* Sorella Agata. As you know, I could never say no to you." Madre Carmela had patted her cheek.

Ever since the homeless women had come to live on the convent's grounds, Sorella Agata had been even busier as she helped them adjust to their new surroundings and began instructing them in making pastries. She was happy, but she had to admit lately she felt once again as if something was missing, much the way she had felt after she had become a nun and was looking for a way to serve God. She had felt a sense of purpose and fulfillment when she was sneaking out of the convent and bringing food to the homeless women. But now that she had helped them and was watching them thrive, she felt her work in that aspect had been completed.

About an hour later, when Sorella Agata was done with her volunteer work at the hospital, her mind returned to what she'd been pondering earlier. Silently, she prayed to God, asking Him to give her a sign as to how she might serve Him best. Perhaps she should devote more time to volunteering at the hospital? No, that didn't feel quite right. Sorella Agata had learned, especially in the past couple of years, to trust her instincts more and more. As she walked toward where she had left her bike, she looked at the piazza in the village and was surprised not to see as many beggars or homeless people as she normally saw. She often saw young women, mostly runaways, when she came into town. If only she could help more people. What if she tried to get money to run a nonprofit shelter? If she received funds, she could expand the size of the former abandoned chapel and turn it into a functioning shelter. She could hire volunteers. Her mind began racing as she thought about how many more women she could save. Madre Carmela had told her once that it was impossible to save every woman, and that Sorella Agata needed to realize that it wasn't her responsibility to save everyone. Sorella Agata knew Madre was implying that she was trying to save herself whenever she rescued another woman who had been forced to live on the street because someone had mistreated or abused her. She was still trying to save herself from Marco. But it was more than that for her. This was Sorella Agata's way of serving God and thanking Him for rescuing her from that horrible cave as well as giving her a new life at the convent. If it hadn't been for Madre Carmela's compassion and generosity, she would not be here. The more Sorella Agata thought about it, the more she became convinced that her next calling was to open a women's shelter. Somehow, she would make it happen.

Her thoughts were diverted to a woman who was sleeping on a nearby bench. She had stunning blond hair that rippled in waves, reminding Sorella Agata of the painting *The Birth of Venus* by the great master of art Botticelli. She wore a long, flowing white skirt that was very dirty and a mariner's navy-and-white-striped off-the-shoulder shirt that had food stains. The woman's face was covered with a balled-up crocheted scarf. She almost looked like a handmade doll whose face hadn't been sewn on yet. Her head rested on a small suitcase.

Sorella Agata knelt by the woman's side.

"Excuse me, miss. Are you not feeling well? May I offer any assistance?" Sorella Agata spoke softly, hoping not to startle her.

The woman turned her head to look at her, but then realized her scarf was still covering her face. She pulled the scarf away and sat up.

Sorella Agata was stunned. "Teresa?"

"Who are you?" The pretty woman scowled. "I don't know any nuns, thank God!"

"Teresa, it's me! Rosalia!" Sorella Agata frantically pointed to her chest, but then realized how absurd that action was since she now looked nothing like the Rosalia whom Teresa once knew.

"Rosalia?" Teresa leaned her face in closer. Her eyes widened. "*Dio mio!* It *is* you!" She laughed and pulled Sorella Agata to her chest, hugging her tightly. Then, she pushed her away and looked at her again. "Are you really a nun now or are you dressed up for something? Carnevale isn't for another two months, so that can't be it. You truly did it, didn't you? You became a nun! Did my fanatical sister have anything to do with this?"

Teresa shook her head as if she were disappointed in her, but Sorella Agata could see she was smiling slightly. She looked just as happy to see her.

"No, your sister had nothing to do with my decision. I guess you should know Elisabetta now goes by Sorella Lucia—the name she chose after she took her vows to become a nun."

Teresa slightly nodded her head. Sorella Agata waited to see if she would ask more about her sister, but Teresa remained silent.

"A lot has happened since I last saw you, Teresa. I know you had a horrible experience when you were a nun, but it hasn't been that way for me, and, as you said yourself, the sisters are different at the Convento di Santa Lucia del Mela."

"True, except for Sorella Domenica. Is she as mean as ever?"

"She passed away last year from a brain aneurysm."

"Hmmm. I'm not surprised. That woman repressed so much anger and hatred. Has anyone else taken her place? Who's the mean nun now?"

"No one. We do have more lay workers at the shop. They're living in the old, abandoned chapel, but Madre and I renovated it so it doesn't look like a chapel anymore. But that's a long story."

"What ever happened to Antonio?"

"He went to Paris. I imagine he must be a chef now." Sorella Agata did her best to sound nonchalant, but she could feel the weight of Teresa's stare on her.

"I'm sure that's a long story as well, right, my friend?" Teresa placed her hand on Sorella Agata's shoulder.

Sorella Agata smiled and placed her own hand over Teresa's. "You don't know how good it is to see you, Teresa! We've all missed you, and Sorella Lucia . . . Elisabetta . . ." Her voice trailed off.

"Is she all right?" Teresa's voice filled with concern. Sorella Agata had been troubled earlier when Elisabetta's name had come up that Teresa hadn't asked immediately if her sister was all right. But now she heard the worry in her voice. And she knew her old friend. Teresa had probably not asked about Elisabetta to protect herself from learning that her sister might be angry with her for eloping with Francesco and then leaving without saying good-bye.

"*Sì, sì.* She's all right. But she misses you, too. I know she regrets how she acted toward you when you were still living with us at the convent. We came to visit you and Francesco, but you had moved. She was so saddened. Why did you leave without saying good-bye to any of us? I thought you had told me we would remain friends even after your marriage?"

Sorella Agata couldn't hide the hurt in her voice. First, she had lost her family, then Antonio, although she knew she had been the one to push him away, and then Teresa.

"I'm so sorry, Rosalia. I never meant to hurt you, or Elisabetta either, but things got pretty horrible for me not long after I married Francesco." Her eyes filled with tears.

Sorella Agata noticed once again how dirty Teresa's clothes were. And she had found her sleeping on the bench like a vagrant.

"Are you living on the streets, Teresa?"

Teresa bit her lip and looked away. She nodded.

Sorella Agata reached over and hugged her. Teresa collapsed against Sorella Agata and sobbed so hard her whole body shook.

"It's all right, Teresa. I'm here. You are not alone anymore. I will help you." Sorella Agata stroked Teresa's hair.

Sorella Agata couldn't help remembering how once her own hair had been this long. She felt a momentary pang of sadness. Sometimes she still missed things from her old life, like running a brush through her long, shiny dark locks, the few pretty dresses she had owned before she became a nun, and of course, her family. While the ache had lessened a bit over the years, especially once she became a nun and devoted herself to helping others, she still thought about them every day. Once a year, she went to the police station and checked in with L'ispettore Franco, always knowing what his answer would be. While she contemplated giving up on asking him if he had received any news, something inside her wouldn't let her, even though it felt like a thousand daggers had been pierced into her chest every time he shook his head and lowered his gaze. And, after that day she believed she'd spotted Marco, she had called L'ispettore Franco, but he had told her they had never gotten word that he had returned to Messina.

"I was such a fool, Rosalia." Teresa pulled herself away. "I can still call you Rosalia, can't I? What does everyone else call you now? Sorella Rosalia?"

"Sorella Agata. Remember, we're supposed to choose new names when we become nuns, just as Elisabetta chose Sorella Lucia."

"I can't think of her as anything other than Elisabetta." Teresa's voice sounded sad.

"You never did tell me what your name was when you were a nun."

"Don't remind me. I blocked that part of my life out of my memory so entirely that I don't even remember what my name was!"

Sorella Agata laughed. "I see your sense of humor is still intact!"

"I'm sorry if I'm being disrespectful. I will call you Sorella Agata, if you wish."

"Please, go on, Teresa. You were saying you were such a fool."

"I was such a fool to have fallen in love with Francesco. He was nothing more than a drunk!"

Sorella Agata then remembered how much he had been drinking at the restaurant after their wedding. She had written it off to his celebrating his marriage, but she also remembered how Teresa had looked embarrassed a few times and had seemed to be scolding him.

"He had a drinking problem even before we were married, but I was too stupid to see it then. I thought he was just having a little fun whenever we went out. But after we got married, I saw it was a daily habit for him. At first, he just got drunk and kept to himself. But then he began attacking me, first with insults, then with his fists." Teresa pulled up her skirt and showed Sorella Agata a three-inch-long scar.

"I have him to thank for this. He cut me with a broken beer bottle. He was convinced I was cheating on him, but he was the one cheating on me with every willing whore in the city of Messina. Finally, one day, he came home sober. I was shocked. I couldn't remember the last time I had seen him sober. He announced to me in a calm voice that he was leaving me for another woman. He told me I had a day to clear out my belongings and to leave our house. It was my turn to fly into a rage. I pounded him with my fists, but naturally, he overpowered me and threw me against the wall. He then stormed out, but not before saying that if he found me there the next day, he would literally kick me out with his own two feet and with just the clothes on my back." Teresa laughed eerily. "He actually thought he was being generous by giving me a day's notice and letting me take my belongings. This has been my home for the past year." She gestured to the bench she lay on.

"So you and Francesco never left Messina? Your sister and I just assumed you had left the city when we didn't find you living at your old residence any longer."

"We had to leave because the landlord, who lived below us, was tired of hearing Francesco yelling during his drunken bouts. We moved closer to the marina. Although Francesco was a drunk, somehow he was able to function at his job at the municipality, so we weren't struggling financially. Before I left, I took all the money he kept in the house, but I was only able to rent a room with what I had, and I went through the money in just a few months. It's so hard to find work. I was cleaning a man's apartment, but then he wanted me to sleep with him, so I never went back. Now I pick-pocket and take whatever charity strangers give me. Elisabetta was right. I should've stayed a nun. At least I would have had a roof over my head, and I wouldn't have lost all sense of dignity."

"Why didn't you come back to the convent, Teresa? You should have known you would always have a place to stay there."

"I didn't know that. I thought after the way I left without saying good-bye to anyone that I wouldn't be welcome. How was I to know that Madre Carmela wouldn't think my actions were selfish and that I had just used her and her generosity, especially when she had been so kind and had taken Elisabetta and me in after I was thrown out of our last convent? And she would have been right to think that about me. I had been selfish, even toward Elisabetta. All I cared about was what I wanted and the wonderful future I was going to have. I turned my back on my own sister. I don't blame Elisabetta if she never forgives me."

"She will forgive you; she has already. I told you she was upset when she learned you had eloped with Francesco, but I think she was more concerned that you were making another mistake. She truly thought you would've been better off had you remained a nun, but she has told me in the years since you left that she realizes that was absurd and that you were never meant to take vows. She said she realized that the reason she was so insistent on your be-coming a nun was that she was afraid she would lose you forever if you didn't also take vows. Please, Teresa, come back with me to the convent. There are people there who love you. You can be my right-hand person in the pastry shop. And who's to say you won't meet someone more deserving of your love than Francesco some-day? Don't feel like your life is over."

"Oh, Rosalia. I mean, Sorella Agata. I don't think I can get used to calling you Sorella! You are now giving me the same advice I gave you once about not thinking your life was over after what that monster did to you in that cave. Isn't it funny how life turns out, my friend?"

"As I've learned over and over again, we can never quite know what is in store for us. So will you come back home with me?"

Teresa nodded her head.

"Good. If you had said no, I would've dragged you back anyway."

Teresa got up off the bench and took her suitcase. She linked arms with Sorella Agata and, while they walked, they laughed and exchanged stories from when they had lived at the convent together, even recalling when they had gone out on double dates with Francesco and Antonio. From behind, one could not tell that eight years had stood between the two friends. For they looked as close as ever.

❧ 27 ❧

Latte di Mandorla

ALMOND MILK

Morning of November 11, 2004

Claudia woke up with the sound of the rooster crowing as she did every morning, but today she didn't immediately get out of bed. She had been up late with Sorella Agata the night before, listening to her recount how she had found Teresa on the streets. Though Claudia had been prepared to stay up the whole night to hear the rest of the nun's story, Sorella Agata had insisted they go to bed.

With much effort, Claudia forced herself to sit up. Stretching her arms overhead, she hit her hands on the wooden cross that hung above her bed. Claudia got out of bed and gently straightened it. She noticed a small tag dangling from beneath the purple silk roses that were tied around the cross. Taking a closer look, Claudia read the small handwritten note in Italian that translated to: *You will always be my rose.*

Was this perhaps a gift to Rosalia from Antonio? Claudia remembered noticing the cross when Sorella Agata had taken her to her room on the day of her arrival. She also remembered the sad expression Sorella Agata had had when Claudia had commented on how beautiful the cross was. Sorella Agata had mentioned that it had been a gift, and it was obvious whoever had written the note was referencing Sorella Agata's birth name, since the name *Rosalia* was derived from the Latin word for *rose.* Claudia also noticed that the silk roses were purple. Hadn't Sorella Agata mentioned that purple was Rosalia's favorite color? Yes, Claudia now remembered it was.

She sighed deeply. Sorella Agata had been through so much in her life. Who would have thought that this slightly plump nun who took such pride in her pastries and seemed to live such a simple life had had so much heartache in her past? And then to learn about the shelter she'd founded for women who had been abused or were homeless. She truly was amazing. Claudia respected the way the nun had managed to find purpose in her life after suffering so much loss.

A half hour later, Claudia was in the kitchen watching the nuns at work. They were making *Latte di Mandorla*—almond milk. From the almond paste that was used to make marzipan and so many cookies and pastries to sherbet and drinks such as *Latte di Mandorla* and even the almond syrup known as *Orzata,* the almond truly was front and center in much of Sicilian cuisine.

One of the older lay workers was holding a strainer lined with two layers of cheesecloth while Veronique, the inquisitive, young apprentice Claudia had met on her first day at the convent, poured almond puree through the strainer. The lay worker instructed Veronique to press on the puree with the back of her wooden spoon so they could extract as much of the liquid as possible. The lay worker wore her hair up in a bun. The gray in her hair was quickly overtaking the blond color it once was. When Veronique was done pressing the puree, the older woman said something to make her laugh, and then the woman struck a pose as if she were still young and was flirting with someone. A thought occurred to Claudia. Could this possibly be Teresa?

"You are a clown, Teresa! Now get back to work."

So it *was* Teresa. A nun with a few wisps of black hair that peeked out from under her habit joined her and Veronique.

"*Dai,* Elisabetta! I am the older sister, so if anyone should be scolding it should be me!"

And this was Elisabetta, Teresa's sister, who had become a nun and now went by Sorella Lucia, but Claudia saw that her sibling still chose to call her by her Christian name. Claudia watched the two sisters, who soon broke out into laughter. Claudia could see that the rancor that had once existed between them when they were younger was now gone. Sorella Agata had been right in telling Teresa when she found her on the streets that Elisabetta would be happy to see her again.

Claudia had met most of the workers in the kitchen, but she had never been good with names, so she hadn't remembered, when Sorella Agata had told her about Teresa and Elisabetta, that they were still here at the Convento di Santa Lucia del Mela.

The two sisters instructed Veronique to pour the almond milk with a ladle into Mason jars. Claudia wondered how much longer the young apprentice had to go until she would be well versed in the art of pastry making. She could see that what Sorella Agata had told her was true: They all thought of Veronique as a little sister. But it wasn't just Veronique. In her time at the convent, Claudia had noticed there was a strong sense of sisterhood among both the nuns and the lay workers.

Her eyes rested on the elderly Madre Carmela. She was seated in a tall wooden chair at a counter. She almost looked like a child in a high chair, waiting to be fed. One of the younger nuns placed a tray of *Tetù,* Clove-Scented Chocolate Cookies, and a bowl filled with icing in front of Madre Carmela. With shaky hands, the old nun dipped the baked cookies into the warm glaze and placed them carefully onto an empty tray lined with parchment paper. Claudia saw the glaze drip onto the nun's habit and onto the floor, and she noticed the younger nun noticed, but instead of pointing it out to Madre Carmela, the younger nun complimented her on her work.

Tears came to Claudia's eyes. She felt silly to be moved by seeing the younger nun treat Madre Carmela with respect. But it was this kind of behavior, which she had witnessed over and over again at the convent these past few weeks, that made Claudia feel like something was missing in her own life. Being here had forced her to reflect on her life back home in New York, and watching these women, who it was obvious cared so much about one another and shared a communal bond of respect and sisterhood, made Claudia realize how lonely she'd been in New York. She had acquaintances, but she was so consumed by her career that she didn't make the time to form more lasting relationships, just as she hadn't made the time for the men she'd dated. Now, she realized she wanted more lasting relationships. Perhaps it was hearing Sorella Agata's story as well that had made Claudia realize how important the bonds of family and good friends were. She found herself phoning home and speaking to her family, which she could tell had surprised them since when she was in New York she only spoke to them a few times a month, if that. She made a silent promise to herself that she would make some changes when she returned.

"Would you like some almond milk?" Veronique stood before Claudia holding a small bowl of *Latte di Mandorla.*

"*Grazie,* Veronique."

Claudia took a sip of the almond milk, which was warm. It tasted nothing like the almond milk she'd had back home.

"This is so delicious!"

"I'm glad you like it. May I ask you what America is like?" Veronique's voice was low, and she glanced nervously over her shoulder.

"It's wonderful. But so is Italy, and especially Sicily. Perhaps you can come to New York some time, and I'll show you around?"

Veronique's eyes opened wide. "I would like that very much. My grandfather has always said he wants to go to New York."

"Before I leave, I'll be sure to give you my phone number. Please, call me if you come."

"*Grazie,* Claudia. Oh, please, don't tell Sorella Agata about this. I wouldn't want her to think I invited myself."

Claudia laughed. "But you didn't. I invited you. And I would tell her that, but I won't mention anything about the conversation."

"I should go. *Buongiorno.*"

"*Buongiorno,* Veronique."

Though Veronique looked to be college-age, she acted younger. Claudia wondered if she would ever make it to New York.

"*Buongiorno,* Claudia. You look as tired as I feel." Sorella Agata walked over to Claudia, holding her lower back.

"Are you all right, Sister? I shouldn't have kept you up so late last night. I'm sorry."

"I'm as much to blame. As I said, my story was long, and I'm still not done with it. My bed has also been giving me backaches recently. I think it's time for a new mattress."

Sorella Agata poured some almond milk that was still waiting to be stored into a small bowl, and sipped it slowly.

"Let's go outside where we won't be disturbed. I've decided to take the morning off so we can pick up where I left off last night."

Claudia was surprised. In her time here, she hadn't seen Sorella Agata take a whole morning off.

"Are you sure the kitchen can spare you?"

"*Si, si.* I need to start taking it easier. Besides, I want to finish telling you the rest of my story. It's been quite draining, to say the least, and you have been so patient."

Claudia noticed the necklace with a small gold crucifix that Sorella Agata wore. Her thoughts turned to the wooden cross with the silk rosebuds that hung above her bed.

"Sorella Agata, is the room I'm staying in normally yours?"

She looked up in surprise at Claudia's question. She nodded.

"You didn't have to give me your room. I feel bad that I've displaced you."

Sorella Agata waved her hand. "Please. Don't worry. I wanted you to be comfortable, and my room is the most spacious of the rooms in the convent. Naturally, as the mother superior, I have the largest room, but I don't need that extra space."

"Thank you, Sorella. That was very generous of you."

Sorella Agata sipped her almond milk.

"May I ask you about the cross that hangs above the bed? I happened to notice this morning the tag with the handwritten note. I remembered you said it was a gift."

Sorella Agata's eyes filled with tears.

"Oh, I'm sorry, Sorella. If you don't wish to talk about the cross, I understand."

Sorella Agata took a handkerchief out from one of the pockets of her habit and dabbed her eyes.

"It is all right, Claudia." She paused a moment before continuing. "Yes, the cross was a gift from someone very dear to me."

"Antonio?"

Sorella Agata didn't answer. After a moment, she said, "Do you believe in miracles, Claudia?"

Claudia shrugged. "I don't think I've ever given much thought to them, so I don't really know if I believe in them."

"Well, God granted me a miracle back in 1980. And it was the perfect night for miracles. You see, it was Christmas Eve. . . ."

28

Pignolata

HONEY CLUSTERS

December 24, 1980

Sorella Agata was rubbing a healing ointment over the burn blisters that were scattered along her arms. Every year when she made *Pignolata,* or *Struffoli,* as the fried Honey Clusters were known on mainland Italy, she failed to escape the splattering oil. It went with her trade, and she had just accepted it long ago.

Once she was done applying the ointment to her blisters, she washed her hands and went back to the kitchen, where huge bowls of *Pignolata* lined the counters. The other workers were either still frying more batches of the Honey Clusters or they were preparing the honey glaze that would coat the *Pignolata.* Sorella Agata walked over to Madre Carmela, who was adding multicolored confetti sprinkles onto the *Pignolata* that had been dipped into the honey glaze and were piled high into either pyramid shapes or wreaths.

"I thank God today is the last day we'll be making *Pignolata.* I don't think my arms can take any more burns," Sorella Agata said as she joined Madre Carmela in adding confetti sprinkles onto another platter of *Pignolata.*

"It will be nice to have a few days' rest after Christmas." Madre Carmela smiled.

"Speaking of taking a rest, why don't you go clean up and rest before midnight Mass. I, and the other workers, can handle finishing up here."

Madre Carmela thought for a moment before nodding her head. "Well, if you're certain you can manage, maybe I will do just that. I've had this fatigue lately I can't quite shake."

"*Si, si.* We always manage. Now go."

Sorella Agata used her motherly, stern voice with Madre, but they both knew she was only joking. She marveled still at how their roles had reversed as both women became older and Madre Carmela slowly, but surely, was losing the energy she had once seemed to have in droves. Sorella Agata worried about her and wondered how much longer she would be able to oversee the duties of the convent and the pastry shop—even with all the help that Sorella Agata and the other nuns and lay workers gave her.

"*Grazie.*" Madre Carmela placed her hands on her lower back as she slowly walked away, but then she stopped and turned around. "Oh, will you be taking *Pignolata* to the patients at the hospital this evening?"

"Of course, and to the women's shelter. I made a few extra batches this year."

"You really have gone above and beyond in your service to God, Sorella Agata. I am very proud of you, and I know God is, too."

"*Grazie,* Madre. I just wish I could do more."

"Don't we all wish that. Please, don't be so hard on yourself." Madre Carmela looked at her with concern in her eyes.

"I'm fine, Madre."

"*Va bene.* I will see you later."

Sorella Agata walked over to a pot of honey that one of the sisters had just taken off the stove.

"I'll take over from here," she said to the nun, who looked relieved to have a break.

Sorella Agata glanced over her shoulder to make sure no one saw her, and then she popped one of the just-dipped honey-coated *Pignolata* in her mouth. Though they were encouraged to try what they had baked, for some reason she never wanted the other workers to see her having one of the sweets merely for the sake of having it. It was one thing when they shared dessert after dinner or needed to try a sweet to make sure it had come out well, but Sorella Agata often sampled the sweets several times. She couldn't help herself. They still had the power to brighten her mood whenever she was feeling down. And today was one such day.

The holidays were still difficult for her, even after all these years of being separated from her family. She was now forty-two years old, and while she had been able to find some inner peace with herself over never finding her family, it still saddened her greatly from time to time, especially on holidays when she remembered how she used to spend them with her mamma, papà, Luca, and Cecilia. She sighed deeply. Had twenty-five years, since she became separated from them, really gone by?

She didn't even notice the tears that had rolled down her face and were now spilling into her pot of *Pignolata* until she felt a teardrop hit her hand. Taking a dish towel, she patted her eyes dry. She shook her head. Today was Christmas Eve. She should be reveling in the celebration of Jesus's birth, not wallowing in self-pity. Sorella Agata composed herself and finished helping the workers with the *Pignolata*.

A few hours later, she was driving the one car the convent owned. It was a blue Fiat that had been donated to them by a local wealthy businessman five years ago. The nuns had become giddy when they had received the brand-new car. A few of the women had taken driving lessons so they could go into town and buy their own baking supplies instead of relying on deliverymen for the larger loads. Before they'd received the Fiat, they were still bicycling into the village or taking the bus if they traveled farther away, for example to Messina, but that rarely happened. Sometimes, Sorella Agata thought about the few times Antonio had taken her to Messina, and for a moment, in her heart she longed to be young again and to look forward to traveling to a big city. But that had been a lifetime ago, and she was no longer that same young woman.

First, Sorella Agata stopped at the Rifugio delle Donne Sant' Anna, the women's shelter she had founded fifteen years ago. With the increase in the profits the pastry shop had seen in the past decade and through several fund-raisers, Sorella Agata had been able to open and support the shelter in town. She had decided to name the shelter the Rifugio delle Donne Sant' Anna after her own mother, whose name was Anna. And she also thought Saint Anne was a good saint for the shelter to be named after, since she was the mother of the Virgin Mary; Sorella Agata wanted the women at the shelter to feel as if they were returning to the arms of a mother who would protect them and help guide them on their road to healing.

Madre Carmela had suggested she name the shelter instead after Saint Agatha, both to honor Sorella Agata for having founded it and because the saint was the patron saint of rape victims and other abused women. But Sorella Agata didn't want so much importance to be placed on the fact that she had been the one to found the shelter. Sorella Agata wanted the work of all the employees and volunteers at the shelter to be celebrated. Each one of them was an integral part of the shelter's success. While she couldn't deny that naming the shelter after Saint Agatha would have been fitting, especially since she had chosen that name when she took her vows as a nun, she didn't want to be treated as a star, whether it was at the pastry shop or at the shelter. Ever since her twenties, when customers had begun taking notice of her *cassata,* she had grown to resent the attention it had cast on her. While she was happy the shop's patrons loved her cake as well as many of the other pastries she made, she didn't feel comfortable being set apart from her fellow nuns and workers at the pastry shop. And likewise, she was embarrassed at the treatment she received whenever she visited the shelter. The patients and even the shelter's volunteers and employees treated her like a celebrity.

"*Buon Natale,* Sorella Agata!" Everyone greeted her as she handed out platters of *Pignolata.*

The newer women seemed surprised that they were receiving something for Christmas, and the glow in their eyes once they realized that someone had thought of them, too, was enough to almost make Sorella Agata lose her composure.

"God bless you!" Many of the women kissed Sorella Agata's hands or embraced her as she greeted each and every one of them.

When she finally left the shelter an hour later, she felt drained. Though she always felt a tremendous sense of fulfillment whenever she went to the shelter and was still proud of all that she had done with it, sometimes the enormity of the women's emotions and gratefulness was almost too much for Sorella Agata. She felt a combination of love and compassion for these women. And sometimes, she was moved and thought about how once she had been as scared as they were.

As she drove on to the hospital, she thought about how the women received intensive counseling at the shelter. They even had a program in which they teamed up with local businesses that were willing to take the women on as apprentices. The women were not paid while they learned a trade, but if the business liked their work and needed employees once their training was done, they hired them. And if the business didn't need employees, the women had the experience to apply to other jobs. Not all the women, however, trained at local businesses. Many of the younger women returned to their families and homes once they had healed from whatever crime or abuse they'd suffered. There were young women who had been in abusive relationships and had run off with their boyfriends or who had been raped as teenagers, as Rosalia had been. She was grateful that times had changed, and families did not expect the women to marry their rapists. A cold shiver ran through Sorella Agata as she thought about how so many women had been expected to do this when she was young.

A thin string of multicolored lights hung from the awning of the Ospedale di Santa Teresa, Saint Teresa's Hospital, to commemorate the Christmas season. After Sorella Agata parked the Fiat in the lot behind the hospital, she pulled out of the trunk a folding shopping cart and began stacking carefully the platters of *Pignolata* she'd brought for the patients. She then made her way into the hospital's main corridor.

She delivered a platter of *Pignolata* to each of the hospital's divisions except for the children's ward. Earlier in the day, a few of the younger nuns at the convent had delivered toys that had been donated through a drive that the sisters had conducted the previous weekend. The hospital would distribute the toys to the children who were patients at the hospital on Christmas morning.

A half hour later, after Sorella Agata had finished delivering her platters, she still had one platter left. She must've miscounted how many she needed. As she rolled her shopping cart down the corridor toward the elevator, she heard soft crying coming from one of the patients' rooms. Sorella Agata peered into the room, but all she could make out were the chapped feet of the patient who was in distress. From her weeping, she could tell it was an older woman. Sorella Agata looked toward the nurses' station so she could alert them to go assist the patient, but the only nurse present was on the phone and, from the sounds of it, was in a heated exchange with someone. Sorella Agata's eyes then fell on her last platter of *Pignolata*. Perhaps they would distract the patient from her pain until a nurse could give her whatever medicine she needed.

Sorella Agata bent over and took the platter out. She walked into the room softly, not wanting to startle the patient. The curtain around the patient's bed was halfway drawn. Sorella Agata tilted her head to try to get a better view of the patient, whose back was turned toward her as she lay on her left side. The woman's hair was all gray and was long, past her shoulders. It was tangled, and it looked like it had been days since a comb had gone through it. At the middle of her head, her hair was flattened, showing she had lain in bed for several days. Sorella Agata mentally shook her head. Couldn't one of the nurses have brushed this patient's hair?

The woman's shoulders shook slightly as she cried, the sound now a low, deep wail.

Sorella Agata spoke softly, hoping not to frighten her.

"*Signora,* are you in pain? I can call a nurse for you, or perhaps I can help you with something?"

The woman's shoulders stopped shaking at the sound of Sorella Agata's voice, and her crying stopped. She held up her hand and waved it, imploring Sorella Agata to leave.

"I'm sorry. I didn't mean to disturb you. Perhaps you would like these. A little Christmas treat."

Sorella Agata gently placed the platter of *Pignolata* at the foot of the woman's bed. This way she could see them. She silently prayed the woman wouldn't be angry and kick them off the bed.

But the woman turned her head and glanced at the platter and whispered, "*Pignolata.*"

Sorella Agata felt a shiver travel through her, though she didn't know why. The air in the hospital was stuffy, as she found it always was whenever she visited.

"*Si, Pignolata.* They're made at the pastry shop at the Convento di Santa Lucia del Mela. If I may say so myself, they're quite good. Here. Let me take off the cellophane and give you a few so you can see how delicious they are."

Sorella Agata took the platter and looked at the table that stood near the bed with an untouched small bowl of pasta on it. She didn't see a knife to cut the ribbon that held the cellophane wrapping in place. Perhaps they had scissors at the nurses' station. She was about to tell the patient she'd be back when the woman spoke.

"Your voice." The woman then turned so that she was lying on her back. When her eyes met Sorella Agata's, fear immediately filled them, but she didn't remove her gaze.

Sorella Agata stared back. The resemblance was quite striking, but naturally, this woman was much older than her mother was. And then, her heart stopped with the realization that suddenly occurred to her. Sorella Agata's mind quickly did the math. Her mother would have been sixty-two now, but this woman looked older—either in her late sixties, or maybe even seventy. Sorella Agata was tired. It had been a long day. She was seeing things. Still, there was something about the woman's eyes.

"Rosalia?" the woman softly said.

Sorella Agata felt slightly dizzy as she whispered back, "Mamma?"

The plate of *Pignolata* fell from her hands as she walked closer to her mother. There was no doubt in her mind now. This woman *was* her mother. The same mother who had rocked her in her arms when she was a baby; the same mother who had sung lullabies to her to help her fall asleep; the same mother who had shared stories and laughed with her as they worked side by side, both in their home and in Papà's shop; the same mother who had listened to Rosalia's dreams for the future.

"It is you! My daughter, my daughter!"

She sat up in bed as Sorella Agata reached her bedside and wrapped her mother in her arms.

"Mamma! Please, don't tell me I'm dreaming. Please let it really be you! You don't know how much I've prayed for this day to come."

"And so have I, my daughter. So have I."

Later that evening . . .

Sorella Agata was driving, making her way back to the convent. Every few seconds, she took her gaze off the road to glance over at her mother and make sure she truly was sitting in the passenger seat beside her. It really was Mamma, and not a ghost. When Sorella Agata had left the convent earlier to distribute her *Pignolata* platters to the hospital patients, never in her wildest dreams would she have imagined she'd be returning home, let alone spending the Christmas holidays, with her own mother. Silently, she prayed to God, thanking Him over and over again. Her mind also kept replaying her reunion with her mother at the hospital and their conversation once they had gotten over their initial shock of finding each other.

Sorella Agata had told her mother at the hospital how Marco had kidnapped her, held her hostage in the cave, and even how he'd raped her. Her mother had wept when she heard all that her daughter had been through. Sorella Agata had also relayed how a group of nuns had found her unconscious after she'd escaped from the cave, and then how she had returned home once her memory was restored only to discover her family had all left Terme Vigliatore. But it was getting late, and she wanted to be able to take her mother back to the convent with her that night. She knew it would take some time to explain to the hospital that this was her mother and that she would be taking her mother home with her. The hospital's administrator had known Sorella Agata for many years now and also knew her story of being estranged from her family when she was young and how she had never given up hope of finding them someday. He agreed to release her mother, but made Sorella Agata promise to bring her back in a few days for an exam. Sorella

Agata's mother was on the mend from pneumonia, and he had been thinking he would be able to release her in a couple of days, although he had been reluctant to do so since he knew she was homeless. Still, as with all the other patients who were homeless, he could not keep them there forever. There were too many sick people and not enough beds.

On the drive home, Sorella Agata promised her mother she would explain the next day, after her mother had had some rest, more about what she'd been up to since they'd been separated. And her mother promised to tell Sorella Agata everything about what had led her back to Messina and why she had been living on the streets. But the suspense was too much for Sorella Agata to bear. She had to ask her mother how she had become homeless and why she was not with Papà, Luca, and Cecilia. Had her father died? But surely, Luca and Cecilia would have looked after Mamma if that had happened. Her heart beat frantically; she was afraid to learn the fate of her family.

"Mamma, I know you are tired and are still recuperating, and I know you have received a great shock in seeing me tonight, but I must ask where Papà, Luca, and Cecilia are. When I was trying to find all of you, our police inspector told me you had moved to Marsala and that Papà had briefly gone to America for work before returning to Sicily. He also told me you had to leave Marsala and were planning on moving back east. What happened? I just don't understand why you were alone and living on the streets. Are they . . ." Sorella Agata could not say it. Could it be that perhaps they all had died?

"All I will say right now, Rosalia, is that I left your father. I'm sorry. I know you have as many questions as I do. But I promise I will tell you more tomorrow. You are right. I need to rest, and the story I have to tell is difficult, I'm afraid to say. Can you bear to be patient a little longer and wait until tomorrow to hear the rest? I'm sorry, my child. I know you have waited all these years, wondering what happened to all of us. But my excitement over finding you has taken what little energy I have left in my body."

"Of course, Mamma. I want you to get well so we can go back to

laughing and sharing stories with each other as we used to do."
Sorella Agata took one hand off the steering wheel and squeezed
her mother's hand.

"You were always the perfect daughter." Mamma smiled and
then closed her eyes. Soon, she was fast asleep.

Sorella Agata's heart winced when she heard her mother say
she'd always been the perfect daughter. For the longest time after
Marco had kidnapped her, she'd blamed herself for the misfortune
that had befallen her family. To hear that her mother had never
thought of her as anything less than perfect made her happy, but it
also stirred up again the pain she'd felt all these years.

When they arrived at the convent, Sorella Agata felt elated. She
couldn't wait to see the shock when she told Madre Carmela and
everyone else that this woman with her was none other than her
own mother. She hoped the commotion that would surely follow
wouldn't be too much for Mamma. She looked so frail, even
though the hospital's administrator and her doctor had assured
Sorella Agata that she was on the mend. Sorella Agata couldn't lose
her again after finding her.

Sorella Agata helped her mother out of the car. Slowly, they
made their way to the convent's front door. Once they were inside,
Sorella Agata could see everyone was seated at the kitchen table. A
few platters of *Pignolata* and *Buccellati* lined the table. Everyone
was talking and sampling the sweets. When they saw Sorella Agata
enter with the older woman, they fell silent.

"Sorella Agata. We were beginning to get worried about you. Is
everything all right?" Madre Carmela asked. "Please, have your
friend sit down."

She pulled out a chair from the table. Sorella Agata did not let
go of her mother's arm until she was seated. Her mother smiled
shyly at everyone. Sorella Agata could sense she was a little nervous. She had repeatedly asked her if it truly was all right for her to
go live with her at the convent. Remembering how her mother had
kept asking her this made her want to cry. She had assured her
mother that everyone would welcome her, and that she had no
cause to worry.

Sorella Agata noticed Madre was looking at her a bit peculiarly.

"I'm sorry if you were all worried about me, but I had an unexpected circumstance arise while I was at the hospital, when I met this woman who was a patient there, recovering from pneumonia. Her name is Signora Anna DiSanta." Sorella Agata glanced at Madre Carmela to see if she would remember that DiSanta was Sorella Agata's surname. But Madre didn't even flinch. She was getting up there in years, and Sorella Agata had noticed the mother superior's memory wasn't as sharp as it used to be.

Sorella Agata continued. "I don't quite know how to say this, since what I have to say will be a shock regardless of how I say it, so I will just say it. This woman is my mother."

Everyone looked from Sorella Agata to the elderly woman, who kept her gaze lowered. No one said a word. After what seemed like an eternity to Sorella Agata, but what was probably no more than a few seconds, Madre was the first one to speak.

"Sorella Agata, please forgive me, but how can you be sure this woman is your mother? Perhaps this lost soul is looking for companionship?" Madre Carmela asked, worry etched all over her features.

"Madre, you know how long I have waited for this day. Do you think I would not know my own mother?"

When Signora DiSanta heard her daughter address Madre Carmela as simply "Madre," she frowned. Sorella Agata noticed, and patted her mother's hand.

"There is nothing to worry about, Mamma. You have always been and will always be my first mother, but Madre Carmela rescued me and has been like a second mother to me ever since I was separated from you and Papà. Madre Carmela is also the mother superior here, so we all call her Madre."

Signora DiSanta turned toward Madre Carmela, and softly said, "*Grazie* for taking care of my daughter when I couldn't."

Madre Carmela merely stared at Signora DiSanta, not quite sure yet whether to accept that this was truly Sorella Agata's mother. Then Teresa spoke up.

"I don't see a resemblance. Of course, if this woman is truly your mother, she is much older now and would look different from you, but I would still expect to find some resemblance. I'm sorry, *signora*. I mean no offense."

Sorella Agata knitted her brows furiously together. She was beginning to get angry that they didn't believe she would know her mother even if a century had passed before they were reunited. She had always favored her father in terms of her looks, so she wasn't surprised Teresa couldn't see a resemblance. Sorella Agata was about to speak up when her mother held up a hand, imploring her to wait. Her mother then dug around in her large straw tote bag, which contained the few belongings she now owned, and pulled out a small, weathered-looking Bible. Opening the Bible, she pulled out a photo and held it up for everyone to see.

Madre Carmela, Teresa, and everyone else quickly moved in to examine the photo more closely. The nuns and pastry workers who had known Sorella Agata before she took her vows, when she was simply Rosalia, gasped. For the young teenage girl in the photo was the Rosalia they remembered and whom they had rescued all those years ago. In the photo, she and her mother stood alongside each other in a garden. Two rosebushes sat on either side of them. Rosalia held one of the roses in her hand and was smiling the most extraordinary, radiant smile.

"*Dio mio.* I'd almost forgotten how beautiful you were, Sorella Agata," Sorella Lucia said, holding her hands to her chest. "I mean, you are still attractive. I mean—"

"Enough, Elisabetta. I think we all know what you meant," Teresa said, shaking her head.

Teresa had tried to call her sister Sorella Lucia when she had returned to live at the convent, but she would always inevitably revert to Elisabetta. Finally, one day she gave up. Madre Carmela asked Teresa to try to call her sister Sorella Lucia at least when they were together with the other nuns to set an example. But it was no use. Teresa continued to forget.

She then turned to Signora DiSanta. "I'm sorry I didn't believe you were Sorella Agata's mother, *signora*. You don't know how happy it makes me, all of us, to finally see you and your daughter reunited. She never stopped searching for you." Teresa embraced Signora DiSanta, who looked momentarily startled.

"*Grazie.* I'm sure this is all a shock to you, as it still is for Rosalia and me. I mean Sorella Agata." Signora DiSanta looked slightly uncomfortable when she referred to her daughter as Sorella Agata. "I'm sorry, my daughter, it will take some getting used to."

Madre Carmela stepped forward. "I think Sorella Agata would agree it is all right if you continue to call your daughter by the name you have always known her by. Don't you agree, Sorella Agata?"

Tears came to Sorella Agata's eyes. Her gaze met Madre Carmela's as she conveyed her gratitude. Once again, Madre had said the right thing, just as she had ever since Sorella Agata had been that lost, young girl struggling to heal and believe in herself again.

"Of course, Mamma. You may continue to call me Rosalia. Just because I have taken vows, does not mean I am not the Rosalia you once knew. I am still her in here." Sorella Agata pointed to her heart.

Signora DiSanta smiled. "I do not want to disrespect you, Rosalia. I am honored that my daughter decided to become a nun and serve God."

Madre Carmela began crying, though it was unlike her to lose control in front of everyone. "I can't believe it, but I cannot deny it now that I have seen the photo. I'm so happy for you, Sorella Agata. After all these years, you and your mother are together again."

Sorella Agata walked over to Madre and embraced her.

"*Grazie,* Madre. You have been so wonderful to me all these years, and now I must make of you one more request. My mother has no place to live. Can she—"

"Say no more." Madre held up her hand. "You know she is welcome here, and she is now as much a part of our family as you were when we first brought you here." She then turned to Sorella Agata's mother and said, "Welcome, *signora.*"

Madre bent over and embraced Signora DiSanta, who was fighting back tears.

"*Grazie.* I will repay you with whatever work you need, once I am stronger. I promise."

"There is no need for you to repay me, Signora DiSanta. Just get well. That is all I ask."

"As you all must realize, my mother has received a great shock, and she is still a bit weak from the pneumonia she caught. I'd like to take her up to my room and let her get some sleep. We can all talk more tomorrow."

"Of course, Sorella Agata. I take it you will sleep on the couch in the sitting room?" Madre Carmela asked.

"I will sleep on the floor in my room. I don't want to leave my mother."

Madre knew no words in the world would persuade Sorella Agata to leave her mother's side for even one second. After all, she was probably still in disbelief that her mother was actually standing here before her after twenty-five years. Poor Sorella Agata. She probably feared if she let her mother out of her sight, she might lose her again.

"I believe there's a free cot in the chapel. I can have a few of the lay workers bring it over. This way you won't put out your back by sleeping on the floor."

"*Grazie,* Madre. *Buona notte.*"

"*Buon Natale,* Sorella Agata. God has given you a wonderful gift this year."

Sorella Agata glanced at her wristwatch. It was five past midnight. In the excitement of finding her mother, she had almost forgotten it was Christmas Eve. And now it was officially Christmas.

"*Buon Natale,* Madre. I nearly forgot it was Christmas. I think I am still in shock."

Madre Carmela went over and embraced her once again, whispering in her ear. "You never gave up hope. And God has rewarded you for your patience."

Sorella Agata blinked back tears. She glanced at her mother, who was talking to Teresa and Sorella Lucia. Though she still looked quite weak, she managed to smile at them and answer their questions.

Keeping her voice low so it wouldn't reach her mother, Sorella Agata said, "I was beginning to lose hope, Madre, I'm sorry to say. And I still don't know what fate the rest of my family members met with. Something tells me I will have more heartache once my mother tells me what happened to Papà, Luca, and Cecilia."

Madre Carmela took Sorella Agata's hands in hers and squeezed tightly. "You are much stronger than the young woman I rescued all those years ago. You will be fine whatever you learn about your family. And now, you will be even stronger with your mother by your side. Remember that."

"I pray you are right, Madre. I pray I can continue to be strong. But I suppose I must be. I have no other choice now that my mother is back in my life. I must be strong for her."

❧ 29 ❧

Torta al Limone di Mamma

MAMMA'S LEMON CAKE

December 25, 1980

Though all the desserts for Christmas had been made and the shop was closed today, Sorella Agata had still woken up shortly before dawn to bake one of her favorite desserts—*Torta al Limone*. It would be a special gift for her mother.

As she stirred the batter, memories came back to Sorella Agata of when she was a child and Mamma would make the lemon cake for her and Luca. As she had told Madre Carmela when they were on their way to her hometown of Terme Vigliatore, when Rosalia had thought she would be reunited with her family, her mother would make the lemon cake for the children's birthdays and their namesake saint's day and sometimes for Easter. It was one of the simple desserts her mother made. But to little Rosalia and Luca, the dessert had felt decadent with its citrus aroma and flavor and its intensely sweet lemon glaze that was drizzled over the cake once it was done baking.

As Sorella Agata stirred the batter, she cried profusely. Usually, she made an attempt not to cry when she felt sad, but her emotions always got the better of her. And it seemed like when she was making her pastries, there was no control, and the tears insisted on coming out. Today, however, she didn't try to stop them; she let them flow freely. With one hand, she expertly beat her batter, and with her other, she dabbed at her eyes with a handkerchief.

But today, she cried because she still could not believe her mamma was here with her. She had found Mamma. Her elation had kept her up most of the night. Once her mother was sound asleep, Sorella Agata had sat up in the cot that had been set up for her in her room, and she had stared at her mother. The moonlight that came in through the sheer window panels that hung from Sorella Agata's window cast an almost angelic light over her mother's tired face. Sorella Agata wanted to stroke her mother's cheek, but she was afraid of disturbing her. She was even tempted to crawl into the bed and lie beside her, but she knew how much her mother needed her rest if she was going to fully recuperate from her recent bout of pneumonia. Sorella Agata was almost afraid to leave Mamma out of her sight, but sense finally came to her, and she knew Mamma wasn't going to vanish into thin air—even if it did seem like she had materialized out of nowhere when Sorella Agata had found herself suddenly face-to-face with her at the hospital. Then, the idea had come to her to make Mamma's *Torta al Limone*. After all, it was Christmas, and she wanted to give her mother a small gift.

An hour later when the cake was done, Sorella Agata poked holes throughout the top of the cake with a wooden skewer. She smiled as she did so, remembering how Mamma used to let her and Luca perform this task. Then when they were done, she poured the lemon glaze—which simply consisted of lemon juice, sugar, and water that was heated on the stove—over the cake. The final touch was to sprinkle a few strands of lemon zest over the cake.

"*Buongiorno,* Sorella Agata. Look whom I found strolling around the corridor upstairs."

Madre Carmela entered the kitchen with none other than Mamma. Though she held onto Madre's arm, she looked better than she had last night. Her eyes held a glow, and she didn't seem as shy of Madre Carmela anymore.

Sorella Agata rushed to her mother's side and embraced her. "Mamma, you are already looking much better this morning. Did you sleep well?"

Signora DiSanta patted her daughter's cheek. "I did, Rosalia. But I must admit, when I woke up, it took a moment for me to realize where I was and that I hadn't been dreaming last night that I'd finally found you."

"It's all right, Mamma. I barely got any sleep. I kept staring at you throughout the night to make sure I hadn't been dreaming as well." Sorella Agata laughed.

"Ah, I'm sorry you did not sleep well because of me."

"Don't be silly. I am fine. Look, I even baked something special for you. This is my small Christmas gift for you, Mamma. Naturally, I had no idea I would be seeing you for Christmas this year, so I could not get you something more."

Sorella Agata picked up the plate with the cake. Her mother placed a hand over her mouth and smiled as she looked at her daughter. She had remembered, as Sorella Agata had known she would. But a tiny part of Sorella Agata had feared that perhaps her mother might have forgotten.

"My *Torta al Limone!* Rosalia, you remembered how to make it?"

"Of course. Since you last saw me, Mamma, I have become an expert pastry chef under the guidance of Madre Carmela. The convent operates a pastry shop, and we do quite well."

Sorella Agata rarely boasted about her work since she was accustomed to remaining humble as a servant of Christ. But she couldn't help displaying her talent and passion for pastry making to her mother. Overnight, she had reverted to the young girl she once was, seeking her mother's approval and praise.

"She's an extraordinary pastry chef, Signora DiSanta. Her pastries are talked about all over our village."

"It makes me happy to see you have done so well, Rosalia, in spite . . . in spite of everything that's happened to you."

Signora DiSanta began to cry.

"Mamma, please don't be sad. Not today. It's Christmas, and we have so much to be grateful for, now that we're together."

Madre Carmela handed a handkerchief to Signora DiSanta and rubbed her back. Sorella Agata could see tears in Madre's eyes.

"I know what will make you feel better. A slice of your *Torta al*

Limone. You can go sit down with Madre at the dining table while I cut the cake."

"It is your *Torta al Limone* now, Rosalia, since you made it." Signora DiSanta smiled.

"Mamma, it will always be your cake. Do you remember how you used to let Luca and me poke holes throughout the cake with toothpicks?" Sorella Agata laughed.

But instead of her mother's joining in her laughter, she looked once more like she was going to cry.

"What is it, Mamma?"

"Let us eat the cake and relax for a bit, and then we will have the talk we promised each other last night."

"*Si.* You must be hungry, Signora DiSanta. Let's go wait for Rosalia in the dining room."

Madre Carmela led her out of the kitchen. Sorella Agata noticed how Madre had called her Rosalia instead of Sorella Agata. It was strange to hear Madre call her that after all these years, but she knew the mother superior was doing her best to make her mother feel as comfortable as possible. Dread began to fill her heart. She didn't know if she was ready to find out what fate had befallen the rest of her family since she last saw them.

Sighing deeply, she cut three thick slices of cake for herself, Madre Carmela, and Mamma. She placed the plates of cake on a tray and then poured a pot of freshly brewed espresso into three cups. As she poured the espresso, she glanced out the kitchen window and was startled to see a bluethroat perched on the ledge. But this couldn't be the same bluethroat who had visited her for so many years. She hadn't seen her friend in so long. Sorella Agata wasn't quite sure when she had last seen the bird. But then a memory returned to her. It had been the morning when she was about to take her vows to become a nun. Not only had the bird stood outside her window as she got ready for the ceremony, but she remembered seeing it flying nearby as she left the convent grounds to make her way to the church where she would be taking her vows. With the distractions her new life had presented to her after she became Sorella Agata, she hadn't realized until many months later that the bird had stopped visiting her. She had assumed it must have died, or perhaps it had finally flown to another home. She had felt sad not to see the bird that had become a welcome sight ever since that day she first saw it sitting on the tree branch that hung outside her window; that day, it had been almost as if it were urging her to leave her room and live again. And that was exactly what she'd done. Sorella Agata had also felt some guilt that she hadn't even noticed the bird's absence for months. But then she'd felt foolish for feeling that way. Now, the bird glanced at her. She was about to open the window to feed it a few crumbs that had fallen off the lemon cake, but it flew away. Opening the window anyway, she looked out, hoping to see where the bluethroat had flown to, but it was nowhere in sight.

After Sorella Agata, Madre, and Signora DiSanta had eaten their lemon cake, Madre Carmela excused herself. Sorella Agata felt the same dread she had felt earlier when her mother had told her they would have the talk they'd promised each other. Perhaps they should wait until tomorrow? It was, after all, Christmas. But she knew her mother was anxious to tell her what she needed to.

"Mamma, perhaps we can put off until tomorrow your telling me everything that has happened since I last saw you and our family. Let's just enjoy the holiday."

Sorella Agata reached for her mother's hand and held it. Her mother placed her own hand over her daughter's.

"Rosalia, telling you what I have to tell you tomorrow won't make it any easier. *Si,* today is Christmas, but I don't think I can wait any longer. Once you know everything, we can move forward and try to be as happy as we can for the time God has decided we will be together."

"*Va bene,* Mamma. It is your story to tell after all."

"As you told me, Rosalia, you know already about how we were forced to leave Terme Vigliatore once your father began losing patrons at his tailor shop. And you know we went as far as Marsala, and Papà went to America temporarily to make some extra money."

"*Si,* Mamma. L'ispettore Franco told me once Papà returned, the vineyard owners could no longer afford to keep you on as laborers and provide room and board, so you headed east. I hoped you were returning to Messina, and we would soon be reunited."

"As did I, my daughter. I will get to that soon. I thought perhaps you might've known more, since L'ispettore Franco had learned we were in Marsala as well as that your father had gone to America. But I could see from what you said last night, the inspector had no knowledge of what I'm about to tell you."

Signora DiSanta paused, taking a sip of her espresso. She then squeezed Sorella Agata's hand tightly.

"Rosalia, Luca is no longer with us. He caught the flu shortly after we moved to Marsala and died."

Even though her mother's grip on her hand was very warm, Sorella Agata felt herself go cold all over. Tears silently dropped from her eyes into her espresso cup. She had known it. She had known Mamma had bad news to relay. Naturally, Sorella Agata had suspected that perhaps her father was no longer alive. He was the oldest of them, after all. But to hear her dear brother Luca was the one who had passed away, and at such a young age. It was just too cruel. He had such high dreams. Worthy dreams of serving the Lord and living by His example, as Sorella Agata was now doing. She shook her head as she began to sob uncontrollably. Her mother stood up and went to her side, cradling her daughter.

"Oh, Mamma! It is so unfair! Why? Why has everything that's happened to our family happened? Though I am a woman of faith, I still struggle to this day to understand it all. And while I feel God had a purpose for me with the work I have done here at the convent and in our village, I still grapple with the pain and suffering we all went through. And now I will never see my brother again!"

"Rosalia, I'm sorry to be delivering this pain to you. We all grieved terribly for Luca, especially your father. I think that was also why he decided to go to America. He needed some time to be alone and get away from all that had happened to our family in such a short amount of time. And I know exactly how you are feeling. My faith has been tested many times, especially when I thought I had lost you forever and then when I lost Luca. But somehow I continued to pray to God and place my trust in Him that I would at least get news someday of what had happened to you. Rosalia, can you ever forgive me for having left Terme Vigliatore without waiting longer to see if you would return home? I never should have left with your father. You don't know how much I have hated myself for that decision. And I have felt that it was my fault as well that Luca died. I felt that if we had remained in Terme Vigliatore, he never would have gotten sick."

"You don't know that, Mamma. People get the flu everywhere."

"True. But that was how I felt. A mother strives to protect her children, and when something terrible happens to one of them, she feels she has failed."

Sorella Agata pulled herself out of her mother's embrace. Madre Carmela's words from the previous night came back to her. She needed to be strong for Mamma. While Sorella Agata was stunned to learn of Luca's death and to realize she truly would never see him again, she couldn't completely collapse. Her mother needed her. She noticed her mother wiping her brow with a linen napkin. She seemed to be sweating profusely.

"Has your fever returned?"

Sorella Agata quickly placed the back of her hand against her mother's forehead. While it was warm, it wasn't burning.

"It's just the anxiety over having to tell you about your brother's death. I'm fine, Rosalia. Please, don't worry."

Sorella Agata went over to the windows and opened one to let in some air. A bird flew through the window and landed on the chair where Sorella Agata had been sitting a moment ago. It was the bluethroat she'd seen earlier.

"*Dio mio!*" Signora DiSanta cried out.

"It is just a bird, Mamma. Don't be afraid."

Sorella Agata walked over to the chair where the bluethroat sat. It looked expectantly at her mother. When Sorella Agata reached the chair, it glanced at her for a moment before flying back out the window it had flown through. But instead of flying away completely, it stayed on the window ledge.

When Sorella Agata turned toward her mother, she was frightened to see how pale she looked.

"Mamma, are you feeling all right? You don't look well. Let me get you a glass of water."

"No, Rosalia, I don't need water. It's that bird. The only time I've seen a bird like that—with those colorful stripes on its chest—was when your brother was ill. You see, when Luca was sick, we saw a bird that looked just like this one."

"It is a bluethroat. The bird has that name because of the blue on its chest, although I never understood why they chose to call it a bluethroat since there are several colors. I remember seeing them in our yard when we lived in Terme Vigliatore. Don't you remember?"

Signora DiSanta shook her head. "No. I don't. I only remember seeing one when Luca was sick. You see, Rosalia, that bird visited him every day."

A shiver ran down Sorella Agata's spine as she remembered how the bluethroat had visited her regularly once she learned her family was no longer living in Terme Vigliatore.

"The bird sat on the windowsill of the bedroom Luca shared with Cecilia at the vineyard in Marsala where we were staying. It was as if the bird were watching over him. At first, I found it endearing, almost as if Luca had a guardian angel. But then when I could see he was dying, I became angry and saw the bird as an omen of his impending death. But then one day . . ." Her voice trailed off as tears filled her eyes. "It was the day before Luca died. He opened his eyes and, though he was so weak, he managed to slightly lift his head and look around the room. Once he saw the bird, he whispered to me that it was you."

"Me?"

"Luca said to me, 'Mamma, look. You know who that is, don't you? It's our Rosalia. She's been visiting me every day. She is watching over me and letting me know I am not alone, and that I won't be alone once I am gone. Remember that, Mamma. And never lose hope that you will see Rosalia again.' "

Mamma shook her head and placed her hands over her face as she cried.

It was now Sorella Agata's turn to hold her mother and console her. She closed her eyes tightly as she hugged her mother and whispered words of comfort. When she opened them again, she saw the bluethroat was still sitting on the window ledge. It lifted its head up, and as had always happened with the bluethroat who had visited her all those years ago, its gaze met hers. Instead of feeling a shiver as she always did when the bird looked at her, Sorella Agata instead felt her heart wince. It couldn't be. The thought she was entertaining was crazy. Could this bluethroat who had visited her regularly all those years ago be the spirit of her dead brother?

She then remembered it had been December when she had first seen the bird. It had been just a few weeks before Christmas, and she had fed the bird *Buccellati,* the popular fig cookies the pastry shop made for the holiday. Mamma had said Luca had died not that long after they had arrived in Marsala. She knew they had left Terme Vigliatore in November. She then remembered how seeing the bluethroat had motivated her to finally leave her bedroom and chase after it in the convent's courtyard. And Antonio. The bird had led her to Antonio, for it was that day when she first met him. Did her brother's spirit live on in the bluethroat? Had he been the one to spark a drive in her to live again when she had been devastated over discovering her family had left without her? Had he led her to Antonio—her dear friend who had encouraged her as they learned how to make pastries side by side and who had loved her so much and helped her learn to trust again? The bluethroat chirped a few times, looked at her for a moment, and then flew away.

Silently, she thanked her brother for looking after her all those years ago and giving her the courage to live again.

30

Taralli all'Uovo

SWEET PASTRY RINGS

Evening of November 11, 2004

Siesta was almost over, but Claudia had not been able to sleep. All she could think about was how Sorella Agata had been faced with sadness once again after her initial joy of finding her mother. Sorella Agata had stopped narrating her story after revealing her brother Luca had died. It had been time to get lunch ready, but she had promised she would pick up where she had left off after siesta. Claudia glanced up at the cross that hung above her bed. The nun still had not said who had given her the cross. Just when Claudia had thought Sorella Agata's story finally had a happy ending after she'd found her mother, she learned the poor woman only had more heartache. Claudia reached for a tissue from the box that sat on her night table and wiped her eyes for what felt like the thousandth time since she'd arrived in Sicily.

"I'm sorry, Claudia. I didn't mean to make you cry."

Claudia looked up to see Sorella Agata standing in the doorway of her bedroom. Though Sorella Agata also looked sad, she wasn't crying for once. Of course, she held a bowl filled with some sweet. Once again, Claudia marveled that the nuns and everyone else at the convent weren't enormous.

"It's all right, Sister. I've always cried easily. I just can't help reflecting on all that you've been through. I don't know if I would've survived everything you have gone through."

"You would have. I can tell you're a strong woman." Sorella Agata smiled.

She came over to Claudia and patted her shoulder before sitting next to her on the bed. She held the bowl of sweets out to Claudia. *Taralli all'Uovo*—sweet pastry rings braided into a circle—filled the bowl. The convent always had *Taralli* on hand. They were often what the nuns and the other pastry workers ate for breakfast since they were perfect for dunking into coffee. Claudia bit into a *Taralli,* and for a moment she forgot about her sadness. The sweets at the Convento di Santa Lucia del Mela truly were a panacea for any sorrow.

"Did you ever see the bluethroat again after that day your mother told you Luca had died?"

Sorella Agata shook her head. "Whenever I am outside, I am always looking for my little friend."

Claudia paused, wondering if she should say anything.

"What is it, Claudia?"

"I saw a bluethroat about a month after I arrived here."

"You did?"

Claudia nodded.

"Are you sure it was a bluethroat?"

"I'm positive. My father is a birdwatcher and, when I was a little girl, he always pointed out pictures of birds in the books he collected on the subject. The bluethroat was one of my favorite birds. It's quite stunning with all the colors that are displayed on its breast. I've never seen one in person since they are mainly found in Europe and Asia, but I know without a doubt the bird I saw was a bluethroat. My father used to make color Xeroxes of the photographs of the birds I liked from his books, and he hung them in my room. The bluethroat was in one of those photos that hung in my room. The day I saw the bluethroat in the courtyard, I remember thinking it was odd that the bird seemed to be staring right at me. And then you mentioned feeling as if the bluethroat that visited you would also look right into your eyes."

Sorella Agata thought for a moment before speaking. "Perhaps Luca decided to visit since I was telling the story of my family again. That is, if the bluethroat is really a sign from him." She sounded sad, but there was also a slight glimmer in her eyes upon hearing that Claudia had seen the bird recently.

"Perhaps, Sorella. What about your father and Cecilia? Please, don't tell me they died as well?"

"No. Well, when I was reunited with my mother, as far as she knew they were still alive; however, I don't know if they are still living now. You remember my mother had told me the night I was driving her from the hospital to the convent that she had left my father?"

Claudia nodded.

"She and my father and Cecilia had moved to Palermo after they left Marsala. Mamma had fought bitterly with Papà as they traveled to Palermo. She wanted to return to Messina to look for me, but he wouldn't hear of it. Their relations had already been strained, since she had not agreed with him about leaving Terme Vigliatore." Sorella Agata shook her head before continuing. "Mamma had not given up on me, and just as Madre Carmela had told me, the jars of blood orange marmalade I found in my child-hood home were her way of letting me know she still believed in me. But she couldn't stay behind. She had Luca and, especially, little Cecilia to think of. And how would she support herself if she didn't leave with Papà? Though she stayed with Papà for twenty years, her resentment toward him grew with each day until she decided she would leave and return to Messina in hopes of finding me."

"So it was true then that your father believed you had gone off with Marco and were going to bear his child?"

Pain flashed across Sorella Agata's face.

"Mamma said he didn't think I had run off willingly with Marco at first, but when he received that letter in my handwriting, he felt he couldn't deny any longer that I wanted to be with Marco."

"But as you said, the handwriting was shaky since Marco had drugged you and forced you to write the letter. Didn't he notice that?"

"Mamma and Luca had noticed and pointed that out to Papà, but he thought they were holding on to false hope and didn't want to think the worst about me. I think he felt that, as the patriarch of the family, he needed to be the one with a sound head on his shoulders. He needed to be the one to get them through this crisis and ensure that he could continue supporting his family. I came to this realization years ago, and I shared it with Mamma. She agreed with me, but told me she had not seen it this way when she still lived with him. Her anger and dismay over not knowing what had happened to me clouded all else. I forgive my father. I know in my heart he never stopped loving me even if he believed the worst about me and felt I had let the family down."

Sorella Agata spoke the last line very quietly. She placed the bowl of *Taralli* on the night table next to Claudia's bed and then clasped her hands in her lap. Her gaze rested on her hands.

"So when did your mother find the courage to leave your father?"

"It was only five years before she and I were reunited. She had some money to tide her over for what she thought would be quite some time, but it only lasted a year. She was renting a room in the house of an elderly lady who needed someone to cook and clean for her. Although my mother was working for her, the old lady still expected her to pay rent, but she didn't give her any earnings for cleaning and cooking. So when my mother could no longer pay her rent, she had no choice but to live on the streets. She was fifty-seven when she left my father, so she was fifty-eight when she found herself homeless. Can you imagine at that late stage in your life suddenly finding yourself without a roof over your head?"

Tears filled Sorella Agata's eyes.

"I can't imagine." Claudia placed her hand over Sorella Agata's.

Sorella Agata sighed deeply before resuming her story.

"Mamma was fortunate to befriend a woman older than she who made and sold silk flowers. The woman showed Mamma how to make them and agreed to share the corner where they sold them. Mamma said that woman was a saint, for if it hadn't been for her, she would have starved and died."

Sorella Agata looked up at the cross above Claudia's bed. Claudia followed her gaze.

"Your mother gave you that cross, then?"

"*Sì.*"

Sorella Agata took off her lace-up black shoes and then stood on the bed.

"Be careful, Sorella."

"It's all right. I'll be fine."

She removed the cross from the nail it hung on and lowered herself back down to the bed.

"See how beautiful the work on these silk roses is? Mamma made these roses and then wrapped them around this cross for me. She gave this to me about a year after she came to stay with me."

Claudia took a closer look, marveling at the stunning silk flowers that were entwined around the simple wooden cross. She glanced at Sorella Agata, whose thoughts seemed to be elsewhere—no doubt remembering when her mother had given her the cross. Claudia was afraid to ask her next question.

"Your mother is no longer alive, is she?"

"No. She died nine years ago. At least God let me have her for fifteen years after we were reunited. Oh, it was a wonderful time, Claudia. We baked side by side, and she even came with me to the women's shelter and helped me with whatever work I did there. She felt it was her way to thank God for reuniting us. She even brought whatever food we could spare at the convent to the homeless people on the streets. Then, when she was seventy-seven years old she died. She wasn't ill. I found her sitting in the courtyard. Her hands were wrapped around silk she was cutting to make her flowers. At first, I thought she had merely nodded off and was sleeping. But when she didn't wake up . . . Well, then I knew Mamma had left me for good this time."

Claudia swallowed hard, fighting back the well of tears that were threatening to surface again. "As you said, at least you did find each other and had that time with her. She died happy."

"*Sì.* But she always felt guilty. When she left Papà, it was 1975, so Cecilia was twenty-seven years old then. Mamma didn't feel too bad about leaving her behind in Palermo, for Cecilia had married a few years before and had even had a son. Mamma had kept Cecilia's phone number and did talk to her a few times the first year after she left Papà, when she was living with and working for that old lady. But then when she was living on the streets, she lost Cecilia's number. My father's number was in the same little notebook that contained my sister's number, so she had no way of communicating with them. When she found herself on the streets, she thought several times she would return to Palermo, but she never had enough money for the train ride. But she did remember their addresses. I tried writing to Cecilia and Papà a few times, letting them know Mamma was with me and we were both safe, but I never received a response. So two months after Mamma came to stay with me at the convent, when she had fully regained her strength after her bout with pneumonia, we traveled to Palermo. We went to the house Cecilia had been living in with her family. The new occupants told us that she and her family, along with my father who had apparently moved in with Cecilia two years prior, had moved because her husband had found work in Trapani. So they had headed back west. They'd left an address with the new occupants, who had been a bit confused as to why they were doing so since the post office would forward their mail. But, of course, Mamma and I knew that was their way of letting us know where they had gone. I suppose Cecilia and Papà never gave up hope that Mamma would return to them someday . . . after she'd found me.

"But it wasn't to be. When I wrote to my sister, the letter was returned to me with a stamp stating that no one by Cecilia's name lived at the address. I tried sending the letter again, but addressed it to Papà and even another time to Cecilia's husband, but each time the letter was returned with the same stamp. All I can think is that either the address was not written down correctly, or perhaps something happened and they were not living at that address any longer. The latter reason seemed more plausible. After all, at this point, Mamma had been away from them for five years, going on six. And the last time she had corresponded with my sister had been four years prior. The owners had told us they had bought the house from Cecilia and her husband in 1978. So who knows what happened in the two years before my mother and I were reunited and tried to find them. Perhaps they decided to leave Trapani. There's no way of knowing. So Mamma felt guilty that she had left them and that she would most likely never see her other daughter and grandchild again before she died. She told me she didn't regret leaving to find me, but she couldn't help feeling bad that she had had to leave another daughter behind in order to do so, even though Cecilia was no longer a child and had her own family."

"Did she also feel guilty about leaving your father?"

"I don't think so. She never said, and, while she admitted to me eventually that she understood my father's motives for leaving Terme Vigliatore, I think whatever love she had once had for him had vanished."

Sorella Agata took a deep breath.

"Marco's kidnapping me changed so many people's lives. Never in a million years would I have thought my mother would fall out of love with my father or that she would leave him. When I think about how happy they were, how happy we all were as a family together . . ." Sorella Agata's voice trailed off as she bit her lip.

"Life can be very cruel," Claudia softly said.

"Ah! We all have our crosses to bear, some more so than others, and I learned a long time ago, I cannot question God's ways. And when I think about all I have done and still have to do to help others and continue God's work, that is what matters."

Claudia was amazed by Sorella Agata's outlook, but she also sensed this had been her way all along of coping with the injustices that life had dealt out to her and her loved ones. This was how Sorella Agata had survived—through her faith and her work in helping others.

"So I take it you have not given up on finding your father and Cecilia someday?"

"I have not. I continue to pray to God to let us be reunited or at least to let me know what happened to them. But I have run up against a wall. Again, as with my mother, I must await a miracle."

"Have you tried doing a search on the Internet? Or how about hiring a private investigator? I know it would be expensive, but they often have success with cases like these."

Sorella Agata smiled. "I have searched their names numerous times on the Internet, but nothing. All I found was Cecilia's marital record. And I simply cannot justify spending the money it would take to hire a private investigator when the pastry shop and the convent need that money."

"But it seems like the shop does well. Surely, everyone would understand if—"

"No, Claudia. It is self-serving. I have made my peace. If God wants me to be reunited with my sister and father, then He will find a way to do so. Besides, there is no guarantee the private investigator would be able to locate them."

Claudia couldn't help wondering if perhaps another reason why Sorella Agata didn't want to hire a private investigator was that she couldn't handle yet another disappointment. But she also knew the nun's priority above all else was to serve others before herself.

"And Antonio? I suppose you never did hear from him again?"

"Antonio came back to the Convento di Santa Lucia del Mela."

"He did?" Claudia asked, stunned.

"Four years ago."

They were interrupted by a knock on Claudia's door.

"Excuse me, Sorella Agata, Claudia." Veronique greeted them with a bow of her head. "I didn't realize anyone was in here. I wanted to change the sheets since I didn't have a chance to do them this morning. I'll come back later." She turned to leave, but Sorella Agata called out to her.

"No, it is all right, my child. Claudia and I can continue talking in the courtyard. I know it's a bit chilly outside tonight, but it's not too cold to take a stroll as long as we wear sweaters."

Sorella Agata stood up, leaving Claudia no choice but to follow her. She found it strange that Sorella Agata hadn't asked her whether she minded continuing their talk outside. Usually, she was very courteous, asking Claudia if she was comfortable and if she could get her any-thing—anything usually meaning sweets of course—and if where they chose to have their interviews was fine since they alternated between the courtyard and the sitting room. In spite of what Sorella Agata had said, it was more than just a little chilly outside today. The average temperature for this time of year in Sicily was in the fifties, but for the past few days the temperature hadn't gotten out of the forties. But Claudia didn't object.

Grabbing their sweaters from the coat closet downstairs, they stepped out into the brisk air. Claudia couldn't help finding it odd that Veronique had mentioned she was going to change the sheets.

"Does Veronique also help with the chores at the convent even though she's an apprentice? Is that part of the bargain you have with all the apprentices at the pastry shop?"

"No, of course not. Other than cleaning up the kitchen after they've learned their pastry making for the day, apprentices are not expected to help the nuns with our chores in the convent. I've told Veronique this many times, but she insists on helping when she isn't apprenticing in the kitchen or shop. So I've given up on asking her not to. She seems content to help us, I suppose because she is grateful for all that we have taught her."

They walked quietly for a little while. Claudia decided to wait until Sorella Agata was ready to begin talking about Antonio instead of prompting her. She could only imagine how hard it would be for her to talk about how it had felt to see him again after so many years had passed since they'd last seen each other. Finally, Sorella Agata broke the silence.

"I love taking walks. It helps to clear my mind."

Sorella Agata breathed deeply before glancing over her shoulder, almost as if to check that no one was within earshot.

"I don't believe you've ever been to the abandoned chapel, Claudia, have you?"

"No, I've just walked by it. I didn't want to go in and disturb the residents there."

"Actually, no one is living there now. I must've forgotten to mention that to you. After I opened the women's shelter in town, I was able to move the women who were staying in the abandoned chapel."

"That makes sense. I should've thought of that."

"Let's go to the chapel. It's getting too cold to remain out here, and it will give us privacy while we talk."

As Claudia followed Sorella Agata to the abandoned chapel, her heart raced in anticipation. She had been dying to know what had happened to Antonio. Although Claudia knew it was not the ending she had hoped for, now that Rosalia was Sorella Agata and naturally there was no chance that their romance would have been resumed, she was still curious to hear where Antonio's life had taken him since he had left for Paris. Had he become a renowned chef? Had he found love again? Or had he never forgotten Rosalia . . . ?

❧ 31 ❧

Torta Savoia

CHOCOLATE HAZELNUT CAKE

January 1, 2000

Sorella Agata couldn't believe it was not only the start of a new year, but also the beginning of a new century. Where had the time gone? In the past thirty-five years since she had started the Rifugio delle Donne Sant' Anna, the women's shelter in town, she had been busier than ever. And then in 1985, her duties had increased at the convent when she had assumed the role of mother superior. At sixty-five years old, Madre Carmela had been getting up there in years and was getting more tired. As Madre's right hand in the convent and the pastry shop, it was only natural that Sorella Agata would become mother superior. But she insisted on still being called Sorella Agata, and she continued to address Madre Carmela as Madre. Sorella Agata could not think of her as anything else.

Some days, she did not know where she found the energy to split her time between the pastry shop and her work at the shelter. She often went to the shelter in the evenings, after siesta, and skipped her evening supper. Although she was tired, the work also renewed her spirit and gave her a sense of fulfillment. The work at the Rifugio delle Donne Sant' Anna had also saved her. For it kept her mind off of the fact that she had not been able to find her family. While she was preoccupied and the ache in her heart had dimmed a bit, it had never completely faded.

But Sorella Agata was human. While she now knew this was God's purpose for her—helping women who had met with some horrible fate in life—she couldn't help wondering from time to time what her life would have been like if she had followed another path. What if she had moved to Paris with Antonio and become his wife? Once these thoughts entered her head, she chastised herself. It was not for her to question the road God had placed her on. Still. When she was whipping up her pastries, she sometimes thought about Antonio, and wondered what had become of her old friend who had loved her so much. Her cheeks still burned when she remembered the look of hurt on his face on that day so long ago when she had turned him away and had been so mean to him. She prayed he had found it in his heart to forgive her, and she also prayed he did not think too badly of her. That is, if he thought of her at all after all this time.

"*Buon anno,* Sorella!"

"Elisabetta! I mean, Sorella Lucia, you scared me."

Sorella Agata placed her hand over her heart. From time to time, she still called her old friend Elisabetta instead of the name she had chosen once she became a nun. Sorella Lucia, as well as Teresa, also forgot from time to time and called her Rosalia. Every time this happened, they would look at each other, smile, and then act as if it hadn't happened.

Strangely though, Madre had never once slipped and called her Rosalia except when she was trying to make Mamma feel comfortable after she'd come to live with them at the convent. For some reason, this sometimes made Sorella Agata a little sad. She would have thought that, if anyone would have a hard time no longer calling her Rosalia, it would've been Madre Carmela. Whenever Sorella Agata would wonder about this, almost immediately afterward she would feel silly and even a little guilty for feeling this way. After all, why should she feel sad that Madre always remembered to call her Sorella Agata? It was who she was now, and to this day, she had never regretted for a second her vocation.

"I'm sorry for startling you, Sorella Agata," Sorella Lucia said, before busying herself with washing a sink full of prep dishes as she hummed a hymn to herself.

"That's all right. I must say I've been more skittish than usual lately. And Happy New Year to you, too. Where are my manners? I was lost in thought when you startled me. I couldn't believe another year is upon us, and that it is the start of a new millennium."

Sorella Lucia stopped humming. She glanced over her shoulder at Sorella Agata, but then returned her gaze to the cake pan she was scrubbing.

"Isn't it funny, Sorella Agata, how the older we get, the quicker time seems to pass, whereas when we were children, time seemed infinite."

"I wouldn't say it's funny, but yes, I suppose someone upstairs is having a bit of fun with us, for once we're aware of how short life really is, the days just seem to get shorter. Then again, it's natural a child would feel that time passes slowly, especially since children can feel quite invincible."

Sorella Agata thought about when she and Luca were children, running around in the back of their house. The days had felt endless, and when they would talk about how they couldn't wait to grow up, it had felt like the future was a long way off. If only she had known then just how soon everything would change, and how short their time together would be—how short Luca's life would be. She prayed for her brother's soul every day, as well as for her mother's. And whenever she was taking a stroll through the courtyard, she looked to see if her bluethroat friend would visit her again. But since the day Mamma had told her about Luca's death, she'd no longer seen the bluethroat.

"Are you all right, Sorella Agata?"

Sorella Lucia had finished washing the dishes and was now drying them off with a linen towel.

"*Si, si.* You know me. My mind is always wandering." When she noticed the look of concern in Sorella Lucia's face, Sorella Agata quickly added, "All the things I have to do here at the shop and at the shelter. Our work is never done."

She smiled, averting her gaze from Sorella Lucia's lest Sorella Lucia realize she was lying. Silently, she said a quick prayer, asking God to forgive her little white lie.

"The nerve!" Teresa came storming into the kitchen, slamming down a large sack of flour onto one of the work counters and sending a haze of flour particles into the air. She coughed.

"What is the matter, Teresa?"

Sorella Lucia went to her sister's side and brushed some flour out of her hair. It still warmed Sorella Agata's heart to see how close the two sisters had become once Teresa had returned to the convent.

"There is a customer in the pastry shop insisting that something tastes off with our *Torta Savoia*. I told him he was mistaken, but he kept insisting. He said there wasn't enough rum in it. Then he asked if we made our own hazelnut chocolate cream or if we were using the version that's sold in a jar. That's when I lost it and screamed, 'Nutella?! We make everything from scratch here.' "

"Calm down, Teresa. He was just a pesky customer. We've had those before. I don't know why you're getting yourself so worked up." But Sorella Agata couldn't help feeling a bit irked by the man's accusations. The Nutella comment especially grated on her nerves.

"What are you talking about? It's rare a customer is dissatisfied with our pastries," Teresa said.

"That's not true, Teresa. We've had patrons question our pastries, especially my *cassata*."

"But they are questioning your *cassata* because it is so delicious and its taste far surpasses that of any others they've had. This pompous idiot is questioning our chocolate hazelnut cake, implying it's horrible and even suggesting that we forgot to add an ingredient or used inferior ingredients like Nutella."

"Nutella is absolutely delicious and a very good substitute if a home cook doesn't have the time to make his or her own chocolate hazelnut cream. But at our pastry shop, we pride ourselves on making everything from scratch. There really is no need to take such offense, Teresa," Sorella Lucia chimed in.

"Well, I cannot be as magnanimous as the two of you. I told him he could leave and never step foot in our shop again."

"You didn't, Teresa!" Sorella Agata exclaimed, shocked that even Teresa would treat a customer in such a way.

"I did. But he wouldn't leave. He said he wanted to meet the chef who had made this mediocre cake. He actually called it mediocre!"

Sorella Agata remained quiet, doing her best not to let this customer's comments get to her the way they had gotten to Teresa. She took pride in her work, though she always strived to keep her pride from turning into arrogance. After all, she worked to serve God, even with her pastry making. But she couldn't help taking some offense at this man's harsh criticisms of her baking.

"He is still in the shop?" Sorella Agata would confront him and defend her cake.

"He is. I'll take you to him."

Sorella Agata and even Sorella Lucia followed Teresa, who was all but running, to the pastry shop. In her mind, Sorella Agata rehearsed how she would calmly tell the customer there was no mistake in how she'd made the cake. She would listen to him, let him have his say, and then once she defended her work, she would offer him another pastry, free of charge. She was not going to engage him like Teresa had—or worse yet—be so rude toward him.

They stepped into the pastry shop, which was full of customers. Quickly, Sorella Agata assessed the workers behind the counter and the line of patrons waiting to be served. The line seemed to be moving along, and none of the other workers looked flustered. At least this customer hadn't rankled any of them.

"He's right there." Teresa pointed toward a man whose hands were clasped behind his back as he looked at a photo of the pastry shop taken back in the fifties. He had a full head of hair, but it was all gray. She had expected the customer to be someone much younger. She then saw him turn to a young, attractive woman who was standing beside him, and he gestured toward the picture with his head as he said something to her. The woman nodded her head, but barely glanced at the photo. Her eyes held a dark, vacant stare, and for a moment Sorella Agata felt a slight chill. There was something familiar about the haunted look in that girl's eyes, and she had a strange feeling in the pit of her belly that something was very wrong.

Sorella Agata made her way toward the man. Clearing her throat, she said, "Excuse me, *signore*. I understand you wanted to meet the chef who made the *Torta Savoia* you are not happy with?"

She waited, but the man did not turn around immediately. The woman beside him glanced at her, but when their eyes met, she quickly lowered her gaze. Then, the man turned around. His eyes held a twinkle, and were those tears she saw as well? For the second time that morning, Sorella Agata pressed her hand to her heart. Surely, she was mistaken. But the eyes that stared back at her and even the smile were the same as those of the young man she had once fallen in love with.

"Rosalia."

His voice had deepened with age, and even had a quality to it, much like that of a smoker. Had he taken up smoking since she'd last seen him? He was staring at her, waiting for her to say something, but she was still too shocked.

"It is so good to see you, my dear, old friend."

As soon as Sorella Agata heard those words, tears quickly slid down her face. He had forgiven her. She could see it in his eyes and hear it in the way he had called her his dear, old friend. She shook her head, feeling as if she didn't deserve his forgiveness. For she had never forgiven herself for the horrible words she had spoken to him all those years ago.

Finally, she said, "I'm so sorry, Antonio."

"You have no need to be sorry."

He stepped forward and embraced her. And in that moment, as memories of the time they'd once spent together came rushing back to her, she was no longer Sorella Agata, but instead was Rosalia—the teenage girl who had briefly given her heart to the young boy who had made her feel safe, special, and loved.

A few minutes later, Sorella Agata, Antonio, Teresa, and Sorella Lucia were chatting away. Well, Teresa and Sorella Lucia were doing most of the talking, filling Antonio in on the changes the pastry shop had undergone in the years since he'd left. Antonio listened patiently and offered a word here and there, but his gaze kept floating over to Sorella Agata, who was still getting over her initial shock at seeing him again. She then realized Teresa had made up the whole story about the disgruntled patron.

"Teresa, why didn't you just tell me Antonio was here instead of coming up with that elaborate story? We're not silly young women any longer."

"What fun would that have been? Besides, I didn't make up the entire story. I didn't recognize Antonio right away, and he did say all those things about your chocolate hazelnut cake."

Sorella Agata looked questioningly at Antonio, hurt evident in her face. He really thought she hadn't added enough rum to the cake and that she had used Nutella?

But just like the times when they were young and Antonio had been so perceptive in sensing her feelings and thoughts, he patted her shoulder reassuringly and said, "I was joking. I remembered how easy it used to be to rile Teresa, and I wanted to see if she'd changed. Needless to say, I was happy to see she hadn't." He laughed.

Teresa swatted his arm playfully. "And you haven't changed either. Well, except for the wrinkles and the gray hair."

Though he had aged, he was still a handsome man, even in his sixties. Sorella Agata then realized that Antonio must've been shocked to see her in a nun's habit, and surely, he would think she had changed considerably.

Never one to exercise delicacy, Teresa blurted, "Well, I'm sure you both want to catch up. Antonio, Elisabetta and I can take your granddaughter back to the convent with us. She looks tired. She can wait for you in our sitting room. We'll keep her company and tell her stories about what a devil you were when you were young."

His granddaughter. Of course. Sorella Agata should have realized when she saw how young the woman by his side was that she had to be his granddaughter. She even noticed that they had the same shape eyes and nose. So he had found someone else to love and had married. She was glad. Sorella Agata had prayed that Antonio would meet a woman who would be kind to him and give him the love he deserved. She had always wanted him to be happy, especially knowing how she'd hurt him. She wondered where his wife was now. Maybe she'd stayed behind in Paris—that is, if he still lived there. Suddenly, a flurry of questions raced through her mind. Why after all these years had he come back to the convent? Surely, it could not have been just to see her?

Antonio looked at his granddaughter. Worry was etched across his features, and he looked as if he was about to turn down Teresa's offer, but then the young girl spoke up.

"That is fine, Nonno. I am tired. I can rest. Take your time talking to your friend."

The girl spoke perfect Italian, but there was a definite French accent. So they did still live in France.

Sorella Agata walked over to her and extended her hand. "I am Sorella Agata. It is a pleasure to meet you."

"I thought your name was Rosalia?" The girl looked from her to her grandfather, confused.

"Ah. Yes, that is, I mean *was,* my name before I became a nun. Once we take our vows, we choose new names."

"I'm sorry, Rosalia. I should have asked—" Antonio looked slightly uncomfortable.

Sorella Agata held up her hand. "Please, don't worry. Teresa and Sorella Lucia still forget and call me Rosalia from time to time."

"*Piacere,* Sorella. My name is Veronique."

Antonio lightly slapped his forehead. "I'm sorry I didn't introduce you sooner. This is my granddaughter. I don't know what is wrong with me today. Too much excitement, I suppose."

"Sorella Lucia, Teresa, please make sure Veronique is comfortable and bring her something to drink and a few of our pastries."

Veronique followed Sorella Lucia and Teresa, and though Teresa had started regaling the young woman with tales of her grandfather from when he was an apprentice at the convent, Sorella Agata noticed it looked as if Veronique's attention was elsewhere. Why was she so sad?

"You must be tired as well, Antonio. Please, let me get you an espresso. Do you want another slice of *Torta Savoia*—that is, if you really had no objections to how it tasted?" Sorella Agata raised an eyebrow.

"Ah! I see it bothered you when you thought you had a customer questioning your expertise? I'm glad to see not everything has changed with you, Rosa—I mean, Sorella Agata."

An awkward silence followed before Sorella Agata excused herself to get their cups of espresso. She cut an extra-large slice of cake for Antonio, but while she was behind the display case, she quickly broke off a small piece of cake and tasted it. Intense hazelnut and rich chocolate greeted her, and the rum was discernible but not overly potent. The *Torta Savoia* was how it should be. Nothing was wrong with it. Antonio had been joking with Teresa after all. Placing the plates of cake slices and cups of espresso on a platter, she carried them out to Antonio, who she saw had stepped outside and seated himself at one of the tables.

"It is still as beautiful and serene here as I remember it." Antonio's eyes scanned the courtyard and gardens.

"Not much has changed out here, but we have made a few renovations, especially in the abandoned chapel where you used to sleep. I will have to take you there later and show it to you."

"I would like that."

They glanced at each other for a moment, and Sorella Agata quickly looked away. Was he also thinking about the time he had taken her to the abandoned chapel, when he had told her for the first time he was falling in love with her?

"Your granddaughter is beautiful."

"*Grazie.* I treasure her."

Sorella Agata was about to ask him about his wife when Antonio surprised her with his next question.

"And you, Rosalia? Are you happy?"

Sorella Agata was about to correct him, but didn't want to make things any more awkward than they already were.

"I am. Since I received God's calling to become a nun and serve Him, I have been so fulfilled. As I'm sure you saw, the pastry shop is doing better than ever, which has helped greatly not only to keep our convent running, but also to support a women's shelter I founded in town."

"I have heard about the shelter and all the wonderful things you have done for those women. Naturally, I was not surprised to hear of your work there after what you'd been through."

"Helping these women has helped with my own healing, just as the pastries helped me find a sense of purpose in those first dark days after Madre Carmela had rescued me."

"How is Madre? I forgot to ask Teresa if she is still alive."

"She is, but I have taken over her mother superior duties. She is getting quite up there in years, and it was too much for her. I am also the head pastry chef at the shop now."

"I heard that as well. And I have heard about the controversy with your *cassata*."

"Who has been talking about me so much to you?"

"Teresa told me about your being mother superior and the head pastry chef now, but I actually had heard about the shelter elsewhere. We have a lot to talk about, but first I must ask you, did you ever find your family?"

"Yes and no."

Sorella Agata told Antonio everything, from how she had been reunited with her mother and had learned about Luca's death to how they had not been able to locate her father and Cecilia.

"So bittersweet, my friend. I'm sorry. You have had more than your share of heartache in this life, and still, you find it in yourself to help others. I always knew you were amazing, Rosalia, but now that I see what a wonderful woman you have become, I am even more floored."

"It has been hard work to get to where I am now. And I still struggle at times, wondering why my family and I have suffered so much. But it is not for us to know God's plans for us. We must place our faith in Him and do our best."

Antonio pressed his lips tightly together. "I suppose you are right. My faith in God has been tested, and I must be honest, I do not know if it will ever be restored."

Without thinking, Sorella Agata placed her hand over Antonio's, which rested on the table.

"We all go through difficult times, Antonio. And we all are tested. Please, do not abandon God. He will be there for you during your most trying times."

Antonio sighed deeply, but remained silent. Sorella Agata removed her hand from his. It pained her to see her old friend like this. She wondered what had happened to make him question his faith.

"So I take it you are still looking for your father and sister?"

"Not actively. I'm afraid I have run up against a wall and have simply not been able to find out more. But I still pray every day to God that if He wills it, as He did with my mother, He might let me be reunited with them someday—or at least learn what became of them. After so many years, I have found a way to make my peace with everything that happened and with the very real possibility that I may never see the last of my surviving family members. That is, if Cecilia and Papà are still alive."

Antonio sighed. "I suppose that is all you can ask for. I am just glad to see you have managed to make a fulfilling life for yourself in spite of your losses."

"Please, Antonio. Tell me all that you have been up to since you left for Paris. I have thought of you often and wondered if you were cooking in some of Paris's best restaurants."

"You thought of me often?" Antonio sounded surprised.

"I have. I hoped you were well and happy. I hoped in your heart you knew that I never meant to hurt you all those years ago. I truly am sorry, Antonio. I never should have told you that you were the same as Marco. How could I have made such a comparison? You were always kind to me and patient. I wasn't in my right mind when I said those words, but mostly, I was scared. You see, I've come to realize, Antonio, that the reason I said those terrible things to you and pushed you away is that I was afraid of letting go of my family—letting go of the idea of finding them. I think part of me thought if I married you and moved to Paris, I would in essence be starting this new life without them. I know you told me the move would've been temporary, and I know you are a man of your word, but it was easier for me to believe you would not have moved back to Sicily. Please know, Antonio, I did care about you, and in my own way, I loved you, too. But I came to see I was nowhere near ready to commit to any man. It was still too soon after what Marco had done to me. You deserved to be with someone who could give you so much more than I could."

"*Grazie* for telling me all of this, Rosalia, I mean, Sorella Agata.

Forgive me, but it is still hard to get used to calling you by a different name."

"I'm sure it must have been a shock for you to learn that I had become a nun." Sorella Agata smiled.

"It was at first. But the more I think about it, the more it makes sense. I often thought about you, too, and only wanted you to be happy as well. I can see, from the way you talk about the work you've accomplished in the shop and at the shelter, you have found peace and contentment in your life. But as your old friend, I must also be frank with you. I can see there is still a sadness in your eyes that has been there since I first met you that day, out here in the courtyard, when you were chasing that bluethroat. And now that you have told me how you still long to be reunited with your father and sister, I know that is where your sadness stems from."

"You always were able to read me so well. The ache was much less when Mamma was here with me. I am so grateful to God that I had that time with her. But enough about me. Please. Don't keep me in suspense any longer. Did you become a great chef? And naturally, you must've married since you have a granddaughter."

Antonio's eyes narrowed.

"Paris was wonderful. It was everything I had imagined it to be and more. I did complete my studies at Le Cordon Bleu, and I was head chef at three renowned restaurants in Paris. So like you, I have been very successful and am proud of my accomplishments. I did meet a very nice French woman whom I married. Her name was Claudette. I met her three years after I moved to Paris. Believe it or not, I was pining for you all that time and would not allow myself to date anyone. The naïve young man I once was believed you would have a change of heart."

Sorella Agata blushed.

"I'm sorry. I shouldn't have told you that. I don't want you to feel bad. As you said, God has His plans for us, and He didn't think we would be a good fit. We probably would've killed each other, each trying to best the other with our baking!" Antonio laughed.

Sorella Agata joined him. "That is true! We were quite competitive!"

"As I was saying, I met Claudette three years after I moved to Paris. We got married two years later. She was a dear woman, very sweet and patient. Eventually, I opened up my own restaurant in Paris. Claudette helped me manage it. We had only one child—a son we named Giovanni. He was all that a father could hope for in a son—kind, honest, hardworking. Giovanni followed in my footsteps and was training to become a chef. He worked at my restaurant in the evenings, and during the day he was in culinary school. When he was twenty-one, he began dating Noelle, one of the waitresses at my restaurant, and then the following year they were married. They had Veronique a year later. We were all so happy, working together at the restaurant, helping Giovanni and Noelle raise Veronique. Our restaurant was doing well, too. But then two years after Veronique was born, there was a fire at the restaurant. It was during the afternoon. Giovanni was prepping for the night's dinner, and Claudette and Noelle were there helping him. I had a meeting with a vendor, so I wasn't there. Fortunately, Noelle's parents were watching Veronique that day. I'm not sure what happened, how the fire got started, but it destroyed the entire restaurant and killed my wife, son, and daughter-in-law. So Veronique was left orphaned at only two years old. I have raised her since. Noelle's parents wanted to raise her, but I was quite staunch in my insistence that I raise her. I think they didn't have the heart to take her away from me after I had lost my wife and son."

"Oh, Antonio! I am so, so sorry! Now I understand what you meant when you said your faith has been tested."

Antonio took a sip of his espresso. "There's more. Although I was upset with God for taking away my wife and only son and making my granddaughter an orphan, I still went to church and prayed. It is what happened later that has made me greatly question my faith.

"After the fire, I took a job working as a chef in a restaurant. I didn't have the energy or the heart to open another restaurant without my wife and son to help me. I also had to think about Veronique. She needed me, and the hours that would've been required had I started another business would've made it nearly impossible for me to be an adequate caretaker. Noelle's parents watched her while I worked at the restaurant in the evenings. They were a godsend.

"But a few months ago, Veronique and I decided to move back to Sicily."

"How old is she? Eighteen?"

"She's only fifteen, but she is often mistaken for being older, even as old as her early twenties. She's very beautiful, as you noticed."

"I did. But I also couldn't help but notice how sad she is, Antonio."

Pain flashed through his eyes.

"I am getting to that. So as I was saying, we moved back to Sicily a few months ago. I bought a small *trattoria,* just outside of Santa Lucia del Mela."

"You have been here for a few months, and you've only come by to visit now?"

"At first, I was busy getting the restaurant up and running. And once that happened, I wanted to come see you, but I must admit I couldn't help remembering how upset you had been with me when we argued, not long before I moved to Paris. I was afraid that maybe you would not receive me so well, even after all these years. Though I knew you didn't mean what you said that day, I didn't want to upset you, and I had no idea where your life had taken you or even if you were still here. So I needed some time to gather the strength to come back here to find out what had happened to you, and, if you were still here, to confront you. But I should've known all along that we would still be the good friends we were all those years ago."

Antonio smiled before continuing. "I thought about leaving Paris and coming back home to Sicily after I lost Claudette and Giovanni in the fire, but I didn't want to take Veronique away from her maternal grandparents, and, as I said, they helped me raise her when I was working. But something happened in Paris that made me realize we could no longer stay there. Veronique is fifteen now, and both her maternal grandparents passed away in the past couple of years. So we made the move.

"One day while I was in my *trattoria,* I overheard the conversation at one of the tables of patrons who were dining there. They were talking about the shelter for abused women that you had founded in town. But I had no idea you were the one who had started the shelter, since they were referring to you as Sorella Agata, and naturally, I didn't know you had become a nun.

"So finally, one day, I had time and decided I would work up the courage to go to the pastry shop to see if you were still there. This was a week ago. I asked one of the nuns behind the seller's window if you still worked there, and she told me you no longer went by Rosalia, but instead were now Sorella Agata. I thought she was mistaken and gave her your full name—Rosalia DiSanta—but she told me that you were the only Rosalia to have worked at the shop. I was quite shocked that you had become a nun, but, as I mentioned before, the more I thought about it, the less I was surprised. After all, you hadn't allowed yourself to be loved by me because of what had happened to you in that horrible cave. So I realized it had been hard for you to trust men, and if you weren't able to fully trust me, then there was a good chance you would never feel completely comfortable trusting another man."

"That is true, Antonio, but my becoming a nun was about so much more than that. I truly received a calling and wanted to serve God to the fullest."

"I can see that now, especially after learning about the women's shelter and the work you've done. I'm sorry. I didn't mean to offend you. I am just being honest about what my thoughts were when I found out you had become a nun."

"Go on."

"After getting over my initial shock, I asked the nun behind the pastry shop window if you were there and if I could talk to you. She told me you were at the shelter. I then remembered the people at my restaurant talking about the shelter and saying that a Sorella Agata ran it. I couldn't believe the irony of all of this and wondered if God had sent Veronique and me back to Sicily for this reason."

"Irony? I'm sorry, Antonio, I'm not following you."

"You were right in noting earlier that Veronique looks sad. She has been through hell. You see, Rosalia, like you were all those years ago when you were just a teenager, my granddaughter was raped."

Sorella Agata once again felt the shiver she had felt when she first saw the haunted look in Veronique's eyes while she stood next to Antonio in the pastry shop. Now, Sorella Agata knew why she had sensed something was very wrong. For Veronique had the same vacant, dark stare Sorella Agata had had when she looked at herself in the mirror for weeks after Madre Carmela had rescued her from the cave. Tears came to her eyes.

"Oh, Antonio, you and your family have been through so much as well. May I ask when it happened?"

"It happened last year. As with you, it was someone she knew, a boy from her school. He followed her as she was coming home one evening. It was winter, so the streets were already dark as she was making her way home on her bicycle. He came up from behind her, caused her to fall off her bicycle, and then he clapped his hand over her mouth as he carried her to an alleyway. I don't know how she was able to pull herself together and make her way back home afterward."

Antonio ran his hand through his hair. Then, he began sobbing.

Sorella Agata stood up and went over to him. She knelt by his side and spoke to him.

"There was nothing you could have done, Antonio. It was not your fault. I, of all people, know about blaming oneself, and it took me a very long time to realize there was nothing I or anyone else could have done to prevent what Marco did to me. And it is the same with what happened to Veronique. Do you hear me?"

"I should have known you would know I was feeling guilty. I shouldn't have let her come home by herself once the sun went down earlier in the winter."

"You can't watch her all the time. Please, don't blame yourself any longer. It will do little good in helping Veronique get the help she needs, and it will only hinder both of you."

"Oh, Rosalia, she still screams at night from the nightmares she has. I've tried to get her therapy, but the therapist told me she refuses to say a word during their sessions together. I don't know what to do to get through to her. I was hoping these last few months, being here in Sicily, would help—the change of scenery and all—but she still seems unreachable. At least she does help me in the restaurant. I think that is a bit of a distraction for her. But I'm afraid it's not much. She has nightmares several times a week. Will you try to help her, Rosalia? Please. She's all I have left, and I'm afraid of what will happen to her once I'm gone someday if she hasn't found a way to come to terms with what happened to her."

"Of course, I will help her, my friend. And I promise you, she *will* get better."

∽ 32 ∽

Fior di Pistacchio

CHEWY PISTACHIO COOKIES

Night of November 11, 2004–Morning of November 12, 2004

Claudia looked around at the interior of the small abandoned chapel. The only features remaining that gave any indication it had once been a chapel were a few stained-glass windows and a life-size statue of the Madonna that stood in the entryway. The other saints' statues that had once surrounded its interior had been moved to the active chapel where the nuns went to Mass. After the chapel had been renovated to provide a safe haven for the women Sorella Agata had first rescued from the streets, the furnishings were kept simple, but there were a few touches that gave it a cozier sense of home like the ceramic vases holding silk flowers that adorned the night tables. Claudia was almost certain Sorella Agata's mother had made these silk flowers. Small paintings depicting Sicilian landscapes such as Mount Etna and the beaches of Taormina hung on the walls. Claudia couldn't help but see the irony in Sorella Agata's relaying the story of her reunion with Antonio here in the chapel where he had lived while staying at the convent and where he had first told her he was in love with her.

"So your apprentice, Veronique, is Antonio's granddaughter."

Claudia said this more as a statement than a question, since it would have been too much of a coincidence that there would be another woman with the name of Veronique, which was uncommon in Italy. She then remembered how she had noticed that Veronique's accent wasn't completely Italian. And, of course, her name was French.

"*Sì*. She is Antonio's granddaughter."

"Does she live here now?"

"Not permanently. She still lives with her grandfather for half of the week, and the other half, including weekends, she lives here. Antonio's home and *trattoria* are just outside of town, and it is easier for Veronique to sleep here while she is studying to become a pastry chef."

"She doesn't seem at all like the young girl you described when you first met her four years ago. I didn't detect any sadness in her; rather she seemed like any other happy teenager who was inquisitive about the world."

"Now, she is like this, and Antonio tells me she was like this before she was raped. Thankfully, she has made enormous strides in healing from her ordeal, and she has learned to put it as much as possible behind her."

"So you were able to help her, then."

"I was. But I must say, for a time, I was afraid I wouldn't be able to keep my promise to Antonio that she would get better. It took Veronique even longer than it took me to engage with the world. I even tried the tactics Madre Carmela had used with me, introducing her to a new sweet every time I spoke to her. In the beginning, Antonio was only bringing her here on his days off from the restaurant, which usually only amounted to one or two days a week. He couldn't spare more time away since the restaurant was still new, and he was trying to keep it afloat to make a new life for himself and Veronique here. He didn't want to leave her full-time with a bunch of strangers either. She was still very mistrustful of everyone, even women. After a month, I could see she seemed to relax more when she came here. She liked going to our sitting room and reading a few of the books we keep in the bookshelves there. I sensed that if she didn't spend more time with me, I would not be able to get through to her. So one day, I asked her if she would feel comfortable staying here for a few days, so I could show her how to bake. I told her this way she could prepare the desserts in her grandfather's *trattoria,* and how wonderful that would be if the desserts the restaurant's patrons were eating were made by her own hands. That was the first time that I saw a flicker of something in her eyes. She said she would like that.

"We started off slowly, and she only stayed for the weekends at first. I began by teaching her the simpler desserts so she wouldn't get frustrated immediately and possibly give up. But I had no cause to worry. She was a rapid learner and eager to move on to the next pastry once she had mastered the previous one. She reminded me so much of myself in those early days when I was getting over my own ordeal and becoming more enraptured with pastry making. After a few months, she agreed to stay half of the week, and I offered her the opportunity to be one of our apprentices. She readily accepted.

"Six months later, I felt that perhaps she might be ready to hear the story of how Marco had kidnapped and violated me. She listened, but said nothing once I was done. I never asked her outright to talk to me about what had happened to her. I knew she had to want to talk about it, and she had to come to me of her own will. A few weeks after I'd told her what had happened to me, she surprised me one evening as I was getting ready for bed. She told me all about her classmate following her on her way home and how he had raped her in that alleyway. She then told me that she had felt different from other girls her age after that had happened to her, and she had hated herself for it. But when she heard I had also been raped and she saw how I had managed to survive and have the life I have, she realized there was hope for her. She cried and told me she wanted to get better and try to move on.

"With her permission, I referred her to a counselor at the shelter I'd founded. I told her I could be present for the first few sessions until she felt more comfortable with the counselor. She was scared, but she decided to trust me. After the first session, she told me she would be fine meeting with the counselor alone. And from that day forward, she continued to get better."

"You gave her something to live for, Sorella Agata, just as Madre

Carmela had given you something to live for by teaching you how to make pastries."

"I didn't realize until I became a nun how brilliant Madre's strategies for helping me to heal were. But isn't that what most of us want and need out of life—a sense of purpose, a chance to feel that we have something to give back to the world? Veronique and I both felt like we were no good after what had happened to us. For a brief time, we let the men who had violated us take away our dignity and sense of self-worth. Besides providing the women at the shelter with a safe haven, I and the other volunteers there work with them to help them realize they still have so much of themselves to give back to the world."

"If you wouldn't mind, Sorella, I would love to see this shelter you founded before I head back to New York."

Sorella Agata's face lit up. "Of course. I would love to take you there and introduce you to a few of the women."

"So you must see Antonio regularly since his granddaughter stays here part of the week. How has it been these past few years since he's been back?"

"He has continued to be the dear friend he was when I needed one the most all those years ago. I, and the other sisters here, have even dined at his *trattoria*—free of charge!" Sorella Agata laughed.

It was good for Claudia to see her laugh after all the tears she'd seen the poor woman shed, which reminded her . . .

"Sorella, I have yet to actually watch you make the *cassata*. I haven't wanted to pressure you, but given that my stay here is almost up, do you think I could watch you make it tomorrow?"

"Tomorrow it will be, but again, I must warn you that you will be disappointed. There is—"

"No secret ingredient. Yes, I know!" Claudia laughed.

The following morning, Claudia woke up early and headed down to the kitchen, anxious to finally witness Sorella Agata make her *cassata*. Claudia tried to keep her expectations low because she knew there was the very real chance she would not discover the nun's secret since Sorella Agata kept insisting there wasn't one.

When Claudia reached the kitchen, she was surprised to see an older gentleman taking a baking sheet out of the oven. Puffy-looking cookies coated in confectioners' sugar lined the baking sheet. Claudia didn't think she'd ever seen cookies that were baked with confectioners' sugar rather than dusting the powdered sugar on the cookies after they had baked. The man looked up when Claudia stepped in.

"*Buongiorno,*" she said, and smiled.

"*Buongiorno.* You must be Claudia." The gentleman wiped his hands with a dish towel and came over, extending his hand. "Antonio Bruni."

Claudia was speechless for a moment before she realized she'd left him hanging with his hand extended. Shaking his hand, she said, "I'm sorry. Need my espresso." She laughed lightly. "I'm Claudia Lombardo, but you knew that already."

Though he spoke heavily accented English, it was much better than Sorella Agata's English. She wondered when he had had the time to learn English since it sounded like he had been kept busy with his culinary training and running his restaurant in Paris and now the one in Sicily.

"*Si,* my granddaughter Veronique and Sorella Agata have told me about you and your book. Veronique is so excited. She can't wait to see the book."

"She's a lovely young woman, and from what I understand, she is on her way to becoming a fine pastry chef, just like Sorella Agata."

"*Si,* she is learning from the best. Me, as well." Antonio laughed boisterously.

"Sorella Agata did tell me you and she shared a friendly competition when you were both apprentices here years ago."

"*Si, si.*" Antonio's eyes seemed to go to that moment in time as he stared at the wall behind Claudia. "Have you seen this photograph?"

Claudia looked to where Antonio gestured with his head.

"No, I don't believe I have." She walked over to the photograph.

It was an old black-and-white photo of the nuns at the convent.

The photo looked like it could've been from the fifties from the style of eyeglasses a few of the nuns were wearing.

"See this young woman here?"

He pointed to where three women were standing, dressed in sundresses. The woman he pointed to had long black hair that was blowing in the breeze. Some of her hair covered part of her face.

"That is Sorella Agata. Or rather, that was her before she became a nun. She went by Rosalia back then." Antonio looked at the photo, smiling.

Claudia moved in closer. "My God, she was absolutely breathtaking. Her hair was so long."

"It was. Beautiful, dazzling black hair. But she is still beautiful. Such an amazing woman."

Claudia looked at Antonio. His eyes beamed as he said this, and she thought she heard his voice catch a little. He still loved her. While it likely wasn't the same passionate love he and Rosalia had once shared when they were young, there was no doubt he continued to care for her very much.

"*Vieni.* You must try the batch of *Fior di Pistacchio* I have made."

Claudia followed him to the counter where the baking sheet of cookies he'd taken out of the oven lay.

"So, I'm surprised Sorella Agata lets you bake in her kitchen." Claudia smiled before taking one of the *Fior di Pistacchio*.

"Eh. She lets me dabble. We did learn in this kitchen side by side all those years ago after all."

"These are so good."

"They are cookies made with pistachios and almonds, soft cookies, not like biscotti. There is another version called *Fior di Mandorla* that is made only with almonds. When Sorella Agata and I were apprenticing here, we tried the *Fior di Mandorla* from one of the best pastry shops in Messina. We memorized how they tasted, and then we came back here and made the convent's *Fior di Mandorla* taste even better than the ones we had in Messina."

Claudia remembered when Sorella Agata had told her about the first time Antonio had taken her to Messina, and she remembered her mentioning the almond cookies. But she didn't let Antonio know just how much Sorella Agata had told her about their shared past.

He looked at his watch. "Ah! I must go. It was nice to meet you, Claudia. *Arrivederci!*"

"It was nice to meet you, too."

She watched Antonio as he walked away and tried to imagine what he must've looked like when he was young. He wasn't in the group photo he had shown her. Maybe he was the one who had taken the picture? From the way he had aged, she was certain he had been a very handsome young man.

An hour later, Claudia was watching Sorella Agata make her famous *cassata*. Claudia had her legal pad in one hand and jotted down all the ingredients Sorella Agata was adding as well as noting her methods, even though the nun's recipe book lay open next to her. Of course, Sorella Agata no longer needed to follow her recipe book after all the years she'd been making her pastries; the book was there more for Claudia's sake so that she could see for herself that the nun was not deviating from the recipe—or adding any secret ingredients.

Although Sorella Agata allowed her other workers to use an electric mixer, she still preferred to beat her cake batters with a wire whisk. Being in her sixties didn't stop her from beating the cake batter with quick strokes, and she didn't seem to tire. Claudia smiled as she watched her and knew she would miss watching Sorella Agata and the other workers whipping up their heavenly creations. Sorella Agata seemed lost in thought as she stared at her batter, and then, suddenly, tears were sliding down her face. Reaching for a paper towel from the dispenser that stood on the counter, Claudia ripped off a sheet and was about to hand it to Sorella Agata when she noticed one of her teardrops spill into her cake batter. Claudia paused as she suddenly remembered all the times she'd witnessed Sorella Agata crying as she baked. She cried when she was making her cannoli . . . her *Torta al Mandarino*. . . . In fact, there were many times Claudia had seen her crying, and it was often while she was making her pastries. There had even been times when Claudia had seen Sorella Agata crying while the other pastry workers were present, but they didn't seem to pay any heed to her. Was it because they had become accustomed to seeing her cry while she worked, and there were only so many instances one could ask her if she was all right without making the situation more awkward than it already was? A thought entered Claudia's mind. Could the secret behind Sorella Agata's *cassata* be her tears? And not just her *cassata,* since Claudia had also noticed that the other pastries that were made by the nun's hands always tasted better than those that were made by the rest of the workers. Sorella Agata's pastries surpassed versions of the pastries Claudia had tried at other pastry shops in Sicily and even back home in New York. No, it was too crazy.

"Sorella, I'm sorry, but may I ask you why it seems you often cry when you are baking?"

Sorella Agata looked up, almost as if she was surprised that she'd been crying and in Claudia's presence. She took the paper towel that Claudia was still holding and dabbed at her tears.

She shrugged her shoulders and sighed. "I'm a silly old woman."

"You're not that old, Sorella."

"It's just . . ." Her voice trailed off as she looked down into her batter. Her eyes filled with tears again, but she managed to keep them at bay this time. "It's just always the same. You would think, after all these years, I would be more accustomed to the fact that my family is not in my life. That is why I cry so much. I am often thinking about them. Even when I found Mamma, and she was living here with me, I found myself crying, thinking about Luca and how I would never see him again . . . thinking about Cecilia and Papà."

Claudia walked over and hugged Sorella Agata, who looked surprised for a moment, but then she returned her hug.

"*Grazie,* Claudia. You are a fine young woman. I will miss you. It has helped me, talking to you about everything from my past. I hope you will come back and visit me again, someday?"

"Of course, Sorella. And I will miss you and everyone else here. But we will be in communication until the book is published. I hope you will be happy with the finished product."

"I'm sure I will be. I can tell, like me, you take great pride in your work and will do an excellent job with the book."

Claudia smiled before adding, "Well, I must admit, Sorella

Agata, it doesn't seem like you added any secret ingredient to your *cassata* recipe—unless, of course, it will be in the icing, since you have yet to make that." She winked.

"Eh! This whole secret to my *cassata* was dreamed up by some fool who wanted to make a big deal out of nothing. That is all."

Sorella Agata poured her cake batter into the prepared pan. Claudia still could not help wondering if there was some mystical explanation for the remarkable flavor of the *cassata* as well as the other pastries. She supposed she and the rest of the world would just never know.

EPILOGUE

Cassata

SICILIAN RICOTTA CAKE

A year and a half later . . .

It was Holy Saturday, the day before Easter. It was such a beautiful day that Sorella Agata decided to take her cake batter and mix it in the courtyard outside. Perhaps the sunshine and fresh air would make her feel better. She slowly walked outside to one of the café tables by the selling windows of the pastry shop. Sitting down, she paused a moment before mixing her batter, letting her eyes rove around the convent's gardens. She noticed the leaves on the trees' branches had multiplied since spring had started weeks ago, and the tulips and daffodils were now all in full bloom. A few birds hopped along the other café tables, looking for crumbs that had been left behind by the pastry shop's customers who had enjoyed their pastries and cappucinos for breakfast. Sorella Agata scanned the tops of the trees, but still no bluethroat was among the birds singing there. Her heart felt heavy as her mind inevitably flashed back to her childhood, when she and her family had all been together for Easter.

Doing her best to push these thoughts from her mind, she began whisking her batter. She was making her *cassata,* which was now even more famous with the publication of Claudia's book six months ago. The book had brought more attention to the shop, and as such, they were busier than ever. Sorella Agata had had to hire more workers. She had even allowed Claudia to include her story in the book, but not all of it. No mention was made of Marco or her rape. Though she was in her sixties, the fear that he would find her some day had never left her. Sometimes, she still wondered if that man she had seen in the homeless women's alleyway had been Marco. Claudia did include in the book that Sorella Agata had been separated from her family as a teenager and had gone to live at the convent, and she'd also added Sorella Agata's byline against her wishes. All of Sorella Agata's proceeds from the book went to the pastry shop and the Rifugio delle Donne Sant' Anna. She was pleasantly surprised at how much the royalties had been. Claudia had done a beautiful job in relaying both Sorella Agata's background and the story behind each of the pastries Convento di Santa Lucia del Mela created. In addition to the breathtaking photos of all the sweets the shop sold, Claudia had also included photos of the other nuns and pastry workers, which made them all giddy with excitement, especially Veronique.

Sorella Agata smiled as she thought about Antonio's granddaughter. Veronique had been a special light in her life, along with the return of her dear, old friend Antonio. They had become as much a part of her family as the other sisters and workers in the shop. She silently thanked God for giving her all of them and for every blessing in her life.

Usually, when she reminded herself of all she had to be grateful for, her spirits lifted and she was able to put aside her sorrows. But today, it didn't seem to help. Again, her mind replayed the scenes from her childhood when Papà would buy lilies for her and her mother on Easter Sunday after the entire family had attended Mass. Then, they would go home and celebrate with the special dinner Mamma had prepared, which usually was a roasted lamb, followed by Mamma's lemon cake. Luca would lead the family in a prayer before they began eating, and afterward, the family would take a *passeggiata* in town.

Sorella Agata stopped whisking her cake batter and wiped the tears that were quickly sliding down her face with the back of her hand. But as soon as she was done wiping them, more tears fell. Several drops fell into her batter without her noticing. She was too tired to try to stop crying, as she did on other occasions when her emotions got the better of her. Maybe that had been her mistake all along—fighting back the tears and sorrow as she repressed her deep pain over what had happened to her with Marco all those years ago and over losing her family. As she let the tears flow freely, they continued to fall into her cake batter.

A taxi pulled up into the courtyard's driveway, but Sorella Agata was so absorbed in her thoughts she didn't hear it until the sound of doors slamming shut reached her ears. She looked up, squinting into the distance. The driver stepped out of the taxi and opened his trunk, taking a wheelchair out. Bringing it to the side of the vehicle, he waited as a woman helped an elderly man sit in the wheelchair. The woman paid the driver and then pushed the wheelchair with the old man down the driveway leading to the convent's entrance. Sorella Agata stood up. She was about to walk toward them when she noticed the man was crying. He was saying something over and over again, but she couldn't understand his words through his choked sobs. The woman, who looked to be in her mid to late fifties, stared at Sorella Agata, her lips spreading into a slow smile. Sorella Agata then noticed the woman's hair, which was cut in a shoulder-length bob. Except for a shock of gray hair that was near the crown of the woman's head, the rest of her hair was a deep, lustrous shade of black. That was odd. While Sorella Agata's hair had several scattered grays throughout, she, too, had a shock of gray at the front. But she barely looked at her hair anymore since she had shorn it when she became a nun and now always covered it with her veil. An image then came to her mind of when she was young and her own hair had been as black and shiny as this woman's hair was. Sorella Agata's eyes opened wide as she dropped her whisk, oblivious to the cake batter that splattered all over her habit. The woman stopped pushing the wheelchair and ran toward Sorella Agata. Once she reached her, they embraced.

"Cecilia?" Sorella Agata pulled away from her sister and took a close look at her face. "It really is you!"

"*Sì,* Rosalia. It is your little sister, Cecilia! How I have prayed for this and thought of you every day since you were taken from us."

Sorella Agata hugged her sister once more before going to her father's side and dropping down to her knees. She took his frail hands in hers. He cried and leaned his head against Sorella Agata's bosom. She could now make out the word he had been repeating: "Rosalia, Rosalia."

She held him close, wiping the tears running down his cheeks with the back of her hand.

"Don't cry, Papà. We are together now."

"We finally found you, my dear daughter. We finally found you."

"You were looking for me, too, Papà?" She couldn't hide the surprise in her voice.

"Ever since your mother left, Cecilia and I have been looking for both of you. I made so many mistakes, Rosalia, and it took me so long to realize I was wrong. Please believe me when I say, I always thought about you and never stopped loving you, even when I believed you had left with that man. I was a fool. How could I have thought such a thing? Look at you. Look at the fine woman you have become."

"Papà! I missed you so much."

Sorella Agata hugged her father and instantly felt the heavy weight that had sat on her heart for the past fifty years begin to ease. She then turned to her sister.

"How did you ever find me?"

"Your book." Cecilia took out of her handbag Claudia's and Sorella Agata's recipe book.

Sorella Agata shook her head. Never in the past fifty years did she think she would be the one to be found. Like Mamma, they hadn't given up on her after all—just as she had never given up hope she would be reunited with them someday.

Cecilia knelt down beside Sorella Agata as the two sisters huddled around their father, forming a circle as they embraced one another. While they were happy to be together again, each of them could not help thinking that the reunion was bittersweet since not all of their family was present. But the trio didn't notice a pair of birds on the table where Sorella Agata had left her *cassata* cake batter. The birds pecked at the drops of batter that had spilled and then hopped to the edge of the table, where they fixed their gazes on the DiSanta family.

A breeze riffled Sorella Agata's veil, causing her to look up. Just when her eyes landed on the birds, they flew off, but not before she caught the flash of iridescent colors on the breast of one of the birds. Closing her eyes, she sent out a silent prayer, thanking God for granting her another miracle. Tears streamed down her face once again, but this time they were tears of joy.

Author's Note

Rosalia's Bittersweet Pastry Shop would not have been possible without the following books, which I used for research:

Bitter Almonds: Recollections and Recipes from a Sicilian Girlhood, Mary Taylor Simeti and Maria Grammatico (Bantam Books, 2002).

The Encyclopedia of Saints, Rosemary Ellen Guiley (Checkmark Books, 2001).

Sicilian Feasts, Giovanna Bellia La Marca (Hippocrene Books, Inc., 2003).

Sophia Loren's Recipes and Memories, Sophia Loren (GT Publishing Corporation, 1998).

Sweet Sicily: The Story of an Island and Her Pastries, Victoria Granof (William Morrow Cookbooks, 2001).

Please turn the page for a very special Q&A with Rosanna Chiofalo, as well as some special recipes from her kitchen!

Why did you decide to focus your novel on a convent of nuns who make pastries?

I came across a book called *Sweet Sicily* by Victoria Granof. I had no idea that in addition to listing the recipes for many of Sicily's famous desserts, the book would also have a history of pastries on the island. When I read the book, I was fascinated to find out that Sicilian convents in the nineteenth century made and sold sweets, mainly to remain afloat, since after the Italian unification in 1860 much of the Church property was confiscated, forcing convents to close. The nuns treated the pastry making as their second vocation. I also learned that many of these convents were safe havens for women who had fallen on hard times, and in the pastry kitchens of these convents, these women found a new lease on life. I then began forming the idea of a young woman who suffers a horrible tragedy, but is rescued by a group of nuns who make and sell pastries from their convent. The pastries help the young woman to heal, and they become her passion. Shortly after I conceived the premise for *Rosalia's Bittersweet Pastry Shop,* I also discovered the book *Bitter Almonds,* by Mary Taylor Simeti and Maria Grammatico, which recounts the true story of Maria Grammatico, who was sent to a convent when she was a young girl in the 1950s. *Bitter Almonds* proved invaluable in giving me a glimpse of how the nuns baked their pastries.

In your last novel, *Stella Mia*, you tackled the difficult subjects of domestic abuse and a mother who leaves her child. And in *Rosalia's Bittersweet Pastry Shop*, your heroine is raped. What was your motivation for touching on this sensitive subject?

As we know, rape is still very much a problem in today's society, but at least there is more public awareness about it now. In the 1950s, when Rosalia was raped, it was a much different time, especially in Italy. I remember my mother's telling me stories of young women in her neighborhood who had been kidnapped and raped. These women were often then expected to wed their assailants because they had been "ruined," and no other man would want them. This was in the forties and fifties. I was shocked when my mother first told me about this horrible custom and could not imagine these poor women having to marry the men who had violated them. What saddened me even more was that often these women's own families encouraged them to wed the men who had attacked them. The shame and the scandal that would ensue if the young woman didn't marry the perpetrator would have been too much for the families of the victims to bear. I couldn't help feeling that little regard had been given to the women when they were forced to marry their rapists; it was as if they were being blamed for the crime's having happened to them—an attitude that is still often carried with rape victims today, unfortunately. I wanted to show how my character not only survived her ordeal, but didn't let it define her or dictate her life. I also wanted to show how one horrible act could have devastating consequences not only for the victim but for all the people in her life—her family and then the man she meets and falls in love with.

In all of your novels, families figure prominently, just as families are at the heart of Italian and Italian-American culture. In *Rosalia's Bittersweet Pastry Shop*, what you did was quite different from your other novels, in that Rosalia's family for the most part isn't present, yet you still manage to convey how much she loves them and how much she has been affected by their absence in her life. Rosalia's heartache over the loss of her family and her yearning to be reunited with them really comes through. Was there any personal connection for you with this angle of the story?

I was inspired by my mother and how she left her family in Sicily behind when she and my father immigrated to the U.S. My mother was one of eight children, and she was very close to her family, especially her sisters. She missed them terribly, and while she eventually adapted to life in America, I think her heart is still in her homeland. I experienced a little of what my mother went through when my husband and I relocated to Austin, Texas, for a year, seven years ago. I wasn't on another continent, and I was only a three-hour plane ride away, but I still missed my family so much and was so sad we weren't living in the same state any longer. So I can't even imagine fully how my mother felt being so far from her family and only seeing them sporadically over the years. My experience made me appreciate even more what my mother sacrificed to give my siblings and me the life we've had.

This was the first novel in which you have elements of magic realism. Is this a new direction we'll be seeing more of in your future novels?

I'm not sure if I will have elements of magic realism in my future novels, but this novel felt like the perfect story to include it. I kind of surprised myself when my editor discussed with me the possibility of using magic realism, and I agreed to do it. But I am glad I did, and I had so much fun with it. If it feels right for future storylines, I would include magic realism again, but it's not like I said to myself, "I want this novel to have magic realism." I want it to feel right, and it definitely felt right for this book.

Do you have a sweet tooth? And what are your favorite desserts? Which are your favorite desserts in *Rosalia's Bittersweet Pastry Shop*?

I think you can't be a Sicilian American and *not* have a sweet tooth! Everyone in my family has a sweet tooth, and when I learned of Sicily's long, rich history with desserts, I understood why every member of my family, going as far back as my great-grandparents, had a sweet tooth. When I was a little girl, I dreamed of my first job being in one of the Italian bakeries that were in Astoria, Queens, where I grew up. And sure enough, when I was fifteen, my first job was at LaGuli Bakery, one of the few reputable Italian bakeries that have survived. Unfortunately, more and more of these Italian bakeries are closing in Astoria, which makes me sad because they were so much a part of my childhood, and I feel like a crucial part of the neighborhood will be lost someday if and when all of these bakeries shut their doors for good. When I graduated from college, I worked at the bakery in The Cellar at Macy's, at the flagship store at Herald Square, until I was able to secure a job related to my college studies. It was wonderful sampling all the different sweets at both bakeries where I worked, and I loved bringing a cake or some other dessert home to my family every weekend. I have so many favorite desserts. I love the old-fashioned, German style custard-filled doughnuts. There used to be a wonderful German bakery in Astoria when I was a child that had the best doughnuts. These German bakeries are harder to find now in New York City as well. I love traditional American desserts such as apple pie, pumpkin pie, and brownies. My favorite desserts in *Rosalia's Bittersweet Pastry Shop* are the *Chiacchiere* (Fried Pastry Ribbons), the zeppole, the *Biscottini da Tè* (Little Tea Cookies), the cannolis, and of course, the *cassata*.

Biscotti all'Anice (Anise Cookies)

Yield: approximately 4 dozen cookies

In my second novel, Carissima, *I also included a recipe for* Biscotti all'Anice. *They are such a popular Sicilian biscotti that I decided to have another recipe for them in this book. The recipe below is slightly different from the one in* Carissima, *and it gives the option of baking the cookies for a softer texture or for a firmer biscotti texture. Either way, they're absolutely delicious!*

3½ cups unbleached all-purpose flour
3 teaspoons baking powder
1 cup granulated sugar
⅓ cup olive oil
1 teaspoon anise oil or 1 tablespoon anise extract
4 eggs, beaten

Preheat oven to 350 degrees. Grease three large baking sheets with butter.

Mix the flour, baking powder, and sugar in a bowl. Add the olive oil, anise flavor, and eggs. Mix into a soft dough.

Turn onto a lightly floured work surface, and divide in four parts. Roll each part into a 12-inch rope, and cut into twelve pieces. Roll each piece between your hands and shape into a crescent. Place cookies an inch apart on greased cookie sheets and bake for 15 to 20 minutes.

For crunchier cookies and for more of a biscotti texture, follow instructions below:

Shape the dough into two 14-inch logs. Bake 15 to 20 minutes. Cut baked logs into half-inch slices. Place the slices cut side down on baking sheet and put back in the oven to toast for 10 minutes.

Adapted from *Sicilian Feasts,* by Giovanna Bellia La Marca (Hippocrene Books)

Chiacchiere (Fried Pastry Ribbons)

Yield: approximately 6 to 8 servings

My mother also makes a version of this recipe (she chooses to make it without the Marsala) and would make it every year for Carnevale, which is when Sicilians usually make Chiacchiere. *They're quite addictive!*

1½ cups unbleached all-purpose flour
1 tablespoon granulated sugar
½ teaspoon baking powder
¼ teaspoon salt
2 tablespoons unsalted butter, chilled (see Note)
1 egg
3 tablespoons sweet wine, such as Marsala (optional)
Vegetable oil for frying
1 cup powdered sugar

Sift the flour, sugar, baking powder, and salt into a medium-size mixing bowl. Cut in the butter until the mixture resembles coarse cornmeal.

In a small bowl, beat together the egg and wine to blend. Pour into the flour mixture and mix until the dough comes together in a ball.

Turn the dough onto a lightly floured work surface and knead for 5 minutes, or until smooth. Cover and refrigerate for 1 hour before rolling out.

Divide the chilled dough into four pieces. Keep the unused portion covered while you work. Roll a piece of the dough very, very thin, dusting the work surface with a tiny bit of flour if it sticks. You should be able to read a newspaper through the dough. Do the best you can while bearing in mind that the thinner the dough, the crispier and more delicate the *Chiacchiere* will be.

Cut the dough into 2-by-4-inch strips using a fluted pastry wheel or a pizza-cutting wheel.

In a large, deep, heavy saucepan, heat 3 inches of oil to 350 degrees using a deep-fry or candy thermometer. Fry the *Chiacchiere*, a few at a time, turning once, until nicely browned, about 45 seconds per side. Drain the cookies on paper towels. Dust with powdered sugar.

Note: The recipe from *Sweet Sicily* calls for lard or vegetable shortening, but I chose to list butter in the ingredients above since many people in the U.S. prefer baking with butter to using lard or vegetable shortening. However, if you wish to use lard or vegetable shortening, you can use the same measurement as is listed above for the butter.

Adapted from *Sweet Sicily: The Story of an Island and Her Pastries,* by Victoria Granof (William Morrow Cookbooks)

Zeppole (Saint Joseph's Day Doughnuts)

Yield: approximately 2 dozen

My father's name was Giuseppe (Joseph), and my mother always made zeppole *every year for his namesake day, which is on March 19.* Zeppole *are my weakness, and every time I attend a street fair, I buy half a dozen* zeppole *and eat all of them before I leave!*

1½ cups milk
One ¼-ounce package active dry yeast
¼ cup granulated sugar
Grated zest of 1 lemon
4½ cups unbleached all-purpose flour
1 teaspoon baking powder
¾ teaspoon salt
½ teaspoon cinnamon (see Note)
Vegetable oil for frying
1 cup powdered or granulated sugar

In a small saucepan, heat the milk to body temperature (it should feel neither hot nor cold when tested with a clean finger). Remove from the heat, add the yeast and sugar, and let sit for 5 minutes, or until the yeast begins to foam. Add the lemon zest.

Sift together the flour, baking powder, salt, and cinnamon into a large mixing bowl. Add the yeast mixture and stir vigorously until the dough comes together. Turn the dough out onto a lightly floured work surface and knead it with gusto for about 10 minutes, or until it is smooth and satiny. Cover and let rise in a warm place until doubled in bulk, 1 to 1½ hours.

When the dough has risen, heat 2 inches of oil in a large, heavy saucepan to 350 degrees on a deep-fry or candy thermometer. Grab a handful of dough and squeeze it gently so some of it pops out the side of your fist between your thumb and forefinger. When you have a piece the size of a walnut, squeeze your thumb and forefinger together to release the ball of dough into the hot oil.

Fry the zeppole, a few at a time, for about 1½ minutes on each side, or until browned on both sides, then transfer them with a slotted spoon to paper towels to drain. Dust with powdered sugar or sprinkle with granulated sugar.

Note: I choose to make these without the cinnamon since my husband prefers them this way.

Adapted from *Sweet Sicily: The Story of an Island and Her Pastries,* by Victoria Granof (William Morrow Cookbooks)

Biscottini da Tè (Little Tea Cookies)

Yield: approximately 3 dozen cookies

What I love about these cookies is that they're quite easy to bake and only require ingredients that most of us have in our pantries, proving that you don't always need an elaborate recipe to have a very delicious sweet.

5 tablespoons unsalted butter or margarine, softened
1½ cups granulated sugar
6 eggs
¼ cup milk
1 teaspoon vanilla
Zest of one lemon
¼ teaspoon salt
5⅔ cups unbleached all-purpose flour

Preheat the oven to 350 degrees.

In a large mixing bowl, cream the butter or margarine and sugar until blended. Beat in the eggs, one at a time. Then add the milk, vanilla, lemon zest, and salt and continue to mix until smooth. Stir in the flour, a little at a time, until the dough comes together in a ball. If the dough is too dry, add more milk, one tablespoon at a time, until the dough comes together. If the dough is too wet, add more flour, a couple of tablespoons at a time, until the dough comes together. Turn the dough out onto a lightly floured work surface and knead for a minute or two.

Pinch off a tablespoonful of dough at a time and roll out, under your palms, on a floured work surface to form a 4-inch-long rope. Bring the ends around to form a circle and cross them over each other, pressing ever so lightly, just to seal.

Place the cookies two inches apart on ungreased baking sheets and bake for 20 to 25 minutes, or until barely golden. Do not over-bake or they will become crunchy, which is good for some cookies, but not these. Cool on a rack.

Adapted from *Sweet Sicily: The Story of an Island and Her Pastries,* by Victoria Granof (William Morrow Cookbooks)

Torta al Limone di Mamma (Mamma's Lemon Cake)

Yield: 8 to 10 servings

One of my favorite "simple" desserts, as I like to call them, that my mother makes is her lemon or orange cake. She can whip it up in no time by hand, and the cake always comes out scrumptious with its intense citrus flavors.

CAKE

4 tablespoons (½ stick) butter, softened
1 cup plus 3 tablespoons granulated sugar
3 eggs
2 cups plus 2 tablespoons unbleached all-purpose flour
2½ teaspoons baking powder
Grated zest of 3 lemons
1 teaspoon vanilla
1 tablespoon whole milk

SYRUP

2 cups freshly squeezed lemon juice, with 3 tablespoons sugar
    dissolved in it

Heat the oven to 350 degrees. Grease and flour a tube pan with a removable bottom.

Cream butter and sugar in electric mixer until pale yellow. Add eggs, one at a time, and beat until well blended. Add flour, baking powder, lemon zest, vanilla, and milk. Beat until well blended.

Pour cake batter into prepared pan. Bake for 40 to 45 minutes, until the cake is a deep golden brown and toothpick inserted into the center of the cake comes out clean.

While cake is still warm, poke holes throughout it with a wooden skewer or toothpick. Pour about a cup of the lemon syrup over the cake. Serve at room temperature, with more lemon syrup drizzled over each slice.

Note: You can also make this cake without the lemon syrup.

This is a family recipe.

Piparelli (Crunchy Spice Cookies)

Yield: approximately 2 dozen cookies

Although these cookies are customarily made for the season of Lent in Sicily, I find they're the perfect cookies to eat during autumn with their deep notes of ground cloves, brown sugar, and honey. Whichever time of the year you choose to bake them, they're always yummy!

4 tablespoons (½ stick) unsalted butter or margarine, softened
¼ cup packed dark brown sugar
1 cup orange blossom honey
2 egg whites (kept separate from each other)
3 cups unbleached all-purpose flour
1½ teaspoons baking soda
¼ teaspoon salt
¾ teaspoon ground cloves
½ teaspoon freshly ground black pepper (see Note)
3 tablespoons chopped Candied Orange Peel (recipe follows)
1 cup unblanched whole almonds

Preheat the oven to 375 degrees. Grease a baking sheet.

In a large bowl, cream the butter or margarine with the brown sugar and honey. Add one of the egg whites and mix until evenly blended. Sift the flour, baking soda, salt, and spices together into another bowl and add the butter mixture, stirring until the dough is smooth and no longer sticky.

Turn the dough out onto a lightly floured work surface and knead in the orange peel and almonds until evenly dispersed. Divide the dough into three pieces and form each piece into a log that is 8 inches long by 2 inches wide. Place the logs 3 inches apart on the greased baking sheet. Beat the remaining egg white lightly and brush the tops of the logs with it.

Bake the logs for 20 to 25 minutes, or until firm to the touch. Remove from the oven and allow to cool for 10 minutes. Reduce the oven temperature to 325 degrees. Slice the logs ¼ inch thick and lay the cookies on the baking sheet. Return to the oven for another 15 to 20 minutes to dry them out. The cookies will become crisp as they cool, so don't overbake them. Cool on a rack.

Note: Although the recipe in *Sweet Sicily* calls for black pepper, I choose to make these without it since I'm a bit finicky when it comes to black pepper.

FOR THE CANDIED ORANGE PEEL (SEE NOTE)

3 unblemished organic navel oranges
2 cups granulated sugar
⅓ cup water
¼ cup corn syrup

Wash the oranges and cut each one into six wedges. Scrape away the pulp (reserve it for another use), leaving the peel with the white membrane attached, and place the peel into a nonreactive saucepan.

Cover the orange peel with cold water and bring to a boil. Boil for 1 minute, then drain off the water. Cover again with cold water, bring to a boil, and drain; repeat the process two more times. This is the only way to remove the bitterness from the peel; you'll be glad you went to the trouble.

Remove the peel from the saucepan and add the sugar, water, and corn syrup to the pan. Bring to a boil over medium-high heat, stirring constantly to dissolve the sugar. When the sugar is dissolved, add the peel, turn the heat down to medium, and boil for 20 to 25 minutes, or until most of the syrup is absorbed and the peel is glossy.

Place a cooling rack over a baking sheet to catch drips, and transfer the wedges of candied peel to the rack. Let cool and dry for 2 to 3 hours, then store in an airtight container in the refrigerator for up to six months.

Note: To cut down on the prep time, the candied orange peel can be made ahead of time. It's worth making your own since it tastes far superior to store-bought candied orange peel.

Adapted from *Sweet Sicily: The Story of an Island and Her Pastries,* by Victoria Granof (William Morrow Cookbooks)

Torta Savoia (Chocolate Hazelnut Cake)

Yield: approximately 12 to 14 servings

I only discovered a couple of years ago the many extraordinary desserts made with chocolate and hazelnut, and this recipe is one of my favorites. The cake was named in honor of the Duke of Savoy, who ruled Sicily for three years during the eighteenth century. As you'll see, the cake is as regal as its name.

SYRUP

½ cup granulated sugar
½ cup water
6 tablespoons dark rum

FILLING

One 13-ounce jar Nutella (chocolate hazelnut cream)
1½ cups heavy whipping cream, divided
1 teaspoon vanilla

CAKE

1 recipe Sponge Cake (see recipe on pages 386–387)

GLAZE

1 cup heavy whipping cream
2 tablespoons unsalted butter, at room temperature
12 ounces semisweet chocolate, chopped

FOR THE SYRUP

Combine the sugar and water in a small saucepan, bring to a boil, and boil until the sugar is dissolved and the mixture is reduced by one-quarter. Let cool, and stir in the rum.

FOR THE FILLING

In a small bowl, whisk the Nutella with ½ cup of the cream to lighten the Nutella. In a mixing bowl, whip the remaining 1 cup of cream with the vanilla until it begins to hold its shape. Add the Nutella mixture and continue to whip until stiff.

TO ASSEMBLE THE CAKE

Line a 10-inch springform pan with plastic wrap. Cut the sponge cake into three half-inch layers. Place one cake layer in the bottom of the pan, brush with one-third of the rum syrup, and spread evenly with half of the filling. Repeat with another layer of cake, another one-third of the syrup, and the remaining filling. Finish with the final cake layer and the remaining syrup. Chill, covered, for 2 hours before unmolding.

MEANWHILE, MAKE THE GLAZE

Bring the cream and butter just to a boil and immediately remove from the heat. Add the chocolate and let sit for 5 minutes to allow the chocolate to melt, then whisk until smooth. This glaze solidifies significantly upon cooling; if it becomes too stiff to work with, warm it over low heat, stirring carefully.

TO FINISH

Invert the cake onto a serving platter and remove the pan and plastic wrap. Pour or spread the glaze evenly over the top and sides of the cake. Allow the glaze to set before serving.

Adapted from *Sweet Sicily: The Story of an Island and Her Pastries,* by Victoria Granof (William Morrow Cookbooks)

Pignolata (Honey Clusters)

Yield: 10 to 12 servings

This is my mother's recipe for Pignolata, *which she made every year for Christmas. I'm proud to now carry on this tradition for the holidays.*

DOUGH

4 cups flour
1 orange, zested
¾ cup sugar
½ teaspoon baking powder
½ teaspoon salt
1 stick of unsalted butter, cut into smaller pieces
6 eggs
1 teaspoon vanilla
Canola or vegetable oil for frying

GLAZE

2 cups honey
1 tablespoon freshly squeezed orange juice
¼ cup sugar
Confetti sprinkles for decorating.

FOR THE PIGNOLATA

Place the flour, orange zest, sugar, baking powder, and salt in a food processor and lightly pulse to blend the ingredients. Add the butter and pulse until the mixture resembles coarse meal. Then add the eggs and vanilla and pulse until the mixture begins to come together into a dough. Take the dough out of the food processor and shape it into a smooth ball.

Pinch off one-inch pieces of dough and roll between your hands to shape into small balls. Place on a lightly floured work surface or on a baking sheet that has been lightly floured.

Add 3 inches of oil to a large, heavy-bottomed pot and heat

over medium heat until the oil reaches 350 degrees on a candy thermometer (or when a small piece of dough dropped into the oil rises to the surface). Place batches of the dough balls into the oil (do not place too many at one time) and fry until the balls are golden brown, about 2 to 3 minutes. With a spider or slotted spoon, scoop the balls out of the pot and place on a plate lined with paper towels to drain.

FOR THE GLAZE

In a large pot over medium heat, bring the honey, orange juice, and sugar to a boil. Stir until the sugar dissolves. Remove the pot from the heat and add the balls. *Be careful: This glaze is very hot.* Stir until the balls are all coated with the glaze. Let cool for about 15 minutes.

With a large spoon, place the *Pignolata* onto a large serving plate or platter. With wet hands, pile the *Pignolata* into a pyramid. Sprinkle with confetti sprinkles.

This is a family recipe.

Cassata (Sicilian Ricotta Cake)

Yield: approximately 12 to 14 servings

While there are several steps involved in making a cassata, *it is well worth your time, especially for a special occasion. For there's no doubt this cake will impress your guests with its decadent, rich flavor. You can find fresh ricotta in Italian food specialty stores or gourmet food specialty stores.*

FILLING

2 cups fresh ricotta
½ cup sugar
½ cup candied fruits, chopped
4 ounces milk chocolate or semisweet chocolate or small
     chocolate morsels, chopped
1 teaspoon ground cinnamon

RICOTTA ICING

2 tablespoons fresh ricotta
2 cups confectioners' sugar

ASSEMBLY

1 recipe Sponge Cake (see recipe on pages 386–387)
1½ cups Marsala wine
½ of a whole candied citron (if you cannot find this ingredient,
     you can leave it out)
¼ cup candied cherries
½ cup sliced blanched almonds

FOR THE FILLING

Beat the ricotta and the sugar with an electric mixer until smooth. Divide in half and add the fruit to one portion and the chocolate and cinnamon to the other. Set aside.

FOR THE ICING

Beat the ricotta and the sugar until smooth and of spreading consistency. Set aside.

FOR THE ASSEMBLY

Place four triangles of waxed or parchment paper on a serving platter under and all around where the cake will be so that the papers can be pulled out after the cake is assembled. Place one cake layer on the waxed paper. Place the Marsala wine in a small spray bottle and spray a third on the first layer. Spread the ricotta and fruit filling on top of the cake layer. Place the second layer on top of the ricotta filling and spray with another third of the Marsala wine. Spread the ricotta and chocolate filling on the second layer, top with the third layer, spray it with the rest of the Marsala wine, and let rest.

Place the citron, if using, on a cutting board and slice thinly. Slice the candied cherries in half.

Spread the icing on the top and on the sides of the cake. Press the sliced almonds lightly over the sides of the cake. Place the citron slices, if using, in a pattern around the top of the cake. Add the cherries, cut side down, to complement the design made by the citron slices. Chill until ready to serve.

Adapted from *Sicilian Feasts,* by Giovanna Bellia La Marca (Hippocrene Books)

Pan di Spagna con Crema Pasticciera
(Sponge Cake with Pastry Cream)

Yield: 10-inch sponge cake and 6 to 8 servings of pastry cream

This cake is the starting point for many more elaborate Sicilian cake recipes. It can be made with or without the pastry cream. If the cake is not filled with pastry cream, a scoop of ice cream on top of a slice is perfect; even an excellent store-bought or homemade jam complements the cake well. Whether you eat it plain or with a filling or a topping, this cake will satisfy your sweet tooth.

The pastry cream can be used for many other desserts as well or even eaten simply with fresh berries. The pastry cream recipe I chose to include is not a Sicilian-style pastry cream, which typically uses cinnamon, lemon zest, and cornstarch, but when testing recipes I found the recipe below was easier on most palates with the absence of the cinnamon.

FOR THE CAKE

6 eggs, separated
¾ cup granulated sugar, divided
1 tablespoon hot water
1 teaspoon vanilla
Grated zest of 1 lemon
1¼ cups cake flour (see Note)
½ teaspoon baking powder
¼ teaspoon salt
Powdered sugar for dusting on top (optional)

Preheat the oven to 350 degrees. Grease well a 10-by-3-inch springform pan and line the bottom with parchment paper, greasing the parchment paper as well.

In a large bowl, with an electric mixer, whip the egg yolks with ½ cup of the sugar, the water, the vanilla, and the lemon zest until light yellow and tripled in volume. Sift the flour, baking powder, and salt directly into the yolk mixture and gently fold in.

In a separate bowl, with clean beaters, whip the egg whites until soft peaks form. Whip in the remaining ¼ cup sugar, a tablespoon at a time, until stiff peaks form. Fold the whites gently into the yolk-flour mixture until no white streaks remain.

Spread the batter evenly in the prepared pan and bake for 35 to 40 minutes, or until the cake is golden brown and the top springs back when lightly touched. Cool the cake completely on a cooling rack before removing from the pan. If desired, dust with powdered sugar.

IF FILLING THE CAKE

With a serrated knife, cut the cake through its center so that you have two layers. Place one of the layers, cut side up, onto a plate. With a spatula, spread the pastry cream on top of this layer of cake. Take the second layer and place it cut side down onto the layer with cream. Dust with powdered sugar.

Note: If cake flour is unavailable, substitute 1 cup unbleached all-purpose flour and ½ cup cornstarch. Sift both the flour and cornstarch well before measuring.

Adapted from *Sweet Sicily: The Story of an Island and Her Pastries*, by Victoria Granof (William Morrow Cookbooks)

FOR THE PASTRY CREAM

2 cups milk
1½ teaspoons vanilla extract
6 egg yolks
1 cup granulated sugar
4 tablespoons flour, sifted

In a saucepan over medium-high heat, bring the milk just to the boiling point, add the vanilla, and remove from the heat. In a large bowl, beat the egg yolks together with the sugar until the mixture is pale yellow, then whisk in the flour. Continuing to whisk, very slowly pour the hot milk into the egg mixture.

Pour the mixture back into the saucepan and, stirring constantly, bring it slowly to close to the boiling point—but do not let it boil or the eggs will curdle and you will have a lumpy sauce. Remove from the heat, cool briefly, then place a sheet of plastic wrap on the surface of the cream to prevent a skin from forming.

Cool to room temperature, then refrigerate until ready to use.

Adapted from *Sophia Loren's Recipes and Memories,* by Sophia Loren (GT Publishing Corporation)

Rosalia's Bittersweet Pastry Shop

Rosanna Chiofalo

About This Guide

The suggested questions are included to enhance
your group's reading of Rosanna Chiofalo's
Rosalia's Bittersweet Pastry Shop.

DISCUSSION QUESTIONS

1. Madre Carmela coaxes Rosalia to talk after her ordeal by introducing her to a new pastry every time she visits her. What is it about the sweets that the pastry shop at the Convento di Santa Lucia del Mela makes that is so enticing to Rosalia? Do you believe they were instrumental in helping her to heal?

2. Rosalia is devastated to learn that her family has moved when she returns home. How do you think you would have reacted if you were Rosalia? Would you have been more angry than hurt or vice versa? Would you have kept longing for your family the way Rosalia does? Do you feel that her family had no other choice but to leave because of their circumstances, or could her father have made a different decision?

3. Although Rosalia is afraid of Antonio when she first meets him and for some time afterward, why do you think she eventually lowers her guard and decides to trust him? What is it about him that makes her realize he is different from Marco and would never hurt her?

4. How have the nuns and the lay pastry workers at the convent become a surrogate family for Rosalia? How do they fill her need to have a sense of belonging? Why is it impossible for them to take the place of her biological family? Discuss the similarities and differences between biological families and adopted families.

5. Do you feel the sisterhood among the nuns and workers is because of the sense of pride they take in their work? Or is it also because many of the women are in a sense "orphans" like Rosalia with no other families to turn to?

6. Is it fair of Antonio to ask Rosalia to go to Paris with him—even if it is only temporary as he says—in light of all that's happened to her? Was it too soon to ask her to make such a huge decision, and do you believe she would have gone with him if

he had asked her at a later date? Do you think Rosalia over-reacted when she learned he and Madre Carmela had not told her he had applied to culinary school in Paris?

7. Why does Sorella Agata feel so compelled to help the home-less women she meets in the alleyway? Do you agree with Madre Carmela when she tells her that it is impossible to save every woman and that it isn't her responsibility to save every-one? How has helping other women in need given Sorella Agata a new purpose and aided in her own healing?

8. Discuss all that Sorella Agata had to give up when she became a nun. What has she gained by her vocation? Do you feel she struggles at times between her identity before she was a nun and her new identity once she has taken her vows? Discuss how her life would have been different if she had not decided to take her vows.

9. After Claudia meets Antonio and hears him talking about Sorella Agata when she was young, before she took her vows, she realizes he never stopped loving her, although now it's more a love comprised of friendship and deep respect and ad-miration. How is the relationship between Antonio and Sorella Agata mutually beneficial, both when they were young and now in their older age?

10. When Claudia first arrives at the convent, she senses a spiri-tual, almost mystical, quality there. Do you believe there was something magical about the Convento di Santa Lucia? And do you believe that it was Sorella Agata's tears that made her pastries taste far better than those made by the other workers?

FAR AIM 2018

FEDERAL AVIATION REGULATIONS

Aeronautical Information Manual

RULES AND PROCEDURES FOR AVIATORS

U.S. Department of Transportation

From Titles 14 and 49 of the Code of Federal Regulations

Updated and published by
AVIATION SUPPLIES & ACADEMICS, INC.
Newcastle, Washington 98059
www.asa2fly.com

D011306J

FAR/AIM
(Federal Aviation Regulations and Aeronautical Information Manual)
2018 Edition

Aviation Supplies & Academics, Inc.
7005 132nd Place SE
Newcastle, Washington 98059-3153

This publication contains current regulations as of June 15, 2017.
The *Aeronautical Information Manual* is current through April 27, 2017.

Visit **www.asa2fly.com/farupdate** for regulation and AIM changes released after
this printing date. ASA provides a free Update service with email notification when
rules and procedures change.

None of the material in this publication supersedes any documents, procedures, or
regulations issued by the *Federal Aviation Administration*.

ASA does not claim copyright on any material published herein that was taken from
United States government sources. The *Aeronautical Information Manual* is reprinted
directly from the government document as an exact facsimile of the FAA publication.

Front cover photo: istock.com/Daviles

ASA-18-FR-AM-BK
ISBN   978-1-61954-536-6

Printed in the United States of America

2018   2017   9   8   7   6   5   4   3   2   1

14

Stay informed with ASA online resources.

Website

www.asa2fly.com

Updates
www.asa2fly.com/farupdate

Twitter

www.twitter.com/asa2fly

Facebook
www.facebook.com/asa2fly

ASA